Mars 2242

Mars 2242

Brian Wilson

BOOKLOGIX
Alpharetta, GA

ISBN: 978-1-6653-0356-9 - Paperback
eISBN: 978-1-6653-0357-6 - ePub

Library of Congress Control Number: 2022909222

⊗This paper meets the requirements of ANSI/NISO Z39.48-1992 (Permanence of Paper)

Cover art by Tori Lehman

1 0 1 1 2 2

To the Dodgen Young Authors Club

Prologue

The air on the observation deck was chilled despite the scorching heat of Venus just a few thousand kilometers below. A scattering of colonists had gathered around the large telescopes hoping to catch a glimpse of something interesting—perhaps a distant quasar, galaxy, or passing meteor shower. Some of the older ones gazed, instead, at Earth, their former home, searching for the places they had known in their youth. There was a collective gasp as an asteroid came into view, someone exclaiming that it was close enough that you could see the robots mining its surface. Immediately, a group flocked to one of the telescopes and took turns pressing their eye into the scope's oculus for a better look. A girl pulled a transparent pad out of her backpack and hurriedly sketched the asteroid. With a quick brush of her finger, the image leaped off the pad and hovered above her as a three-dimensional hologram.

Amid the excitement, a young girl and her grandfather made their way to an open telescope at the far end of the observation deck.

"Where to?" the little girl chirped, her small hand already on the telescope's keypad. "Earth? You still haven't shown me all the continents yet. We've been learning about them in school."

"Not this time, darling. There's something else I want to show you." The old man gazed into the distance at a tiny red speck in the ink-black sky. He exhaled slowly, seemingly lost in thought. His granddaughter reached for his hand and drew back as she felt the clamminess of his palm. He smiled uneasily and typed *Mars, Sector 7 G* into the search panel.

"Stand back," he said. "This will take a couple minutes."

The motor whirred and clicked as it swung the telescope into position. Upon locating Mars, it paused before making a series of small adjustments. Finally, a green light switched on, indicating that it was ready.

"Okay. You can look."

The girl pressed her dominant eye into the oculus and blinked as the image came into focus. "It's beautiful," she gasped. "Mars, isn't it?"

"Yes—Mars. I was there once," said the grandfather with a tinge of sadness in his voice. "It wasn't pleasant."

"But," protested the girl, "I thought nobody lived there. I thought—"

"There's a lot you don't know yet, but I think you're ready now. Switch the magnification to ten thousand times and tell me what you see."

"I see a mountain, and I think I see a canyon too."

"Okay. Now boost magnification to twenty-five thousand and move slightly south-southwest. Now, what do you see?"

"There's a settlement of some kind, but the buildings are all in ruins. It looks like no one lives there anymore."

"Exactly," remarked the grandfather. "But when I was there, a long, long time ago, it was different. I was a prisoner—a convict—and I had to do hard work every single day. There was a war and a lot of people died, but they'd just bring in new convicts to replace the ones who'd been killed. To them, we were expendable."

"You were a prisoner?" gasped the girl. "What did you do?"

The old man smiled wryly. "Oh, I can assure you I wasn't the killer they claimed I was. Back in those days, all someone had to do was report you, and the government believed the worst. Really, I think all they wanted was just an excuse to send people up there to work in the mines. They couldn't have gotten anyone to do it otherwise. You know, Mars is very far away from Earth, and it's cold there, and you can't breathe the air. For a long time, we also thought it was lifeless, but we were wrong about that."

"You mean like aliens?" asked the little girl.

"Aliens?" the old man chuckled. "Yes, but probably not like any that you've ever imagined."

"What were you mining for?"

"Iridium, uranium, and a bunch of other stuff we had run out of on Earth. They were in that mountain, Olympus Mons, which was really a long-extinct volcano. A small amount was used to fuel the colony, and the rest was sent to Earth."

"How did you get away, and what happened to the colony? And what were the aliens like?"

"That's the story I'm going to tell you. It involves a rebellion, a mysterious scientist, and even the pyramids of Egypt. And there was a girl, not much older than you, who came to save us. Interested?"

"Yes!" exclaimed the girl. Her grandfather sat down in a pod chair and cleared his throat with a raspy cough.

"It was during the third prisoner rebellion on Mars, in the year 2232, that a small group of scientists, engineers, and convicts deserted our little colony. They left without telling anyone, and to be honest, we all assumed they had died in the harsh Martian climate. Their leader was Dr. Artemis Burke, a mysterious scientist who was possibly even insane. She was helped by strange alien beings who looked like tiny lights. Years later, we started hearing rumors of a rival colony.

"And then for some reason—I still don't know exactly why—we were attacked by fast-moving robots that looked like spiders, only larger. We were no match for them, and a lot of us died. In the end, our survival depended on a girl who had been born on Mars fourteen years earlier to convict parents. Her name was Megan—no last name—just Megan. If it hadn't been for her and a few other very brave people, you and your mother wouldn't have been born. This is her story, and it begins on Earth, in a city we called New York."

Chapter 1

Escape

New York City, 2242

It was six o'clock. Fourteen-year-old Megan paced the floor of her apartment anxiously as she plotted her escape. Agnes Starch, the stern white-haired government chaperone assigned to supervise her, stood rigid as a board, her back pressed firmly against the closed oak door, her eyes following Megan's every move. She had fallen for one of Megan's tricks before and was not about to let it happen again.

Megan couldn't afford to wait—she was already late for an important meeting with the other kids who had been born on Mars. The press had dubbed them the Wonder Kids when they first arrived on Earth years ago, but as the years ticked by, fewer and fewer people seemed to care or even remember them. Now someone was trying to kill them. They needed to figure out who. With her limp, it would take at least twenty minutes to reach the abandoned warehouse. She had to act now.

She glanced quickly at Agnes and the front door. Agnes glared back at her with furrowed eyebrows, her skinny wrinkled arms folded defiantly across her chest as if to say, *Just try something, I dare you.* A vent a couple meters away blew chilled air in her direction, gently rustling her hideous blue and white polka-dot dress. Suddenly, Megan knew exactly what to do.

She hurried to her bedroom and quietly closed the door. With a screwdriver in hand, she climbed from her bed onto her dresser, reached up, and removed the screws from a vent cover in her room. Standing on her tiptoes, she peered inside the now exposed ventilation shaft. Yes, it was just wide enough for someone her size to climb into, and better still, it led back toward the living room, to where Agnes was guarding the front door. With a snap of the wrist, Megan flung the screwdriver as far back into the shaft as she could manage and jumped back down onto the bed.

Bang! a loud metallic thud echoed through the apartment. Hurrying, she jumped inside her closet and partially closed the door, leaving an opening just large enough to look out of.

"Megan!" Agnes's voice shook with anger. Megan heard the clicking of shoes against the hardwood floor and a whoosh of air as the bedroom door flew open. Through the crack in the door, she saw Agnes go immediately for the open ventilation shaft, climbing on top of the dresser without using so much as a chair or the bed for help. She was remarkably spry for an old woman, and Megan knew she would have to be quick.

She slipped unnoticed out of the closet and crept silently toward the bedroom door. She wished she were fast, that she had never suffered the debilitating effects of polio as a young child—fast, like her friend Harper who had been the fastest one at her school and who had nearly qualified for the Olympics. Fortunately for her, though, what she lacked in speed she more than made up for in intelligence and cunning.

Agnes seemed convinced that she had gotten into the ventilation shaft, despite the fact that it would have been nearly impossible with her bad leg. Megan limped silently out of the room as swiftly as she could manage. As she unbolted the front door and turned the polished stainless-steel handle to leave, she heard Agnes once again scream her name. Megan smiled. She had fooled the old bat yet again.

Megan took the express elevator down to the lobby and exited the building onto Liberty Street. The road bustled with activity as pedestrians hurried home from work or sought out one of the district's many restaurants, their photoluminescent suits and dresses beginning to glow in the fading daylight. A strikingly beautiful woman with glowing neon-orange hair brushed past her, her dress changing from lime green to aquamarine in the blink of an eye.

There were also cyberpunks—heavily tattooed teens and twenty-somethings clad entirely in black. They were the dropouts, alienated loners who pretended to want nothing to do with society but who clung tightly to its fringes. Their garments gave the appearance of austerity but were, in fact, interlaced with dozens of trendy electronic devices. Others wore shirts and dresses that monitored their heart rate or glucose level, displayed moving graphics, or emitted fragrant scents as they walked.

And then there were the ones who lacked financial resources, wards of the state like Megan, who wore clothes completely devoid of electronic fibers and high-tech devices. She found it ironic that the state housed her and fed her but provided little in the way of clothing. Her faded blue jeans, white linen shirt, and denim jacket looked as though they belonged to a bygone era, a sign to anybody who saw her that she was different and perhaps somehow less worthy as a citizen.

All around her, reflective steel and glass skyscrapers soared into the darkening sky, their shimmering exteriors reflecting neighboring buildings. Brightly lit billboards showcased full-motion advertisements, as street vendors hawked their wares to people walking by. Below it all lay the ocean, dark and polluted, an ever-present reminder of just how much sea levels had risen over the past two hundred years. The streets, restaurants, stores, apartments—everything was suspended by massive steel cables strung between the skyscrapers.

Dodging an oncoming street vendor, Megan inadvertently stepped into the street and was nearly struck by a bus that seemed to come out of nowhere. Sensing her presence, it swerved at the last instant and continued quickly on its way. She tripped and fell back onto the sidewalk. She had been mere centimeters from death, but not a single person had so much as raised a finger to help her. *Had people always been so cold?*

As she picked herself up and dusted off her jeans, a thin, slightly transparent man with a neatly groomed beard and emerald-green eyes marched through the crowd toward her, his suit flickering as he passed through solid bodies. He was a holographic pitchman, the latest in advertising.

"Hungry for something delicious?" he said, smiling as he looked Megan in the eye. "How about an exciting new Dreamburger—this week only for forty-nine credits? A deal like this is too great to miss!"

"Can you just get lost?" asked Megan sarcastically.

"Hungry for something delicious?" quipped the hologram again, oblivious to her question. Without missing a beat, it flickered and then disappeared into the crowd in search of potential customers.

Megan turned back toward the road and watched a fleet of yellow driverless taxis whiz quietly by. She wished she could take one, but it would be too risky. The government installed biometric screening devices in all public vehicles to identify passengers, so there would be a record of her movements. Few cars had drivers these days as most people opted for the automated taxis. They were cleaner, faster, and safer to operate than traditional vehicles, and the fact that they communicated wirelessly with the city grid meant that it was impossible to get lost, at least theoretically.

She pressed on, her limp slightly worse than before. If she hurried, she just might make it to the warehouse before her friends gave up and left. Calling wasn't an option either; she had every reason to believe that the government was bugging her phone. The same government that rescued her from Mars, that raised her, that provided her with a basic, but functional, apartment. It was her benefactor and her warden, but lately she had begun to think that she would be better off without it.

Reaching the intersection of Liberty and the West Side Elevated Highway, she turned left and headed south toward Battery Park. The buildings were dirtier here, less modern, and more industrial. Factories spewed black smoke into the air with reckless disregard for the environment, and trucks bearing coal and scrap metal rumbled by like tanks on a battlefield. There were huge piles of trash everywhere, with people rummaging through them in search of anything that could be recycled and sold. Even the people looked seedy with their greasy hair, dirty hands, and cheap secondhand clothes with broken electronics. They had the look of defeat in their eyes, as though the joy had been stamped out of them, and they looked desperate.

Megan nervously exited the West Side Highway and limped down a stairwell leading to the waterfront. Beneath the elevated highway, rows of tents, crates, and corrugated tin shacks lined a narrow unlit street suspended mere centimeters above the ocean. It flooded whenever there was a storm, and scientists were predicting that it would be completely underwater in another decade or two. At the other end of the street lay a boarded-up automotive factory and several abandoned soot-stained warehouses.

A boy and an old man were fishing near the stairwell that Megan had come down, their clear nylon lines extending out into the filthy water. In the distance stood the Statue of Liberty, blackened with soot, the water now covering her ankles. She had stood for something once, but those days were long gone. Further out still, a barge power station relentlessly processed coal and depleted iridium into electricity to be consumed by the city's homes and high-tech devices, but the people who lived here stood to gain little from it.

As she limped on, the boy turned and stared at her. She

felt uneasy, unwelcome. A group of older men, maybe in their forties or fifties, came out of a tent and stood in the middle of the street, blocking her way. *Show no fear*, she thought, remembering what Harper had taught her. *Look them in the eye and keep walking.* As she reached the men, one, a skinny toothless guy in rags, stepped in front of her.

"What do you got?" he asked. "There's a toll if you want to pass."

"I don't have anything," Megan replied defiantly. "Leave me alone."

"It don't work like that, missy. By the looks of you, you aren't rich, but you aren't poor neither. Now hand over yer credits or we're going to have some fun with you." The other men snickered as one with a lazy eye pulled out a pair of rusty pliers. He opened and closed its jaws menacingly, the cutting edges making a metallic click each time they snapped together.

Megan thought fast. "Okay," she said. "I wish you hadn't made me do this." She reached into her back pocket and pulled out a fake badge with her holographic image on it. Printed boldly across the top were the words STATE INTELLIGENCE SERVICE. "I'm an undercover agent on my way to a drug bust. There's a drone watching me at this very moment, and if you don't let me pass, I'm going to order it to vaporize all of you."

The men looked confused and began muttering among themselves. They were trying to convince themselves that it was a bluff, that the young lady in front of them was just a girl, clearly too young to work for State Intelligence. Megan lifted one of the lapels of her denim jacket and spoke into it. It did not contain a transmitter, but the men in front of her did not know that.

"Hold your fire," she said, just loud enough for the men

to hear. "I'm going to give them one more chance." Then, looking the toothless man in the eye, she issued a threat.

"You're obstructing an official SIS operation. If you don't leave, we will be forced to eliminate you. You have ten seconds to vacate this street."

"She's bluffing," chided one of the man's friends. "Look at her, she's just a kid."

"I don't know, Ben," said another. "Some of them agents look pretty young these days. It's one of their tricks, and you know how they have their drones up there."

"You have five seconds to walk away," Megan warned, warm sweat trickling down the back of her neck. If this didn't work, she would be in serious trouble.

"Well, all right, little lady," said the toothless man. "We'll be on our way, I reckon. We was just playing with you anyways." The men left the street and crossed a vacant lot to where some boys were picking through a heap of trash. Megan took a deep breath and continued walking.

When she finally reached the warehouse where the meeting was taking place, she gave a shrill whistle and waited near the rear entrance. The door opened and her friend Harper waved her inside. She had a rosy complexion and bright, shiny red hair that bobbed as she moved.

"What took you so long?" she asked.

Megan shifted uneasily. "It's hard to be fast when you have a bum leg. Sorry—I did the best I could."

"Okay," said Harper. "I knew you were fine, but the others weren't so sure. Oh, and there's bad news. Come inside and we'll talk about it."

Chapter 2

The Meeting

Megan followed Harper down a long dusty corridor, carefully stepping over shards of broken glass on the smooth concrete floor. The walls were covered with blood stains and graffiti—some old, some new—all of it telling the story of drifters and gangs that had called this place home. As they turned a corner, the stench of urine hit them like a fetid avalanche, and Megan hurriedly covered her mouth and nose with a handkerchief.

"Vagrants," Harper muttered, her voice echoing slightly. "I've never understood why they won't take better care of the places where they sleep." She pulled out a chem-light to illuminate the darkening passage. "We're almost there," she whispered. "Watch out for the trip wire I set."

Megan stared at a spot on the floor illuminated by the

chem-light. A wire of woven steel filaments was stretched taut across the passageway, just a few centimeters above the floor, one end attached to a crumpled aluminum can beside the wall. *Explosives*, Megan thought. One false step and an intruder would be blown to bits. She knew her friend was resourceful—after all, Harper was an actual SIS agent—but she still had trouble imagining her as a cold-blooded killer.

Finally, they reached a door at the end of the corridor. Harper knocked once, paused, and knocked twice more. The door slowly creaked open, revealing a boy on the other side. He was tall and thin, around fifteen years old, and he wore a simple white T-shirt and jeans.

"Any luck?" he asked.

"Yeah, Megan's with me," replied Harper. She stepped inside, and Megan followed. The room was huge, like an airplane hangar, and it was filled with machine parts and broken outdated robots encrusted in dust and cobwebs. Once upon a time this facility had produced thousands of finely crafted automobiles, but it had been abandoned decades ago when the company was forced to file for bankruptcy amid rising production costs and government regulations. On the other side of the room, a small group of kids was playing cards beneath a rusty lamp that resembled a showerhead.

Megan smiled at the boy who had opened the door. His name was Bryce, and he had dark hair and brown eyes like hers. She often wondered if he was her brother. They had both been born on Mars and taken from their parents when they were still babies. Of course, so had Harper and everyone else gathered here tonight. But there was something different about Bryce, something in his mannerisms and demeanor that reminded her of herself.

"Hi, Bryce," Megan said softly with a smile. "Sorry I'm late."

"I'm just glad you made it. Did Harper tell you the news?"

"No. What news?" Megan looked at Bryce and then at Harper. Harper looked away.

"It's Violet. She's dead," continued Bryce. "I'm so sorry. I know how close you two were."

"Not Violet!" gasped Megan. "Not her. It must be a mistake."

Harper's voice sounded distant as she explained what happened. "We found her this morning under the bridge. She'd been shot." Tears streamed down Megan's face, and she sank to the floor. Harper knelt beside her and put an arm around her. Although they looked nothing alike, Harper had been like an older sister to her, protecting her and making sure she had everything she needed. She was nineteen, the oldest of the Wonder Kids, as they were called, and the only one with any memory of having lived on Mars.

"I knew this would be hard for you," she said. "She was a wonderful girl, and she didn't deserve to die like that."

"I dreamed last week that there would be another killing," said Megan, "but everything was different, and I didn't think it was Violet."

"I know," said Harper. "We're all going to miss her."

"That leaves eight of us," commented Bryce sadly. "Maybe seven. We haven't heard from Darius."

"Why didn't the SIS protect her? I mean, isn't that their job?"

"I'm sorry, Megan," said Harper. "Whoever's doing this is very good—a professional. Maybe someone within State Intelligence is even helping them. We're all going to have to be very careful if we want to survive."

Bryce sat down beside them. "What I want to know is how they're getting their information."

"We need to make a plan," added Harper. She stood and helped Megan to her feet. "Let's talk with the others."

"Wait," said Megan. "You go on, Bryce. We'll be right there. I need to say something in private to Harper." Bryce nodded and left them.

"What is it?" asked Harper.

Megan pressed an index finger against her lips, pulled back Harper's hair, and whispered into her ear. "Do you think the informant could be one of us?" Harper turned quickly and looked Megan in the eye.

"I've wondered the same thing," she exclaimed softly. Megan stared into her eyes but said nothing. Harper's eyebrows lowered as she pinched the point where her nose met her forehead. "If you're right, we can't say a thing. Not now, anyway. Not until we have some proof." She thought silently and then added, "Block it out of your mind. If you don't, the twins will read you like a book. They're getting more powerful every day."

Megan nodded silently.

"Okay. Let's go," Harper said, and they walked over to where the others sat playing cards. Harper sat on an overturned bucket and leaned forward. A teenage boy with brown skin and glasses drew a card from the deck, studied it briefly, and then stared into the bright blue eyes of a small boy with straight blond hair and demanded an answer.

"Ace of clubs," answered the younger blond-haired boy, grinning triumphantly. He was joined by another boy who looked exactly like him, his identical twin. They high-fived each other and stood grinning like mirror images of each other.

"That's the entire deck!" exclaimed the older boy in disbelief, his glasses making his eyes appear artificially large. "Nobody's ever gone through an entire deck without missing." His name was Wiley, and Megan had always liked him. He had an easy smile and a playful way about him even in the most stressful situations. When the going got tough, he laughed. Megan wondered how anyone could be so positive and felt grateful that he was in the group. Without his encouragement and sense of humor, their group likely would have broken up long ago.

"That was incredible," continued Wiley. "Nice work, Spencer. Jack, do you want to try?"

Spencer's towheaded twin fidgeted before responding. Like his brother, he had bright pale blue eyes and an angelic face. At eleven years of age, they were the youngest of the Wonder Kids, and the fact that they had even survived the trip to Earth was something of a miracle. Harper had been nine when she left, the others just three or four. The twins, on the other hand, had been strapped into a spaceship shortly after their first birthday, their tiny bodies subjected to nine months of weightlessness. Removing the twins at such a young age was dangerous but necessary. With rebellion brewing, the colony was no place for children, and evacuating them all to Earth was judged to be the only realistic solution.

Jack hesitated for a moment and then spoke. "I can't do that."

"Well, neither can we," said Wiley. "But you'll never know how good you are unless you try."

"I have something," announced an ebony-haired thirteen-year-old clad entirely in black and wearing way too much eye shadow. Her jacket, studded with electrically charged spikes, screamed *keep your stinking hands off me,* and a luminescent tattoo of a snake winding its way down her forearm and hand reinforced the message. She was Raven, a troubled genius, and Megan didn't trust her. She hung out with cyberpunk thugs and drug addicts and was possibly one herself. She reached into her pocket and pulled out a blue feather. "Watch," she said, and she placed it on the concrete floor.

Raven glared at the feather. It twitched, rose slightly, then fell back to the ground. She glared at it again, more intensely this time, as though she hated it with every fiber of her being. The feather rose swiftly off the floor and floated upward until it rested against the ceiling.

"Amazing," gasped Wiley. "Just imagine the possibilities."

Megan shifted uneasily. The thought of Raven possessing the ability to use telekinesis frightened her. Using only her mind, Raven held the feather firmly against the ceiling for several more seconds and then released it. It fluttered gently back to the floor.

"That's a huge improvement," remarked Harper, her eyebrows raised. "Have you been practicing?"

"Not really. It just comes naturally, I guess."

"Well, I'd like to see what you can do with some other items," interjected Wiley. "Just imagine if you could lift a chair or a person." Megan did not want to imagine this. One of the twins—possibly Spencer—glanced at her curiously. Megan quickly thought of something else, a movie that she hoped to catch later in the week. The boy looked away, uninterested.

Harper stood up. "There's a reason why I asked you all to be here tonight. There's been trouble on Mars. The oxygen supply to the colony—to where we were born—has been cut off. People are dying."

"Our parents!" gasped Wiley.

Raven exploded in fury, a shock of charcoal-dark hair whipping across her face. "What do you mean *our parents*? We don't even know who they are, idiot. As far as we know, they were nothing but human garbage—criminal lowlifes whose only reason for being on Mars was to avoid the death penalty. They would have died in the mines years ago."

"Yeah, maybe that's so, Raven," protested Wiley, "or maybe some of them were actually decent people who just made one terrible mistake in their lives. Maybe they even loved us and didn't want to give us up." He was clearly angry, his face and neck turning red.

"Then why don't any of us have last names?" demanded Raven. "Do you know anyone else who doesn't have one? I'm Raven—that's it. No family name because I have no family. Just like you." What she said was true. Each of the Wonder Kids had only one name, a first name, as the government never saw fit to officially give them a surname. Megan sometimes lied and called herself Megan Swann after the Hans Christian Anderson story, and the name had stuck, but deep down she felt an emptiness, a deep sense of abandonment that came from not belonging to a family. She wished Raven would just shut up. It was bad enough having just lost one of her best friends.

"Stop!" screamed Harper. "Just stop. Nothing good is going to come out of arguing over who our parents were. We'll probably never know. The important thing right now is that you know what's going on up there. There's talk of a rescue mission—a *top-secret* rescue mission—and I'm going to try to be a part of it."

"But won't everybody already be dead?" asked one of the twins. They looked so much alike that Megan couldn't tell which one had spoken.

"We think they're getting a little air, but not much. There's probably, like, one generator that's still working. But they have another problem—they're under attack."

"By who?" asked Megan. "Are they fighting each other?"

"I don't know. Maybe. I hope to know more soon."

Bryce spoke up. "Did you know about this, Megan, that something was going to happen?"

Megan squirmed uncomfortably. "Sort of. I've been having some strange dreams lately—about Mars, but not the colony. In my dreams, I'm there, and there's a woman. She wants to talk with me, but the more I walk toward her, the farther away she seems. I swear I didn't know anything about the colony being under attack."

"Did anybody else pick up on it?" asked Harper. The twins, Bryce, and Wiley all shook their heads no. Raven spit on the floor.

"Okay," continued Harper solemnly. "There's something else we need to talk about—strategy. I don't think you're safe in your apartments anymore. Those of you who want to hide should keep the location of your hideouts to yourself. That way, if one of us gets captured, we can't be forced to say where you are." Wiley and Bryce nodded. Harper continued, "I'll be staying in plain sight since I'm pretty well protected. I'm going to continue working at SIS headquarters in Langley, so you'll know where to find me if you need me. You know the signal."

"Can you get us guns—the kind that shoot exploding titanium rounds?" asked Raven with a raised eyebrow. She no longer seemed angry. Her moods tended to change quickly and without warning—sunny one moment, stormy the next. "It would be nice if we could protect ourselves."

Megan had a thought, and one of the twins glanced at her suspiciously.

"That's not going to be possible," replied Harper. "Only agents get guns. Your best bet is going into hiding."

"Great. You really seem to care about us," Raven sneered sarcastically.

She's afraid, thought Megan. *Interesting. Would an informant want them armed? It seemed unlikely.* Megan again caught one of the twins looking at her. She shifted her thoughts to dinner and hoped they hadn't gleaned too much.

"I'll be in my spot in the attic above the old library on West Fifty-Sixth Street," said Megan. "That is, if Agnes doesn't lock me in. I don't care if any of you know." Harper turned and gave her a stern look.

"Well, I'm not saying where I'll be," interjected Wiley, "but let's just say that I'll be near at hand. If any of you need me, just concentrate on the Statue of Liberty until you can picture it in your mind. I'll get the message."

"And I'm the snake," added Raven. "Any snake will do." The others nodded and reminded each other of their own signal images. Megan felt slightly jealous as she was the only one of them who couldn't detect these telepathic signals. She was on her own, although she had a few tricks up her own sleeve.

"Okay," said Harper. "We'll meet back here in a month. Keep your eyes open. Bryce and Wiley, you go first, then the twins, then you, Raven. Leave fifteen minutes apart. Megan and I will leave last after we know everyone is safe."

Slowly, the others snuck out of the warehouse and disappeared into the night. Some, like Wiley, seemed confident, while others looked nervous. When, at last, Raven vanished into the darkness, Harper pulled Megan aside. "I want you to take the long way home, not up the steps to the elevated highway. It's too dangerous for you."

Too dangerous for you. Megan felt her back stiffen with anger. She disliked being told what she could and couldn't do, especially when it was obviously about her leg. "Don't underestimate me, Harper. I can take care of myself."

"I know you can. Sorry. It's just that you're the closest thing I have to a little sister, and I want to take care of you. Take this." Harper handed her a black retractable umbrella the size of a small purse. "It's bulletproof, and the tip can deliver an electrical charge." Megan hesitated. "Please," insisted Harper. "You probably won't need it, but you'd make me feel a lot better if you had it.

"Also, there's something I need to tell you," she said. "Something important."

"Okay," said Megan. "Shoot."

"I want to go on this mission, but my intuition says it's going to be you."

"Me?" exclaimed Megan. "But I'm only fourteen. And you're an agent."

"I know. But I've been hearing the voice again and it's clearer than ever. It says you're the one."

Megan fidgeted nervously. She had always been curious about Mars, but she had never wanted to go back. She remembered no one—her parents, her caretakers, the people who put her on a ship to Earth—they were like a fairytale to her, a story with few, if any, details. Harper, on the other hand, was different. She was nine when they were evacuated. Though she never met her parents—she, like the others, was taken from her mother immediately after birth—she had vivid memories of a scientist named Dr. Burke who had raised her, taught her, and protected her.

She remembered living underground in a concrete-reinforced bunker and leaving the colony only once when Burke had taken her to see Olympus Mons and the mines. They had ridden in a truck with enormous tires, and she recalled seeing other trucks carrying convict laborers and wondering if her mom or dad was on one of them. She also recollected the landscape, a sweeping red plain, pitted with impact craters, and an enormous mountain with steep sides rising above it all.

"Harper, has the voice ever been wrong?"

"Never."

Harper had lived with this little voice her entire life. It spoke to her, sometimes only once or twice a year, sometimes more frequently. She had learned to trust it. When she was a child, it influenced her choice of friends, gave her answers during tests, and warned her of danger. Later, it steered her on the path to becoming an SIS agent and helped her rise far above what would have been normal for someone her age. It was never wrong. She wondered if it was intuition or if it had something to do with being born on Mars. The other Wonder Kids, with the exception of Megan, could send messages to each other telepathically, and Megan had her mysterious dreams, but only Harper heard the voice.

"*Never*," repeated Harper. "I'm going to ask my supervisor what he knows. I'll call you as soon as I know something."

"Okay. And Harper, I'm not really going to hide in the attic above the library. I just said that to throw off the informant, if we have one."

"Good thinking. I'll be in touch."

Chapter 3

Unexpected Trouble

By the time Megan left the warehouse, it was completely dark outside. Most of the streetlights were broken, and the ones that still worked cast a pallid yellow glow, barely enough to light the street. Darkness concealed tents and shacks that she knew were only meters away. She was tired and her limp had worsened. Passing the shantytown again, this time at night, frightened her, though she hadn't been able to admit it to Harper. It was tough being disabled. People either pitied you or didn't take you seriously. She heard something to her left, close at hand, and prepared for an ambush, remembering that a punch to the throat was one of the most efficient ways of disabling an attacker.

Suddenly, a mangy brown dog charged out of the darkness and lunged at her, growling and baring its fangs.

Panicked, she kicked it hard on the nose, causing it to retreat momentarily. As it swung around to attack again, she whipped out the retractable umbrella that Harper had given her and pushed the button on its side. Instantly, it expanded to form a flexible shield around her. The dog looked confused as Megan regained her footing and shoved the now-open umbrella into its snarling face. She tried to hit it with the electrically charged tip, but the dog was nimble and darted away. There was shouting within the surrounding community, and she could hear the sounds of people running. She didn't know what to do. *If only Harper were here,* she thought. *I should have listened; I should have taken the long way home.*

Bang, bang, bang! Three shots erupted from nearby. There was a yelp, and the frenzied canine sank to the ground and became still. The shouting stopped. Harper stepped out of the darkness and took Megan by the arm. "Stand back or I'll shoot," she shouted at a figure lurking in the shadows. "Don't worry, Megan. I'll get you out of here."

At that instant, Megan heard the screeching of tires and turned just in time to see a pair of bright headlights barreling toward her. There wasn't time to move, and the glare was blinding. She closed her eyes and braced for impact. Just in the nick of time, the vehicle's automated drive system slammed on the brakes, and it skidded to an abrupt stop.

"Get in!" screamed Harper as she opened the door. Megan dove inside, and the car took off like a rocket, its tires throwing up black smoke as the rubber spun against the asphalt street. Still shaking with fear, she felt warm tears roll down her face. Harper had been right all along. She was easy prey with her damaged leg. Gradually, her fear turned to anger and frustration as she confronted this reality.

"I'm sorry," she cried. "I don't know what I was thinking. I'll listen to you next time."

"You did great, Megan. Don't beat yourself up. Now let's get you home and erase the car's data log. We don't need anyone knowing where we've been." As they drove up an access ramp and onto a side street, Harper squeezed her eyes shut and pinched her forehead with her thumb and index finger.

"What's the matter?"

"Migraine. I've been getting them a lot lately."

"Is it bad?" Megan had never had one before.

"Yeah, but I'll get over it," replied Harper. "I get them whenever I hear that little voice—the one inside me."

"What's it saying now?"

"That there's work to be done."

A short time later, they arrived in front of Megan's apartment unit. An agent was waiting outside for them. His name was Hendrix—Megan had seen him before and knew that Harper couldn't stand him. *Arrogant jerk* was how she described him.

"I see you found her," he said to Harper. "Where was she?"

"I promised her I wouldn't tell," said Harper. "She got in a little trouble and called me for help. Everything's okay now."

Hendrix looked irritated. "Well, tell that to Agnes. She got fired for letting her leave the apartment." He turned to Megan. "Does that make you happy?"

Megan felt a small pang of guilt for costing Agnes her job, but she wasn't about to admit as much to this agent who treated her like she was barely there. "I feel just fine, thank you," she said, not looking at him.

"I'll take it from here, Hendrix," Harper said, grimacing.

"There's been a change of plans," answered Hendrix. "I'll be guarding her tonight. In the morning, she's going to have a guest. The director himself wants to speak with her."

This is big, thought Megan. *This is Mars-big.* It looked like she might be going there after all.

Chapter 4

The Assignment

That night, Megan dreamed that she was a prisoner in a small boat, her hands and feet bound with rope. A large man with unkempt hair and an overgrown beard sat behind her, straining against the weight of the oars as he rowed the boat forward. A guard sat in the bow watching her, his eyes lazily opening and closing. Seagulls chattered noisily in the distance.

She could hear the rhythmic slapping of the oars against the water as the boat rose and fell on each passing wave. The sun's rays danced on the water's surface, causing her to squint. It seemed too real to be a dream. She was unafraid. Soon, an island became visible in the distance, and as they approached, she noticed the silhouetted figure of a woman standing on a pier. She was middle-aged, with dark eyes and strands of gray in her hair. She smiled at Megan and held out a hand.

Suddenly, the pier and island disappeared, and they were standing alone in a bleak, reddish landscape strewn with rocks and craters. Megan felt an icy chill pass through her as though she had been plunged in freezing water. Then, the mysterious woman began shrinking rapidly, growing smaller and smaller until she disappeared into a tiny glowing speck.

Megan awoke suddenly to the scent of freshly brewed garrack. She rolled over to glance at her clock and groaned. It was already ten o'clock.

Her memory of the dream faded quickly as the events of the previous evening came back to her. As she put on her slippers, she felt a twinge of pain in her bad leg and remembered the dog charging her. She had been lucky—it was large and could have torn her to pieces. As much as it pained her to admit it, it was a good thing Harper was there to save her. She opened her bedroom door and saw a tall man with neatly combed hair standing with his back against the front door.

"Oh, it's you," she muttered. "I was hoping you were only a dream. Hendrix, right?"

"Good morning, sunshine," the agent quipped sarcastically, ignoring the slight. "Yes, Hendrix is my name. Go turn on the news. There's something you need to see."

What a jerk, she thought.

She poured herself a cup of hot garrack and took a sip. Nasty but nutritious. *Now what to have for breakfast?* She brushed her fingers across an LCD screen on her refrigerator and selected the icons for an omelet and juice.

"Good morning, Megan," replied a soothing voice straight out of the machine. "How would you like your omelet?"

"Two eggs, cheddar cheese, and some diced tomatoes and onions."

There was a pause as the kitchen's computer scanned its inventory. "I'm sorry. We're out of tomatoes," it said with a twinge of regret. "Would you like me to make you one without them?"

"No, thanks. I'll see if there's one in the garden."

She opened a large glass door to her balcony and walked outside to the small garden that she shared with a neighbor. The plants were mostly stunted and covered with a fine gray powder. She ran her fingers along a stem until they felt a ripe tomato, and she plucked it. It wasn't large and shiny like the genetically modified ones sold in stores, but it was her tomato, grown from seeds planted by her own hands.

She wiped a coating of gray dust off the tomato, revealing a beautiful reddish-orange fruit. Smog was a constant nuisance these days, not just because it made breathing difficult, but because it deposited a grayish dust on virtually everything it touched. It even got inside people's homes, ruining rugs and chairs and making vacuuming a twice-a-day chore.

She placed the tomato in a pot and set it aside for a moment. Moving to the edge of the balcony, she put her hands on the railing and stared at the ocean below. She remembered stories about when there were still dolphins and how they would jump and play right here in front of her balcony. They were extinct now, the victims of pollution and overfishing. The thought saddened her. There was a distant squawk, and she scanned the horizon for seagulls. She had fed them from her balcony only a couple of years ago, but now they, too, were becoming scarce as the pollution worsened.

She walked back inside and began washing the tomato in the sink. The kitchen's computer interrupted her. "Lethal pathogens detected," it announced in a pleasant, soothing voice. "Please discard. Would you like for me check your inventory for a replacement?"

Megan sighed and tossed the contaminated tomato into her compost chute. "Yes."

"Very well then," the voice continued. The refrigerator's display panel suddenly lit up, displaying a list of possibilities.

"I'll have the omelet without tomatoes."

"Very well. It will be ready in two minutes. By the way, you are running short on milk and eggs. Would you like for me to place an order?"

"Yes, please," Megan answered. "Thanks." She felt a little silly thanking a computer, but she always found it difficult to accept anything without being courteous.

"Turn on the news, sunshine." It was Hendrix again, and he was obviously losing patience. "The director will be calling any minute, and you might as well know what's up."

"Can't it wait until after breakfast?"

"No. Turn it on now or I'm coming in there to do it for you."

She hesitated, not wanting to give him the satisfaction, but then flicked on the monitor above the oven. The news scrolled slowly across the display:

> Martian base Opportunity II on the verge of suffocation. Massive power failure. Oxygen production falls to near zero. Inhabitants await rescue as the American Commonwealth, Pacific Alliance, and Trans Europa plan mission.

A 3-D image of Opportunity II materialized on the display. Beside it towered Olympus Mons, an immense volcano with steep, cliff-like sides rising to a height surpassing that of Everest. It had been dormant for more than a million years, but recent photographs had shown smoke rising from its caldera, suggesting that an eruption was imminent. She remembered what Harper had told her the night before, only now it seemed more real and threatening. That dome-covered settlement had been her home, the place where she had been born and where she had taken her first steps. Perhaps her parents were still there, fighting to stay alive so that they might see her again.

She recalled her dream and guessed that the island represented Mars. And the woman—*Who was she? Her mother? Burke? And why did she always disappear?* Like most of her dreams, its meaning was shrouded in symbols and metaphors. She didn't understand it, but she had a hunch that Harper was right, that she would somehow be going to Mars as part of the rescue mission.

The oven chimed twice, and the computer announced that the omelet was ready. Just as she was about to take a bite, Hendrix rudely interrupted.

"Too late, sunshine. Leave the meal—the director's coming online." She stared at him in disbelief. "I'm serious," he continued. "If you don't, you'll be sorry. You could end up losing this apartment and have to live on the streets. Not a pretty picture with that leg of yours."

"Okay," complained Megan. "I'm coming." She returned her breakfast to the oven and crossed into the living room.

Hendrix's open briefcase lay on the glass table beside an empty chair. "Begin transmission," he said, switching on the case's holograph feature. "Have a seat."

A blue light within the briefcase glowed softly and brightened. Individual rays of light then shot out from the device toward the middle of the room and interacted with each other until they began to form a three-dimensional figure of a man. At first, it appeared faint and slightly bluish as it flickered in and out, like static on a radio. Gradually, the image stabilized to reveal a small bespectacled man with gray hair and a solemn, slightly threatening expression. It was Ross Herrington, director of the SIS. He surveyed the room before turning his attention to Megan.

"What do you remember of Mars, Ms. Swann?" he asked, skipping pleasantries.

"Nothing at all, sir," she replied. "I was only four when I left."

"Of course, Ms. Swann. Of course." He looked at Hendrix. "Agent Hendrix, would you be so kind as to leave the apartment for a while? This will be a private conversation."

Hendrix looked perplexed. "Don't you want me to guard her, sir? She escaped just last night and put herself in great danger."

"Rest assured that Ms. Swann will not be a flight risk, Agent Hendrix," interjected the director bluntly. "Am I correct?" Megan nodded uneasily. Herrington gave her the creeps both in person and as a holograph. "That will be all, Hendrix."

Hendrix glanced suspiciously at Megan before exiting the apartment.

"Thank you, Megan," continued the director. "You don't mind if I call you Megan, do you? After all, you don't actually have a last name, do you?"

"It's okay," she answered with a twinge of nervousness.

"Megan, I trust that you've seen the news about our

colony on Mars. Do you have an idea why I would want to talk with you about it?"

"No, sir," she replied. "I mean, I was born there, but I don't see how that matters now."

The director pressed his fingers together and made the shape of a pyramid. It was an odd mannerism meant to convey power. "Oh, it matters greatly, Megan." He stared at her, grinning like a chess player about to declare checkmate. "You see, there's someone up there, on Mars, who we believe is behind all the trouble. Her name is Dr. Artemis Burke. You've heard of her, no doubt?"

Megan nodded uncomfortably.

"Megan, let me be frank. The president believes that Burke and her cronies have created their own settlement. They're now in the process of eliminating the competition—us. The prize is the stockpile of mineral resources we've mined there, and we believe she's intent on killing every last colonist to get it."

Megan didn't like where he was heading and considered attempting another escape. She fidgeted and looked around the room for something to use against Hendrix should he try to stop her.

"Don't even think about fleeing," warned the director, as if reading her mind. "I've got drones watching your apartment at this very moment. If you try to leave, I will kill you. Now think: you can either help us save the colony—and everybody in it—or die. And Megan, there's something else. Your parents are alive, or at least they were when we last had contact with the colony. If you help us, I think the president will be willing to issue them each a pardon. Now, what's it going to be?"

It was too much for her to process, but she knew that there was only one possible answer. She looked the director in the eye. "Okay, I'll help. What do you need me to do?"

Herrington grinned confidently. "You're going to accompany one of our agents on the mission to the colony. We think Dr. Burke would be more agreeable to negotiations if we brought you along. She held you as a baby, cared for you. Who better to speak to her than you?"

It was beginning to make sense. Just as the police would get a violent criminal's wife or mother to talk him into dropping his weapon and coming out with his hands up, Megan would be used to act on Burke's emotions so that they could draw her out and kill her. They might even use her as a bargaining chip.

She nodded her head. "I'll do it. Just one question, though. Why me and not one of the others?"

Herrington took off his glasses, wiped them, and put them on again. "I've been observing you for more than a decade, Megan, and quite frankly you're the only one of the Wonder Kids who could pull this off. You're brave and you have the ability to think quickly on your feet. Raven's smart but unstable, and the twins are too young. Wiley and Bryce lack creativity. The other choice would be your friend Harper, but we have other plans for her."

"Okay. When do I start?"

"Meet us at headquarters in Langley in four hours. I'll have Harper there to explain the details. There's a taxi waiting outside. Oh, and by the way, Megan, the omelet smells delicious." Megan felt her blood run cold. *A hologram that could smell?* That was scary. The hologram shimmered and disappeared. She heard a soft purr and felt a furry face press against her leg. It was Angel, her cat. She reached down and picked her up, gently stroking her soft white fur.

"Computer, see if Mrs. Mitchell next door can visit Angel while I'm gone. I know that you'll take good care of her, but she does like to have people pet her. And please order ten more bags of cat food."

"I can assist you with that," the voice answered pleasantly. "You know you can always count on me."

After packing her luggage and changing into her faded jeans and T-shirt, Megan turned off the lights, pulled the door shut behind her, and took the elevator down to the first floor. As she exited the complex, she relished the warm summer breeze and the sound of waves beneath her feet. She made her way down the narrow metal pedestrian bridge and met the air taxi that was already waiting for her.

Chapter 5

Headquarters

The State Intelligence Service headquarters in Langley was housed in an enormous concrete building that looked more like a fortress than an office complex. It had few windows.

Megan entered the lobby through bulletproof steel doors and immediately noticed a sharply dressed young woman with red hair hurrying toward her. It was Harper, and she was trailed by two M-20 wielding guards in camouflage fatigues, who struggled to keep up with her. The guards' fatigues changed colors as they moved, morphing to mimic the colors of their surroundings. They were green and brown as they walked past a series of potted trees and shrubs, then white as the wall behind them as they neared the entrance. Dark sunglasses hid their eyes while similarly changing colors to blend in with the surroundings.

Harper reached Megan first. "Megan," she said. "We have to move fast. Come with me." They hurried through a maze of hallways to her office, a small unassuming room with a desk, two chairs, and a computer connected to a monitor that took up most of one wall. A poster of Mars, with the sun rising behind it, hung on a wall behind her desk. Harper closed the door behind them, leaving the guards outside.

"Well, I was right about you getting picked for the mission. How do you feel?"

Megan shrugged her shoulders. She knew that Harper was disappointed at not being chosen. After an uncomfortable silence, she spoke. "I don't want to go, but the director isn't leaving me much choice."

Harper hugged her and whispered into her ear, "I'm sorry you've been dragged into this. I'll do whatever I can to help. Now put on your game face. We can't let them see us like this." She stepped back from Megan and stood with her back straight like a soldier at attention. "You can do this, Megan. It's in the government's best interest to deliver you to Mars safely. And if Burke really is still alive, she's not going to hurt you either. She loved you. She loved all of us."

There was a knock and the door swung open abruptly. Hendrix sauntered in, wearing a sharply tailored brown suit and expensive leather shoes, grinning from ear to ear. He plopped down in a chair and propped his feet on Harper's desk as though he owned it. "Good news, sunshine," he smirked, glancing at Megan. "You're looking at your chaperone for the Mars mission."

"What?" cried Harper in disbelief. "They chose *you*?"

"Yeah, go figure. Looks like I'm getting a promotion. Maybe I'll even get an apartment as nice as your little friend's." He leaned back in the chair and laughed. "Imagine that—Agent Stanley Hendrix going to Mars. How do you like that, sunshine?"

Megan was disgusted. "I don't need a babysitter," she said angrily, "and I sure don't need you."

"The director begs to differ," Hendrix said, raising his eyebrows for emphasis. "Anyway, I think you'll come to like me. I'm a good friend to have when there's trouble. Just ask your friend over there."

Megan already knew the story. Hendrix was the best shot in the service. He could knock a leaf off a tree from a hundred meters, and he had won the agency's marksmanship award for the past five years. And he never missed an opportunity to brag about it.

"Yeah, you're a good shot as long as nobody's shooting back," Harper remarked coolly. "But we both know the real reason you're going is because the director is your uncle."

Hendrix laughed. "Have it your way, ladies. But seriously, sunshine, I'd show some respect if I were you, because whether you like it or not, you're stuck with me for the next six months." He stood up and straightened his tie. "See you in a few minutes. They're flying us out to the launch site this afternoon." He smirked and left the room without closing the door behind him.

"What a jerk," remarked Harper. "He's like forty years old and still thinks he's God's gift to the world."

"Lucky me," said Megan. "Looks like it's going to be a long trip."

Harper looked at her sadly. "Oh, Megan, I wish we could just chat like we used to, but there's not enough time. The president has already assembled his team, and you're leaving tomorrow. The ships are fast—I think they're fusion-powered. You'll reach Mars in about three months, which isn't bad for a trip that used to take nine. Oh, and don't mention Burke to anyone, not even the other participants in the mission. You can tell anyone who asks that you're a senior officer's kid and a Junior Cadet with special clearance. The director asked me to make that very clear. Got it?"

"Got it," Megan replied. She was nervous. She would almost certainly be the only kid on the mission, and the thought of being supervised by Hendrix made her uneasy. Even if they did make it to Mars, what then? Would there be a fight? With her bad leg, she'd be easy prey. And what if it turned out that Burke wasn't even there?

"I'll do the best I can, Harper. Anything you can do to help would be great."

"Okay," continued Harper. "Time's up. We're going to have the Space Administration's people get you suited up for the trip, and I'll be talking with you throughout the mission." Harper handed her something thin, like a manila folder. It had a flexible LCD display on which words flickered. "All the files associated with Burke and the Mars colony are loaded on this. Read it, memorize it. You'll have plenty of time. Oh, and one more thing. Watch out for the spiders."

"Spiders?" Megan gasped. "On Mars?" She hated spiders. "Don't they require oxygen?"

"Sorry, I can't explain now, but it's all in the report."

As Harper hugged her again, Megan saw tears welling up in her friend's eyes and wondered if they would ever see each other again. She wiped a tear away from her own face and followed Harper to the door.

"Guards," ordered Harper. "Please escort Ms. Swann to the parking lot. Megan, I'll be thinking about you. Good luck."

Chapter 6

Arrival at the Launch Site

The typical astronaut spends years preparing for space travel. Megan had less than a day. After exiting SIS headquarters, she and Hendrix were driven by car to a small airfield near Washington, DC. Their vehicle's air conditioner was broken, and the heat inside was stifling. She wiped a drop of sweat from her forehead and reached to open a window, but Hendrix stopped her.

"Don't open that," he barked. "You'll get dust on my new suit."

"But it's hot."

"Not for me, sunshine. This suit has a built-in cooling system."

"Well, that's great for you," said Megan, "but I'm the one sweating over here."

Hendrix smirked and looked out the window. "Not my problem, sunshine," he muttered indifferently. He reached into his blazer and pulled out a small silver cylinder. He gave it a twist and a holographic image of a cube materialized above it. The cube was comprised of smaller cubes, each one a different color. With his free hand, he manipulated the smaller cubes until they began to form patterns within the larger cube. He became completely engrossed in the puzzle and ignored Megan as though she weren't even there.

Sensing the awkwardness, their government escort, who was in the front seat, interrupted. She was young and pretty and seemed irritated by Hendrix's rude behavior. "I'm really sorry about the air conditioner. It's been broken for a month, but nobody's bothered to fix it. Try this. It's a can of compressed cold air. You spray it on yourself."

"Thanks." Megan took the can and felt immediate relief as she sprayed her face, neck, and arms with it. Besides being icy cold, it also had a pleasant scent like spring flowers. Hendrix looked up as though to ask for some but then returned his attention to the puzzle. *He's too proud to ask,* thought Megan. *Serves him right.*

The young escort smiled at Megan. "This is where the president boards Air Force One," she explained, pointing. The grass along the runway was newly mowed, and there was a large gray control tower with tall, darkened windows along the top floor. "They've been using this site for the past sixteen years. Do you see that aircraft over there, the one that looks like a cross between a jet and a helicopter?" Megan nodded. "That's what's going to take you to the launch site."

"Is that what the president flies in?" asked Megan.

"No, he has his own jet that's much nicer. This one's strictly military, but it gets the job done," explained the escort. "Be prepared to be blindfolded during the flight. You're not allowed to see where they're taking you. We're taking your phone too."

"Okay," sighed Megan. The thought of being blindfolded made her uneasy, like she was a captive rather than a valued asset to the mission. She wondered if Hendrix would have to wear one too. "Will you be accompanying us?" she asked hopefully.

"Sorry," replied the escort, brushing hair away from her face. "I wish I could, but I have to stick with the car. I'm afraid it's just going to be you, Mr. Puzzle Boy over there, and the pilot."

Hendrix looked up annoyed. "Watch it, princess," he muttered angrily. He switched off the holographic puzzle and put the tiny cylinder back inside his jacket. "I don't appreciate being talked to like that." Megan rolled her eyes.

When the vehicle stopped, they exited and approached the drab, olive-green helijet beside the runway. Megan noticed the words *CAS Air Force* printed boldly on its side. Tucked under its wings was a pair of laser cannons and several air-to-surface missiles. With retractable propeller blades inside each wing, the helijet was a modern attack aircraft designed to take off and land like a helicopter but fly with the long-range, high-speed performance of a supersonic jet. It was a surprising choice of aircraft for a civilian operation, and Megan guessed that there must not be a runway where they were going.

As she followed Hendrix into the rear compartment, she noticed that the windows had been painted over so that they couldn't see out. She wondered why her escort had mentioned the blindfold. Maybe she hadn't known. The air inside was stale and smelled of diesel. Straps hung from the ceiling. Megan sat in a chair away from Hendrix and waited for takeoff.

The pilot was stern and said nothing other than to remind them to strap themselves into their seats before takeoff. There was a low roar and the helijet rocked jarringly from side to side as it rose into the air, its rotors making a rapid thumping noise. When it had risen forty or fifty meters, Megan could feel its jet engines turn on and the thumping noise die down. It drifted slowly to the right and then there was a loud clattering as the rotors retracted into the wings. Hendrix smiled and winked at her. "Get ready, sunshine."

Suddenly, and with a jolt, the craft took off like a shot. Megan grabbed the sides of her seat and dug her fingernails into the fabric. The force of the acceleration pushed hard against her, and she closed her eyes and tried to feel which direction they were going. *South*, she thought. *Definitely south*.

The flight took a little more than an hour. It was warm inside the aircraft, and she was exhausted. Slowly, she drifted off to sleep and began to dream. In her dream she was walking beside the older woman with dark eyes whom she remembered from her previous dreams. Her hair was mostly brown but had streaks of gray. They were walking together across a rust-colored desert and the woman was trying to tell her something. Then the scene changed and Megan found herself strapped into a seat as everything shook around her. There was an explosion, and she gasped. She awakened covered in sweat and trembling.

"Sweet dreams?" Hendrix asked, grinning.

Megan was still shaking. She had no idea where they were now. The aircraft decelerated and she could hear the rotors moving into position for landing. Just as during takeoff, it swayed back and forth like a pendulum as it descended, and there was a light bump as they touched down on the tarmac.

"We're here," shouted the pilot. "You can take off your harness and exit through the door. Watch your step as you get out!" Megan climbed down the steps ahead of Hendrix and surveyed their surroundings. They were on some kind of a base, and surrounding it was a forest of blighted pine trees. The air was hot and sticky with humidity. She blinked as her eyes adjusted to the sunlight. The details of her dream had melted away, but the terror lingered.

They were met on the tarmac by Chief Project Engineer Daryl Kang. Kang greeted them politely and thanked them for taking part in the mission. He was wearing a white lab coat and seemed surprised that Megan was so young, prompting her to wonder how much he really knew about the mission. He drove them in a sleek, solar-powered three-wheeler to a two-story rectangular building near the launch site, where technicians fitted them for survival suits. The suits were orange to blend in with the Martian terrain and though filled with insulation, they were formfitting and flexible. A metal gasket surrounding the neck area allowed for an air-tight fit with the helmet and visor.

Afterward, they visited Kang's laboratory where he handed Megan a black duffle bag full of travel supplies like toothpaste, thermal socks, and a pillow. The lab was small and cluttered. Robotic parts and circuit boards lay everywhere so that it was difficult to walk around without tripping over something. A fly buzzed erratically around the room looking for a way out. Opening the bag, Megan smiled as she pulled out a pair of furry brown bunny-rabbit slippers. "I love them," she exclaimed, taking off her shoes and trying them on. They fit perfectly. "Thanks!"

"One of the toughest things about space is keeping your sanity," explained Kang. "We've found that a sense of humor really helps. When people crack up there, it's usually because they haven't had enough mental stimulation. The other thing is fitness. You'll be in zero gravity, and your muscles will atrophy quickly if you don't work out."

"But how do you work out?" asked Megan. "Wouldn't the weights be weightless?"

"Good point," acknowledged Kang. "Actually, it's easy—we use resistance bands and isometrics. There are exercise pods in all of our ships that make use of these. The tough part is disciplining yourself to work out every day. No exceptions. Some of our best conditioned astronauts work out two or even three times a day."

Hendrix reached into his jacket and pulled out a nine-millimeter semi-automatic pistol. The letter H was inscribed on its handle. "I'll be carrying this onboard the ship," he stated bluntly. "It's SIS regulation."

Kang raised an eyebrow disapprovingly. "That's a Night Hawk. It fires exploding rounds—too dangerous inside a ship." He opened a closet door revealing a vast selection of firearms and ran his hand across a row of pistols until it stopped at one with a red handle. "Take this one. It's a Remi 540. Never jams and the rounds don't explode, so it would be a lot safer around the ship."

Hendrix took the red-handled pistol and aimed it at an exit sign down a long hallway. "Okay," he said, "but

I'm bringing my Night Hawk along too, for when we reach Mars."

Kang agreed and said that they could lock it in a gun vault on the ship for safekeeping until they got there.

"Megan," continued Kang, "I want you to have something too." He handed her what looked like a small, yellow industrial nail gun. Its rubberized grip had a checkered pattern like a diamondback rattlesnake. "It's an electro-static immobilizer—L-Stat for short—a kind of stun gun. Use it only in extreme emergencies. It sends a nonlethal electric pulse that disrupts the central nervous system. You can hit a man up to two meters away and he'll be completely useless for up to ten minutes, enough time to get help." Megan took the gun, felt the grip, and ran her finger along it. It would be nice to have a means of defending herself should the need arise.

"Wait a minute," said Hendrix. "I don't want her carrying any type of weapon, even if it's nonlethal. That's why I'm here." He snatched the gun from Megan's hand. She was mad enough to kick him but didn't get the opportunity. He handed the weapon back to Kang and made him put it away.

"Sorry for the misunderstanding," said Kang. "If you'd please follow me, I'll take you to a mock-up of the ship so you can see where everything is. We'll also issue you your flight suits for when you're on board the ship." He walked briskly down the hall with Hendrix right beside him. Megan followed as fast as she could, but with her limp she couldn't keep up.

"Wait," she yelled, frustrated. Hendrix turned around, clearly disgusted, but Kang told him to go on ahead.

"I've got something that might help her," he said. "We'll meet you in the supply depot. It's just up the hall."

Satisfied, Hendrix proceeded without them while Kang walked back to where Megan was standing.

"I sense that you and Agent Hendrix don't like each other," he said. "Come with me. There's something I want to give you." They went back to Kang's lab, and he reopened the closet containing the firearms and took out the L-Stat stun gun.

"Don't tell anybody that I'm doing this," he said, "but I want you to have that stun pistol. Keep it hidden."

"Thanks," said Megan, relieved.

"It needs time to recharge between firings," continued Kang, taking it back out of the weapons closet. "So, aim carefully."

"How long until it can be fired a second time?" asked Megan.

"Several minutes. It depends on temperature, humidity, and other factors like that. Go ahead and try it. See if you can hit that fly over there."

Megan took aim at a bristly green-and-black fly on the wall and fired. There was a sudden flash, and the fly fell to the floor twitching. "I like it," she said, surprised. Guns made her uneasy, but this one wasn't lethal, at least not to humans. She hoped that she wouldn't have to use it, but it made her feel more secure slipping it into her duffle bag. "Can I try it on Hendrix?" she joked.

Kang smiled. "No. He probably deserves it, but you can't do that. It's not a toy." He closed the armaments closet and locked it. "Okay, let's get you a flight suit. Follow me."

When they reached the supply depot, Hendrix was already dressed in a black Commonwealth of American States Space Administration flight suit that marked him as a member of the ship's security team. It was basic, a plain jumpsuit with pockets and a zipper down the back. "What do you think?" he asked, turning around.

"Much better than the suit," replied Megan sarcastically.

Hendrix laughed. "Don't be jealous, sunshine. You're getting one of your own."

A female attendant measured Megan and handed her a black flight suit like the one Hendrix had on. Putting it on, she was surprised to find that it was lightweight and comfortable. It was easy to move around in, like athletic wear.

"It says you work for the Space Administration now," remarked Kang, pointing to a patch on her left shoulder. Megan liked that. She smiled. It made her feel important and less like an SIS puppet.

Glancing around the room, she noticed men and women of all shapes and sizes collecting their flight suits. Kang explained to her that engineers and flight operators wore blue, maintenance wore red, and soldiers and security personnel wore black. There were other colors too, but Kang was talking so fast by now that what he said barely registered. Instead, she turned her mind to what awaited her: the moment of lift-off.

With the sun only beginning to rise the next morning, Megan boarded a shuttle to the launch pad. The shuttle was long and white with multiple cars attached, like a train. Hendrix was beside her but did not speak. He gazed out a window, lost in thought. They were crowded in, among dozens of other security and military personnel, all standing, all wearing black flight suits with the blue and white Space Administration patch on the shoulder. Although she was nervous, her thoughts began to wander. She thought about the dream she had on the way down to the launch site. She had been on Mars one moment and then in an explosion the next. What could it mean? She closed her eyes and tried to clear her mind.

The atmosphere inside the shuttle was one of nervous chatter.

"Hey, have any of you heard of that new restaurant on Mars?" joked a burly man with a moustache. "Great food but no atmosphere."

Megan's mood brightened slightly. In the distance she could see three launchpads, each with its own control tower and spacecraft. The ships looked nothing like the original pencil-shaped rockets sent to the moon during the Apollo program over two hundred fifty years before. Each was huge and gray, and there were no letters, flags, or words printed on the outside. Resembling prehistoric insects, their bodies were tubular and sleek, with low, flat cockpits on top that flared outward like the heads of venomous snakes. Instead of eyes, they had windows that were tinted black to offer protection from the sun's intense glare outside of Earth's atmosphere. Large, triangular wings jutted outward from their bodies, and a low vertical wing rose along each cockpit's roof like a long dorsal fin. Powering each ship was a fusion reactor that ran along the entire sixty-meter length of the ship, with the actual turbine engine located at its base. How long these ships had been in production and how much they had cost, Megan could only wonder.

A few minutes later, they arrived at the launchpads. It felt good to exit the crowded shuttle. As people began chatting nervously before heading to the spaceships, she noticed that the crew members in black had military-style haircuts and the steely-eyed gaze of marines. She felt out of place. *Strange,* she thought. *Who are these people?*

Mixed in among them were others wearing different

colors—some tall, some short, some young, some old. Even the youngest were still years older than she was. She noticed a young woman, perhaps in her midtwenties, standing apart from the others and staring inquisitively at her. She wore black-rimmed glasses and had long hair that cascaded down her back. As their eyes met, the woman walked over to Megan.

"You look like you could use some help. Which ship are you on?" she asked.

"The *Intrepid*," answered Megan, "but I don't know which one it is. They all look the same to me."

"It's the one over there," said the woman, pointing to the ship furthest from them. "The *Intrepid*. I like that name. I'm on ship two, the *Icarus*." She paused and glanced around nervously. "My name's Paige. You look a bit young for this mission. Do you know what you're doing?"

"I'm a reporter," said Megan. "I look younger than I actually am. I'm going to be writing about the rescue mission, and I'd love to ask you a few questions." She shook hands with Paige and noticed a small tattoo on her wrist. It was less than two centimeters across, but she could see it clearly—a pyramid with an eye above it. "How about you? Will this be your first time on Mars?"

"No, I've been there before, but it wasn't as dangerous then."

"What did you do there?"

Before Paige could answer, Megan noticed another crew member, also in blue, watching them from several meters away. The man quickly looked away when she made eye contact with him. He was standing next to a much larger man whose back was facing her. Paige also noticed and immediately became flustered.

"I'm sorry—I shouldn't have come over here," she

stammered. "I'm not allowed to talk to you without permission." She slung a heavy duffle bag over her shoulder and added, "Be careful, Megan. We're counting on you. I'll do everything I can to help you once we reach Mars."

"Wait," said Megan. "How do you know my name? Who are you?"

"A friend." The woman glanced at the man now walking toward her and added, "I know you're not a reporter, Megan. We'll talk on Mars. Stay safe and be careful who you trust."

"Who can I trust?"

"That's hard to say," replied Paige. "Sorry. Gotta go." As she turned to leave, the man who had been watching them caught up with her and put a hand on her shoulder.

As they walked away, Megan noticed the man whisper something in her ear. Paige quickly glanced back at the large man whose back had been facing them. He was now looking directly at her, his blond hair blowing in the wind, and she looked scared.

Who is this guy? thought Megan. From a distance, it looked like something was wrong with his face, but she couldn't tell what. She stepped toward him to get a better look, but just then a crowd of people walked between them—and when they left, he was gone.

Chapter 7

Lift-off

Inside the *Intrepid's* control tower was a freight elevator that carried the crew members up four stories to the ship's main entry port. There was something about being inside that crowded elevator, creeping steadily upward, that felt final to Megan. There was no turning back.

She yearned for a friend to talk with, but everybody on the elevator seemed preoccupied or unapproachable. Hendrix appeared to have already made an acquaintance—an attractive brunette in her thirties with some kind of a tattoo on the back of her neck that was mostly concealed by her ponytail. The woman's blue flight suit suggested that she was either an engineer or a flight operator. He was showing off for her, imitating how he would draw his gun in a shootout, and she seemed to be enjoying the show. *If she only knew what a jerk he was*, thought Megan.

The elevator continued rising until, at last, there was a loud clank and the doors jolted open. In front of them stood an open hatch just large enough to accommodate one person at a time. Megan stepped cautiously inside, her eyes gradually adjusting to the dimness of the light.

The ship's interior was spotless and smelled like disinfectant. There were white walls, surprisingly large open spaces, and comfortable chairs. The ship was standing on end, so its normally horizontally oriented interior required steps and ladders for the crew to reach their assigned positions. An attendant helped Megan to her seat, which to her great disappointment was right next to Hendrix. *Figures*, she thought. She lay back against the soft upholstery and ran her fingers along the armrests. Looking up, she noticed a triangle and an oval crudely scratched into the vinyl cover of the seat in front of her, and a feeling of déjà vu swept over her. It reminded her of Paige's tattoo, but she knew she had seen it somewhere else too. Suddenly, everything looked strangely familiar, but she couldn't put a finger on it. A sense of dread came over her.

"Hendrix," she whispered. "Something's not right. I have a bad feeling about this."

Hendrix turned and looked at her as though she were an idiot. He was clearly annoyed. "It's too late to back out now, sunshine. Just close your eyes and try not to think about it."

He whispered something to his female friend who was next to him, and she laughed. *Oh great*, thought Megan, *now they're talking about me*. They hugged and the woman left, climbing down a ladder to where her seat was.

With only minutes to go before lift-off, an attendant with short, cropped hair climbed in beside her and strapped her firmly into her seat.

"Is everything okay?" Megan asked.

"Everything looks good," he answered. "Don't take off your safety harness until we tell you to. You'll need to put on your helmet now." He smiled and moved on to the next person. Megan positioned the helmet over her head, wondering what good it could possibly do if the ship crashed and burned. Her fear was growing stronger by the moment. A male voice came over the intercom. *"This is mission control to Mars Expedition 105. Do you copy?"*

One by one the captains of the three ships responded with *"Copy that."* The voice from mission control resumed, clear and calm. *"We have sunny skies and excellent visibility. Looks like a great day for a lift-off. Is everybody ready?"*

Megan fidgeted in her seat. Suddenly, she remembered the dream. The chair she was sitting in at this very moment was identical to the one in the dream, right down to the scratch. She desperately looked around for the attendant but couldn't find him.

"Turning on engines," mission control announced. There was a long, low rumble as the main engine warmed up, and the entire spacecraft shook. Megan was beginning to panic.

Had the dream been trying to warn her that the ship was doomed? She began pulling at her harness, trying to escape. "Let me off this ship!" she screamed. "Please, somebody help!"

Hendrix was shouting back at her, but she couldn't make out what he was saying. The noise around them grew to a roar as the engines prepared to blast them into space.

She could barely hear the voice of mission control over the intercom, but it was clear that they were nearing the moment of lift-off.

"Ten, nine, eight . . ."

She twisted a latch on her safety harness, and it popped open.

"Seven, six . . ."

As she tried to step out of her seat, she felt strong hands pulling her back down into it. She looked up. It was Hendrix and the attendant. They were gripping her by the shoulders and refastening the safety harness.

"Five, four . . ."

"Do not get out of this seat!" yelled the attendant.

"Three, two . . ."

Megan closed her eyes and prepared for the inevitable. She could hear frantic scrambling as the two men raced to their seats.

"One, zero."

It didn't seem possible that everything could end in an instant.

"Ignition, lift-off."

The noise of the engine escalated until it reached a frenzied high-pitched shriek. She thought she could hear the other ships lifting off, the earth trembling beneath them, the crescendo of fusion-powered rockets ripping the air. As her own ship's engines roared at a near-deafening pitch, she felt it rise off its launchpad. Then there was an explosion so enormous that it drowned out every other sound. Emergency lights flashed around her and an alarm blared, but curiously there was no smoke or fire.

The ship rose into the atmosphere, shaking at first but then steadying. Despite the numbness in her arms and legs caused by the safety harness, she felt the force of the lift-off pressing against her like a thousand-kilogram weight. She began to hyperventilate. Gripping the armrests with all her might and gritting her teeth, she held on as long as she could manage and then blacked out.

When she awoke a short time later, surprised to be alive and curious at how calm everything had become, her breathing had slowed and was almost back to normal. She glanced at Hendrix beside her, but he was looking the other way. The top part of his flight suit was drenched in sweat. *He's going to be seriously pissed off*, she thought. *I wonder what happened.*

A tranquil female voice on the intercom announced their status. *"We've departed Earth's stratosphere and will be entering the ionosphere in approximately sixty seconds. Please remain seated."*

Looking around, Megan noticed that some of the crew members were already taking off their helmets. As she reached up and pulled off her own, she was relieved to find that not only had the force of lift-off diminished, but her hair was floating weightlessly around her. She let go of her helmet and smiled as it levitated like a helium-inflated balloon. She tapped it with her left hand and it sailed right until she caught it with her other hand. She began batting it back and forth slowly between her two hands, enchanted by the weirdness of it all.

I'm alive, she thought. *We're going to Mars!*

"Are you all right, sunshine?" It was Hendrix, who had turned around in his seat. Strangely, he sounded sincere. She felt embarrassed that he had had to help restrain her and worried that he'd never let her live it down.

"Yeah," she sighed. She waited for one of his sarcastic remarks, but it never came. She placed her helmet in a container in front of her seat and tried to relax. The voice on the intercom returned a few minutes later giving them the okay to leave their seats. All at once, the crew began unbuckling themselves and swimming through the compartment as though underwater. They seemed happy. Even the ones who had looked unapproachable earlier were now laughing and playing.

A young woman with long black hair twirled and did a flip in midair, causing Megan to smile for the first time since boarding the ship. She slid out of her seat and kicked her feet, propelling herself forward, slowly at first and then more quickly. Having never experienced weightlessness, she moved haphazardly, bumping into walls and equipment, but gradually, she improved. The key was controlling your speed. A gentle push off a wall was all that was needed; even the subtlest flick of a finger could be enough to propel you forward. She smiled. For the first time in her life, she felt like her injured leg wasn't a liability.

Pushing off a wall, she suddenly found herself drifting toward a tall, muscular man with blond hair. He had the strangest face she had ever seen. There was something peculiar about his eyes—they were a deep blue, just like his flight suit, and never blinked, and his eyelashes were just a little too long. She recognized him—he was the man she had seen earlier, the one Paige had seemed scared of.

The collision was inevitable. She hit him square on the chest and began apologizing immediately, but the man said nothing. He merely gazed at her with an odd, curious stare that made the hair on the back of her neck stand on end. She pushed off him firmly and sailed to the other side of the compartment, putting as much distance between them as possible. She wondered why he hadn't said anything. *Was he mute? And what was the matter with his eyes?*

She did her best to put him out of her mind, reminding herself that everybody was probably a little out of sorts after the launch, and continued practicing her movements. She tried staying in place by moving her arms in circles as though treading water, but with limited success. The only sure way to remain in place was to hold onto something. She watched Hendrix on the other side of the compartment. He was trying to do a somersault but couldn't rotate all the way around. The attractive woman with brown hair was beside him, coaching him, the tattoo on her neck now clearly visible as her ponytail floated upward. It was a pyramid, etched in black, with an eye transposed over it.

Strange, thought Megan. *It's exactly like the one Paige had on her wrist. But what could it mean?* At least Hendrix's sudden interest in the woman might mean more unsupervised time for her. She watched other passengers glide like fish through the compartment and marveled at the grace and beauty of their movements. It was easy to tell that, for many of them, this was not their first time in space.

She soon found herself having fun, but it was shattered by the arrival of a silver-haired woman with tears in her eyes. The woman glided to a stop beside a man whose eyes were also filled with tears.

"I'm so sorry, Neil," the woman said. "It happened right at the moment of lift-off. They're gone." They hugged. A sudden chill crawled up Megan's back and onto her neck and shoulders. She approached them cautiously, afraid of what she might find out.

"Excuse me," Megan said, addressing the woman nervously. "I couldn't help overhearing you. What do you mean 'they're gone?'"

"The *Icarus*—it exploded during lift-off. We don't know why. The captain will be making an announcement in a few minutes."

Megan instantly thought of Paige, who had only wanted

to help her. She closed her eyes and felt a tear slide not down, but sideways across her face. She now knew what the dream had been trying to tell her.

Chapter 8

White House Debriefing

SIS Director Ross Herrington was fifteen minutes late to the White House. After passing through security, an armed guard quickly escorted him to the Oval Office where the president's most trusted advisors were seated around a long rectangular table.

The president stood bent over at the waist with his hands pressed against the table, impatiently tapping the wedding band around his left ring finger against its surface with the rhythmic ticking of a clock. He was a tall, dignified man with graying hair and deep wrinkles, and he wore a freshly pressed suit with a small red carnation placed neatly on the lapel. His black shoes were so finely polished that Herrington could have seen his reflection in them if he had tried. He looked angry.

"I'm glad to see that the director feels that attending this meeting is worth his while," the president quipped sarcastically. "As we were discussing, the Mars launch was a disaster. We lost one of the ships—the *Icarus*. What do you make of that, Mr. Herrington?"

Herrington nodded an apology and took a seat just to the president's right. He was breathing hard. For the past two hours, he had been working feverishly to cover up any evidence of government involvement in the *Icarus*'s destruction. Of course, he was merely doing what the president had ordered him to do, but the others in the room did not know that. The Mars mission was an operation that Herrington and the president ran covertly, a closely guarded secret shared only by the two of them. He interlaced his fingers and placed his elbows on the hard, cold table, and prepared to speak.

"This comes as a shock, Mr. President," he remarked, feigning surprise. "The *Icarus*. That's where we placed the bulk of our military resources." He took off his glasses and wiped his forehead. "Is the mission even still possible?"

"What do we tell the press?" gasped a tiny middle-aged woman in a luminescent green-and-gold blazer. Her yellow-dyed hair was tied into an enormous bun that made her look ridiculous. Her name was Penny Rose, White House press secretary, better known as the president's lapdog because she did nothing without asking him first. She was stupid and easy to manipulate. Herrington scribbled her name in his notebook and circled it. She would be useful in the cover-up, especially since she suspected nothing.

"Tell them only that a rescue mission has been

launched," replied the president. "Say nothing of the accident."

"Do we know that it was, in fact, an accident?" demanded a loud man in a military uniform. He was Secretary of Defense William Blythe, formerly the president's most trusted advisor but now one of his most vocal critics. He had a thick neck, piercing gray eyes, and grayish-brown hair, trimmed short like the grass on a putting green. Herrington hated him, the way he refused to collaborate with the SIS, and how he publicly questioned the president's motives. He had been especially difficult to work with since the Commonwealth's failure to prevent Trans Europa from seizing Antarctica a year ago—a loss that Blythe blamed on the president. Everybody in the room knew that the two men hated one another, and it would be just a matter of time before the president replaced him with someone more pliable.

"Not at this time," answered the president. "An investigation is already underway. Herrington, I need you to put together a team to analyze the surveillance video."

Herrington nodded and pretended to write in his notebook. Surveillance video—he was way ahead of the president on that one. He had placed his own nephew on the *Intrepid*, and he had also already obtained footage of the lift-off. Nobody would suspect what had actually happened, not if he could help it. Not even the secretary of defense. Yes, he was sure of that.

"Yes, sir," he replied solemnly. "I'll put my best people on it."

"Mr. President," interrupted Blythe. "With the loss of the *Icarus*, we've lost our electric pulse bomb. This is serious. We won't be able to stop their robots without it. We've also lost the bulk of our Special Forces unit. There's not a rescue mission without them."

"I agree," replied the president, obviously irritated. "This will not be a rescue mission. Our primary goal will be to secure the stockpiles of uranium and other raw materials and bring them back here."

Blythe spoke again. "My sources report that the Pacific Alliance will be launching their own mission in the next few days. Trans Europa will need more time, but we expect that they, too, will soon be headed to Mars."

The president paused and looked each man and woman at the table in the eye. "That's exactly why we need to get there first. I don't want any other nation to get to those stockpiles before we do. Our ships are faster, so I like our chances. Herrington, what's your latest intelligence from the colony?"

Herrington flipped open a small glass tablet and set it on the table in front of him. He pressed a button, and writing flashed on its screen. "Sir, we believe a war has broken out between factions within the prisoner population. The oxygen level is low, but there's still enough to last a few months. Most of the power is down. We also know that robotic spiders have breached the base. Intelligence confirms that they disable their victims by attacking their legs and severing the tendons. Once the victim is immobilized, they move up the body to finish the job. It appears that they feed on the bodies, especially the blood."

Penny Rose wrinkled her nose in disgust.

"Mr. Herrington," asked a sullen-faced advisor with a thin nose and bangs. "Who's operating the robots, and how can they ingest human flesh? It doesn't make sense. And why is this the first time we're hearing about this?"

Herrington closed the screen on his tablet. "The spiders, which are robotic, seem to generate power through biomass. We believe they recharge their batteries by gobbling organic matter—in this case, blood. In effect, they're autonomous because as long as they're able to harvest biomass, they require no human assistance. We know that the Pacific Alliance had been using much simpler robotic insects to spy on operations, but those were nothing like this."

"Do we have any idea who's behind them?" asked Rose.

Herrington paused and closed his eyes. "The SIS strongly suspects an outside group, probably nongovernmental. Private companies have been running their own space missions for decades. We're in the process of bugging their communications and infiltrating them with spies."

"So, nobody's getting rescued?" interrupted the press secretary.

"If we're going to rescue anybody," the president continued calmly, "it will only be a few scientists and engineers, the ones with the most knowledge about mining operations. There's simply not enough room on the ships for everybody. Again, our primary objective is the raw material that has been mined. Our technology, our way of life, and our position as the world's most powerful nation depend on it. Otherwise, it's back to the Stone Age."

Secretary of Defense Blythe shook his head. "With all due respect, I strongly disagree, Mr. President. If there's room for uranium, there's room for people. I say we forget about raw materials and try our best to save every Commonwealth citizen trapped on Mars. It's the right thing to do."

The president glared at his nemesis. He wasn't used to people standing up to him. "Mr. Secretary," he said sternly, "the decision has already been made. If you don't like it, you're welcome to resign immediately." There was an uncomfortable silence.

Blythe collected his belongings and rose from his seat. "Very well then, Mr. President," he said. "I resign. I refuse to be a part of this any longer." He pushed his chair in. "Be warned, though, Mr. President: I will do whatever I can to put a stop to this operation." He walked quickly to the door and was met by a neatly groomed guard who escorted him out of the White House.

The president looked at each of his remaining advisors one by one. "Is there anyone else who wishes to leave?" There was a nervous cough from someone at the table, but nobody got up to leave. "Okay then. We'll carry on as planned. Are there any questions?"

The secretary of the Interior raised his hand. He waited for the president to acknowledge him and then spoke cautiously. "Mr. President, what are we going to do about the ones we can't bring back?"

"They are not our primary objective," repeated the president. "As far as we're concerned, and as far as the public needs to know, they're already dead."

The meeting ended a few minutes later.

As the various advisors and staff members went on their way, the president approached Herrington. "Mr. Herrington," he said. "I'd like to speak with you privately." He placed a hand on Herrington's back and walked him into an adjoining room and closed the door behind them. "Mr. Herrington, I want you to initiate Protocol 231 right away. See to it that the surveillance video from the launch site clearly shows Burke placing an incendiary device near the *Icarus*. We'll release it to the press tomorrow morning, which should give us our citizens' support. Can you do that for me?"

"Of course, Mr. President," replied Herrington. "I already have the surveillance footage. The operative who placed the explosive is a dead ringer for Burke, and I can adjust her image digitally to make her look even more like Burke if necessary."

"Good. There's something else that I want you to do. Use the avatar. I want you on Mars to ensure that everything works out as planned. Will that be a problem?"

"No, sir. The avatar has been working well. It's quick and strong, and the Earth to Mars transmission delay is now less than a second due to a new proton accelerator we installed. I'll conduct another test this afternoon."

"How many people on Mars know about it?" asked the president.

"No one, sir. I've kept it hidden in a secluded room beneath the colony."

"Very good, Herrington. I knew I could count on you. You're like a brother to me. There is, however, one more matter to iron out."

"What's that, sir?"

"I think it's time to eliminate the remaining Wonder Kids. If anybody figures out what we're doing, it's likely to be one of them—especially the older ones. What's the name of the one we put on board the *Intrepid*?"

"Megan. She'll be our bargaining chip."

"Okay. She'll be allowed to live for now, but I want the others gone. If we make Burke angry enough, we just might be able to lure her out for a fight. We'll deal with Secretary of Defense Blythe later."

Chapter 9

The Avatar

Herrington hurried back to SIS headquarters in Langley. He walked briskly down a maze of plain white hallways with concrete floors, ignoring everybody he passed. When at last he reached an elevator, he took it to the basement and then activated a hidden switch to take it down one more level to a secret chamber beneath the building's foundation.

As the elevator's steel doors opened, he glimpsed a large black chair attached to a supercomputer in the middle of the room. The walls were bare, and the glare of fluorescent lights caused him to squint. Above the chair was a retractable helmet connected by wires to the computer. Herrington removed his jacket and tie and sat down in the chair. He pressed a button, and it tilted back into a reclining position. He reached up and pulled the helmet down over his head.

A retractable probe emerged from inside the helmet and pressed firmly against his scalp. He felt a flash of pain as a bundle of wires shot out from the probe and entered his skull through a hole that had been drilled there for this very purpose, and that was now usually hidden by a flap of artificial skin and hair. The wires coursed through his brain until they linked themselves to tiny computer chips embedded into his cerebellum and frontal cortex.

The pain was intense. He vomited and passed out.

When he regained consciousness, he had a headache, but the pain had mostly subsided. A pair of virtual reality goggles now covered his eyes, its lenses showing a three-dimensional view of an entirely different room. The view was surreal; he was seeing it from the perspective of another being—a remotely controlled cyborg called an avatar.

He could plainly see its arms, hands, legs, and feet as though they were his own. He opened and closed his right hand. The avatar's right hand opened and closed. He tried other movements, and the avatar mirrored his actions perfectly each time. Next, he tried moving its hands and feet by thought alone, while remaining motionless himself. It worked. He willed the avatar to stand up, walk to a door, and open it. The avatar moved quickly and powerfully and executed each command to perfection. It had in effect become an extension of Herrington's own mind, a sort of second body, and it would now enable him to operate on Mars without actually being there.

The avatar exited the room and closed the door. It followed a dark narrow shaft steeply upward until it reached a hidden panel in the wall. It pressed its hypersonic ear to the panel and listened for signs of life on the other side. There was nothing. It pressed a switch, and the panel quietly slid open, revealing a dimly lit corridor. A man and a woman lay dead on the floor, covered in blood. Curious, it knelt beside them and examined their wounds. Their ankles were slashed, a sign that the spiders had gotten them. Farther up their bodies, on their necks, were puncture wounds where the spiders had siphoned their blood.

Satisfied, the avatar rose and proceeded down the corridor toward a large freight elevator spattered with blood, making a crunching sound as it stepped on the dead man's outstretched hand. Reaching the elevator, it got inside and pressed a button that began its ascent to ground level. As the elevator rambled slowly upward, the avatar noticed its own slightly blurred reflection in its steel doors. The face was mostly human, with a small nose and deeply set eyes. The skin was a light cream color, and there was something about it that seemed fake. *Was it the lack of facial pores? Or was it the absence of wrinkles in the corners of its eyes?* It was hard to tell, but something about it was obviously different and not entirely human.

The elevator jolted to a stop and its doors hissed menacingly as they opened. The avatar emerged into a room with large glass windows. Outside, a dark sky loomed overhead, the reflection of stars gleaming on the surface of the clear polymer dome that protected the colony from Mars's unforgiving atmosphere. It approached a door marked "exit" but was startled by the sound of footsteps.

"Halt," shouted a young man with a rifle. He was wearing a black security officer uniform and had long greasy hair that looked as though it had not been washed or trimmed in weeks. "Who are you? What's your business here?" Although the young man was trying his best to act tough, it was clear that he was terrified.

"My name is not important," answered the avatar in a voice not unlike Herrington's. "I wish to go outside."

"Why haven't I seen you before?"

"Relax," said the avatar, offering a smile. "I'm not here to cause trouble. I want to help."

"Do you have any weapons?"

"Yes. There's a plasma grenade in my left pocket. You may have it if you would like."

The officer approached nervously. "I'm going to need you to turn around and stand facing the wall. Place your hands on the wall in front of you." The avatar did as it was told. It felt the officer reaching into the pocket.

"Where is it?" the man asked, turning the pocket inside out. He was confused. With blinding speed, the avatar seized the man's arm and spun him around. It grasped him by the throat and squeezed with inhuman strength. There was a gurgling sound and then a snap. His neck was broken. The avatar let the man's limp body fall to the floor with a thud. It opened the door and stepped outside. Stars shone overhead.

The avatar scanned the horizon until it could make out the silhouette of a large volcanic mountain in the distance. The reddish ground outside the dome was illuminated for several meters by spotlights, but beyond that lay darkness. Inside the dome was a compound consisting of low concrete buildings, one of which was damaged and on fire.

Something moved nearby, and the avatar observed a large robotic spider emerging from the shadows. It crept forward cautiously, stopped, and seemed to consider its options. It thought that the avatar looked like food, but there was something about its composition that just wasn't right. It scurried back into the shadows and disappeared from view.

The avatar turned and strode back inside the building from which it had come. It took the elevator down to the lowest level, got out, and found the hidden panel in the hallway. Returning to its secret room, it lay back in its reclining chair and went dormant.

In his own secret chamber millions of kilometers away in Langley, Virginia, Ross Herrington removed the virtual reality goggles from his eyes and flipped a switch that caused the bundle of wires inside his head to disengage and retract into the helmet. He felt pain, but it did not bother him. Taking off the helmet, he dabbed a small puddle of blood from his scalp and repositioned the flap of synthetic skin to cover up the hole in his skull.

He exhaled deeply, satisfied that the avatar was in perfect working order. He wouldn't need to use it again until the *Intrepid*—along with Megan and his nephew—landed on Mars twelve weeks later, but he would be ready when the time came.

Chapter 10

Voices

Back at SIS headquarters, Harper was angry and confused. She had received an anonymous report from someone close to the president informing her that one of the ships had exploded during lift-off, killing everyone on board. It had also warned her to get out of Washington.

Her initial reaction was one of fear. Megan could be dead already. She was worried for her friend and felt vaguely responsible. She wished that she had tried harder to get assigned to the mission herself, wondering if there was anything more that she could have done. Yet deep down, she felt as though Megan must still be alive. There had been no little voice, no intuitive warning that something was wrong.

She left her office accompanied by two SIS agents. One, a tall outgoing man named Davies, was easy to get along with and seemed to like her. He was very handsome with wavy blond hair and the ruddy complexion of a surfer, and he always smelled of cologne. The other agent, a serious woman named Adams, was the opposite in every way. She was short, stocky, and unpleasant, and she did not wear deodorant, which made her difficult to be around on hot sunny days. Although they were her equals in rank and supposedly her partners, Harper suspected that they were really there to keep an eye on her.

Together, they walked through a nearby park as they did every day on their way to lunch. The park was a shady place of majestic oaks and elms that had managed to survive despite the poor air quality, and it was one of the few places where the songs of chirping birds could still be heard. There were ponds, fountains, and walking trails, and the entire park was surrounded by a long cast-iron fence that made it feel like a secluded island in the center of the city.

As they passed a group of excited schoolchildren racing toy sailboats on an algae-covered pond, Harper closed her eyes and concentrated. *What was going on? Was Megan safe? And why the betrayal? What could her bosses possibly have against her?*

Davies and Adams were engrossed in a conversation and weren't paying attention to her. They were beginning to argue. Suddenly, her inner voice spoke: *Everything is okay. Megan is okay. You are in danger, but a way out is about to present itself.* She relaxed slightly.

The voice came as a whisper, but one so close to the ear that she could hear nothing else. *Harper, help me,* it continued. *I need you. It's time you knew the truth. Come home — to me.* She was startled. She had always assumed that the voice was part of her, like intuition, but now it sounded different. It had never spoken to her like this before, like it was coming from another person, someone speaking to her from inside her own brain. She pinched her forehead with her thumb and index finger, closed her eyes, and held her breath, but the whispering continued. *Come home, come home, come home.*

She felt the urge to leave immediately. "Adams," she said abruptly, "I can't go to lunch right now—I'm feeling a little sick. I'm going to go back to the office and lie down for a while. I'll see you when you get back."

Adams and Davies looked at each other, unsure of what to do. "We can go back with you," offered Davies hesitantly.

"No," said Harper, "go have lunch. Don't worry about me—I'll be all right." Adams was about to protest, but Davies softened a little. "Okay. We'll just pick something up. See you back at the office in ten minutes."

Harper turned and began walking back toward the park's gated entrance. Although she couldn't see them, she felt sure that her partners were watching her and clutched her stomach for dramatic effect. Just then, out of nowhere, a jogger in a gray hooded jacket came crashing into her, knocking her to the ground.

"Sorry, sorry," he exclaimed. "Are you all right?" He tried to help her up, but she resisted and got up by herself. As she glanced at his face, she noticed that he was young and had gray eyes that matched the color of his sweatshirt. Something briefly shimmered deep inside one of his eyes. Electrical interference. She had seen this before. He was wearing a micro-screen embedded directly into his cornea, a tiny technological marvel that allowed the wearer to relay everything he viewed to a computer for analysis. *A spy,* she thought. She reached into her jacket and wrapped her fingers around the grip of a small handgun. She placed a finger on the trigger.

"I'm fine," she answered, cautiously. The young man seemed to back away from her. Adams and Davies both rushed toward them, but not before the man secretly handed her a brown envelope. "It's for you," he whispered, and then he sprinted away in the opposite direction from which he had come. Davies raced after him in pursuit, and soon both men disappeared from sight. Adams stayed with Harper to make sure she was uninjured.

"We just got a call from Herrington," she told Harper. "He wants to meet with you immediately. I'll be going with you." She touched a hand to her ear and listened to an incoming message. "It's Davies. He was unable to catch up with the guy who ran into you."

"It was no big deal," Harper replied, still shaken. She slid the envelope into her back pocket. "I mean, it was just an accident." She dusted herself off and brushed her hair with her hands. Adams said nothing. She looked nervous, which for her was unusual. There was something about this upcoming meeting with Herrington that made her uneasy.

Moments later, a sleek black car arrived to take her to Herrington. It was one of a dying breed, a car that still actually used a human driver. The driver was ugly, with a large head and enormous ears supported on a small wiry body. He had a single tuft of hair near the back of his head but otherwise was bald. She climbed into the back seat, followed by Adams who sat beside her. She opened the envelope, making sure to keep its contents hidden.

"Who's that from?" asked Adams.

"A friend. Don't you get letters?"

Adams looked slightly embarrassed and turned to stare

out the window. Harper pulled out the letter. It read as follows:

Dear Ms. Harper,

You are in extreme danger. Do not go to see Herrington. He intends to kill you.

There is a major conspiracy involving the Mars colony and the woman who raised you. If you would like to know the truth, you must go to Mars. A company called Space Innovations will take you there, but it must be you who goes and no one else, and you may tell no one where you are going. The company is located near Sydney, Australia, and they do not know who you are. We have submitted a résumé for a computer technician required for a private Mars mission that leaves in eight days. The résumé is for one Shannon O'Reilly. You will be supervising a shipment of microchips and integrated software systems. Go—the truth and the Red Planet await.

Godspeed,
X

Do not go to see Herrington. He intends to kill you. Harper read that part again and again, trying not to look at Adams or the driver. Suddenly, the voice inside her spoke once again. *Get out now.* She put the letter back inside the envelope, folded it in half, and put it back in her pocket.

This is weird, she thought. Peeking at the driver, she noticed his eyes watching her in the rearview mirror. She ventured a quick glance at Adams, who was staring at her as though she were an insect about to be swatted into oblivion. She could tell there wasn't much time.

Feigning a yawn, she put her left hand to her mouth and then swung her elbow back savagely into Adams's neck, knocking the wind out of her. She then drew her handgun and jabbed it into the base of the driver's neck. "Pull over!" she screamed. As he slowed the car and began moving to the side of the road, she could hear Adams gasping for breath.

"Don't worry, you're going to be all right," she told the older woman, who was clutching her own throat with both hands and struggling for air. "Breathe slowly and deeply."

The car came to a stop beside a robotics factory, and Harper struck the back of the driver's head hard with her pistol, knocking him unconscious. She tried to open the door, but it was locked.

"How do I get out of here?" she yelled, but Adams was unable to answer. She fired a shot into the window, shattering the glass, and then kicked out the remaining fragments. Climbing through the now-open window, she sprinted down a nearby alley and hid behind a rusty trash compactor that smelled of rotting food. In a matter of minutes, the authorities would know what had happened and would send drones to locate her. Then it would just be a matter of time before the police found her. From there, she'd either be executed on the spot or sent to a maximum-security prison to await execution later. Neither prospect was appealing.

She took out her phone, pried off the back with her fingernails, and removed its memory chip, before inserting a new one that would be harder to trace. She called her friend Wiley, second oldest of the Wonder Kids, and he answered immediately, as though he had been expecting her call.

"Wiley," she whispered hoarsely into the phone, "I need you to pick me up at the corner of Sixth and Benson right away. Will you do that for me?"

"Of course. I'm leaving now."

"Bring my escape bag." She switched the phone off and pitched it into the trash compactor, then began running as hard and fast as she could toward the intersection where Wiley was to meet her. It was roughly two kilometers away, and she knew that Wiley could be there in ten minutes. If she ran her fastest, she could be there in nine. Her legs burned and her lungs felt as though they would burst as she sprinted to the intersection, but she did not slow her pace.

When at last she arrived, she hid behind a thick hedge until Wiley pulled up in his battered red E-Varo just moments later. Exhausted, she charged out of the hedges toward his car, opening the passenger side door and jumping in before it had even come to a stop.

"Go!" she yelled, climbing into the back seat and getting as low as she could. Wiley was sweating profusely and looked terrified. He hit the accelerator, and the vehicle sped off down the road.

"Did you bring my bag?"

"Yes. Here." He tossed a bag the size of a large purse back to her and continued driving. "Where are we going?"

"The airport," said Harper, struggling to regain her breath. "But you're going to let me out a couple blocks away so nobody sees you."

"Okay. What kind of trouble are you in, Harper?"

"I think they want to kill me. You and the others are

probably next, so stay out of sight at all costs. Will you warn the others for me?"

"Of course. You can count on me. Why didn't you contact me telepathically?"

"Because I think someone may have found a way to listen in. Maybe it's one of us. I don't know."

"You think it could be me?" Wiley asked, stunned.

"No, not you," Harper assured him. "I trust you completely. But somebody. Just be careful."

She sat back and opened the bag, taking out a pair of scissors. Looking at herself in the rearview mirror, she snipped off her long curls and applied black dye until not a trace of red remained. Satisfied, she spoke to Wiley in her best Irish accent. "Thanks for the help. I've got to go now. You might not hear from me again for a long time. Now get lost. We're both in a lot of trouble."

Chapter 11

Anya

It was on day three of her journey to Mars that Megan became aware of just how inadequate her training had been. Almost everybody else on board the ship had trained for at least two years to go into space. She had been given a day. Things that she normally took for granted now became major challenges—brushing her teeth, eating, drinking, bathing, even trying to stay in place while reading. Nobody seemed interested in helping her or even in getting to know her, at least not until she met Anya.

On the day they met, Megan was practically starving. It wasn't just that the food was bland and lacked texture—zero gravity made eating nearly impossible. During her first meal aboard the *Intrepid,* she swallowed a bite-sized morsel of chicken parmesan only to feel tiny bits of it floating back up her esophagus and into her mouth. It almost made her sick. Now, after practically fasting for the past day and a half, she returned to the ship's dining compartment with the realization that she was going to have to eat no matter how unpleasant the experience.

The dining compartment was a long, narrow room with rounded corners and a row of stainless-steel benches that the crew could strap themselves into, but most of them seemed to prefer floating weightless instead. They were grouped in twos and threes, and they kept from floating off from each other by tethering themselves with short cables to a handrail running the length of the room. It was noisy—people chatting, maintenance robots scurrying about, kitchen staff shouting orders at one another—as Megan slipped quietly through the air toward where a food service robot was handing out shrink-wrapped trays of compressed thermo-stabilized food.

There were only two choices: cheese sandwich with wilted lettuce and tomato or soggy chicken with green beans. As she waited for the man in front of her to take his meal, a tiny drone sidled up beside her and slipped a monitoring device securely onto her wrist. She was startled.

"What's this?"

The man in front of her turned around, annoyed. "It monitors your caloric needs, vitamin and mineral deficiencies, stuff like that. You haven't seen one before?"

"No. What does mine say?"

"Sorry, miss. I'm not a dietician. The robots take care of all that. Now excuse me—I have to join those people over there." He nodded toward a group near the ceiling. "Gotta go."

Megan felt sad and alone. Nobody invited her to eat with them. She wished Harper could be with her now. The robot handed her a tray and spoke to her without emotion.

"Your vital signs show that you are low on carbohydrates

and essential vitamins. I recommend the cheese sandwich, which is enhanced with a multivitamin complex." She took the sealed tray in her hands and gently pushed off a wall, allowing herself to drift to an unoccupied corner of the compartment where she could eat alone.

She looked around. Everything was wrong. The food was strange—it was odorless, compressed into small blocks, and sealed in tight-fitting plastic. She opened her package and was disappointed to discover a small tightly compressed cube of bread and cheese coated with something like wax to seal in the nutrients. It looked disgusting. She broke it in half and took a small bite, trying hard to force it all the way down into her stomach. It didn't taste bad, but then again, it didn't taste good either. Crumbs scattered haphazardly around her despite her best efforts to capture them. They floated away from her in all directions.

Suddenly, another crew member—a cargo specialist—shouted at her angrily from across the room. "Hey, what do you think you're doing? No crumbs!" Megan felt embarrassed and apologized. Just then, a friendly face appeared. It was Anya.

"First time in space?" she asked.

"Yeah. That easy to tell, huh?" replied Megan nervously. She held onto the ceiling to keep from drifting away.

"How much training did you receive?"

"About half a day's worth." Anya raised an eyebrow, surprised. "How about you?"

"Two years, and that was before my first mission. I've already been to Mars twice. By the way, my name is Anya. You look like you could use a friend."

"I'm Megan. I can't tell you how great it is to meet you.

Nobody else even seems to notice me unless I do something wrong."

Just then a service robot launched itself in their direction, stopping in midair before turning its mechanical head to face Megan. "Be mindful of your crumbs, please," it chirped in a shrill, metallic tone. "Tiny crumbs create huge problems."

"Get lost, drone," ordered Anya, raising a hand as if to swat it. It screeched and spun around quickly before jetting off to the other side of the room. Megan looked confused.

"What's the big deal about crumbs?"

Anya explained that once crumbs spread out in the air, they were almost impossible to track down and eliminate, even for a service robot. That meant that they were free to lodge themselves inside delicate equipment or get into crew members' eyes. Much worse was the threat posed by runaway droplets of water. Even a small droplet could cause vital electronic components to short out and burst into flames. Larger blobs of water, like what you'd expect to find in a small cup, could levitate and drift into your face, filling your sinuses and creating a drowning sensation. Anya then demonstrated the proper way to remove food from its packaging and how to eat it in the safest manner possible. Megan was grateful for the help, but she was even happier to make a friend.

"Do you like this food?" she asked.

"Not particularly, but it's okay once you get used to it," answered Anya. "So, what brings you to Mars? You must be important if they're sending you without any real training."

Megan looked uneasily at her feet. She didn't know what to say. Her mission was top secret, but she didn't want to start off on the wrong foot with her new friend. And she couldn't help remembering how Paige, the young woman she'd met as they prepared to board the ships, had seen through her lie about being a reporter. "I'm really not allowed to say," she finally offered hesitantly. "I wish I could, but I can't."

"That's okay," said Anya. "I understand. I have a few secrets of my own. Hey, I forgot to mention that I'm a biologist. I work in the research lab, mainly with plants and insects. Would you like a tour?"

"Yeah, I'd love to. When?"

"How about now? That is unless you'd rather eat that nasty sandwich."

Megan took one last bite of her dinner and used all the muscles of her digestive tract to force it down. She balled up what was left inside the discarded wrapper and placed it inside a waste disposal vacuum before following Anya out of the dining compartment and through a series of winding corridors until they reached an open freight elevator.

As they went inside, she was surprised to see that its top had been completely removed, allowing them to see all the way to the top of the elevator shaft.

"Watch this," said Anya with a gleam in her eye. She descended to the floor, bent her knees, and pushed hard off it with her legs. She sped upward through the open ceiling to the top of the elevator shaft like a soda bubble and then did a fancy swimmer's somersault, catapulting herself out an open door and onto the ship's second floor. Megan was impressed.

"Come on," shouted Anya. "It's fun!"

Megan did exactly as her new friend had done, leaving out only the somersault at the top, and she quickly found herself hurtling out the open door onto the second floor. She smiled at the thought that her disability didn't matter here, that she could be as swift and graceful as anyone on the ship. She pushed off the wall to catch up with Anya, who was now slightly ahead of her.

"How much farther?" she asked, nearly breathless.

"Not far. Just around this corner."

When they reached a closed metal door marked CAUTION: EXPERIMENTS IN PROGRESS, Anya opened the door carefully but did not go inside right away.

"You first," she whispered.

Megan gently nudged the wall opposite the lab door and glided slowly inside. Once in, she noticed that one entire side of the room had a transparent glass wall separating them from a narrow chamber of plants growing on the other side. Droplets of water clung to the inside surface of the glass, but Megan could clearly make out dozens of bright green plants growing in containers. Some were secured to what would be considered the floor, while others were attached to walls or the ceiling. Mesh fabric prevented the soil from leaking from the containers, which were transparent to allow the scientists to observe the roots.

On the other side of the room were control panels, test tubes and beakers secured to the wall with nylon fasteners, and a metal cage with something small and furry inside. A window with thick glass looked in on them from the back of the room, behind which was some sort of observation chamber. Anya went to a control panel and clicked a button marked SIMULATED RAINFALL. A fine spray of mist soon enveloped the foliage inside the greenhouse chamber.

"Don't worry," said Anya, "the water's safely behind

the glass, and that glass is absolutely bulletproof. Oh, and if you hadn't figured it out yet, that's the greenhouse."

Megan studied the plants carefully. Labels identified them by type. There were various types of beans, green and red peppers, cabbage, and strawberries as well as several tree seedlings. Holes in the glass wall opened into arm-length rubber gloves that allowed the scientists to touch the plants inside without spilling drops of water into the rest of the ship.

Megan turned back to the other side of the room, curious about what was in the cage. "What's in there?" she asked. A small mass of curled up brown and white fur hovered eerily inside. It was balled up as though hiding or sleeping.

"That's Shem, our vervet monkey. He's helping us better understand the effects of space travel. He's a great climber and very fast, but the zero gravity conditions have been hard on him."

"Is he lonely?" asked Megan.

"He's a monkey, not a person, Megan. We feed him and do our best to keep his spirits up, but he probably won't survive the mission. They almost never do. Right now, he's sleeping, so let's try to be quiet."

"What do you do in here?"

"I'm in charge of the greenhouse. Bugs are actually my specialty, especially arachnids. I find out how well they can handle things like weightlessness and cosmic radiation and where they encounter problems, I try to find solutions. I've constructed an entirely self-sustaining ecosystem—plants, soil, bugs, bacteria. It's amazing to see how they interact." She stuck her hands through two of the holes in the glass wall and slipped them into the thick rubber gloves protruding to the other side. Reaching into a container, she gently pulled back a bright green leaf on one of the bean plants. Beneath it, a fat black spider with a red spot like an hourglass on its belly clung to the plant's stalk.

"Beautiful, isn't she?" mused Anya, softly caressing its shiny back. "You'd think the lack of gravity would make it impossible for them to function, but it turns out they're just fine."

"What type is it?" asked Megan, raising her eyebrows in surprise.

"This one's a *Latrodectus hesperus,* or black widow. Her venom is fifteen times stronger than a rattlesnake's, so you need to use gloves when handling her. Look closely. Can you see her fangs?"

Megan pressed her forehead against the glass and stared. "They're huge," she whispered.

"They use those to puncture their prey and deliver digestive enzymes. Basically, they liquefy their prey's bodies and suck up the resulting fluid."

"That's terrible. What happens if they bite you?"

Anya's face lit up with excitement. "Their venom is comprised of neurotoxins—substances that affect the nervous system. At first, you'd only feel a pinprick, but after a few hours, you'd start cramping all over. Then it becomes difficult to breathe. Then delirium sets in. Pretty soon you're ranting like a madwoman. Cool, isn't it, the way something so small can take down something much larger than itself."

Megan was beginning to feel uncomfortable and even a little nauseous. She backed away from the glass and rubbed her forehead. "You're interesting, Anya. Have you always liked spiders so much?"

"Yes, always. I love them. It's fascinating, I mean, what these tiny things can do. Did you know that there are even robotic spiders with military applications? What a brilliant idea! They're on Mars right now, and they've invaded the colony!"

Suddenly, Megan became interested. "So, you know about those?" she asked, astonished. "I thought that was classified information."

"I know a lot of things that would surprise you," Anya answered with a wink, and then her demeanor became extremely serious. "How old are you, Megan?"

"Twenty."

"Right. Twenty." Anya grinned slyly.

As Megan squirmed a little uncomfortably, a large, unmarked container on the other side of the lab started shaking vigorously and its lid twisted slightly. Then it stopped. A dull scratching noise arose from within as though something was trying to get out, and it vibrated again.

"What's that?" Megan gasped, startled. The lid seemed ready to pop off. She floated over cautiously to investigate, nervous at what might be inside but glad to divert Anya's attention.

"Don't open that box," ordered Anya sternly.

"Why?"

"I can't tell you. Just don't do it."

Just then, Megan became aware of a pair of eyes staring at her through the observation window. She only caught a brief glance, but she was sure someone had been there. They were gone when she looked up. "Someone's watching us," she said, alarmed. "I could swear I just saw somebody through that window." She pointed at the window, not daring to take her eyes off it.

"Megan, I think it's time you left," said Anya. She propelled herself toward Megan and took her by the arm. "See you at breakfast tomorrow?"

Megan forced a smile and managed a weak *thanks* but an uncomfortable feeling had swept over her. As Anya held open the door for her, the hair covering the back of her neck rose just enough to reveal a tiny black tattoo of a pyramid and an eye, but it happened so quickly that Megan failed to notice.

Chapter 12

Danger Stalks the Wonder Kids

Herrington was elated following his successful test run of the avatar. Now in his seventies, he had lost most of the vigor of his youth, but in the guise of the avatar, he had felt invincible. He showered and took a pill to dull the pain in his head. Elation giving way to exhaustion, he picked up his phone and dialed a number. The phone rang twice before a man with a low gravelly voice answered.

"Yeah."

"It's me," said Herrington. "Show a little respect."

"Sure, boss," came the reply, revealing a slight southern drawl. The man's voice seemed detached and impersonal.

"I want them all dead within a week. Get your three best assassins on the job right away."

"I understand." There was a click and the line went dead. Herrington closed his eyes and drifted off to sleep, completely untroubled by the order he had just given. That night he dreamed he was on Mars, this time in person, and he smiled for the first time in years.

A few hours later, deep into the night, a man dressed entirely in black crept silently along a row of hedges next to a small house at the edge of a wooded park. Using a serrated knife, he severed the home's electrical line, disabling its alarm system.

With the stealth of a cat, he stole his way around the side to a window that he had been informed would be unlocked, then knelt in the tall grass beneath it. He took out a sleek black pistol and screwed a silencer onto its muzzle. He steadied his nerves. He did not like killing children, but he had his orders and knew what must be done.

With gloved hands, he gently nudged open the window and climbed inside. The room was vacant, its floor consisting of hundred-year-old oak slats that creaked and groaned with every step. Placing one foot carefully in front of the other, he proceeded to the door and opened it slowly. Just down the hall was a closed bedroom door. He adjusted the dark ski mask covering his face, wiped the sweat off the back of his neck, and then inched his way steadily down the hall until he reached the door.

Suddenly the floor squeaked loudly, and he heard movement on the other side. He turned the knob and rushed inside. There was a thud followed by blinding pain as something heavy crashed down onto his head, and he fell groaning to the floor.

It was a trap. He had been hit from behind. A teenage boy stood above him holding a baseball bat, ready to strike again. It was the one they called Wiley. The man groaned again and rolled over onto his side, holding his head in his hands.

"Who are you and why are you here?" demanded Wiley, waving his bat wildly and breathing hard. He flicked on a lamp and squinted as his eyes adjusted to the light.

"My name is . . ." began the man in black, and then he fell silent and stopped moving.

Wiley waited for what seemed to him an eternity and then knelt down to check for a pulse. It was a mistake. The man grabbed him by the arm and yanked him to the ground where he struck a knockout blow with his left fist to the boy's jaw. Rising to his feet, he walked across the room to where his gun had fallen. As he bent down to pick it up and finish the job, a voice interrupted him.

"Agent Munroe," it said in a confident southern drawl, "did that boy almost get the best of you?"

"No, sir, Mr. Irons" replied the man in black, alarmed. "I mean, he got in a swing, but he didn't hit me that hard. Not much of an athlete if you ask me."

"Well then," continued the other man slowly, stepping into the room, "it is time you finished the job." He was a tall heavy man in combat fatigues and a cowboy hat, and his face was deeply pitted, as though it had been worked over with an icepick. A neatly trimmed goatee covered his chin.

"Yeah—yes, sir," stammered the assassin. He picked up his weapon, walked over to where the boy lay on the ground, and took aim. There was a sudden *thwoomp thwoomp,* and the assassin sank to the floor, dead, his blood forming a dark puddle around him.

The man in the cowboy hat and camouflaged fatigues slipped his still smoking gun into its holster and picked up the unconscious boy and threw him over his shoulder. He stepped over his dead partner and carried the boy outside where he tossed his limp body in the trunk of a waiting car.

One down, four to go, he thought as he switched on the ignition and pulled away. The decision to take the boy alive had not been his own; Herrington had called back a few minutes before with the change of plans. Irons had been mildly disappointed, but he knew better than to defy a direct order. A beam of moonlight briefly illuminated a long, jagged scar on his left forearm and another on his neck. He reached into a pocket, pulled out a phone, and dialed a number without looking. A low female voice answered.

"Yes?"

"There has been a change of plans. You are going to take the boy alive. I'll take care of the girl. Meet me at the library on West Fifty-Sixth when you are ready."

"But what about my orders, sir?"

"Those orders have changed. Just do as I tell you."

"Yes, Mr. Irons," came the perfunctory reply, and she hung up.

Irons dialed another number. This time the voice on the other end was that of a middle-aged man.

"Sir?"

"Bring the twins to the library on West Fifty-Sixth. Make sure that they are unhurt. I'll meet you there in one hour."

Irons closed his phone and continued driving to where he knew the one called Raven was hiding. *What a stupid name,* he thought. He stretched his arms and cracked his knuckles. This one was beginning to master telekinesis and would be the toughest to catch; he had to be prepared for anything.

When he arrived at the water tower behind the abandoned automotive factory, Irons slipped out of his car silently and sent it down the street where it parked itself a few blocks away. The boy in the trunk would be waking up soon, so he had to hurry. Crouching in the shadows and using an infrared scope, he scanned the factory's windows, moving quickly across them until he caught a glimpse of a face. He zoomed in for a close-up. It was a girl, about thirteen or fourteen, with straight black hair and a glowing amber stud in her nose. A reflective tattoo of a snake gleamed eerily on her neck, its eyes glowing with reddish phosphorescence. It was Raven—he knew it. Slowly and carefully, he crept along a low concrete wall behind the water tower until he reached a boarded-up entrance. Then, using a pry bar, he tore off boards until there was an opening large enough for him to squeeze through.

Irons's wide-brimmed cowboy hat tumbled to the ground as he squeezed through the narrow opening. He tried to reach it but could not. Cursing angrily, he left it outside and continued on his way. Raven would know that he was coming, but if he executed his plan perfectly, it wouldn't matter.

The room was dark, but his night-vision contacts allowed him to see everything clearly, albeit with a greenish glow. He pulled out a stun gun. All around him were grimy discarded machine parts, many large enough to hide a person waiting in ambush. He heard a pitter-patter of tiny feet and turned to look. A rat with wet matted fur scurried to the safety of a broken pallet where it disappeared from view.

Irons stepped cautiously over a puddle and then around rusted machine parts until he reached a closed metal door marked STAIRWELL. It creaked menacingly as he pushed it open. As he stepped inside, the stench of putrid air engulfed him. He took a deep breath and smiled. The smell reminded him of his childhood home. Undeterred, he scaled four flights of stairs and stepped out on the floor where the girl was hiding.

"I know you are here, Raven," he called loudly in his Virginia drawl. "There is no use tryin' to hide. Come out now and let us get this over with."

"Leave me alone!" shrieked Raven from an unseen corner as a pile of boxes flew into the air and exploded into a storm of papers that rained down on him. He waited for them to settle and stepped forward eagerly.

"You have grown stronger, Raven. Show me what else you can do."

Instantly a hundred-kilo machine part rocketed past him and crashed violently into the wall beside him, shattering, and sending shrapnel everywhere. Irons dove to the floor and shielded himself behind a steel control panel. He scurried toward the floor's assembly line and crawled along a row of dusty conveyor belts until he reached the windows. Glancing through an opening, he saw the girl. She was a mere three meters away, but she couldn't see him.

"This is your last chance!" shouted Raven, with a hint of fear in her voice. "You have no idea what I can do to you!"

Irons grinned. He was thinking the same thing as he aimed his stun gun at her chest and fired. The girl dropped to the floor, writhing in pain. Her assailant moved swiftly and covered her mouth and nose with a chloroform-soaked handkerchief. The girl jerked her head twice and passed out.

Two down, three to go, thought Irons as he picked up her limp body and hoisted it over his shoulder. He pulled out his phone and ordered his car to meet him in front of the factory. Soon Wiley would no longer be the only one in the trunk.

Irons arrived at the library a short time later, carrying Raven over one shoulder and Wiley over the other. Both were unconscious. He was pleased to find the remaining two assassins already there.

A tall boy, about fifteen years old, with dark hair and closed eyes, lay still on the floor, his hands and feet bound with wire. Beside him stood a slim athletic woman in black fatigues, her bright orange hair tied in a ponytail. A balding fat man in an iridescent gray suit sat in an uncomfortable plastic chair calmly smoking a cigar. A wide grin broke across his face when he saw Irons, and he let out a long puff of smoke and chuckled. The woman seemed annoyed. Nearby, a pair of nearly identical blond-haired boys stood in a corner talking softly with one another while casting glances at the others around the room. Irons tossed the two unconscious Wonder Kids off each of his shoulders onto the carpeted floor. Then he took off his hat.

"That one is called Raven. The other, I believe, is Wiley. Is that correct, boys?" he asked looking at the twins. One of them nodded yes while the other stared at the three bodies on the floor. "What an entirely inappropriate name for someone so easy to catch," Irons remarked sarcastically. "Is your boy alive?" he asked, glancing at the woman.

"Yes. Unconscious, but alive."

"You've done good work—both of you," he said after a pause. "I'll see to it that Herrington gives you both a most generous raise."

"Much obliged," answered the fat man. He took another puff on his cigar and blew the smoke upward toward the ceiling. The woman looked away, disgusted.

"What is the matter, Ms. Smith?" asked Irons, staring at her. "Does the smoke bother you, or are you just concerned about Agent Jones's health?"

The fat man began laughing so hard that tears streamed down his cheeks, but then his laughing turned into a fit of coughing. Irons continued speaking calmly while removing something from inside his jacket.

"I can assure you that you need not worry about the harm smoking will cause him." He raised a silver revolver and pointed it at the fat man's chest. The man ceased coughing as panic filled his eyes. There was a single blast, and he fell backward off his chair, dead. The woman gasped.

"Do not worry, Ms. Smith," Irons continued coolly. "That just leaves more for you and me." He turned toward the twins, who were now visibly shaken. "They were exactly where you said they would be. All of them." The boys nodded but said nothing. Their eyes looked tired, but their hands were trembling.

"Now, I promised that I would send you to Mars if you cooperated," Irons continued, staring them in the eye. "I lied."

The twins looked stunned. That Irons might deceive them hadn't crossed their minds. Was it possible? They had read his mind during their previous encounters with him, but not once had there been even a hint of betrayal. Had he somehow fooled them? As they stood face to face with their betrayer, they suddenly realized the precariousness of their situation. *You go left, I'll go right*, thought Jack. *Run.* Spencer turned to his brother and nodded. Then they ran for their lives, one darting to the left while the other sprinted behind a row of bookshelves on the right.

"Seize them!" shouted Irons, pulling out his stun gun. "We must not let them get away!"

The orange-haired woman dashed after one of the boys and caught hold of his jacket, but he got away when she tripped over a trash receptacle and fell. At the same instant, Irons spun around and fired a bolt of electricity at one of the boys as he ran past him. There was a flash and a scream. The boy sank to the floor and writhed in convulsions as the electricity surged through his small body.

The lights suddenly went out and darkness filled the room. Irons blinked but his night-vision contacts refused to activate—something was wrong. There was a low moaning from behind him, but he couldn't identify its source. He felt his way along a wall to where he thought the exit was and waited.

"Did you get him?" asked the woman, picking herself up off the floor. "Where are you?"

Irons did not reply. He lay on his side across the exit waiting for the other boy to cross. He waited silently in the dark, like a snake, confident that his prey would soon come this way. Minutes passed, but he remained motionless. Finally, something bumped against his shoulder, and he reached out blindly and grabbed hold of a foot. He twisted it violently and heard a boy's scream. With the swiftness of a python, he quickly subdued the boy with a choke hold and held him until he passed out.

"I got him!" he yelled. "Both of them. Turn on the lights!"

The female agent fumbled through a bag and pulled out a chem-light and gave it a sudden twist. A pale-yellow glow illuminated her corner of the room, and she searched until she found a light switch. When the lights came on, both she and Irons were shocked by what they saw. There in the middle room where three of the Wonder Kids had been lying unconscious, only two remained.

"It's Wiley," said the woman. "But how did he get loose?"

"It is this one," replied Irons gruffly, nudging Raven with his boot. She stirred slightly. "She untied him with her mind—remarkable. I should have seen that coming."

"But she's out cold," interrupted the woman, baffled.

"No, she only wants us to think she is. She has been awake the whole time. She and the boy." He put the stun pistol back in its holster and pulled out his revolver. "Agent Smith, I do appreciate your service, but you now know far too much for me to allow you to live." He aimed and fired.

The woman staggered backward to the wall and struggled to stay on her feet. She reached for her own gun, but Irons fired twice more, and she sank to the carpeted floor as the blood ran out of her body.

Irons took out his phone and dialed a number.

"This is Agent Irons," he said calmly. "I need assistance at the old library on West Fifty-Sixth. I have four of the five children, and we need to remove them at once."

"Yes, sir," came the reply. "We'll be there shortly."

Chapter 13

Trouble Aboard the *Intrepid*

Meanwhile, Megan was settling into a routine aboard the spaceship Intrepid. Now three weeks into the journey, all but a few precious minutes of her days conformed to a rigid schedule set by the officers running the ship—wake-up, exercise, breakfast, training drills, lunch, guard duty, assigned readings, dinner, clean up, sleep. She saw Hendrix infrequently, usually in the mornings, but he had a habit of disappearing for long periods of time with his new friend, the mysterious lady with the pyramid tattoo. She suspected they were in love.

The week before, the ship's chief security officer noticed her and assigned her guard duty. He was a small, compact man in his fifties with little patience and even less interest in small talk. After ascertaining that Megan was part of his team, he immediately put her to work patrolling the ship. Her job was to keep an eye out for anyone or anything that looked out of place. Spies, he said, were the biggest threat. Catching them required constant surveillance and even trickery. He said that Trans Europa and the Pacific Alliance were continually trying to sneak their spies onto Commonwealth missions and that the Commonwealth was probably doing the same to them.

Meals were a little better now that Megan had somebody to eat with. She and Anya met for lunch and dinner nearly every day. Despite the awkwardness of her experience in the greenhouse, she enjoyed Anya's company and liked her more and more. They told stories, joked about the other crew members, and Anya kept her up to date on the latest with Shem. Yet something about her new friend continued to trouble Megan: how had she known about her age? After all, for years people had commented to Megan that she looked older than she really was.

One evening she could stand it no more.

"How did you know I'm not twenty?" she asked abruptly before scarfing down a food cube. She raised an eyebrow inquisitively and half grinned.

"Oh, I did say that, didn't I?" replied Anya. "Don't make too much out of it. I wasn't being serious."

"But you were," insisted Megan. "And I'm not twenty. I'm fourteen. I'm just wondering how the girl who works in the greenhouse would know something like that about me."

Anya smiled. "I can't say, Megan. Let's just say there are some things you weren't meant to know. But I can tell you that I'm a friend and that I'm here to help you."

Megan blinked, stunned. That was the same thing Paige had said to her before they boarded the ships.

"Do you know who my parents are?"

"No. But I might know someone who does."

"What . . ." Megan began to ask, but Anya touched a finger to her lips and motioned for her to be quiet.

"No more questions," she said, shaking her head. "I would like to be your friend, but you're going to have to trust me." She looked at her seriously and then added, "Don't turn around. Your chaperone is coming to join us, and he has company."

Megan stared straight ahead, pretending not to notice as Hendrix saddled up next to them. She was surprised to find that she was happy to see him, but that happiness was short-lived.

"Well, if it isn't Mary Poppins!" he exclaimed sarcastically, tugging at Megan's shoulder-length ponytail. He turned to Anya. "And what is your name, lovely lady?"

"Anya," came the reply coolly.

"I think I'll call you Freckles. It suits you." Hendrix chuckled and turned toward Megan. "They're opening the sports pod tomorrow morning. It's a huge cylinder in the middle of the ship with room for twenty people. Just think, boxing and wrestling in zero gravity!"

Megan wrinkled her nose in disgust.

"They also have gymnastics. Or how about dodgeball?" offered Hendrix with a wink. "I mean, come on, wouldn't you love the chance to fling a ball at this handsome face?"

"Not really my thing," said Megan. "Who's your lady friend? I've been noticing you two together since we boarded the ship."

"This is Cassandra. She's a flight engineer. Quite an athlete too." The woman beside him flashed a brief close-lipped smile that caused the sides of her eyes to wrinkle slightly. Her pyramid tattoo was, for the moment, hidden beneath the collar of her exercise jacket. Megan wondered why she didn't make more of an effort to be friendly. Anya looked on inquisitively.

"We've been working out twice a day," continued Hendrix. "Resistance bands and stationary bikes mostly. You should try it."

As Hendrix bragged about his many athletic accomplishments, Megan thought she noticed something strange in the way Cassandra and Anya looked at each other. It was as if they knew each other. Perhaps it was their body language or the way their eyes met and quickly parted once they had made contact.

Just then Anya coughed and excused herself. "Sorry—I've got to go," she said hurriedly. "It was nice meeting you both." As she pushed off a corner where the wall met the ceiling, her ponytail shifted ever so slightly to the left, momentarily revealing the pyramid tattoo on the back of her own neck. This time, Megan noticed.

"Sure, Freckles," Hendrix said as he watched her float off toward the exit. He smirked. "See you around." He turned to Cassandra and whispered something in her ear. She squeezed his hand and kissed him on the cheek before gliding off in the opposite direction from where Anya had gone.

"Megan," began Hendrix, tilting his head to the side, "I asked Cassandra to leave because I need to speak with you privately."

"Okay."

"There's news from headquarters. There's been activity around the colony. It's robots—spiders that move like the real thing, only they're much bigger and deadlier. It seems that's what's been attacking the colony. We've got them on film. Here, watch this."

He pulled out a small device and pulled the top and bottom halves apart, revealing a clear polymer screen. The screen turned blue, and a 3-D rendering of the colony materialized in front of them, the same as the one she'd seen on the news back in her apartment.

The screen flickered and changed views, zooming in on a small portion of the dome. There were dark spots moving across it. The screen flickered again as one of the spots came into focus. There it was—a spider, made entirely of mechanical parts. It was about as large in diameter as a dinner plate. Its head turned side to side, scanning its surroundings. A metallic leg reached out and tapped the dome's clear surface, and then it stopped.

"What's that dark stuff on the back of its head?"

"That's blood, sunshine. These things kill. They go for your legs first. Once your tendons are slashed and you fall to the ground, they stab you in the neck with a sharp metal tube and drain all your blood."

"How do you know this?"

"There's footage of them doing it. Terrible stuff. Believe me, you don't want to see it."

"Can we kill them?"

"You can't kill what was never alive to begin with, but I'll stop them, all right. I'll blow 'em to bits!" Hendrix unzipped a pocket and pulled out his semi-automatic handgun with exploding rounds and grinned.

"You're not supposed to have that on the ship," Megan said sharply. "Kang said—"

"Well, Kang's not my daddy." He slid the gun back inside his flight suit. "There's more." He swiped a finger across the screen and a new image appeared. It showed what looked like a swarm of green and blue sparks streaking across a night sky.

"What are those?"

"We have no idea," said Hendrix. "But I suspect we're going to find out."

The next day, while she was on duty, Megan thought about what Hendrix had shown her. So, Harper and Anya had been right—there were spiders on Mars, or at least robots that looked and acted like them. The thought of facing one terrified her. Her bad leg could make her an easy target. She would have to find a way to outsmart them. *But how?*

She also wondered about Anya and Cassandra. *Could they be spies? Undercover agents?* It was impossible to tell. She became so lost in her thoughts that she didn't notice the man watching her until it was almost too late. She would have missed him entirely if it hadn't been for a small service droid that nearly ran into her.

Turning quickly to dodge it, she glimpsed a tall, muscular man in a pale-blue flight suit staring at her. He had blond hair and broad shoulders, and there was something odd about his eyes. She remembered seeing him when she met Paige, and that Paige had seemed scared of him, and she had seen him again shortly after lift-off when she collided with him. He had stared at her then too, saying nothing. And now, here, he was doing the same thing again. *Was he a stalker? A predator?* She was scared. Noticing a repairman nearby, she got an idea.

"Excuse me, sir. Can you help me?" The repairman looked up, surprised and a little annoyed.

"That guy behind me is looking for someone to fix a thermostat. Can you help him?"

"What guy?" asked the repairman, a little more annoyed than before.

"Him." Megan turned to point at her stalker, but he was gone.

"He was just there a second ago," she stammered awkwardly. "I'll let you know when I see him again."

"Okay, little lady," he muttered sarcastically. "Anything you say."

Slowly and steadily the days aboard the *Intrepid* ticked off like hours on a clock. Sometimes Megan dreamed, and sometimes she did not. When she did dream, she saw the same dark-haired woman as before, always waiting or reaching out to her as though for help. But now she had company. The man with the strange eyes—the one whose stare made her skin crawl—was with her. His gaze was so penetrating as to be terrifying. She awoke from these dreams drenched in sweat, her heart racing, unable to go back to sleep. After a few such nights, she found herself exhausted and sleep-deprived.

The food continued to be a problem. It was still bland and unappetizing, and she found herself hungry all the time. It became almost unbearable by the third week. She couldn't wait to have something other than dehydrated compressed meals in bags or cubes, with their dry, tasteless vegetables and rubbery slices of meat. She was tired of life in zero gravity and missed being able to walk, even if it meant having to limp.

Getting to sleep at night was a challenge too. There was always noise. Robots scampering along walls with magnetic feet while performing maintenance tasks. Repairmen assisting the robots. Control panels humming. The clanging of metal tools banging into stainless-steel walls. She longed for a quiet place where she could relax.

To conserve their precious water supply, the crew was

limited to one fifteen-second shower a week. As the water went down the drain, it was instantly recycled and sent back into a membrane surrounding the ship's outer walls that served as protection from solar radiation blasts. Before long, the ship began smelling like a giant sweaty locker room. Anybody could take an air shower whenever they wanted—a process by which you stood inside a narrow plastic tube and had your body strafed with compressed scented air so that it felt like you were being attacked by a tornado—but the general consensus was that these were too painful to be worth the effort. It was easy to spot someone who had just taken one because their skin was red all over.

Nevertheless, what Megan dreaded most was the mysterious, creepy man who continued eyeing her from afar. She noticed him more and more as the days turned into weeks. His face was always expressionless, yet his gaze, through those bizarre eyes, haunted her. When she caught him staring, he no longer tried to leave or look away. He stood his ground and watched her every move. She asked the head of security who he was.

"His name's Vic," came the reply. "Weird guy. Apparently, he's involved in a top-secret project that's above my clearance level. Kind of a mission within the mission. That's all I know. Why do you ask?"

"I've caught him staring and . . ." Megan paused. Complaining about a fellow crew member suddenly felt lame, and she didn't want to appear weak. "Never mind. I thought maybe I knew him from somewhere, but I was mistaken."

Each day she went about her routine, always keeping an eye out for the mysterious "Vic." She asked Anya and Hendrix to watch her back, but Hendrix laughed at her and Anya just shrugged it off as nothing to worry about.

Feeling frightened and alone, she kept her L-Stat stun weapon close at all times.

Chapter 14

Phantom Apparition

The night after Hendrix showed her the pictures, Megan had a dream. She dreamed she was standing on a beach with reddish rust-colored sand. Before her stretched a vast, shimmering sea. A small girl was crying. She approached the girl and asked her what was wrong. As she spoke with the girl, she realized it was Harper, only she was five or six years old. She had lost a bracelet while swimming, and now it was too deep for her to retrieve it. Megan told her not to worry—she would find it. She dove into the cold blue water, breaking the surface with a gentle splash. She swam deeper and deeper along the sandy bottom until she saw something gold sparkle in front of her. It was the bracelet. She scooped it up, gripping it tightly in her fingers, but before she could turn around, something large and dark caught her eye, and she swam toward it.

As she got closer, she could make out an outcropping of rocks with a gap in it—a cave. Pieces of an old wooden shipwreck lay scattered and crumbling in the sand around it, and hundreds of tiny silver fish darted in and out of the cave's narrow entrance, their shiny bodies reflecting the sun so that they appeared as bright specks of light.

She grabbed onto the sides of the cave's entrance and pulled herself inside, where it opened into a larger space. At first it was dark and quiet, but gradually the interior lit up with an eerie reddish glow. She noticed a series of crude drawings and markings on the walls. The markings reminded her of ancient Egyptian hieroglyphs, and the drawings were mostly of people and animals. She swam closer to one and noticed that the people were under a dome, just like the one she had lived under on Mars. There were spiders attacking them, and there was a girl in the middle holding something that looked like a small child with a tail.

Suddenly she felt the need for air. As she swam back toward the cave's entrance, she saw a pair of eyes staring at her from a dusky corner. In a flash, something dark rushed toward her, kicking up sand and silt so that she couldn't see it clearly. She panicked, frantically kicking to get away, desperate for air. Swimming as fast as she could, she caught a brief glimpse of a shadowy figure behind her. It was gaining on her. She reached the mouth of the cave and had almost escaped when an icy hand grabbed her ankle and began pulling her back inside. Her lungs felt like they were going to explode. She held onto the sides of the cave and fought as hard as she could to escape, but it was to no avail. The rock was slick with algae, and she lost her grip. As she was pulled back inside, she turned around and looked her assailant in the eyes. It was the mysterious dark-eyed woman, the same one she had seen in dreams a hundred times before. Then something clicked in her brain, and she knew.

Burke, she thought. *It's Dr. Burke!*

The water vanished and the cave's interior faded away, replaced by a landscape of red dust and rock. Not only could she not breathe, but her skin was freezing and felt as though it would crack. "Don't be afraid," said the figure. "Breathe. Just breathe."

She awoke with a shiver. Unable to get back to sleep, she opened her sleep pod and got out. The dream had meant something, but its meaning eluded her, and she couldn't shake the feeling that someone or something very scary was after her.

Chapter 15

Space Innovations Inc.

At the very moment that Megan awakened from her dream, Harper arrived in Australia. She couldn't believe her incredible luck in getting through so many security checkpoints without being identified. Before exiting the airport, she pulled a small compact mirror out of her purse, looked at her reflection, and sighed. Her beautiful long red locks were gone, replaced by a mop of glossy hair loosely tied into a ponytail. Her complexion was darker now, thanks to a pigment enhancer, and she had applied a tiny artificial mole above her left eye and a fake tattoo of a shamrock on her forearm. Even her friends would have a hard time recognizing her now.

She exited the airport and hailed a taxi, which quickly swooped over to the curb to pick her up. It was a solar-powered, driverless model with voice-recognition software and a talking console. You seldom saw them around New York or Washington anymore, but they were still standard fare in Australia. She opened the door and got in the backseat.

"Hello. Welcome to Sydney!" quipped a pleasant, yet slightly robotic voice with an Australian accent. "Please state your name and destination."

"Shannon O'Reilly," Harper answered. "Destination: Space Innovations."

"That will be two thousand credits," said the voice. "Please enter your international pay code on the keypad." Harper entered the information as instructed. "Thanks, mate," replied the voice. "Sit back and enjoy the scenery. We will be arriving at your destination in precisely thirty-five minutes."

Space Innovations' headquarters was situated in a busy neighborhood on the outskirts of Sydney. Harper's taxi stopped in front of a stainless-steel building shaped like a tadpole lying on its side. The sun's rays glared brightly off its silvery exterior so that she had to squint to look at it. Behind the building lay reddish desert scrub—the Outback.

She walked to the front door and stood motionless as a robotic arm retracted from the steel wall and scanned her face. There was a flash as it took her photograph, and a voice asked her to identify herself.

"Shannon O'Reilly," she replied, hoping that her faux-Irish accent was convincing enough. "I'm here for my interview." The door slid open, and she stepped inside. The lobby was spacious and clean, with curved walls, a vaulted ceiling, and a red-carpeted floor. A life-sized photograph of a rust-colored Martian landscape covered one whole wall, while another was decorated with color-changing light fixtures that swayed hypnotically like sea anemones. A receptionist sitting behind a polished wood counter welcomed her.

"Ms. O'Reilly," the woman exclaimed. "We've been expecting you. I'll let Mr. Bridges know you're here." She swiped a finger across a glass screen on the counter and whispered something into it. A few minutes later, a man wearing a suit made of woven metal filaments strode through a pair of double doors and greeted her.

"Welcome to Space Innovations. I'm Dave. I own the company, and I'm also one of the pilots."

"Shannon," came Harper's reply. "Nice to meet you."

"Well, Shannon," Bridges continued, "I must say you come highly recommended. We hadn't expected to be interviewing for this spot so close to lift-off, but our computer systems operator seems to have disappeared into thin air. We were lucky to have such a highly qualified candidate for the job show up when you did. Can you tell me a little about yourself and why you want to go on this mission?"

"Sure," answered Harper, and she went into a long story that she had fabricated during her trip to Australia. She explained that she had been born in Ireland (now part of Trans Europa) but moved to the American Commonwealth as a child. Though she looked young, she was actually twenty-eight. She said she majored in computer systems in college and later updated the Space Administration's communications links with the data-collection satellites orbiting Jupiter and Saturn, claims that were supported by forged documents. She had read up on computer systems during the long flight, so she was able to make it seem as though she knew more than she really did.

Bridges took notes and nodded occasionally. He seemed impressed.

When she was done, Bridges stood up and shook her hand. "Shannon," he said confidently, "we've already done a background check on you, and everything looks great. I'm completely satisfied that you're the right one for the job. It's yours if you'll take it. I guarantee you won't regret it."

"That sounds wonderful," Harper replied. "My only question is safety. I mean, I've read the news reports about the colony on Mars losing oxygen and how there's a rescue mission underway. Do you think we'll be safe?"

Bridges smiled. "Shannon, all I can tell you is that this is a private operation and that we are going to an entirely different part of Mars where some very exciting things are happening. And no, you shouldn't be in any danger. Basically, this is space tourism—we're taking a bunch of very wealthy customers on the adventure of their lives. You'll never even have to leave the ship, although we do offer a Mars walk for our paying guests."

"Well, in that case, count me in," Harper said. "When do we launch?"

"A week from today. Will that be a problem for you?"

"Not at all." She wondered how she was going to learn everything about the ship's computer systems in seven days, but the voice inside her told her not to worry. Everything would work out okay.

"Can I see the ship?" she asked hopefully.

"I'm afraid not," replied Bridges. The actual ship is at the launch site, and it's not easy to reach. But we have a simulator module that should give you a good idea of what to expect. All the ship's software applications are perfectly replicated on it. It's basically a three-quarter-sized model." He turned to the receptionist. "Erin, would you please show Ms. O'Reilly to the module?"

"It will be my pleasure," said the woman behind the counter. "Please follow me."

Chapter 16

Discovery

We all have a circadian rhythm that tells us when to sleep and when to be active. It's like an internal clock, and it is affected by environmental cues such as sunlight and temperature. When it's disrupted, problems such as cardiovascular disease and neurological disorders are common. In space, the problem is magnified. There is no night or day. To remedy this, the *Intrepid*'s lighting was set to dark during night hours, dim in the wee hours of the morning, and increasingly bright as the day progressed.

When Megan awoke from her nightmare, she judged by the faint light outside her sleep pod that it was about 4:30 a.m. She climbed out, slipped on her flight suit, and tied her hair in a ponytail to keep it out of her face.

Without warning, a gray spherical-shaped robot the size of a basketball spun toward her and hovered motionless in front of her. It hummed and beeped softly as it scanned her face with a laser. She closed her eyes tight and waited. She knew that it was merely assessing her physical and mental health, but she wished it would go away. She felt the warmth of the laser as it moved across her face, and she tried to relax. She slowed her breathing and concentrated on turning off her mind, but memories of the nightmare lingered. She tried thinking of her apartment, her garden, her cat. Then there was a beep, and it was over. She opened her eyes just in time to see the robot jet off in search of someone else emerging from a sleep pod.

A short time later, she entered the dining compartment and was surprised by how many people were already there. They were everywhere, talking, eating, stretching. It was the early shift. She noticed Anya tethered to her usual corner beside a young security officer with dark, serious eyes. They were talking and casting glances her way. Megan approached, curious.

"Hi," said Anya. "This is Ob. He's my friend. He's been helping me keep tabs on Vic." Megan was surprised. So, Anya was sharing her secrets with other people, people she didn't know. She offered a guarded hello and introduced herself.

"I already know who you are," said Ob, his necklace floating eerily up around his face. "Anya asked me to do this for her. I've been following Vic and found out where he spends most of his time—that is, when he's not following you."

"Oh?" exclaimed Megan, eyebrows raised.

"He followed you for over an hour yesterday, and you had no idea."

Megan felt her blood run cold as the fear returned. *How had she not noticed?* She wondered if he was here now, spying on her, and was about to turn around when she thought better of it.

"Is he watching us now?" she asked nervously.

"No," said Anya. "You're safe."

Ob whispered, "We think you should try to talk with him. Maybe that's all he wants, and he's been looking for the right moment when nobody's around."

"Okay, but where and when?" asked Megan. "And what if he's dangerous?" She took a deep breath and exhaled slowly. Deep down she knew that a confrontation was inevitable.

"I don't think he wants to hurt you," added Anya. "Just find out what he wants." She placed a hand on Megan's wrist. "I'll give you a transceiver. If anything goes wrong, just say the word, and Ob and I will be right behind you. You need to do this, Megan. You can't live in fear of him any longer."

"She's right," said Ob. "We'll be nearby. I carry a gun, so you'll be safe."

"Okay," replied Megan. "I already said I'd do it." Deep down she knew they were right. If she did nothing, fear would follow her everywhere she went. She strengthened her resolve to confront her stalker. "But it's got to be on my terms, not his."

"Right." Anya smiled, nodding. "Ob, now tell Megan what you told me."

Ob explained that he had followed Vic the night before. He had seen him go into the cargo bay where he disappeared from view. There had been two doors, not counting the cargo unloading hatch, so he must have gone into one of them.

"I watched those doors until an hour ago," he said. "He never came out."

"Then that's where I'm going to find him." A look of determination crossed Megan's face. "I'll go there tonight. If I catch him while he's asleep, at least I'll have the element of surprise on my side."

"I'll be right behind you," said Anya with a gleam in her eye. "I'll meet you outside your sleep pod at zero two hundred hours." The three of them then ate their breakfast and planned their mission.

That night, Megan couldn't sleep. She had set her pod to open at precisely zero two hundred hours. When its lid finally retracted, she looked around for Anya. The crew compartment was dark except for a few dim lights. At first she saw no one, but then Anya was right there in front of her, floating silently in the dark with one hand on the pod to anchor herself.

"Thanks for coming," whispered Megan nervously. "Where's Ob?"

"Keeping an eye out to make sure Vic isn't already up. Are you ready?"

"Just a sec." Megan closed her eyes and mentally rehearsed the plan. Yes, if she was going to catch Vic off-guard, this would be the best time to do it. She strapped on her L-Stat and checked to make sure it was fully charged. Back at the launch site, Kang had told her that one shot could incapacitate a man for ten minutes, and she had a feeling that she would be needing it tonight. Hurrying, she grabbed a pair of infrared night-vision goggles and prepared to follow Anya to the cargo bay.

"Okay," whispered Anya. "Let's go."

Anya pushed off the sleep pod and drifted through the darkness like a ghost, with Megan following close behind.

Together, they made their way through the compartment toward the lab, dodging walls, wires, and pieces of equipment bolted to the floors. A few maintenance workers and service robots worked quietly in the dark, seemingly unaware of their presence.

A few meters short of the lab, Anya stopped. She pulled out a set of the ship's blueprints and motioned for Megan to come close.

"I don't think you should go this way," she whispered softly. "If someone's in the lab, they'll wonder why you're there. We should split up." She pointed to a spot on the blueprints. "The kitchen. It also connects with the cargo bay. There shouldn't be anyone in there at this time of night. You go that way. I'll go through the lab. Meet you inside the cargo bay in about ten minutes."

Megan nodded. Part of her wasn't sure if she could trust Anya. Fighting to calm her nerves, she propelled herself stealthily through the ship until she reached the entrance to the kitchen. Its heavy metal door was locked. She inserted a keycard and gave the door a gentle push. It creaked slightly as it opened. Inside, it was dark except for a few small green plasma lights on the ovens and storage cabinets. She paused, waiting for her eyes to adjust, and then went inside.

Pantry doors and shelves lined the kitchen's walls, and a long stainless-steel cutting table occupied the center. There was a knife rack mounted on the side of the table, its blades held in place by magnets. She searched for the door to the cargo bay but couldn't find it. On the floor lay several large boxes secured to the floor with cables. She silently propelled herself along the kitchen's perimeter, looking for a door or hatch.

Just then, she noticed a ball of light speeding toward

her and spun around. It was about the size of a pea, and it hovered in front of her momentarily before darting behind a stack of boxes on the other side of the room. It was fast and quiet. Curious, she followed it. She loosened a cable holding the boxes down and squeezed herself behind them. The tiny orb of light was there, perched on the handle of a circular gray hatch. She brushed the light away and pushed open the hatch. A soft reddish glow emanated from within.

Inside were more boxes—row upon row of them. There were also tools, machines, and an all-terrain vehicle with giant rubber tires. All were secured with cables. She could see the massive steel door used for loading and unloading the ship. She quickly looked around the cargo bay for Anya, but her friend was not there yet.

She noticed the two doors that Ob had mentioned. One, marked RESTRICTED ACCESS—DO NOT ENTER, was slightly ajar. As she glided toward it, another tiny speck of light darted past her. This one was blue. Her eyes tracked it around the cargo bay until it hovered in place. She wondered if it could be some type of firefly that had escaped from the lab or that had gotten in before lift-off.

She turned her attention to the slightly open door. *Could it have come from in there?* Without waiting, she pushed the door open the rest of the way. Darkness stared back at her. She put on her night-vision goggles and inched forward cautiously.

The room looked like a cross between a lab and a warehouse, with equipment scattered everywhere. What seemed like dozens of brightly glowing specks dotted the walls. She slid the night-vision goggles onto her forehead and marveled at their brightness. Suddenly, one streaked across the room like a tiny comet and stopped in front of her. The others followed and quickly surrounded her. They were beautiful, like fireflies, and they began changing colors, from yellow to green to red to violet. She tried to touch one, but it was fast and darted away. They lingered for a few seconds and then launched themselves around a corner toward an unseen section of the compartment.

Megan followed but was careful to keep an eye on her surroundings. Vic could be lurking anywhere, and he could be dangerous. She drew her L-Stat and held it close to her body so that it couldn't be taken away from her easily.

As she rounded a corner, what she saw shocked her. Three bodies hovered motionless in the air as though sleeping. She crept closer. Two were female, one was male. They were young, probably teenagers, and they appeared not to be breathing. Tubes running from their arms, legs, and chests connected them to a series of machines and computers.

She turned to look behind her and recoiled in terror. There was Vic, three meters away, glaring at her with those strange eyes. His muscles bulged beneath his flight suit.

"Get away from me," she screamed, "or I'll shoot!"

Vic said nothing but held his hands out to his sides as though offering her a target. A glowing speck settled on his shoulder, then another, and then another. Within the span of several seconds, he was covered in glowing, crawling specks. He stared into her eyes. Megan backed away slowly, keeping a finger on the trigger. At last, Vic broke the uneasy silence.

"I've been waiting for you," he said. "The prophecy said you'd return."

Chapter 17

Where Are the Passengers?

For a solid week, Harper trained at Space Innovations. She worked all day, every day, and late into the night trying to get a handle on her job. She studied manuals, dissected virtual models of the ship's computer system, and practiced on simulators. The simulations, which replicated emergencies like a solar radiation blast, were a fiasco. Again and again, her best efforts to correct hypothetical problems resulted in total destruction of the ship. She worried that someone would notice and take her off the mission, but nobody seemed to notice or care. It was as though they were purposely ignoring her. Only a few even bothered to introduce themselves, and when they did, they invariably gave her a quick excuse for why they had to rush off to some other place. For the most part, she trained alone.

The simulator module was huge. If it was only three-quarters the size of the ship, as Bridges had claimed, then the actual ship would have to be enormous, nearly a hundred meters long. Corridors ran through it like a vast maze, with dozens of compartments with locked doors. Signs painted on the doors explained each compartment's purpose: PARTS WAREHOUSE, KITCHEN, DINING COMPARTMENT, CREW QUARTERS, ENGINE ROOM. One sign baffled her: LIVESTOCK.

Farm animals in zero gravity? How was this even possible? Occasionally she heard people inside the various locked compartments, but she couldn't make out what they were saying. Her own workstation, the computer terminal, was long, narrow, and had a low ceiling on which she often bumped her head. Computers ran from floor to ceiling all along the terminal, with hundreds, if not thousands, of switches, knobs, and blinking indicator lights. It was impossible to keep up with all of them. She wondered how she would ever be able to keep the system running in the event of an emergency.

On the fifth day of her training, she was greeted by a woman in a white lab coat. She was at least a couple decades older than Harper—probably in her thirties or forties—with long hair and thin gray glasses on whose lenses flitted tiny digital images. She introduced herself.

"Shannon, I'm Dr. Beaudet, Head of System Operations. You'll be working for me. How's everything going so far?"

"Fine," Harper lied, shaking her hand. "It's a little different from what I'm used to, but I'll have it figured out soon."

"Good," said Dr. Beaudet. "I want you to take inventory

of all the different types of software loaded on the computers. That ought to keep you busy for a while. Wait a minute." She tapped her glasses with her index finger and scanned something that was being projected onto them. "Sorry. Gotta go."

She left abruptly, the heels of her hard-soled shoes clicking on the shiny metallic floor. Harper breathed a sigh of relief. If only she could keep this up until the ship launched, she'd be okay. If something went wrong a few thousand kilometers out into space, well, it wasn't like they could just turn around and bring her back. They'd be stuck with her. Still, she had a lingering fear that something might go wrong, something that she would be expected to fix. If she couldn't do it, would anybody else be able to?

On the morning of lift-off, a car arrived to pick her up from Space Innovations and take her to the launch site. The robot driver wouldn't tell her where she was going, only that there was no charge. They drove to the edge of the city limits and then turned onto a dusty gravel road that led into the Outback, Australia's vast and mostly uninhabited interior. The ground was dry and rust-colored, speckled with low-lying shrubs and boulders. Cracks ran across its surface where the soil had dried out and eroded.

This looks a lot like Mars, she thought. Gazing into the distance, she noticed first one, then two, kangaroos grazing lazily near a massive sandstone outcropping. She had always wanted to see one. She smiled. Gradually, though, the redness of the vast Australian desert turned her thoughts toward Mars and what lay in store for her once she got there.

She wasn't afraid. Part of her was curious to find out

what had happened to Dr. Burke and why the colony was under attack. She wanted to walk on the planet's red surface and explore its dry riverbeds in a way that she hadn't been able to when she was little. For her, it was home in a way that Earth never could be, and she knew that she would never truly be happy until she returned there.

Mostly she was scared for Megan. Megan barely remembered Mars, and now she was being sent there as a pawn in a dangerous power struggle between forces she didn't fully understand. She didn't trust Herrington and the others to protect her. Megan was like a little sister to her—she had looked out for her since they arrived on Earth as young children, and she felt that it was her job to protect her. She knew about the spiders and hoped that she could get there in time to save her friend.

Her inner voice had become strangely silent in recent days. It had done nothing to help her learn the ship's computer system, nor had it commented on the people she met.

She pressed a button, and the back of her soft leather seat gently tilted back until she was in a reclining position. Slowly she drifted off to sleep until a loud noise coming from outside the vehicle awakened her.

She peered out the windows and watched as a pair of wings retracted from beneath the car and locked into place. The robot driver spoke. "Seat returning to upright position. Fasten safety harness and prepare for take-off."

The back of her seat folded upward, returning her to a sitting position as the vehicle rapidly accelerated. She felt it rise off the road and into the air. Outside, the landscape rushed past her in a blur. She sat back, tightened her safety harness, and yawned to equalize the pressure in her ears as the vehicle increased its altitude.

"Do not be alarmed," the robot driver reassured her. "All systems are normal. We will arrive at your destination in less than an hour." *This is nice,* she thought, and she relaxed to the hum of the engine and the sight of clouds through her window. *I really need to get one of these someday.*

When they touched down on a small runway deep in the Outback an hour later, she noticed a few small buildings and a towering structure that loomed over everything else. It was the launch site. The ship, *Ares III*, stood ready for lift-off. It was enormous, over a hundred meters tall, with a bulging cargo bay on its underside and an observation deck on top. Four solid rocket boosters protruded from its sides. It looked old, and indeed it was. The *Ares III* had been one of the original cargo ships to ferry men and supplies back and forth to Mars over seventy years ago. The crew, made up of only twenty-five people, was also there, having arrived in separate vehicles. Not a single camera, journalist, or news drone was present—everything about the place screamed of secrecy.

She walked briskly from the runway to the launchpad. The air was blisteringly hot despite a faint breeze. She looked at the other crew members. Most were young, probably twenty-five and thirty-five years old, although there were a few with graying hair. All wore loose-fitting navy-blue flight suits like her own. A few seemed nervous. They looked over the ship and made small talk while fanning themselves with sheets of thin, rigid plastic. Some glanced at her when they thought she wasn't looking, but she noticed. SIS agents always noticed. Hearing footsteps behind her, she turned. It was Dr. Beaudet.

"Ready?" asked the older woman, her lab coat rustling slightly in the warm breeze.

"Ready as I'm going to be," replied Harper, trying her best to appear confident.

Beaudet continued, her brow furrowed to show that she meant business. "When we board the ship, everything should look familiar. It's exactly like what you've experienced in the simulations." She held a pair of binoculars to her eyes and squinted at a man high up on the control tower. After a while, he gave her a thumbs-up. "Okay," she said. "We've been given the go-ahead to board the ship. I'll see you inside."

After a brief announcement, the crew members took an elevator up the control tower and filed into the ship one by one. Dr. Beaudet was right—as Harper strolled through the ship, everything looked familiar. She found her seat near the back of the crew compartment and strapped herself in.

Minutes turned to hours as they waited for the ship to launch. Harper got out of her seat and made her way to the observation deck. Peering through a window, she noticed several trucks near the launchpad that hadn't been there when she boarded the ship. A farmer wearing a wide-brimmed hat was herding cows and goats into a temporary pen that had been set up beside the ship, and she noticed a crate of chickens in the back of one of the trucks.

"Looks like a regular barnyard out there," she remarked to a fellow crew member who had also come over for a look. She was petite and had short brown hair. "I take it the animals are coming with us?"

"Don't worry," replied the crew member. "They'll be penned up in the cargo bay."

Harper introduced herself as Shannon O'Reilly, Computer Technician.

"It's good to meet you. I'm Windsor," said the other woman, extending her hand. "I'm the copilot. I actually help fly this thing."

"Interesting name," remarked Harper. "Sounds like a castle."

Windsor smiled. "Wait till we get to Mars—you're going to love it! Well, that is, everything except for the cold, but you'll have an insulated suit to protect you from that. Did you know it's colder than Antarctica there? A lot colder."

Windsor explained that even though the ship could practically fly itself, they always had a couple of pilots on hand in case of emergencies. She had been with the company on fifteen missions, including fourteen to Mars and one to the moon. She also led expedition walks on Mars for their wealthy clients. "Would you like to go with us?" she asked.

"I'd love that," said Harper. "Do you think Bridges will allow it?"

"You'll be my assistant. I'll just tell him I need extra help. It will be fine."

"Great. I really hope it works out," she said, her mind already drifting to thoughts of Mars. She wondered if Dr. Burke was still alive and if she had really become the killer the SIS claimed she was. *If so, could she still be trusted?*

An hour later, an announcement blared over the ship's intercom. It was finally time for everyone to return to their seats and strap in for lift-off. As Harper and Windsor made their way to the crew compartment, they walked past the passenger compartment. The door was open. Inside, the compartment looked luxurious, with reclining leather seats, paintings on the walls, and even plants that looked too real to be artificial, although of course they were. To Harper's surprise, nobody was in there. She turned to Windsor and exclaimed, "Where are the passengers?"

"Harper, we're not carrying tourists this time," replied Windsor.

Harper froze. "Harper? Who's that?"

Windsor grinned slyly and said, "We know who you are and why you're here." Just then, two men came up behind her and grabbed her by the arms. Dr. Beaudet was with them.

"Administer the medication," she said sharply. Harper winced as a hypodermic needle pierced her neck. "You're going to sleep now, Harper," continued Dr. Beaudet, "and when you wake up, we'll probably already be on Mars." Harper felt a tingling sensation in her neck that gradually spread down her spine. "We'll take good care of you; there's nothing to worry about." Beaudet paused and then added, "I look forward to seeing you in about three months."

Harper slouched to the floor as her legs lost the ability to support her. Her mind was growing hazy. She stared up at Windsor glassily and asked, "Who are you people? Did you write the letter?"

"I did," answered Dr. Beaudet, "but let's not worry about that now." Her face was becoming blurry and distorted, and Harper blinked to try to bring her back into focus.

"Does Bridges know?" Harper asked, her voice becoming slurred. She saw Dr. Beaudet's lips move in reply, but she couldn't hear her. She lost consciousness and drifted off into a long, deep, and dreamless sleep.

Chapter 18

Price of Knowledge

This can't be happening, thought Megan as she pointed her L-Stat's muzzle at Vic and prepared to squeeze the trigger. She hoped the electric charge would be enough to disable him. Tiny specks of light continued to swarm around him, their bluish glow illuminating his eyes and making him appear even more sinister. She had been surprised by his statement about a prophecy and wanted to know more.

"What do you mean, 'the prophecy said I'd come'?" she demanded. Her hand trembled as she aimed the compact weapon. She forced herself to look him in the eye. "What prophecy?"

"The prophecy that was written thousands of years ago," said a voice behind her. "Our founder, Dr. Burke, discovered it in a cave on Mars. It's the reason we're all here." She recognized the voice immediately—it was Anya. She wanted to turn around, but she was afraid to take her eyes off Vic.

"What? I don't understand," she stammered, confused. "Come on, Anya. We've got this guy!"

"Megan," replied another voice, this one male. "Put down the gun and nobody will get hurt." She wasn't sure who this one was. *Ob?* They had her surrounded. Vic's gaze was penetrating, as though he were trying to peer into her very soul. Images began flooding her mind— pictures of Mars, of a rebellion, of someone trying to shield her from an assailant. She felt time slipping away and knew that she had to do something fast.

"Why is he looking at me like that?"

"He's syncing his mind with yours. You should let him," replied Anya.

Megan felt a montage of thoughts flicker through her mind in rapid succession, like a deck of cards being shuffled. Was Vic sifting through her memories to find something? She panicked.

"Stop!" she yelled, pointing the L-Stat directly at Vic's face. Specks of blue light shot off him and gathered in the space between them. "I'll shoot!"

"They won't let you," responded another voice behind her, this one female. It wasn't Anya.

Megan knew that if she was going to act, she had to do so immediately. She fired at Vic and the swarm. There was a bright electric flash, and she felt a sudden jolt of pain. Then she passed out.

When she awoke, she had no idea how much time had passed or where she was. Vic was gone. So, too, were the specks of light and the three levitating teenagers connected to machines. Anya, Ob, and the woman who was Hendrix's girlfriend were beside her. *What was her name? Cassandra? Yes, that was it.* She felt groggy, as though she had been hit over the head, and she struggled to remember what had happened.

"Who are you people?" she asked faintly, trying to remain conscious. Her head ached and her muscles felt tight and sore. She guessed that somehow her weapon's electrical charge had been turned against her.

"We're the good guys, Megan." It was Anya, and she sounded sincere. "We're guardians of the prophecy. We call ourselves the Sacred Order of the Pyramid." She pulled down the collar of her flight suit and revealed a small tattoo of a pyramid and eye. "We believe you're special and that you're the one the prophecy says will save us and restore Mars's ancient civilization."

Anya handed her a bottle, and she took a sip. Her headache was gradually lessening. On the other side of the compartment, Cassandra was speaking quietly with a young man Megan didn't recognize.

"Who's Vic?" Megan asked after an awkward pause.

"Vic was one of your caretakers on Mars," said Anya. "He held you when you were a baby, watched you take your first steps. He tried to protect you during the rebellion. When they did finally take you away—you and the rest of the children—he thought he'd never see you again."

"Okay, but why was he following me and staring at me all the time?"

"He had to be sure, Megan. We all did. We had to know if you were really the one the prophecy spoke of. Vic was trying to sync his mind with yours to find out. He can do that. He's a descendant of an ancient Martian race that is now almost completely extinct. There's only a small group of them left."

"And those kids I saw back there—the ones hooked up to the machines—were they alive?"

"Yes," said Anya, "very much so. They're being held in a state of suspended animation for their own safety. Don't worry about them. They're volunteers, and Vic's preparing them for greatness."

"How? I don't understand."

Anya looked her in the eye as she explained. "Megan, Vic wants to show you something, something that will change your life forever, but there will be a price. The life you had will be gone. Whether you realize it or not, you're in the hands of destiny now." She clipped something onto her utility belt and called the others over. "Let's go. We'll take her back to her sleep pod and then help Vic prepare the transmission.

"Okay, Megan, " Anya continued calmly while pulling out a small hypodermic needle. "I'm going to give you something to help you sleep. You'll be a little groggy in the morning. See you at breakfast."

Afterward, as she lay drifting off to sleep inside her pod, Megan reflected on the night's events. Could the prophecy be real, or was it just a story Anya and Vic were using to control her? And just what were those tiny flying lights anyway? She wanted to find out more and whether the others, like Hendrix, were also in on it. Although she wasn't sure if she could trust them, she suspected that Vic and Anya could help her stay alive once they reached Mars, so she resolved to at least pretend to go along with whatever their plan was.

At breakfast the next morning, Anya joined Megan at their normal place in the mess hall. Her magnetized lunch tray made a loud click as she set it down on the metal tabletop, and she tore open one of the food bags that had been fastened onto it. Its label read, REHYDRATED RICE AND BEANS, HEAVILY SPICED. She pulled out a medium-sized cube of compressed rice with a few reddish-brown lumps that must have been beans and took a bite.

"Sleep well?" she asked.

"Not really," said Megan.

"Are we still friends?"

"I don't know. Are we?" Megan glanced around her to see if Ob or anybody else from last night was with her, but she was alone.

"Megan," said Anya, "we're here to help you. We have proof that your own government is behind the attacks on the colony, not Dr. Burke. The prophecy said you'd come. We're going to help you save the colony and then try to recruit the survivors to our side."

"Do you think I'll find my parents? Are they still alive?" Megan asked nervously.

"Maybe, but we have other matters to be concerned with right now. Ob says that today we're getting our assignments for when we reach the colony. You're not going to like it."

"Why not?" inquired Megan.

"According to the commander, we're not saving anyone. We're just picking up rocks."

"Rocks?"

"Yeah, rocks," Anya repeated. "Cadmium. Iridium. Iron. Uranium. Not exactly what you expected, is it? They say the colonists are already dead, but we know that's not true. Vic picked up their radio transmissions several times last night."

"What about the spiders?" asked Megan. "What if they kill everyone before we get there?"

"There are lots of them—even more than we expected," continued Anya. "It will be a tough fight." Then she leaned close and whispered in Megan's ear, "Don't worry. If some of the colonists have survived this long, they can make it a little longer. We're going to get you into that colony one way or another, and we'll deal with the spiders when we get there. We have a secret weapon."

"What?"

"You'll find out soon enough."

Later that day, an announcement blared over the intercom. *"All security team members report to the J-deck immediately."*

Megan dropped what she was doing and hurried to the J-deck where a couple dozen men and women in black flight suits hovered silently around a large man in combat fatigues. It was Colonel Krueger, their commander. She nudged her way through the surrounding crew members until she could see him clearly. His expression was solemn. Someone coughed nervously, and then he spoke.

"As every one of you knows, we lost the *Icarus* during lift-off. That means we also lost our Special Forces unit, the guys trained to do most of the fighting. Now it's just us." He paused to let the words sink in. Megan listened intently and tried to hide her discomfort. Ob was beside her, nodding as Krueger spoke, and she noticed Hendrix on the other side of the room.

Krueger continued, "We will be the ones who secure the landing zone and protect the mission. We will guard the mining convoy and attempt to retrieve survivors from the colony if there are any. If this mission succeeds, it will be because of us." He paused again and scowled. "Are you with me?"

The team erupted in shouts and cheers as men and women high-fived each other and did their best to appear brave. Megan wondered how Herrington could allow her to be assigned to such a dangerous mission. After all, she was his pawn, wasn't she? She would be useless to him if she died. She looked for Ob, but he was already gone.

Krueger spoke again. "You are no longer just security guards. From now on, we train to fight. Each one of you, regardless of your job assignment once we reach Mars, must be prepared for battle in the event that we are attacked. You will meet me in the cargo area every morning at zero five hundred hours starting tomorrow."

When the meeting was over, Hendrix surprised her by sneaking over and putting an arm around her.

"Get off me," she said, irritated.

"I'm just being friendly, sunshine."

"It's Megan." She glared at him. "My name is Megan. If you want me to answer you, call me by my real name."

"Okay," said Hendrix. "Have it your way." He grinned and nodded at a passerby. *He's always got to be the cool one,* she thought. *I'll bet deep down he's just as scared as me.*

"I'd like to know something," said Megan. "Is your uncle aware of what we're being asked to do?"

"It doesn't work like that, sunshine—I mean, Megan." Hendrix's expression changed to one of seriousness. "We're part of a mission, and we do what we're told. I don't ask for special treatment."

"But what about me? Isn't the reason I'm here to lure out Burke?"

Hendrix looked surprised. "I don't know anything about that," he ventured, clearly startled. "Who's Burke?"

Oh my God, she thought. *He really doesn't know.* She wondered if his uncle even cared about him. Probably not. Hendrix was an obnoxious show-off, and Herrington probably considered him an embarrassment. Maybe putting him on this mission was a way of getting rid of him. She suddenly felt a little sorry for him.

"You need to get on the radio with your uncle right away," she said firmly. "Tell him that we've been recruited to fight, and that the colony is overrun with mechanized spiders. If he wants to keep us alive, he needs to get us off this assignment."

Hendrix nodded calmly, but she could tell that he was bothered. He was beginning to realize that she knew more than he did and that his uncle had withheld vital information. He muttered a quick "Okay" and turned to leave.

Chapter 19

Powers Revealed

Herrington had changed his mind about the Wonder Kids. At the last minute, he had contacted Irons, the lead assassin, and told him to take the children alive. He knew about their powers. Unlike most of his colleagues, he was confident that they had nothing to do with the supernatural and were not the result of having been born on Mars. He suspected that someone very clever had tampered with their brains, and he wanted to find out how it had been done.

By taking the Wonder Kids alive, Herrington had defied the president. He needed to be careful. He had them secretly moved to a remote location where a team of surgeons and scientists could dissect their brains. Whether they lived or died was of little consequence—if they survived, he might be able to ransom them to Burke and her people, but if they died it would make his life easier because he wouldn't have anything to explain to the president.

When Spencer awoke, he was cold and his head throbbed with more pain than he had ever experienced before. It felt as though an ax had split his skull wide open, and the pain was so intense that he could barely think. He surveyed his surroundings. The room he was in was tiny and had a concrete floor. The walls were gray and bare. Across from him was a heavy steel door with a small opening through which food could be passed. There were no windows, and the smell of fresh bleach stung his nose. He wondered if he was in prison.

As he sat alone shivering, he thought he heard the muffled sobs of a girl coming from another room and wondered if it was Raven. He also wondered where his brother Jack was. Closing his eyes, he tried to contact him telepathically. Nothing. Tears streamed down his face as he lay back down on the hard, cold floor. The pain quickly overwhelmed him, and he passed out.

The next day he awoke again, hungry and thirsty. A sandwich and a cup of water had been placed beside him. His head still hurt, but his mind was clearer than it had been the day before. After drinking the water and devouring the sandwich, he tried once more to contact his brother but got no response.

He sent out thoughts to the other Wonder Kids as well but was equally unsuccessful. Glancing down, he noticed a small pool of dried blood where he had been sleeping, and he reached up and touched his head. It was bandaged in gauze. He probed the bandaged area with his fingers until he hit a spot at the base of his scalp that was especially sensitive. He winced in pain, grew dizzy, and blacked out once again.

When he woke up the next time, he had no idea how long he had been unconscious. Raven was sitting on the floor on the other side of the room with her back against the wall. He noticed that, like him, her head was bandaged. As he pulled himself up into a sitting position, she immediately turned on him.

"Why, Spencer? Why did you do it? Why did you and Jack betray us?"

At first, the boy was groggy and didn't understand, but gradually the memories began trickling back—a man in a suit, a briefcase full of money, promises that he and his brother would be safe back on Mars with unlimited powers of the mind. He and Jack had succumbed to temptation and sold out their friends to a man in a hat and a charcoal grey suit.

"I don't know," he managed awkwardly. "I'm sorry." He turned his face away from her and concentrated on his brother, thinking over and over, *It's me, I need to know if you're okay,* but there was still no response.

"You're trying to communicate with him," observed Raven coldly. "But you can't, can you?" The boy tried his best to ignore her and continued directing thoughts toward his brother, but he knew she was right.

"What about you?" he asked finally.

"No." She turned her face away from him and stared at a wall. "I can't move things anymore, either." There was a long pause, and then she continued. "They did something to us. We're not special anymore."

After sitting in the room for what seemed like hours, they heard a faint conversation down the hall. A man said something inaudible followed by a woman's voice that said, "Yes, they're both awake now." Then they heard heavy footsteps coming toward them. The door opened suddenly and a tall, thin, middle-aged man with gray hair and glasses entered frowning.

"Do you know who I am?" he asked, glancing first at Raven and then at Spencer. The boy shook his head while the girl did her best to ignore him. "My name is Ross Herrington, Director of State Intelligence."

"Why are you keeping us here?" asked Spencer. His voice sounded weak and timid.

"Let's just call this a little experiment," answered the man with a slight grin. "I want to find out what makes you tick."

"What about the others? Are they alive?"

"The older boy died in surgery, but the younger one—your twin—might live."

"Bryce?" gasped Raven, glaring angrily at Spencer. "You killed him!"

"No," interrupted Herrington, "I killed him. I had the same surgery performed on him that was performed on the two of you. You lived, he didn't."

"What surgery?" demanded Raven. Though weak, she looked as though she was considering taking a swing at him.

"We went into your brains to find out what makes you different, why you can do the things you can. What we found was exactly what I suspected—Computer chips. They were embedded in your frontal cortex and wired to your brain stem. Remarkable feats of engineering."

"I don't remember anybody operating on my head," said Raven. "And even if they did, how could a microchip make me able to move things just by thinking about them?"

Herrington cleared his throat and stared down at the two children he had found so remarkable before but who were now completely unremarkable. He grinned sheepishly. "The chips were undoubtedly implanted in you when you were very young, possibly babies. Ever heard of someone named Dr. Burke?"

Spencer nodded, his eyes wide with surprise.

"That's who did this to you. That's who made you freaks."

"Who are you calling a freak, you twisted bastard!" shrieked Raven. She strained with all her might to rise to her feet but lacked the strength. She sank back to the floor, gasping for breath. "You . . . let . . . me . . . out of here!"

Herrington chuckled and knelt down in front of her. "You are a little tiger, aren't you?" he said, smiling. Then he turned to Spencer and continued. "Your telepathy could easily be explained by computer chips that are synced with one another. As for your friend's telekinesis, that's a little harder to understand. I'm guessing that her chip also allowed her to manipulate magnetic fields. We still have some work to do on that one. I'll let you know when I know for sure."

"What's going to happen to us?" asked Spencer, his voice shaking. He was beginning to realize the hopelessness of their situation.

Herrington grinned again, revealing a row of abnormally pearly white teeth. "I think I might just let you live, but you'll need to do something for me first."

"Don't make any more deals!" sneered Raven.

"Do what?" asked Spencer.

"I'll let you live as long as you promise to never say a word about what happened here to anyone."

"What makes you think I'd stay quiet?" demanded Raven.

"Your friend Bryce."

"But he's dead."

Herrington looked her in the eye. "I can bring him back. Not as a human, but as a cyborg. He'll still remember everything from when he was alive, but he'll have a body that can last a thousand years. Through him, we'll advance science into realms never thought possible."

"Why would you do that for him?" asked Spencer. "I thought you wanted us all dead."

"Because he's the guinea pig, idiot," charged Raven. "The test run. They'll make the mistakes on him and get it right before trying it on jerks like this guy who want to live forever."

"Can you do this for me too?" asked Spencer hopefully. His mind was now turning quickly, trying desperately to find a way to survive. He wanted his powers back, and he still hoped to be able to save his brother. Raven would be a distraction and probably couldn't be saved anyway—her mouth would see to that—so he ignored her. He turned toward the State Intelligence director, awaiting his answer.

"Hold tight, little guy," replied Herrington. "That time will come. But as I said before, you'll need to do something for me first."

Chapter 20

Training Begins

Megan awoke early the next morning to the beep of her alarm clock and a gentle increase in the ambient light.

She had dreamed again of the underwater cave with the drawings and markings and suspected that they might have something to do with the prophecy. Her hands had been bound. She remembered noticing spiders clinging motionless to the cave's walls, and the same woman she believed to be Dr. Burke watching her from a dark corner.

Suddenly and without warning, the water vanished and one of the spiders leaped onto the cave's floor and scurried toward her. Panicking, she managed to slip one of her hands out of the rope and was about to run when she noticed a gun by her feet. It was orange and had a short, stocky barrel. She reached for it, but the mysterious woman stopped her.

"It won't work," she warned. "You'll need something bigger."

As she gradually awoke to the sound of the alarm, images from her dream quickly faded, but she continued to hear the woman's warning: "You'll need something bigger." That phrase played itself over and over in her mind.

Finally, she forced herself out of the pod. She glanced at the time. Zero four thirty hours—4:30 a.m. That left her just a half hour to get dressed and ready for combat training. She would need to be quick.

She arrived at the cargo bay ten minutes early. A small group of security team members dressed in black was already there, along with someone in a pale blue jumpsuit who was tethered to the ceiling away from the others. He was tall and had broad shoulders and blond hair. She couldn't see his face, but she knew it was Vic. "What on Earth is he doing here?" she wondered aloud, whispering the words. She pushed off the wall and drifted toward him.

"Why are *you* here?" she asked sharply, ignoring pleasantries.

Vic said nothing but pointed toward a large crate secured to the floor with straps.

"I don't understand," said Megan, annoyed. She was in no mood for his cryptic games. She looked away, not expecting a response, but he surprised her.

"Guns. The crates are full of guns, but they won't be enough. You'll need something bigger."

Images from her dream flashed back to her. "Why are you helping me? What is it that you want from me?"

Vic did not answer. He stared across the cargo bay at the vehicle with the enormous tires while his fingers typed notes on a tiny electronic device. He was clearly ignoring her, so she tried a different approach.

"The guns won't be enough for what?" asked Megan. "The spiders? Yes, I know about them."

Vic leaned closer and whispered, "Thousands of them. By now, maybe tens of thousands."

"So, what am I supposed to do?"

"Stay away from the colony. Come with me instead." He stared at her with laser-like intensity, sending chills down her spine. "But the others can't know."

"Wait," she began again, but he cut her off.

"Not now. We'll talk later. You have more pressing things to worry about at this moment." He rotated his body until he was hanging upside down, like a huge bat. He pushed hard off the smooth metal ceiling with his feet and glided away from her.

Megan thought about what he had said about the spiders—that there were thousands of them, maybe tens of thousands. She had expected to go to the colony with the rescue team but was beginning to have doubts, no matter what the prophecy supposedly said. Perhaps it would be safer to trust Vic. As she considered her options, she looked around the room.

By now, black-clad security team members were all over the place. She counted at least two dozen, which surprised her because she hadn't noticed nearly that many during the previous six weeks. She wondered if some of them were dual-purpose crew members—mechanics or technicians under normal circumstances, but soldiers when circumstances demanded it. Their faces were mostly young and reflected a mixture of anxiety, excitement, and fatigue. A few spoke quietly among themselves.

What she needed was an ally. Hendrix had not yet arrived, and she wondered if he had overslept. Two men on the other side of the large open space caught her eye. One looked younger than all the others—possibly eighteen or nineteen—and his face reminded her of Bryce. The other was older and had a closely trimmed reddish-gray beard. She took a deep breath and launched herself toward them.

"Hi, I'm Megan." She held out her hand and smiled.

"Gregor," replied the young man. He shook her hand and introduced his friend.

"This is Cain." The older man nodded and looked away. A long scar ran sideways across his neck as if someone had once tried to slit his throat. He seemed hostile. There was an awkward silence until the younger man, Gregor, broke it.

"So, you're with us? I don't remember training with you before."

"I'm a late addition. It's nice meeting you."

"Bet you can't shoot straight," quipped Cain gruffly, hardly concealing his disdain. She thought quickly and made up a story.

"I can shoot. I've put in my time at the range."

"But can you hit someone while being shot at?" countered Cain. "There's a difference." She felt the hostility in his voice. Then he added, "Not a lot of people can."

Just then she felt a sturdy hand on her shoulder. It was Hendrix. "This one shoots just fine—almost as well as me." Cain's face suddenly lit up, and he became pleasant.

"Cowboy! Well, who dragged you in here? I thought you'd be asleep until at least noon!"

"What's going on, Slow Trot?" said Hendrix grinning. "You givin' this little lady a hard time?"

"Well, can you blame me? Look at her. She's a kid. Am I supposed to put my trust in that?"

"Looks can be deceiving, my friend," continued Hendrix smoothly. Megan was surprised at just how happy she was that he had shown up. She wondered if he had really ever been as obnoxious as she had thought.

"Hey, sunshine," he said to her with his head cocked to the side. "Go fetch Cain and me each a water bottle. And get one for the kid too."

Same old Hendrix, she thought, smiling inwardly. Then she got an idea. "Hey, Gregor," she said. "Can you come with me?"

"Sure."

She pushed off the wall and glided to a spot where she could be a comfortable distance away from both Hendrix and Vic. When she stopped, she was happy to see that Gregor was still with her. As she glanced at him, she noticed that he was handsomer than she had previously thought.

"I hope you realize I'm not getting them water," she remarked offhandedly, trying her best to act cool.

Gregor laughed. "Good! I like a girl with backbone. What's the deal with Hendrix? He's kind of a jerk around the gym."

"He's okay, I guess," said Megan. "Brags too much, but you get used to it." Gregor nodded and rolled his eyes. "Hey, do you know these people?" she asked, motioning toward the other security team members.

"Sure, most of them."

"Would you mind telling me a little about them? I only know Hendrix and Ob."

"Ob," replied Gregor, shaking his head. "Quirky guy. Not much of a sense of humor, but he seems all right. You see those three over there?" He pointed at a group near the entrance. Megan nodded.

"The big one in the middle is Fletch. He's a fighter. Takes crap from no one. The one on the right wearing a beret is Smithwick. We call her Wick. Tough gal who knows what she's doing. She's a veteran of both Arctic Wars. The one on the left is Wolfson. Clever fellow and a geologist. A little squirrely, though."

"What about Cain?"

"He's my mentor. Comes off as a bit abrasive, but he's a good teacher and he has a ton of medals for his combat experiences. I've learned a lot from him."

"Do you know how he got that scar on his neck?"

"Yes," said Gregor, but before he could say another word, Colonel Krueger entered the cargo bay wearing a mini-propulsion jetpack that he used to move around the room. He inspected each team member one by one as they saluted him. When he spoke, it was in sharp, quick bursts, like rounds fired from a machine gun.

"Here's the way it works," he barked. "On Mars, we stick together or die." He grabbed a pry bar off the wall and popped the clasp off the crate Vic had pointed out earlier. Removing the front panel, he revealed a dozen or so new M-25 assault rifles with silencers.

"Grab one and load up," he commanded. "All of you." He reached into his pocket and pulled out something small and silver. He gave it a twist, and it suddenly tripled in size, expanding like an umbrella. Eight thin mechanical legs protruded from its underside. Krueger tossed it into the air, whereupon it quickly glided to the ceiling and clung to it with grippers attached to each leg. "You have thirty seconds before it's armed. Now go kill it!"

Megan lunged toward the crate but didn't have anything to push off of. Others got there first. Hendrix and another man grabbed ammunition clips and jammed them into the closest available rifles. Gregor had also taken out a weapon and was attaching a scope when the spider-like contraption made a hissing noise and scurried behind some boxes.

"Hurry!" Krueger shouted. "It's armed. Get it before it gets you."

The spider shot out from the other side of the boxes and hurled itself at a terrified young man. It was Gregor. He didn't have time to fire off a shot; the spider thrust a hollow needle into his thigh and injected him with its venom. He lost consciousness immediately.

Megan reached the crate and pulled out a rifle and clip. A barrage of muffled shots erupted as Hendrix fired his weapon at the shiny metal arachnid, but it scurried away with the loss of only a leg.

It lunged at Megan, causing her to drop the clip before she could load it. She pushed off the crate with her good leg and drifted backward, her eyes fixated on the spider. It was fast— she wasn't going to be able to get away.

There was a sudden *thwoomp* and then another. She felt the metallic spider grab her leg with its pincers and almost fainted.

Just then, a final muffled shot rang out, and the robot exploded into hundreds of tiny fragments. Colonel Krueger came to Megan's side, his outstretched hand clutching a still smoking pistol. He looked each soldier in the eye, moving from one to the other and prepared to speak. Vacuum robots had already begun the task of cleaning up the tiny fragments now floating around the cargo bay.

"That's what just one of these little devils is capable of. Now imagine facing twenty."

Or ten thousand, thought Megan. *We're in serious trouble.*

Gregor was still unconscious, but he began to stir. A medic went to check on him, but Krueger called him off.

"Leave him. He's fine. That robot was only a trainer. No poison, just tranquilizer. Your only chance depends on killing these things," snapped Krueger. "Now let's get on with your training." He fixed his gaze on another crate and gave his propulsion pack's remote a quick tap that propelled him toward it.

Reaching the crate, he popped the latch and threw open the lid. Inside was a row of yellow Taser Carbines—a small but powerful weapon that delivered a massive electric charge. They operated similar to Megan's own tiny L-Stat stun pistol but were larger and designed to kill. Beside them lay a plasma rifle, an extremely destructive weapon that fired bullets with the same impact as explosive shells. It was large and intimidating, with an accelerator mounted underneath and a laser-guided scope on top. Harper had once shown her how to use one, blowing up a wrecked car with a single shot. Now Megan knew what the woman in her dream meant when she had said, "You're going to need something bigger."

"I need that gun," she whispered to herself. "And I know exactly who can get it for me."

Chapter 21

A Convenient Escape

Herrington had a problem, and he knew it.

Three of the recently captured Wonder Kids had yielded the microchips that he had suspected were inside them. The technology powering them was unlike anything he had ever seen. The chips, which were a blend of living tissue, computer components, and nanofibers, linked their users' consciousness in a way that he could scarcely believe. It allowed them to interact seamlessly and undetected through mental telepathy, completely negating the need for external communication devices, devices that could be easily hacked or destroyed. The military and political implications were huge—the government would pay billions for something like this.

But there was a problem. He couldn't offer it for sale without the president knowing that he had gone behind his back. He had told the president that all the Wonder Kids except for Megan were dead. Herrington paced the floor anxiously and picked up his phone. He called Irons, his chief assassin.

"Have you found the boy?" he asked in a low voice, glancing around to see if anyone was listening. "And is there any word on Harper?"

"No, boss. The boy could be anywhere. He is scared. He will hide in a hole if he has to. As for Harper, we have not heard a thing. She is either hiding or dead."

"We need to tie up these loose ends, Irons. They could spell trouble for us if they get in touch with the right people."

"I agree. Do you have any ideas?"

"I do. I say we let the girl, Raven, escape and follow her with tracking satellites. She just might lead us to them."

"She is a smart young lady, boss. What about her telepathic abilities? She almost killed me while I was apprehending her."

"She can't do that anymore."

"Oh?"

"She has lost that ability now that we've removed her chip. As for the escape, we must not make it easy for her. If it's too easy, she'll figure out that we're setting her up. When you're done, get over here right away."

"Yes, boss. I understand. But I want more money."

Herrington let out a breath of hot air. "Okay. You'll have your money soon enough." He clicked off the phone. Now even Irons was becoming a problem, a problem that he would have to deal with soon enough.

A few hours later, Raven was awakened by the sound

of her cell door opening. An orderly in white hospital scrubs entered and knelt beside her. He had a surgical mask over his mouth and nose, but she could see his eyes clearly. They were small, dark, and beady.

"Come with me, miss," the man said sharply. Spencer was beginning to stir.

"Where am I going?"

"To clean up. Shower. Brush your teeth. Change into a clean gown."

Raven stood up nervously. She wondered if they were planning to operate on her again. The orderly stood beside the door motioning for her to step out. She exited the cell slowly, peeking around the corner to see if there were others waiting for her outside. Instead, all she saw was a long narrow hallway with dingy, unpainted walls. At its end, it branched out into three separate passages. She followed a few steps behind the orderly, looking around for anything that could be used as a weapon.

"The locker room's this way, miss," said the orderly. He pointed to the right. "There's the door. I'll wait for you out here. You have twenty minutes."

She approached the door cautiously and gave it a push. As the door opened, what she saw was encouraging. A row of grimy sinks with dusty mirrors lined the wall in front of her. Several bathroom stalls were on the right; behind them was a large open area with a tile floor and showers.

She noticed a chair on which someone had neatly stacked two large towels, a clean hospital gown, a toothbrush, and toothpaste. On one of the sinks lay a bar of soap and a small metal file for smoothing fingernails. She walked over to it and blew dust off the mirror. Her reflection startled her. Her hair was shaved off, and the scar where the surgery had been performed was covered by a thick white bandage stained reddish-brown with blood. Her eyes were bloodshot, and her earrings had been removed. She sighed and washed her hands.

It's all over, she thought. *They've won.*

As she walked toward the showers with the bar of soap, a skylight in the ceiling caught her attention. It was dark outside, but she detected a faint glow of moonlight. Beneath the skylight ran a thick metal water pipe, about four meters above the floor. She studied the skylight closely — its frame seemed to be held in place by nothing more than four ordinary screws. She looked back at the sink. The file just might work as a screwdriver. *But how to get up there?*

When Spencer awoke, he was startled to find Raven missing. He was afraid to be alone in this place, and even Raven — who was furious with him — was better than nothing. He sat up, pulled his knees to his chest, and wrapped his arms around them. He wanted to cry but could not. Exhausted, he closed his eyes and imagined he was somewhere else. He sat like that for hours until the cell door opened, and the orderly stepped inside.

"You have a visitor."

Not the SIS director again, he thought. To his surprise, it wasn't Herrington; it was a boy being wheeled in on a gurney. The boy's head was shaven, and he had a bandage covering half his scalp.

"Jack!" Spencer leaped to his feet but stumbled. He was surprised at how weak he had become. He got up again, hurried to the gurney, and stared at the boy's face. A blanket was pulled up over his chest and chin, but there was no mistaking that it was his brother.

Jack's eyes flickered open and then closed.

"I'll leave you two together for a while," said the orderly before exiting the cell and locking the door behind him.

"Jack, I was so worried about you," said Spencer, hugging his brother. "We've got to get out of here."

"Shhhhhh," whispered Jack, his eyes still closed. "We need to be very careful."

Meanwhile, in the locker room, Raven had been cutting the two large towels into strips with a sliver of broken glass that she had found. When she finished, she tied them together into a crude rope. By her reckoning, she only had about ten minutes left. Once the rope was complete, she cut off the water to one of the sinks by turning a rusty knob connected to the water pipe beneath it. Next, she disassembled the faucet and tied the spigot handle to the rope's end to add weight. Then she turned on the other sinks full blast to cover any noise that she might make trying to escape.

She hurried to the skylight, surprised at how much energy she now had. She was running on adrenaline, and she knew it wouldn't last long. Where the water pipe ran beneath the skylight, there was a small on-off valve that stuck out a few centimeters. She fixed her eyes on it and tossed the rope upward, hoping to wrap it around the pipe so that it caught on the valve.

The first three tries failed, but she caught it on the fourth try. Holding the rope in both hands, she lifted her feet off the floor to test its strength. It held her. She took a deep breath, warmed up her arms, and clinched the small metal file between her teeth. Then, with all her remaining strength, she grabbed onto the rope and fought her way to the top.

There's no way I'm letting them get away with this, she thought as she wrapped an arm and both legs around the pipe.

She took the file out of her mouth and fit it inside the groove of one of the screws. It was a perfect fit! She turned the screw counterclockwise until it loosened and fell to the floor and then attacked the remaining screws in the same way. Finally, when all the screws were out, she pushed the skylight upward with her feet until it popped loose and tumbled out onto the roof outside.

With the last of her strength, she climbed through the open hole in the ceiling and emerged onto the roof, which only had a slight incline. Its gritty texture irritated her bare feet, but she knew better than to slow down. She ran stealthily along the roof until she noticed a workman's ladder propped against it. It looked as if luck had finally turned her way.

She took a moment to survey her surroundings—the building she was on was smack in the middle of an old industrial park filled with decrepit abandoned factories and warehouses. Not a single light shone in them, and the stench of sulfur filled the air. With renewed hope, she scurried down the ladder and disappeared into the night.

———

After escaping from Irons and the other two agents in the library, Wiley had returned to the abandoned warehouse where he and the other Wonder Kids used to meet. He hoped Harper would be there, but of course she was not. Then it hit him that the twins had likely told about the warehouse too. Reluctantly, he left and crept over to the nearby shantytown where nobody asked questions. Half of the people there were fugitives anyway. He found an unoccupied spot under the bridge and settled in for the night.

As he lay dozing, he wondered why the twins had done it. What could have possibly made them want to betray the group? Had they not been nice enough to them? The only one who had been mean was Raven, but she was mean to everyone. He wondered where Harper had gone and why she hadn't been in touch. And what about Megan? How long until she would be on Mars? He hoped Raven and Bryce were still alive. He had tried again and again to contact them telepathically, but there was never an answer. In fact, nobody was responding.

Yet something inside him was telling him that they were still alive, and no matter what, he would have to save them. He began to formulate a plan.

The last time he had seen Harper, she was running from the SIS, the same organization that she worked for. What if it was behind all this? Going to the president wouldn't do any good—if the SIS was in on it, then odds were that the president was too. Instead, he would write down everything that happened and take it to the press. Once they got the word out, whoever was trying to kill him would have no place left to hide.

Back at the secret facility where Herrington's surgeons had operated on him, Jack pretended to sleep while his brother Spencer paced the floor of their narrow cell. Finally, he made his move.

"Spencer."

"Yeah."

"Help me out of this bed. I want to sit on the floor."

"But . . ."

"Just do it. Please."

Spencer couldn't understand why his brother would prefer sitting on the cold, hard floor to lying in a cot, but he did as Jack requested. He took hold of his brother's arms and raised him to a sitting position, then helped him onto the floor. Jack's legs were weak, and he collapsed immediately. Spencer wrapped the blanket tightly around him and sat down beside him.

"Are you feeling better?"

"Lean closer, Spence." The boy was confused but did as his brother asked. Jack whispered in his ear. "There are cameras all over the place. Be careful."

Spencer turned to look at him, but Jack warned him to look straight ahead and just nod.

"We never should have told Mr. Irons where to find the others," added Jack. "I wish we could undo that, but we can't." Spencer nodded in agreement.

"Can you still hear people's thoughts?" This time Spencer shook his head side to side.

"You know what's weird?" Jack went on. "Even though they operated on me, even though they took something out, I can still hear what they're thinking. And guess what—Raven escaped. And Bryce is alive. They told you he was dead, didn't they?"

"Yes," whispered Spencer. He was beginning to think that they might have a chance, but he played it safe and continued to stare at the wall in front of him. "How do we get out of this place?" he asked softly.

Jack hesitated. "There must be a way," he said. "If Raven got out, we can too. But it's going to be hard. After losing one of us, they're going to be extra watchful."

Chapter 22

Contagion

To Megan, it was beginning to seem like the voyage would never end. The ship's living quarters were crowded, and the stale air reeked of waste and body odor. Worse still was the boredom. As the excitement of life in space wore thin, boredom set in and many of the crew began growing tired of each other's company. Tensions increased steadily, resulting in grudges and petty squabbles. The mess hall, once filled with friendly chatter, was now mostly silent.

Each morning at zero five hundred hours, Colonel Krueger pushed them to their limits in training exercises. While most of the others hated it, Megan looked forward to it. Anything to break up the monotony was welcome, and besides, she knew that what she learned might save her life once they reached Mars.

Besides strength and endurance training, Krueger taught them how to eliminate blind spots in the event of an attack by standing together back-to-back and shooting outward away from themselves. They analyzed maps of the landing site to identify the best places to take cover and battle simulated spider robots. All the while, though, they were painfully aware that the spiders they would encounter on Mars could be very different from the ones they were training with, and rather than just sedating you with a tranquilizer, the real ones would kill you.

Around week eight, reports began coming in from their sister ship, the *Argo*, that many of its crew had become sick with mysterious symptoms. Megan learned about it from Miles, the ship's physician assistant, at breakfast one morning. Miles was a nervous, energetic young man who wore thick glasses and had curly red hair. He wasn't usually much for small talk, but he was helpful and attentive to the crew members who came into sick bay for treatment. Megan had been in just once for a routine checkup. Anya told her that he specialized in contagious diseases and was interested in how certain germs were evolving on Mars. She had worked with him on occasion in the research lab and insisted that he was quirky but harmless.

As he and several of the medics and nurses were eating, Megan overheard him telling them about the illness and how the *Argo*'s doctor wasn't sure what it was. He suspected it was spread by an insect but was perplexed because they hadn't seen any on the ship. Suddenly, Megan remembered the tiny flying lights. *Could they be insects?* She waited until they were almost finished and introduced herself.

"You probably don't remember me, but I'm Megan."

The young man's glasses nearly slipped off his head

when he turned around. He looked startled. "Hi," he mumbled confusedly, pushing the glasses back over his eyes. "Oh, sorry about that. Darn things are too big for me."

"Is this a bad time?"

"No—yes—I mean I have to get back to sick bay, but I have a minute."

"I wasn't trying eavesdrop, but I couldn't help over-hearing you say that people are getting sick on the other ship from insect bites."

"Uh, that's right," stammered Miles nervously. "But there's no telling. It's just a theory. They might have been harboring a pathogen. You know, when they boarded the ship. And it stayed dormant until just recently."

"Is there a type of firefly that can do that?"

"Uh, no. Fireflies don't bite. Aren't you friends with that biologist lady, Anya? She could tell you that."

"Interesting. It's just that—"

"Why are you asking?" interrupted Miles. "Have you seen one around here?"

"Maybe. To be honest, I'm not sure what I saw."

"What did it look like?"

She remembered back to the night she encountered the lights as they swarmed around Vic. "Like a tiny bright light that flies. And they could change color."

"They?" asked Miles, his eyebrows raised in surprise.

"Well, maybe I saw more than one." Realizing how crazy she must sound, she added, "As I said before, I'm not really sure what I saw. Maybe it was a dream."

"Yeah, probably," replied Miles. "I'd be surprised if any insects got in. There's a better chance that something could have escaped from the lab, but fireflies? I don't think so." He shook his head for emphasis. "You know," he continued, "a single virus can replicate itself many thousands of times. They have all sorts of bizarre and wonderful strategies that allow them to mutate and spread to other hosts."

"That's interesting, Miles. Is it okay for me to call you Miles?"

"Uh, sure."

Megan thought he still looked uncomfortable, although terrified might be a better way to describe it. By the looks of him, he didn't talk to girls often.

"So, what's this illness like, the one they're getting on the other ship?" she asked. "Is everyone all right?"

Miles explained that the infected crew members had tiny patches of swollen, red skin as though they had been bitten by something small. The disease looked a lot like the flu except that within three or four days, its victims were unconscious. A few revived, but their pupils were extremely dilated, and they behaved strangely. The *Argo*'s doctor believed it to be an insect-borne virus, but the usual medications had no effect, and no matter how hard they searched, they found no trace of insects on the ship.

"That's scary," Megan remarked when he was finished. "Keep me informed. I'll let you know if I see anything."

Miles had more news the following week. At first it was good. More of the patients had awakened. But something was wrong. They exhibited poor judgment, had slow reaction times, and were careless in their work. Some became aggressive. It was as though they weren't themselves anymore. The ones who had not awakened slipped into a coma and had to be put on life support. To make matters worse, half of the crew members began showing signs of being infected.

Later that same day, Megan went to visit Anya in the lab. She was drawing a blood sample from Shem, the vervet monkey, who had sensors stuck to his head and chest. The furry primate didn't seem to mind; in fact, it seemed happy to be receiving the attention. It picked up a letter cube and showed Anya.

"That's a C," she explained. Shem turned the cube to another letter and shoved it in front of her face. "A."

Shem was growing increasingly excited. The monkey turned the cube over again and showed her.

"That's a T. Yes, I know, Shem, it spells *cat*."

Shem was now shaking the sides of his metal cage and shrieking enthusiastically. Anya turned to Megan.

"We've been reading him a story about a cat," she said with a twinge of regret. "Now he wants a real one." She turned back to the tiny primate. "Okay, Shem. We'll see about getting you a cat, but you need to wait until we're home."

Megan remembered the first time she had seen Shem, curled up like a small furry ball, sleeping. Afterward, Anya had told her that he was just an animal and not to feel sorry for him—*Don't get too attached. Lab monkeys almost never survive these trips* was how she phrased it.

"But I thought you said—"

"Shut up, Megan. He doesn't know."

Shem froze and stared at them.

"It's okay, Shem," continued Anya in a reassuring tone. "We're done for the day. I'm going to give you some medicine to help you sleep. Sweet dreams." She inserted a hypodermic needle into his arm and pressed down on the plunger. The vervet monkey let go of its cage and seemed to relax. Within seconds it was sound asleep.

"Sorry about that," said Megan awkwardly. "I didn't know."

Anya smiled. "A primate understanding human speech? How could you have known? It's not like we share that with the general public."

"How much does he understand?"

"About as much as a young child. Maybe a little more."

"That's incredible! I sure hope he lives. You're going to give him the cat if he does, aren't you?"

Anya didn't answer. She was processing the blood sample. When she was done, she dabbed the blood with a cotton swab and smeared it onto a rectangular glass slide. She then stuck it in a refrigerator.

"So, what's up?" she asked.

Megan blinked and refocused her thoughts on the virus that was afflicting the *Argo*. She wanted to know if Anya had any ideas about what was causing it.

"I heard Miles told you about the virus," said Anya. "Is that true?"

"He said the *Argo*'s doctor thought it was a virus, but Miles wasn't so sure. Do you think it's a virus?"

"I was wondering why some of the patients who woke up are acting strangely," continued Anya, as she took off her gloves. "A virus might explain that."

"Oh?" exclaimed Megan.

Anya's face lit up. "Viruses are amazing," she explained. "Some can hijack your brain and change your behavior so that it benefits them. Endoparasites do the same thing." She switched on an electronic device and clicked away on its keypad. A holographic model of a caterpillar materialized above it. "I studied this moth in Brazil. A certain type of wasp parasitizes it when it's in its caterpillar stage. The wasp bites it and injects eggs into its abdomen.

When the time comes, baby wasps burst out of the caterpillar, but some stay inside and control its nervous system, making it actually defend the newly hatched wasps. Weird, huh?"

"That's nasty," exclaimed Megan, wrinkling her nose in disgust. Then she became serious again. "Anya, I need to ask you something. What were those lights flying around Vic? Are they insects?"

"Okay," sighed Anya, hesitating for a moment. "I guess it's okay for me to tell you. We call them Light Beings. They're an alien lifeform that we encountered on Mars. They're smart—a lot smarter than we are—and they're certainly not insects. Dr. Burke found them when she discovered the prophecy in a cave near the colony. Somehow, she was able to communicate with them."

"Why are they on the ship with us now? Did you guys bring them?"

"No," said Anya. "You don't understand, Megan. We don't control them. They come and go as they please—even right through the walls of the ship."

"Are they what's making everybody sick?"

"Yes—probably. But they're part of the prophecy too, and they've been helping us just like they helped the Ancient Ones a long time ago."

"And what exactly is this prophecy?" asked Megan. "Does it say what's going to happen?"

"Well," said Anya, glancing around to make sure no one else was listening, "it's more like a history. It begins a long time ago—possibly millions of years ago—when Mars was more like Earth. It had oceans and rivers and forests. An ancient race of people lived there. They built a civilization that lasted for thousands of years, up to the time of the troubles."

"What troubles?"

"Wars, crime, pollution," said Anya. "The Ancient Ones lost their respect for each other and for their environment. Eventually, the atmosphere was destroyed and there was no more oxygen or protection from solar radiation. The forests died, as did the animals and fish. The Ancient Ones were forced to abandon their cities and live underground in caves. Then there was a plague, and almost everyone died.

"That's when the Light Beings showed up. They helped the Ancient Ones build a spaceship so that they could escape their dying planet. A group of the survivors used it to travel to Earth about five thousand years ago, where they encountered humans. The humans thought they must be gods and worshiped them. They made one of the Ancient Ones their supreme leader and called him Pharaoh. Because of him, they built great pyramids, majestic palaces, and tall obelisks pointing to the sky. Sound familiar?"

"Yes," said Megan. "I learned about ancient Egypt in school, but I didn't know they were Martians."

"Just the leaders were," continued Anya. "Over time, the Ancient Ones and humans married and had children, and after a few generations you couldn't tell the difference between them because they looked the same."

"What did they look like originally?" interrupted Megan. "Do you know?"

"Like Vic. He's the last of the Martian race, descended directly from the Ancient Ones."

"Vic's a Martian?"

"Yes, Megan, and I've probably told you too much already. No more questions. And please don't tell anyone what I've told you. Promise?"

"I promise," replied Megan, "but I need to know just one more thing first: what does the prophecy say about me, and what's going to happen when we get to Mars?"

"We've already told you everything we know—just that you'd come, and Mars will be reborn as a living planet sometime in the future. A lot of the future parts were missing though, as if somebody wanted to keep it a secret. All I know is that we've got to get you to Mars. The rest will work itself out."

Chapter 23

The Pandemic Spreads

The next week, Miles brought more disturbing news.

The *Argo*'s captain had radioed in that he and just a few others were the only ones still untouched by the virus. They had barricaded themselves inside the cockpit and were low on rations. They might be able to hold out for a week or two, but unless a rescue mission could be mounted, they would eventually have to come out to get food and water, and that meant coming into contact with infected and dangerous crew members.

Privately, Anya was now convinced that the Light Beings were to blame. "The first time I encountered them," she told Megan, "Vic was there, and they bit me. It was on our previous mission to Mars. It felt like something was scanning my mind, reading my thoughts. Cassandra, Ob, and I were the only ones it happened to, and we all got sick for a little while, but then we were fine. It was as if they decided we were all right and let us go. Now, apparently, they don't feel the same about the *Argo*'s crew."

"What does Vic say about them?" asked Megan, perplexed. "I mean, as a Martian, he might have a different perspective."

"He says they're on our side and not to worry."

It was the next day that the first crew member onboard the *Intrepid* became infected. A flight engineer complained of feeling weak and dizzy. Anya escorted her to the ship's doctor, who began an immediate quarantine. He placed the woman in an isolated sleep pod and ordered Anya to stay with her just in case she, too, had become infected. Miles, who seemed more nervous than usual, drew blood samples for analysis, and the doctor sent maintenance robots to sanitize anything the woman might have touched in the past couple of days.

Over the next several days, more crew members fell ill. Megan was concerned but not overly scared. After all, the swarm had confronted her in the open but had done nothing. At least it seemed that way.

And then it happened. As she showed up for training one morning, she noticed a red spot on her arm. Her head began to throb and her arms and back ached. Krueger called the doctor, and the doctor sent a service robot to tow her to sick bay, where she was placed in an isolation pod. Her headache became so severe that she could barely think, and the light coming in through her pod's tiny observation window only worsened the pain.

It was a relief when night came, and the lights were turned off.

That night she dreamed she was on the deck of a ship. The sky was dark and icy rain fell in torrents, blown sideways by gale-force winds. The ship, one of those ancient Spanish galleons, rose and fell on the ocean waves. The waves were tremendous—up to forty meters tall—and Megan had to hold onto a rope with all her might to keep from being tossed overboard. All around her lay sick and dying men, their moans and prayers unintelligible in the howling wind.

Lightning flashed, and she saw a figure standing on the bow. It appeared to be a woman beckoning for help. Megan let go of the rope and staggered forward clumsily as the ship rocked side to side. She had made it only a few steps when a huge wave broke over the gunwales and nearly swept her out to sea. A wood railing was all that held her, and it was beginning to give way. Just then, a hand reached out to her. She looked up and saw the dark-haired woman. Vic was behind her.

"Take my hand, Megan!" yelled the woman, and she grabbed it. Vic and the mysterious woman pulled her back onto the ship where she lay gasping and trembling.

"Now get up," the woman called out to her. "Just breathe. We're counting on you."

She reached into a bag hanging by her side and pulled out a tiny glowing speck. She blew on it, and it landed on Megan. The next instant, she felt a quick, stabbing sensation as it bit into her arm, and then her entire body began to relax and grow warm. The rain stopped. The wind died down. She rose to get a better look at the woman who had saved her, but she was gone.

Dr. Burke, she thought. She ran to the other side of the

ship and saw Vic and Burke drifting away in a small lifeboat. She waved frantically to them, but they didn't respond.

She watched as the little boat disappeared from sight, and then the water turned to rock, and the ship disappeared. She awoke, feeling helpless and afraid.

I need Vic, she thought. *He can help me.* She was drenched in sweat from the fever, and the headache returned. She tried to bang on the inside of the pod with her fist but didn't have the strength. It was like being buried alive. Eventually, the pain in her head became too much to bear, and she passed out, this time drifting into a deep and dreamless sleep.

Chapter 24

Bellamy

Still hiding among the vagabonds at the shantytown, Wiley returned each night to the abandoned warehouse to see if Harper had returned. He had given up trying to contact the other Wonder Kids telepathically, as nobody had responded to him. He realized that all of them except for Megan were likely dead, and Megan was now probably halfway to Mars. He had also stopped trying to understand why the twins had betrayed them. None of that mattered anymore. All that mattered now was exposing the truth.

At this point, all Wiley could be certain of was that there was a plot to get rid of all the kids who had been born on Mars. He didn't know why anybody wanted to do this or who was behind it, but it was obvious that someone had a motive for killing them.

After eight days of hiding, he decided to visit the offices of the *New York Tribune* and speak with a reporter there. To keep from being recognized on the street, he paid a woman who lived under a nearby bridge to cut his hair short and dye it blue. Then, he traded his clothes for discarded cyber-trash rags and darkened his eyebrows with charcoal dust.

His disguise complete, he ventured up the stairs beside the shantytown and onto the West Side Elevated Highway. He didn't dare take a taxi, as the scanning devices they employed would easily see through his disguise and alert the police, and he wasn't sure if he could trust them.

As he walked along the side of the road glancing at the ocean below, quick driverless taxis whizzed by him in a blur, but he kept walking straight ahead until he reached the section of the city dominated by shiny glass and steel skyscrapers that stretched high into the sunlit sky.

Finally, he came to one with a towering sign that said NEW YORK TRIBUNE. A guard stood outside the door. Taking a deep breath, he pushed open the door and stepped inside.

Inside was a spacious lobby with exotic plants from all over the world and a reception desk in the middle. A woman with silky pink hair and a luminescent green dress sat at the desk answering people's questions.

After waiting several minutes, Wiley approached her.

"I need to speak with a reporter," he said, trying not to sound nervous.

The woman looked him over with a raised eyebrow as if to say, *What are you even doing here?* and then asked, "What type of news do you wish to report?"

Wiley flashed a quick look back at the guard by the door and said, "The confidential type."

"Okay," answered the receptionist, "let me see who's available." She pressed a series of buttons on a console and then flashed a big fake smile at him. "Mr. Bellamy will see you. He's on floor one hundred fifty-seven, office 4A. You can take the elevator or the stairs."

The stairs? thought Wiley. *Who would be that crazy?*

"Thanks. I'll take the elevator."

"Oops, I forgot," said the receptionist, feigning surprise. "The elevator's out of service. You'll have to take the stairs."

When he finally reached Mr. Bellamy's office, Wiley stood for a moment outside his door and caught his breath. Then he knocked.

"Come in," a man shouted. Wiley opened the door, surprised to see that the office inside was tiny and windowless. The smell of tobacco and soy sauce hit him immediately.

"Mr. Bellamy?"

"Yeh, what do ya want?" the man asked gruffly. He was smoking a cigar and leaning back in a reclining chair, his large belly nearly bursting through his shirt. His feet were propped up on his desk, where an assortment of papers, computers, and bags of leftover lunches lay scattered aimlessly. He didn't look as though he could walk up two flights of stairs, let alone a hundred fifty-seven.

"I have a story for you," said Wiley. "A news story."

Bellamy took the cigar out of his mouth and looked the boy over. *Just another cyberpunk flunky,* he thought. *Probably wants to rat out a drug dealer who sold him some bad stuff. I'll bet the receptionist made him take the stairs.*

"Well, what is it? I don't got all day."

"My name is Wiley," said the boy. "I'm one of the ones

who were born on Mars before the rebellion. You guys used to call us the Wonder Kids."

Bellamy's expression changed from indignation to interest. He leaned forward and stroked his whiskered chin. "Go on," he said. "I'm listening."

"Somebody's been killing us one by one. A few days ago, I was kidnapped by a guy named Irons, a military type. I escaped, but my friends weren't so lucky."

Bellamy coughed. "Have you gone to the police with this?"

"No," answered Wiley. "I'm not so sure I can trust them. I think the government might be involved."

Bellamy softened and allowed Wiley to tell his whole story. When Wiley finished, the reporter stood up and paced the floor excitedly.

"This is big," he said with a worried tone, "but I can't help you if that's all we got. I mean, I could get arrested for printing this kind of story." He inhaled deeply through his cigar and blew the smoke out the side of his mouth. "I mean, I want to help you, but I can't. What you need is someone who can support your story. An alibi." He paced the floor again and stopped.

"There's only one way we can do this. You've got to find one of the other Wonder Kids. Then we'll go see a former government official I know who has suspicions of his own. He'll know what to do. Then, and only then, will I consider writing your story. Got it?"

"Got it," sighed Wiley. He was disappointed by Bellamy's answer, but at least there was hope. With a little luck, Harper might turn up yet.

"Oh," added Bellamy, "and take the elevator down to the lobby. It works just fine."

Chapter 25

The Plan

It was night when Megan awoke, but she had no idea which night. Had it been a day? A week? A month? She didn't know. The door to her isolation pod was open, and Vic hovered just outside gazing at her, expressionless, as though observing the outcome of an experiment.

"How are you feeling?"

She stretched her fingers and scrunched up her toes. The headache was gone, but she felt weak, and her neck was stiff.

"Okay, I guess." She grabbed the sides of the pod and pulled her weightless body out of it. "What happened?"

"Don't worry about that. We need to concentrate on getting you back into shape for when we reach Mars."

"Yeah," sighed Megan. "Am I still sick?"

Vic turned and propelled himself ghostlike toward another pod. "No."

As she rounded the pod, she noticed two bodies pressed limply against the ceiling. One was Miles.

"Are they dead?"

"No," Vic whispered. "I silenced them temporarily so I could help you."

"Where's Anya?" she asked. "Is she okay?"

"She's fine," said Vic. "They have no reason to bother her."

"Who's they?"

"Light Beings. They have a way of shutting down anybody they're not sure of. It's how they identify you as friend or foe. Once they've concluded that you're alright, they leave you alone."

Right, thought Megan. *The Light Beings. Anya told me about them.* She remembered what Anya had told her about Vic too—that he was a Martian, a direct descendant of the Ancient Ones.

"Did you wake me up or did they?" she asked.

"I did."

Megan gripped his arm. "If you helped me, you can help the others. We can save them."

"They're not my concern," replied Vic. He wasn't looking at her. "And there's nothing I could do anyway. The only reason you're okay is because they remember you."

"Who remembers me? The Light Beings?"

"Yes. They remember you from Mars, when you were a baby."

"Can you call them off?"

"No, but there is something you can do."

"What?"

After a long pause, Vic pulled out a small brown bag like the one in the dream and handed it to her. "This isn't an antidote, but it seems to help. Give the sick ones an injection and leave. Dispose of the needles. Nobody can know about this, not even Anya."

"Okay. What's going on, Vic? What is it that I'm supposed to do on Mars? Does the prophecy—"

"I can't tell you. Not yet, anyway," he replied sharply. "But I will help you. Also, understand that this is a trade. I'm helping you in exchange for your full cooperation once we get there."

Megan felt trapped. What else could she do? She nodded. "Okay, deal."

Vic stared at her fiercely. "If you double-cross me, I'll come back and kill everybody, and there won't be a thing you can do about it." A chill ran up her spine. The real Vic was far scarier than anything she had imagined.

One by one, she opened the isolation pods. A woman was in the first one. She opened the bag and found nine hypodermic needles containing a bluish liquid that glowed faintly. She removed one and injected it into the woman's arm. She stirred but did not awaken.

Megan turned around to ask Vic a question, but he was gone. She injected seven more crew members as they slept in their pods before finally arriving at Gregor. So, he, too, had been infected. *What an unlucky guy,* she thought. Inserting the needle into his shoulder, she pressed down on the plunger. The young man took a sudden breath, opened his eyes briefly, and closed them again. Confident that she had done everything she could, Megan hid the brown leather bag inside an air vent and navigated her way back to her isolation pod.

The next morning, she watched through the pod's observation window as three uniformed officers moved from pod to pod checking on patients. Anya was with them; the others she didn't recognize. They were talking with the doctor, who was shaking his head as though he had just awakened from a terrible night's sleep. Miles was also awake and was hovering above one of the pods, observing a patient. Then she saw one of the crew members she had injected the night before. He was out of his pod stretching and seemed okay. Another officer began opening the other pods. He reached Megan last.

"Megan, are you awake?" he asked. It was Ob. Anya rushed to join him.

"Yes. How much time has passed?"

"Eight days," said Anya, relieved. "I didn't think they'd hurt you, but when you stayed under so long, I wasn't sure."

The doctor checked her pulse and scanned her with a handheld magnetic resonance imager. There was a series of rapid clicks followed by a long beep.

"Do you remember anything?" Anya asked after the doctor left.

"No," lied Megan, remembering Vic's threat and wondering how much Anya and Ob really knew. "Not a thing."

"We've missed you at training," added Ob. "I think some of the guys wish they hadn't been so hard on you. Are you ready to come back?" He held out his hand.

"Just as long as you have my back," replied Megan. Anya and Ob helped her out of the pod, and she began stretching her arms and legs, which felt stiff and sore. The doctor examined her and pronounced her cured, although he insisted on keeping his patients in sick bay for an extra day.

Megan resumed training once the doctor released her. At first, she struggled to keep up and had to be helped, but as her strength returned, she found herself able to do more and more, and soon she was back in top form.

Under Krueger's leadership, the team became proficient at blasting away all the robotic spiders he threw at them, and they seemed confident in their ability to protect the landing party. However, Megan knew deep down that they were not ready and that nothing could prepare them for the thousands of actual killer spiders that awaited them on Mars.

The *Intrepid*'s sister ship, the *Argo*, was still in distress—its captain and a handful of others surviving on emergency rations in the cockpit. The rest of the ship was filled with unconscious or infected crew members. Then one morning the captain reported that they were out of food. With the Mars landing a week away, they had no choice but to risk leaving the cockpit in search of provisions. That was, unless the *Intrepid* could mount a rescue mission.

There had been talk of such a mission, but the idea had been scrapped to prevent infecting more people. Back on Earth, mission control decided that the only solution was to ask one of the remaining uninfected crew members to leave the cockpit and bring back enough food and water to last them to the end of the voyage. Of course, this meant that the unhappy "volunteer" would likely become infected too.

Megan sought out Krueger. "Is it possible to get someone from our ship over there?" she asked.

"Possible, yes," replied Krueger, "but that person would almost certainly get infected."

Megan's eyes lit up. She had longed for a way to prove

herself, and this looked like a perfect opportunity. "But what if that person had already been infected?"

Krueger's eyebrows furrowed as he considered her question. "That just might work. I'll talk with the captain. Still, I'd feel better knowing that you weren't going alone. We'll need to recruit others."

Gregor immediately signed on to help once he heard the news, as did another guy named Ridge. He was older and had experience in hand-to-hand combat. Both men had been infected and had recovered. Nevertheless, Anya had her doubts and didn't want Megan to go.

"It's not the Light Beings I'm worried about," she said. "They'll most likely leave you alone. I'm concerned about the *Argo*'s crew. The reports say that some of them have become highly aggressive. What if they turn on you?"

"I know," said Megan. "Don't worry about me. I'll have Gregor and Ridge there to help me. Everything's going to be fine."

After receiving approval from mission control, Krueger announced that the rescue mission would proceed at dawn. Megan and the others studied the *Argo*'s blueprints and mapped out the best route for getting supplies to the cockpit.

They would have to enter the *Argo* through a hatch near its cargo bay, which was on the opposite end of the ship from the cockpit. This meant that they would have to navigate their way through a long no-man's-land of infected crew members, any one of whom might attack without warning.

Early the next morning, they received a report that the *Argo* and *Intrepid* were within a hundred meters of each other. The three would-be rescuers suited up to leave the *Intrepid*. Each put on a bulky insolated spacesuit, boots, gloves, oxygen tanks, and a jet propulsion pack. Last came the helmets.

At zero five thirty hours, the hatch inside the cargo bay opened, and Megan and the others climbed in. Inside was a pressurization chamber, with steel walls and handles that they could hold onto. The door closed slowly behind them, and a voice crackled over their transceivers. The voice was Krueger's.

"Are you ready?"

"Ready," Megan said, giving a thumbs-up to her team-mates. Her heart was racing, and she felt a slight tremor in one of her hands. "Let's go."

Chapter 26

Rescue

"Initiating decompression." Krueger's voice sounded crisp and clear over the transceiver.

A hatch on the other side of the chamber began to slide open, and Megan glanced outside. It was dark. Even with her insolated spacesuit, she could feel the temperature dropping rapidly and began to shiver.

"Commence spacewalk," said Krueger.

Megan held her breath and pushed off the interior wall of the pressurization chamber. She drifted quickly away from the ship into the endless void of space and prepared to switch on the propulsion pack. The *Argo* was below her, its massive gray hull dotted with red and white lights. She looked to her right.

There in the distance was Mars, so large that it now dominated the coal-black sky. The sun shone bright against its western hemisphere, revealing a full spectrum of reds, browns, and oranges. It was now so close that she could make out craters and even mountains and canyons. Everything about it seemed strange and inhospitable. She spun around slowly and searched the darkness around her for a tiny bluish star, Earth, but could not find it.

When she looked back at the *Argo*, Gregor and Ridge were already halfway there. They had opened the wings on their propulsion packs for stability, and the faint glow of burning gas could be seen in their exhaust pipes. She flattened her body and opened her pack's wings, then pointed a laser scope at the ship and clicked ENGAGE TARGET. She felt an immediate jolt as the propulsion system switched on, and within seconds she had reached the hatch to the *Argo*'s pressurization chamber. Ridge had managed to unlock it. They got inside and shut the hatch.

"We're inside," she said into her transceiver. "Initiate pressurization."

Gradually, the chamber repressurized, expelling excess nitrogen and filling with breathable air. Megan and her comrades opened a hatch on the other side and squeezed themselves and their gear through the narrow opening and into the ship's cargo bay. A dazed crew member swam through the air toward them and stared at them as if in a trance. It was a guard.

"Who are you?" asked the female guard, blinking erratically. Her pupils were dilated to the point of being huge, and she moved unevenly, as though her coordination was gone. "What are you doing here?"

Megan and Ridge struggled to get out of their spacesuits and took off the propulsion packs, but Gregor kept everything on in case of an emergency.

"We're here to help you," said Megan, removing her

helmet, but the guard did not seem to be listening. She gazed confusedly at the hatch and then back at Megan.

"Have we landed? Are we there yet?"

"Not quite. We're still a few days out from Mars. We're here to help your captain and to make sure everyone's safe."

"My . . . name . . . is," stammered the guard before pausing. "I don't remember."

"We need you to help us," said Megan. She noticed a stun baton on the guard's utility belt and hoped she wouldn't pose a problem. "You're just a little confused right now. Can you take us to the kitchen? We need to gather some food and take it to the cockpit. Otherwise, your captain won't be able to land the ship."

"No!" snarled the guard, suddenly becoming agitated. "This is my ship, and you need to leave now! If you don't, I'll sound the alarm, and the others will come, and then you'll be sorry." She stared wildly at Megan and began growling in low guttural tones like an animal.

Megan pulled out her L-Stat and pointed it at the woman, whose shoulder-length blonde hair floated around her. She was clearly infected and could not be reasoned with. Megan decided to try one more time.

"I said take us to the kitchen."

The guard lunged at her, and Megan fired. A bolt of electricity struck the guard squarely in the chest, causing her body to stiffen. She thrashed about in convulsions, foam spraying from her mouth until her eyes rolled back and she went limp. Ridge grabbed a cable and tied the now incapacitated guard to a pallet secured to the floor.

"Quick," said Megan. "We might only have a few minutes."

She kicked the wall beside her, propelling herself toward

a door. Ridge followed close behind. As they neared the door, they noticed several crew members floating aimlessly, their eyes closed. *Were they dead or unconscious?* Another was conscious but took no notice of them. She pushed open the door, only to find her way blocked by a tall, lanky man whose eyes were as black as coal. He stared at her menacingly and reached out to grab her.

She placed a finger on her L-Stat's trigger but knew that it needed more time to recharge. What was she to do? Suddenly it occurred to her—objects in motion continue moving in a straight line unless a force is applied. Newton's First Law of Motion. On Earth, that force is gravity, like when you throw a ball it eventually falls to the ground unless someone catches it. But not here; not in space. Here, objects would fly in a straight line forever unless they ran into something. The key would be leverage.

The man tried to grab her, but she dodged him just in time. She then grabbed ahold of a pipe and smashed both of her feet into his chest. It was a perfect hit. He tumbled backward down the corridor, arms flailing, with Megan following just out of reach behind him. As hard as he tried, he couldn't stop. When they reached the kitchen, she lunged for the door and just managed to catch its handle as her would-be attacker continued plummeting down the corridor. She gave the handle a twist and opened the door.

What she saw inside shocked her. Bags of food, water bottles, knives, and tools were floating everywhere. At least a half dozen crewmen were in there too, some unconscious, others devouring whatever they could reach.

She kept a hand on her L-Stat and hoped it was ready to fire. A large man turned and glared at her, but then he went back to eating the food. *Okay,* she thought. *It's now or never.* She began grabbing water bottles and anything else she could reach and stuffed them into a sack. Just then, she felt a hand on her shoulder and twisted around to see who it was. It was Ridge. Megan blew a sigh of relief.

"What are you doing?" he snapped.

"Shhhh." Megan put an index finger to her lips. A woman looked up, followed by a man. They stared at her with extremely dilated, vacant eyes, the veins in their necks bulging. The woman bent her legs and pushed hard off the ceiling, hurtling fast toward Ridge like a torpedo.

Megan coiled and sprang at her, smashing into her and knocking her back to the ceiling. She then pushed off the wall in front of her and flew quickly toward Ridge and the door, grabbing another water bottle on the way.

"Let's get out of here!" she screamed, desperately pushing off anything she could find.

Together, they exited the kitchen and raced toward the cockpit. She was drenched in sweat, her flight suit clinging to her like plastic wrap, and her eyes stung. Ridge was now in front of her. They rushed past the mess hall and sleeping quarters, seeing dozens more crewmen, some conscious, others not.

A strong, stocky man shouted "Stop!" and began chasing them. Others followed. Where the corridor ended, she turned left into a new one and continued scrambling desperately until she passed Ridge and moved into the lead. Her lungs felt like they were going to burst, but she pushed on until they reached the cockpit.

"Open the hatch!" she yelled, pounding her fists against it. "We're from the *Intrepid*. We've got water and supplies!" She glanced behind her. The mob was now only meters away. The hatch opened and someone inside grabbed her.

"Get in!" cried a shrill voice. As she squeezed through

the opening, she felt Ridge's hand pressed against her as he tried to enter too, but then he was gone. Their deranged pursuers had grabbed him and pulled him back outside. The hatch slammed shut. She quickly glanced around the cockpit, noting four crew members—the captain, a female copilot, and two young men who appeared to be mechanics.

"Open the door!" she yelled, trying to pull the hatch back open. "We have to save my partner!"

"No," said the captain roughly. "They've already got him." He pried her hand off the hatch and forced her to turn her head so that she had to look him in the eye. The sight of his wide, dilated pupils made her blood run cold.

"But," she whispered, horrified, "we can save him." She could feel the blood coursing through her veins as her heart pounded faster and faster. Then she gasped, "You're one of them!"

The captain stared blankly past her and hesitated. She noticed that one of the mechanics was out cold. The other was counting his fingers and babbling incoherently. It was too late—the Light Beings had gotten them. The mission had failed, and now she had to get back to the *Intrepid. But how?* She handed the sack of water bottles to the copilot.

"Take it," she said, trying her best to sound calm. "I've got to leave. Do you have anything I can use? You know, to protect myself."

"You're not going back out there," ordered the captain, snapping back to life. His eyes flashed black. She drew the L-Stat and hit him with a single burst of electricity. He gritted his teeth and shook convulsively. When she looked back at the copilot, she was surprised to find that her eyes looked normal. Scared, but normal. She felt sorry for her.

"I didn't want to do it," she said, motioning toward

the captain. "He left me no choice. I can't stay here—I need to go."

"I understand," said the woman, her voice shaking. She must have realized that her situation was dire. "Take this. It's a pulse grenade—it kills with shock waves but won't harm the ship." Megan started to reach for it but then drew back her hand.

"No, I don't want to kill anyone. I'm going to wait five minutes and go out."

She concentrated on slowing her breathing and tried to imagine how Ridge was doing outside. He was strong and knew how to fight; it was still possible that he was alive and capable of helping her, but she had to be prepared to go it alone. The stun gun was still recharging—in another minute or two it would be ready. The captain had lapsed out of consciousness and was floating like a rag doll beside his seat.

"I'm infected, aren't I?" asked the copilot, her voice shaking.

"Possibly," said Megan. "But I was too, and I recovered. We just need to get someone over here who can land the ship."

"That's not a problem. Mission control can land it remotely. I just wonder what's going to happen when we get there."

Megan nodded. The same thought had occurred to her. She wondered if she would ever get to go home again, or if she was destined to die up here in space or on Mars. All she could do was her best. Feigning confidence, she put her hand on the hatch.

"Wish me luck."

Chapter 27

The Swarm

With the hatch partially open, Megan poked her head out to see if the coast was clear. She noticed Ridge's body floating limply several meters away next to a fire extinguisher. *Was he dead or merely unconscious?* Several crew members hovered behind him, staring at her, just waiting for her to come out. Their pupils were dilated like the others', making their eyes look huge and sinister. One, a skinny bearded man with rat-like facial features, seemed to be looking at something above her.

Sensing danger, she twisted around to see what it was, but it was too late—a powerful hand grabbed her by the hair and yanked her upward from behind.

The pain was sharp. She tried to get away but could not; his grip was too tight. She twisted her arm around and pointed her L-Stat behind her to shoot him, but her assailant suddenly let go of her hair and grabbed her by the wrist, squeezing so hard that she could feel the bones breaking like twigs. The gun slipped from her hand, and she watched helplessly as it floated away from her.

"Let me go," she gasped. "I'll give you anything you want."

Her attacker was now jamming his thumb into the soft tissue of her wrist and wrenching it from side to side causing her to writhe in agony.

"Let me go!" she cried again, begging. She could hear heavy breathing behind her and felt each warm breath on the back of her neck. Her attacker pushed her into the corridor toward Ridge, but he continued to hold onto her. She caught a brief glance of his short, fat, hairy hand as he pushed her further down the passage.

Her L-Stat was less than a meter away now, so close that she could almost feel its checkered grip. She looked at the infected crew members and counted three men and a woman. One was holding a long pole with a small yellow canister attached to its tip. Ridge's eyes were starting to open, and she noticed one of his fingers twitch.

"Why are you doing this?" she shrieked, still struggling against the pain. "We're just trying to help you."

The man pulled her arm over her head and turned her around so that she was facing him. His wide dilated pupils stared back at her. He had chubby unshaven cheeks, and his breath smelled foul.

"What do want?" she pleaded again, her eyes filling with tears.

"Everything," he whispered coldly. Then he grinned, revealing a chipped front tooth. She wished she had her gun—she could envision herself shooting him right between the eyes and making a dash for the cargo bay.

"I'll give you my propulsion pack if you let me get my partner out of here."

The man loosened his grip. She glanced at Ridge and noticed that his eyes were now partially open.

"A pack?" whispered the man in a raspy voice. His hand was sweaty, and Megan sensed that he was having trouble holding onto her. He seemed confused and agitated. After a pause, he said, "I want your ship."

"Let my friend go and you can have it."

He nodded. The skinny rat-faced man grabbed Ridge by the shoulders and gave him a shove, causing him to float slowly toward Megan, but a little to her left. *He's headed right for my gun*, she thought. She could only hope that he would have the wherewithal to use it.

"Okay, that's it," she said. "Now let me go. I'll get you the pack, and you can have my ship." Her voice trembled and her wrist throbbed, but she was determined to be brave.

Ridge was getting ever closer to her gun, a fact that seemed to elude their captors. Suddenly, she sensed her opportunity. The stocky man let go of her to wipe the sweat off his hands. Ridge was now within centimeters of her weapon. *Grab it*, she thought. His eyelids were drooping, and he was, at best, only half-conscious. She held her injured wrist close to her body, knowing that it was badly broken, and wondered if she would be able to shoot left-handed.

To her amazement, Ridge's hand shot out and he batted the L-Stat toward her. She caught it and fired once at the stocky man's chest. His body stiffened and his head jerked back as though he had been struck by lightning. The man with the pole hurled it at her, but the projectile missed, its yellow canister shattering against the wall behind her and bursting into jagged, leaping trails of blue and white electricity.

"Go!" gasped Ridge. "You can't save me. I'm too far gone." Suddenly, his eyes widened as he noticed something behind her.

"Get out now!" he yelled, shielding his face with his arms.

Megan turned but saw nothing at first. Then a shrill, high-pitched screech, like metal tearing pierced the air, and a stream of thousands of tiny blue lights snaked its way through the corridor and surrounded them. She froze. The noise was almost deafening.

She aimed her gun but did not pull the trigger. She remembered what Vic had said. They remembered her. The swarm was upon her now, hovering around her neck and shoulders, descending to her feet, and then running back up along her body toward her face. Each tiny light was but a speck, and they moved in unison as though they were a single entity.

She waited for a sting or a bite, but nothing happened, so she began searching for a way out.

The others were frozen, afraid, holding onto stationary objects. After several seconds, the swarm left her and settled on the stocky man, who was still recovering from being shot by the stun gun.

Suddenly, he began screaming even louder than before. It then split into two smaller swarms, one advancing toward Ridge and the other toward the man who had thrown the electric spear. She glanced at Ridge. He was curled into a ball, shielding his face with his arms. The Light Beings had begun landing on him, and she noticed a particularly large one on his wrist. She rubbed her own injured wrist and was surprised to find that it no longer hurt, even when she twisted it from side to side. She looked back at Ridge. The partial swarm was now flitting up and down his body, as though examining him. A large bead of sweat trickled from his forehead, and then he, too, started screaming.

The time had come to make her move. She had to get back to the *Intrepid*, and it would be impossible to take Ridge with her. The risk was too great.

She gave the wall beside her a firm shove and sailed down the corridor toward the exit. At first, her hollow-eyed assailants failed to notice, their attention fixed on the swarm, but then one saw her. He sprung off the wall and began hurtling toward her with a super-human burst of speed.

She glanced at her L-Stat. A red light indicated that it was still recharging. Her pursuer would catch up to her in just a matter of seconds. She could try to kick him with her good leg, but without leverage it wouldn't do much good.

Suddenly, the two throngs of glowing specks reunited into a single swarm and engulfed him. He let out an inhuman shriek and began flailing at them like a wild animal. A few seconds later, his body went limp and his eyes rolled back in his head. The swarm then left him and proceeded toward Megan, surrounding her, but she kept on going. Now completely engulfed by the swarm, she continued winding her way down the narrow corridors until she reached the cargo bay. Gregor was waiting for her.

"We've got to go now!" she screamed.

"What's that?" exclaimed Gregor, noticing the swarm.

"I don't know, just go!"

"What about Ridge?"

"He's gone. We can't save him. Help me into my suit." The Light Beings had moved away from her slightly. She felt guilty as she maneuvered into the spacesuit that Gregor held for her. Ridge should have been going back with them. She couldn't understand why the Light Beings had turned on him, and his screams still burned in her mind. As Gregor attached her propulsion pack, they momentarily left her and pressed in around him. He seemed on the verge of panic.

"Ignore them," ordered Megan. "I don't think they want to hurt us."

"I don't like this," Gregor stammered nervously. His face was pale as a sheet. They put on their helmets. The swarm then switched back to Megan, darting in and out between her arms and legs.

"Get in the pressurization chamber," she yelled. "Now!"

"With these things on us?"

"Yes!"

Suddenly, two of the crewmen who had been chasing her burst through the hatch into the cargo bay. One of them had a taser carbine.

Megan shoved Gregor into the chamber and clamored in behind him, locking the hatch from the inside just in time. They heard a loud *thwoomp* and then an explosion as the taser carbine's blast hit the other side of the now-closed hatch.

Gregor called out, "Initiate depressurization," and the chamber went dark except for the glowing specks, which gradually changed in color from blue to violet to red. There was shouting and banging on the other side of the hatch, but then a slow hissing sound filled the chamber and the temperature dropped precipitously. Two large steel doors slid apart on the other side of the chamber, revealing a dark sky filled with dazzling stars.

"Commencing spacewalk," shouted Gregor over his transceiver.

Megan steadied her breath and emerged from the pressurization chamber. Still gripping the sides of the now-open door, she could see Mars below her. Its rugged, crater-strewn surface was clearly visible, and she knew that she'd be stepping onto it in just a few days. She turned to her right and, spotting the *Intrepid*, let go and found herself floating once again in the wide-open vacuum of space.

All around her, stars glistened in the distance like tiny diamonds. The swarm turned red and then blue again. She marveled at their beauty and the way they flew so close to each other without colliding. She tested her injured wrist by making a fist and rotating it from side to side. No pain and a full range of movement—it was as if nothing had happened. She mouthed the words *thank you*, then stared transfixed as they broke off into thin tendrils and wound themselves around her like scarves, covering her entirely.

Then, just as she was about to activate her propulsion pack, Krueger's voice crackled over the transmitter.

"Come in, Megan. Do you copy?"

"Yes, I hear you."

"What are those lights around you? Are you okay?"

"I'm okay. I don't know what they are, but they're not hurting me."

"We only see you and Gregor. Where's Ridge?"

"He's gone. We lost him."

There was an uncomfortable pause and then Krueger spoke again. "Okay. Return to the ship."

She glanced at Mars once more and wondered what the future held. More horrors, more loss of life?

Lost in contemplation, she barely noticed as the swarm pulled away from her and disappeared in the direction of the red planet. She wondered if she would see them again.

Switching on the propulsion pack, she flattened her body, extended the stabilizer wings, and pressed down on the accelerator. Soon, she was back inside the *Intrepid's* pressurization chamber, awaiting the moment when she would have to face the consequences of failing at her mission.

Once re-pressurization was complete, the doors slid open with a hiss. Colonel Krueger was there waiting for her. He floated past Gregor, who was taking off his helmet and spacesuit, and came to a stop beside Megan.

"I'm sorry we put you in this situation, Megan," he said looking away. "You did the best you could."

"But—"

"Don't worry about Ridge. We'll be on Mars in two days. We'll see what we can do for him then."

Chapter 28

The Warehouse

Wiley felt that his only hope was to find Harper, and he had no idea where she was. The last time he'd seen her, he had dropped her off at the airport. *They want to kill me,* she had said. *The SIS. You and the others are probably next.* She had warned him against using telepathy, hinting that they might have found a way to listen in. But he had been desperate, so he used it anyway, and nobody had answered. Now, the only hope seemed to be to wait for Harper to return.

He slept during the day but returned each night to the abandoned warehouse to see if Harper had come back. He did not go inside. Instead, he lay on his belly behind parked coal trucks and garbage bins and watched from a distance.

Finally, after keeping watch for eight nights, he spotted

a shadowy figure on the roof. It was a bald girl wearing a white gown, and she was fast. He watched as she darted out of the shadows and scurried down a ladder to the side entrance. Then she went inside.

He followed her, tiptoeing and keeping an eye out for any sign of danger. When he reached the side door, he opened it slowly and navigated his way down the darkened corridor to their hideout. When he got to the end, the door was open. Inside, the girl stood panting, her back arched forward as she placed her hands on her knees. Her back was facing him.

"Harper?" he whispered, and the girl spun around. To his surprise, it wasn't Harper, but Raven. She was wearing a dirt-stained hospital gown, and her head was shaved and bandaged. She grabbed a section of pipe to defend herself and was about to strike when she recognized him.

"Wiley!" she gasped. Her voice was raspy and thin. If it weren't for the snake tattoo on her left arm, thought Wiley, he wouldn't have recognized her. There were stiches along the side of her head, and there was dried blood on her gown. He ran over to hug her, but she pulled away.

"The twins are alive," she said between breaths. "Bryce is dead. I escaped, but they operated on all of us and removed computer chips from our brains. This guy, Herrington—he's the SIS director—he says that's what was giving us our powers. Now they're his." She sat down and put her hands over her face. "I look horrible, don't I?"

"No," he answered cautiously. He sat down beside her but didn't try to put an arm around her. Raven had always been peculiar like that; she didn't like to be touched.

"I've been to see a reporter," he said. "His name is Bellamy, and he says he knows someone who can help us."

Raven acted as though she hadn't heard him. "They took my powers," she stammered. "I'm not special anymore." She turned her face away from him so he couldn't see her cry. Wiley got up and switched on a light. Not knowing what to say, he tried explaining about the reporter again.

"Raven, we need to go to the press; we need to get this story out there. People need to know. If the head of the SIS is in on it, there's no telling how high this goes. Come with me. I know a place where we'll be safe, and then in the morning we'll go see the reporter. Everything will be okay." She let him help her to her feet and then did her best to wipe the tears from her cheeks.

"One more thing," said Wiley. "Thanks for saving me back at the library. You didn't have to do that."

As they stepped back out into the darkened hallway, the silence was shattered by police sirens and the sound of the front door being bashed in. Seconds later, they heard shouting from the other side too, and the sound of a helijet hovering directly above the warehouse. A man's voice thundered ominously over a loudspeaker. *"We have you surrounded. Come out with your hands up."*

"This way," shouted Raven, and she raced back inside the hideout. Once Wiley was inside too, she bolted the door and started pinching her gown with her fingers. "Unbelievable! They must have bugged it," she said. "Follow me!"

They ran into the large open space that resembled an airplane hangar, and Raven pulled out a crate from under a pile of discarded machine parts. She opened it. Inside were firefighter suits, complete with helmets and oxygen tanks. She ordered Wiley to turn around and then took off her hospital gown and put on one of the firefighter suits.

"Grab one and put it on!" she yelled, pointing to the

box. "Put it on over your clothes." While Wiley did as he was told, she dragged out a large plastic barrel, pried off its lid, and using all her strength, just managed to tip it over. "Fire accelerant," she said as liters of yellowish liquid splashed across the floor. "Don't let any get on you. We're going to torch this place!"

"How are we going to get out?" asked Wiley, moving quickly to avoid the growing puddle of accelerant that had almost reached his shoes. The smell was strong, like kerosene.

"Just stick with me. I have a plan."

Chapter 29

Like Wolves Moving in for the Kill

Raven had gone back to the warehouse, just as Herrington had suspected. Now, his tracking satellite detected two live bodies inside, and he was sure Wiley was with her. With his prey now trapped, he called Irons.

"Yes, boss," came the reply.

"We've found the girl and probably the boy too," said Herrington coldly. "They're in a warehouse by the waterfront, sector 3141-A, southwest corner. I've already deployed a police unit to prevent them from escaping, but I don't want them arrested. I want them *dead*. Follow the coordinates I sent you and see to it that they're eliminated. Dump their bodies in the ocean and kill any witnesses, including police officers."

"With pleasure," said Irons. "However, there is still the matter of money."

"Just do it," replied Herrington. "You'll get your money." He hung up the phone.

Sitting in his car a kilometer away, Irons grinned. He knew that he had the old wolf in the palm of his hand.

When Irons arrived, police units had positioned themselves on either side of the warehouse. A helijet was hovering above the roof, its engines roaring noisily. He approached a young lieutenant who seemed to be in charge, flashed a badge, and asked for a status update.

"We've got the exits sealed, sir," shouted the lieutenant, "but we don't know who our suspect is. We were told only that he's a violent criminal and should be considered armed and dangerous. He might have an accomplice with him."

Good, thought Irons. *The less they know, the better*. Killing cops was a tricky business, and he would prefer not having to do it. "That is correct. The suspect should be considered armed and highly dangerous," he informed the officer in his southern drawl. "I am afraid that you will need to use deadly force."

"Yes, sir." The lieutenant radioed his officers surrounding the warehouse and ordered them to break down the doors. The helijet was now directly overhead, making it difficult to hear. A voice boomed from the chopper's loudspeaker. "We have you surrounded. Come out with your hands up."

Irons placed his hand on a gun that he kept hidden inside his jacket. He knew that he could not allow the boy and the girl to be taken into police custody.

Guessing that they would use the side entrance, he jogged to where two police officers were preparing to batter down the door and flashed his badge. "Federal agent," he shouted, fighting to be heard over the roar of the helijet. "This is my investigation. I will be going in first." An officer nodded, and in the next instant the door burst off its hinges as the battering ram struck it with a loud thud. Irons drew his gun and walked cautiously forward into the dark corridor. At first he saw nothing, but then smoke began to fill the narrow passage.

The lieutenant's voice rang out over the police radio. "Get out of there!" he screamed. "The warehouse is on fire!"

The two officers retreated, but Irons pressed on. He pulled out a handkerchief and held it over his nose. By the time he neared the end of the corridor, the smoke had become so thick that he was forced to drop to his hands and knees and crawl. The heat was infernal, and he didn't know how much longer he could take it.

He reached a closed door at the end of the hallway and fired a bullet through its locking mechanism before pushing it open. He crept inside, wincing as flames leaped around him. The walls and the roof were engulfed in flames, and smoke was everywhere. He began coughing uncontrollably and felt his throat swell shut. Dizziness set in and he dropped his gun. Just before he passed out, he saw what looked like a pair of firefighters hurrying toward him, their faces concealed by masks.

Wiley grabbed Irons by the arm and began dragging him. Even with the firefighter suit on, the heat was intense, but the smoke was even worse. "He's too heavy," he shouted. "Help me."

Raven was only a step or two in front of him, but he could barely see her. "Leave him!" she yelled, but he couldn't hear her. He continued dragging Irons down the narrow corridor, straining against the man's weight. He knew that the building was surrounded by cops, but if they emerged from the burning building with Irons in tow, it would look like they really were firefighters, and they might just be able to complete their escape.

When they finally burst through the side door, Wiley dropped Irons's arm. Two officers were poised just outside the door. "Get this man to a hospital," Wiley yelled through his mask, and each grabbed an arm and dragged Irons to safety. As the police disappeared around a corner with Irons, Raven took off her mask and pointed to the doorway of a building behind the warehouse.

"In there," she said, and she took off running. Wiley followed her, struggling to match her speed. They entered the building unseen and then exited out the back. They raced from building to building until they were at least a kilometer from the burning warehouse and too exhausted to move.

"You're a genius," said Wiley, panting.

"Yeah, I know," said Raven. "And you're an imbecile. You should have let that man burn."

Chapter 30

The Prophecy

The night after she returned from her mission, Megan tossed and turned until she finally drifted off to sleep. She dreamed she was in a cold, damp cave. She was holding a torch in her right hand, its reddish-orange flame lighting up the cave's interior and casting long shadows. A few spiders scurried along the ground—real ones, not robots.

As she looked around, she noticed that the walls of the cave were covered with drawings and indecipherable writing that looked like hieroglyphs.

A series of pictures revealed the story of a small settlement growing into a large city and then falling into disuse. The surrounding forest died, a nearby river froze over, and the people moved underground. Above them, their city crumbled, and the ruins were buried over time by dust storms. Then the people living underground started dying in large numbers until most of them were gone, and the survivors divided into groups and waged war against each other.

She walked a little farther and saw a picture of the Light Beings. Another showed some of the people building a spaceship and flying away. It was the prophecy, exactly as Anya had described it. Suddenly, she heard footsteps and looked up.

She crept forward cautiously. Rounding a corner, she glimpsed a small, dark-haired woman kneeling beside another drawing. She seemed to be reading the inscriptions.

"Dr. Burke?" she called out nervously. "It's me, Megan. You've been trying to show me something, haven't you?"

Burke turned and stared at her with a piercing glare. "Go to the colony, Megan. Return to where you were born. The prophecy has ordained it."

"How do I get there?"

"Use the tunnels. Get inside the dome."

"But what about the spiders?"

"Trust me. Just go. A way to defeat the spiders will present itself."

"Okay. What do I do when I get there?"

"You'll know what to do when the time comes," replied Burke. "Follow me."

Burke walked deeper into the cave where the spiders were larger and more numerous. A few scurried along the walls and ceiling. She pointed to a spot, and Megan drew the torch closer to illuminate it. There was a drawing of an erupting volcano, beside which was written something indecipherable. She turned and looked at Dr. Burke.

"Everything must be destroyed before it can be rebuilt," continued Burke. "It's what the prophecy says must happen. But the destruction that Vic brings is evil and must be stopped."

"What is Vic planning to do?"

"A virus wiped out most of the Martian race thousands of years ago. He's found surviving remnants of the virus and is multiplying them in cryo-containers. If he has his way, he'll bring them to Earth to infect every man, woman, and child."

"Why?" asked Megan.

"Revenge. He blames humans—especially me—for corrupting the last underground Martian settlement. He was born and raised on Earth, unaware of his Martian ancestry, and he left for Mars at the same time I did. We became friends, but what I wasn't prepared for was him falling in love with me. I told him I wasn't interested, that I only wanted to be friends, and he was deeply hurt. He had always been something of an outcast, never fitting in or finding love. He became sullen and resentful. Around that time, his fellow Martians learned of his presence and revealed themselves to him.

"They knew who he was and exactly where to find him. I suspect the Light Beings told them. When the last prisoner revolt started, they asked him to come live with them. They told him that they needed people because there were so few Martians and that he should bring as many good ones as he could find. He disagreed, but they insisted. Not knowing where to start, he came to me and begged me to help.

"I said I'd go. Our colony seemed doomed anyway, and I didn't want to have anything more to do with it. I gathered a group of some of the colony's best and brightest, and when the time was right, we made our escape. The plan was to bring along you and the other children, but you were captured and sent to Earth.

"When we reached the Martian settlement, I began helping them however I could. I loved my new home and decided to stay. But I never forgave the people back at the colony for stealing my children. You were mine, after all—all mine! I was the one who saved you when they talked of letting you babies die. I raised you and loved you. So how could they say I wasn't your mother? How could they take you away?

"The Martians had been living a bleak underground existence, but using my knowledge and contacts on Earth, I transformed it into something beautiful. We brought in more people from Earth as well as plants and animals. At first, Vic supported us, but he changed his mind when humans began to outnumber the Martians and they elected me as their leader. He was jealous, and he still hadn't forgiven me for his unrequited love.

"It was only a matter of time before the colonists found us and destroyed us, so I launched a preemptive strike. I've manufactured thousands of fast-moving robotic spiders to attack and destroy their colony. And that's where we are now, Megan. I don't like what Vic is doing, but I swear I'll kill every man and woman in the colony if I can—especially the ones who took away my children!"

"But why kill them?" asked Megan. "Don't you already have what you want?"

"No," replied Burke, "We're not safe until they're gone. The prophecy says Mars will be reborn as a living planet. There will be oceans, forests, and breathable air. But it's just us, not them. And that's why you're here now—to help fulfill the prophecy. We need your help."

Megan looked at the picture of the volcano again and noticed a dome in the distance. It was the colony, Opportunity II. The next picture showed a girl standing inside the dome. She had something with her—a small animal, possibly a monkey or a squirrel. She searched for the next picture in the sequence, but it was heavily faded and impossible to make out.

"Just remember to breathe," added Burke. "And have faith."

Megan turned around to ask another question, but Burke was gone.

What am I going to do? she thought. *Find Vic and stop him?* She couldn't let him bring the virus back to Earth. And then there was Burke. If she was serious about killing everyone, wouldn't that include her parents, if they were still alive? And her friends' parents too, come to think of it, not to mention any number of innocent bystanders. That would be terrible. She knew she had to stop them but had no idea how.

Chapter 31

Final Preparations

Megan awoke with a jolt. She was beginning to believe that what Dr. Burke had told her in the dream was true.

She checked the time. Zero four thirty hours—4:30 a.m. She exited her sleep pod and set out to find Vic. He had threatened to kill everyone if she didn't go with him once they reached Mars, but her instincts, as well as the dream, were telling her to go to the colony instead.

She decided to try to compromise with Vic. Maybe they could make a deal. If he let her go to the colony first, she would promise to join him afterward. If he refused, she would blackmail him. She would threaten to tell Krueger and the captain about the three teenagers he was hiding. It was a gamble, but she didn't see any other way.

She navigated her way down the ship's winding passageways until she reached the cargo bay and the compartment where she had confronted him before. The ship was buzzing with activity as dozens of crew members and maintenance robots prepared for landing, but none of them paid her any attention.

She had to hurry—the ship was to land later that day. Reaching his compartment, she jiggled the door's handle, but it was locked. Then she knocked. No answer. She pulled out a tiny electronic code scrambler that she had stolen from Hendrix and held its magnetic strip to the door. There was a sudden pop and the lock opened. She pushed open the door and felt along the interior wall until her fingers found the light switch and flicked it on.

The compartment was empty, save for a few boxes secured to the floor. The equipment, the unconscious youths, and the Light Beings—they were all gone.

"What have you done with them, Vic?" she murmured to herself. "And where have you gone?" Part of her was relieved that he was gone. If she was lucky, maybe he wouldn't turn up at all until it was too late and she was already on her way to the colony. She returned to her sleep pod and lay inside until it was time for breakfast.

At zero six hundred hours sharp, she reported to the cargo bay where Krueger was to give them their final instructions. Gregor was already there when she arrived, as were Hendrix, Krueger, Ob, and the rest of the security force. Except one—Vic. She grabbed onto a cable secured to the wall and clipped it onto her flight suit before settling in next to Ob.

"Where's Vic?"

"Shhh," he said, holding a finger to his lips. "Krueger's about to speak."

"Attention," barked Krueger as he made his way to the front of the enclosure. "The ship lands in ten hours. As soon as we're down, make your way to the cargo bay and pick up your weapon. You'll be helped into an exoskeleton and body armor. Then stand by for orders. When the main hatch opens, we'll spread out around the ship in teams of three, back to back, just like we've practiced. Once we've secured the area, the extraction team will be given the green light. Half of you will accompany them to the mines and stand guard as they load everything onto trucks. The other half is coming with me to the colony."

"Yes sir!" everybody shouted at once.

"Wick, Jones, Fletch, Hendrix, Wolfson, and—uh—Megan, you're coming with me," continued Krueger. "The rest of you are on rock patrol."

Megan was relieved. She didn't know what she would have done if they sent her to the mines. Then she remembered the prophecy and realized that going to the colony was her destiny, so of course she would be assigned to go there.

She wondered if she would find her parents. Strangely, she felt no connection to them, probably because she had no memories of them, but she was still curious. She was also worried about Vic. Would he follow through on his threat to kill everyone? She decided to tell Hendrix about him. He was a good shot and just might be able to protect her. For now, though, the important thing was getting inside the colony. She could deal with Vic later.

Before leaving the cargo bay, everyone had their head shaved. This was necessary to ensure a proper connection with the EEG sensors inside the caps that would be worn under their helmets. The sensors communicated with the brain's neural networks and allowed the wearer to control his or her exoskeleton, and they had to be placed directly against the scalp.

They needed the exoskeletons to compensate for the loss of strength and bone density that they had experienced during their three months of weightlessness; daily exercise and calcium injections weren't enough. In fact, the exoskeletons would do better than just restore lost strength; they would make their users strong and agile, better even than the world's best athletes. She was sad to lose her hair, but the prospect of gaining superhuman strength thrilled her. Besides, her hair would grow back.

A robotic barber took measurements and then began shaving off her hair with a pair of rotating razors. Clumps of brown hair floated around her face, tickling her ears, until another robot sucked them up with a vacuum hose. It felt strange to be without hair; her scalp felt cool in the air-conditioned room. She returned to the passenger compartment, hoping to find a familiar face, but none of her friends were there.

Friends, she thought. *They're certainly not my friends if they're helping Vic kill everyone on Earth.* Just then, a messenger robot bumped into her shoulder and handed her a note.

"For you," it said.

There was a sketch of a pyramid and an eye on the front of the folded-over piece of paper, just like the one tattooed on Anya. She opened it carefully and read.

> Change of plans. You're going to the colony without me. Anya will go with you. She'll tell you what to do once you get there. I stashed a plasma rifle in a duffel bag under your seat. You'll need it. Don't be afraid. The prophecy says you'll reach the colony alive. Nothing can kill you before you arrive there. I

will come for you once you've completed your task.

—Vic

She folded the note and stuffed it in a pocket, then strapped herself into her seat, the same one she had tried to escape from during lift-off. She noticed a duffel bag secured under the seat and unzipped it just enough to see the barrel of a plasma rifle inside. She tried to relax, allowing her head to sink into the chair's cushioned headrest, and was about to fall asleep when she was interrupted by a voice.

"Excuse me, miss." It was an attendant. She opened her eyes.

"Yes?"

"There's a message for you." He handed her a small portable holograph generator with a note that said CONFIDENTIAL. He left, and she looked around. The seats nearest her were empty, and nobody seemed to be paying her any attention. She wondered what was taking Hendrix so long. Curious, she switched the device on and pressed a button that said PLAY MESSAGE. After a pause, a familiar but unfriendly voice greeted her. It was Herrington.

"Are you alone?" he asked.

"Yes."

"Okay. Wait just a moment."

At first the image was interrupted by static, but it gradually stabilized. The director's holographic image looked around her for eavesdroppers and then whispered.

"You're landing today. I arranged for you to be put on the team going to the colony. Have you received your orders?"

"Yes."

"It's important that you reach the colony alive. Don't take any unnecessary risks."

"What do you mean by unnecessary?"

"Stay close to Hendrix. Never leave the group."

"Will Dr. Burke know that I've arrived?"

"We believe so. She most likely has at least one spy on your ship."

Of course, Burke's spies are on the ship, thought Megan, fighting the urge to roll her eyes. *Tell me something I don't know.* Then it dawned on her—Herrington probably had his own spies as well. At the very least there was Hendrix, his nephew, but if he was a spy, he was a really bad one.

"Can I speak with Harper?" she asked.

"No," replied Herrington coldly. "Megan, I have your friends. If Burke gets to you before we get to her, tell her that. And tell her that I'm prepared to kill every last one of them."

"That's not fair!" she exclaimed, accidentally raising her voice. Several crew members turned to look at her. She regained her composure and whispered, "I've done everything you asked me to."

"I know," said Herrington. "And if you just keep doing that, they might live. I'm prepared to make a deal."

She felt trapped. Her mind was racing, and she didn't know what to do. If Herrington really did have her friends, there would be no reason for him to keep them alive after Dr. Burke was dead. She decided to change the subject.

"What about my parents? You said they're alive."

"One of them is, but she won't be much longer if you don't make it to the colony in time. Remember, no unnecessary risks."

There was a click, and the image vanished. Megan sat staring at where it had been for what seemed like several minutes. *Okay,* she thought. *I'm ready. Let's do this.*

Chapter 32

Wiley and Raven

Raven felt weak. It didn't help that she was wearing a heavy firefighter's suit or that her head still hurt from the surgery. She had been on the run for over a week. It irritated her that Irons was still alive, and she could barely look at Wiley without wanting to strike him.

They had stopped and were hunkered down in a rusted-out equipment shed with no food and nothing to drink but rainwater.

Raven traded her firefighter's suit for a pair of old denim overalls that she found hanging from a peg. It reminded her of something Megan would wear—cheap and out of style.

Wiley didn't want to go back to the shantytown. It was too close to the smoldering remains of their old hideout, and he was sure Irons would be looking for them there.

Instead, he planned to visit Bellamy again as soon as possible, hoping that the feisty reporter could find them food and a better place to stay.

That night, Raven went out for water and didn't come back. Wiley knew she was mad at him and went to sleep wondering what he was going to do. Without Raven, Harper and Megan were his only hope, and it didn't look as though either of them would be turning up anytime soon.

The next morning, he awoke to find Raven sitting on a stool on the other side of the shed eating a sandwich. She was wearing a wig of shoulder-length green hair and had on new clothes—a flashy red dress and a pair of black leather boots—and she seemed relaxed.

"Here," she said, tossing him a pastry, "you look hungry."

He unwrapped the pastry and devoured it greedily, licking the icing off his fingers. He wasn't sure if he was happier to see her or the food.

"Thanks," he said. "Where did you get the food and those clothes?"

Raven rolled her eyes. "Where do you think?"

You stole them, thought Wiley, feeling uneasy. His stomach growled and he asked if she had more, but she just laughed, opening her hand to reveal a wad of bundled-up credits.

"Don't worry," she said. "I've got enough here to buy meals for a month. But first, let's go see that reporter you were talking about."

They arrived at Bellamy's office just before closing time. Bellamy was impressed by the scar on Raven's head and listened attentively to her story. Then he took the cigar out of his mouth and flashed a big, toothy grin.

"We're going to nail that bunch of lowlifes to the wall,"

he said, punching the air in front of him. "Every one of 'em—including the president, if he's in on it. This story's going to make me millions! But first, we need to get you kids someplace safe." He fumbled with an electronic device on his desk and then spoke into it. "Get me William Blythe," he barked impatiently. "Tell him it's urgent and that I've found a solution to his problem."

Chapter 33

Landing on Mars

Landing on Mars is no easy task. Its atmosphere is extremely thin—only one percent of Earth's—which means that a ship can't fly in on wings the way an airplane does. In fact, it's so thin that it can't even open a parachute. But it is just substantial enough that a ship using downward-pointing rocket thrusters can't land without creating dangerous turbulence.

To make matters worse, its atmosphere is also shallower than Earth's, which means that there isn't much room for a ship entering it to slow down before hitting the surface. To solve this problem, the *Icarus* and her sister ship, the *Argo*, would orbit Mars multiple times, briefly entering and exiting its atmosphere at each pass, each time slowing a little. Finally, on the last pass, the ships would deploy hypersonic inflatables, large balloon-like objects that expand and stiffen to increase drag, thus slowing the ships further. Simultaneously, the ships would fire their rocket thrusters in the opposite direction, away from Mars's surface.

At this point, flying robotic tugs would launch from Mars and intercept each incoming ship, latching onto its sides with enormous electromagnets and stabilizing its descent.

But were the tugs still functional? And would they even launch? In theory, they should since they were automated, but what if they had been sabotaged?

These were the questions burning in most people's minds as they changed into their survival suits, strapped themselves into their seats, and awaited the first pass into Mars's atmosphere. Megan closed her eyes and thought of her cat back home, imagining herself stroking its soft white fur. She wondered if her neighbor, Mrs. Mitchell, had found time to visit her and hoped that her apartment's computer was taking good care of the place.

With its first pass, the *Intrepid* shook so violently that Megan thought it was coming apart. There was a low dull roar accompanied by periodic banging sounds. Her vision blurred as she gripped the sides of her chair and gritted her teeth. The ship was now enveloped in a fiery ball of plasma with heat so intense that she felt herself sweating heavily inside her insulated survival suit. This continued for several minutes and then stopped as they exited Mars's atmosphere.

The ship repeated this process a dozen times, each time losing speed. Finally, on the twelfth pass, they descended all the way through Mars's atmosphere and headed for the landing zone. They had decelerated to around twenty thousand kilometers per hour, half their original speed.

Megan began to feel gravity pulling at her, gently at first but then more insistently. Having been weightless for over three months, its return made her feel heavy.

Several kilometers above Mars, the ship deployed its inflatables and slowed so suddenly that Megan felt like she was going to be torn out of her seat. Her shoulders stung from the pressure against them, and she struggled to catch her breath. The thrusters ignited, and she felt another surge of deceleration; but this time as the ship slowed, it began swinging back and forth erratically.

Turbulence, she thought. *Where are those tugs?* She closed her eyes and waited.

Within seconds there was a sudden thud, jolting the ship to one side and then another, and the *Intrepid* began to stabilize. It was the tugs. The fact that they had deployed was a huge relief to everyone. Megan stretched her aching neck by dropping her head to each shoulder and allowing gravity to do its work. Everything felt heavy, but she was beginning to enjoy the sensation. It almost reminded her of being back on Earth.

Minutes later, there was a gentle thump as the *Intrepid* touched down on the landing pad, and the crew cheered.

I'm on Mars, she thought. *Now the real danger begins.* She felt her lungs tighten and her pulse accelerate. *Robotic spiders—thousands of them.* She knew the prophecy said that she would survive to get inside the colony, but she wondered what would happen after that. Did they really have a chance?

A robotic voice over the intercom interrupted her thoughts. "*Attention,*" it snapped. "*We have arrived at our destination. Security personnel are to report immediately to the cargo bay. Everybody else remain seated until further notice.*"

She unbuckled her safety harness and climbed out of

her seat. It felt good to be on her feet again, but she was surprised at how heavy her arms and legs felt. *Shouldn't they feel light?* she wondered. *After all, Mars's gravity is only thirty-eight percent of Earth's—or at least that's what Miles had said.* She still felt weak as a baby. Several other members of the security team were already in front of her making their way to the cargo bay.

Summoning all her strength, she threw the duffel bag containing the plasma rifle over her shoulder and hurried after them. She stumbled once and had to grab onto someone's seat. "Excuse me," she stammered nervously, her thoughts again turning to what awaited them outside. Fear began to gnaw at her stomach, and she felt light-headed. Would she be able to do this? Did she have the strength? *Don't be silly,* she thought. *This is what I've trained for. It's now or never.*

Krueger was waiting for them when they arrived in the cargo bay. Gregor and Cain had put on body armor and were selecting their weapons—taser carbines. Megan noticed Vic standing in a corner near the all-terrain vehicle with the giant rubber tires. He looked calm, as though there were nothing to fear.

"Megan," said a cheerful voice behind her. She turned around and saw Anya, who was wearing an exoskeleton and body armor. "Guess who's coming with you to the colony?"

"You?" exclaimed Megan, trying her best to act surprised. "But how? You're not security."

"There was a last-minute change. As a biologist, I qualify to serve as a medic. Ob's going too. I'm here in case someone gets hurt." Then she leaned closer and whispered, "Plus, there's something I have to do there."

As Megan looked over the young woman's mechanized

suit, she noticed that she was also carrying a large pack on her shoulders that she assumed was a medical kit.

By now most of the security team was wearing exoskeletons and body armor. They looked strangely robotic as they moved about the room testing their newfound strength.

Megan opened a locker containing a stiff, light exoskeleton and put it on over her survival suit. A technician slathered her scalp with a thick, viscous lotion and fitted her with a cap containing millions of tiny EEG sensors.

"You're set," he said, examining the exoskeleton's external power pack. "Walk around and use your hands and arms so you get used to it. It's learning to read your brain waves even as we speak."

Adrenaline surged through her body, and she felt her strength magnify with each movement. Picking up a hefty metal wrench off the floor, she bent it as though it were made of aluminum foil and tossed it aside. Then she put flexible body armor on over the exoskeleton and crossed the room to where Krueger was preparing to give final instructions.

"Okay, listen up," said Krueger in his customary no-nonsense tone. "We're in the landing zone. The volcano is five kilometers straight in front of us. The colony will be to the east, about a kilometer beyond a low flat hill. There should be emergency vehicles and a control tower that we can use for cover—that is, unless the enemy has already claimed them." As he said this, he loaded a clip into his taser carbine and switched off the safety.

"What are we going to do about the *Argo*?" asked a voice. It was Vic. Everybody stopped and stared. Nobody had seen him for two days, and they certainly didn't think he was part of their team. He wore no body armor, no exoskeleton, and had no weapon. Krueger seemed irritated.

"The *Argo* has been locked down remotely to protect its crew," he said. "We'll get in there and rescue the survivors as soon as we've accomplished our primary mission." He paused, looked each person in the eye, and then spoke again. "Put on your helmets and adjust your airflow. You have enough oxygen to last two hours, and we'll be bringing additional tanks with us."

At once, everyone fastened their helmets to their survival suits and made sure that the seam was airtight. Megan twisted a knob on her regulator and heard a brief high-pitched whine as oxygen filled her helmet. She inhaled cautiously, relieved to find her lungs filling with air.

Krueger continued, this time speaking into a transceiver inside his helmet. His voice sounded distant and muffled, as though far away. "When that door opens," he said, nodding toward the main cargo hatch, "secure the perimeter as quickly as possible. Is everybody ready?"

"Yes, sir," the team answered in unison. Megan had picked up a taser carbine and now held it close to her body. She wanted to break out the plasma rifle from her duffel bag but knew it was too early. People would ask questions. The tension was growing.

Krueger said something inaudible into his transceiver, and then the giant steel doors of the hatch began to open slowly. As the Martian landscape materialized in front of them, Megan gasped in astonishment.

Chapter 34

Unexpected Chaos

The steel doors were now all the way open. Outside the ship, the Martian landscape spread out like a vast orange and red desert, its surface scarred by impact craters of varying sizes. Rocks littered the surface, casting long shadows like stripes across the terrain. In front of them, a huge cone-shaped volcano, Olympus Mons, loomed forebodingly, smoke billowing from a newly formed crater in its caldera. It looked closer than five kilometers away. Megan nudged Hendrix, who was standing beside her.

"I thought it was supposed to be farther away," she whispered into her transceiver. "Is our map wrong?"

"Negative," snapped Krueger instead of Hendrix, his voice muffled by static. "It just looks like that because it's so big. It's three times as tall as Mount Everest."

Taller than Everest. Megan stared in amazement at its

peak, which was partially obscured by clouds. She could see tendrils of smoke rising out of it and wondered if an eruption was imminent.

Sensing her concern, Krueger put a hand on her shoulder. "Don't worry," he said. "It hasn't erupted in a million years and scientists say it won't blow again for at least a hundred million more." Then he switched his transceiver back to the group and addressed the whole team. "Everything looks A-OK. Move out."

Megan was the first to step onto Mars's surface. Her foot sank several centimeters into rust-colored dust, and she thought she heard a faint crunching sound as she broke through the layer of permafrost.

She looked quickly to her right and noticed a concrete warehouse and several small equipment hangars. Bulldozers, trucks, and other large vehicles sat idle, half buried in sand and dust. A control tower, some twenty meters in height, rose above the other structures. She was surprised to see yellow and green lights glowing brightly from its observation deck and from the corners of the landing zone. *Must be solar-powered,* she thought. It looked a lot like any small airport on Earth, except that red dust was everywhere and the surrounding landscape looked entirely alien.

The sun hung low in the sky and was beginning to set. It looked smaller than it did on Earth, and its light was pallid and weak. She hurried around to the front of the ship and took cover behind its nose.

"No sign of trouble," she called into her transceiver. Seconds later, Smithwick and Wolfson joined her. Anya was right behind them.

"Where are they?" exclaimed Wolfson. "I mean the spiders, where are they?"

Then, someone—Megan couldn't tell who—began

shouting over the transceivers. "We have an emergency! It's the *Argo*!" She poked her head around the *Intrepid*'s nose and pointed her carbine toward their sister ship. A small emergency hatch under its cockpit hung open, swaying from side to side. She noticed a mesh ladder on the ground and footprints—lots of them. Suddenly, the sound of gunfire filled the air. Megan sprinted toward the *Argo* and reached the open hatch in time to see four figures fleeing in the direction of the volcano. One turned and fired back at the ship.

"I'm hit," cried a voice. Megan started to move in the direction of the injured man, but something caught her eye. Just above the open hatch, a woman lay dead, her eyes staring blankly back at her. She had either been killed before the hatch was opened or had suffocated or frozen to death afterward. *Could it be the copilot?* She hoped not. She spoke into her transceiver.

"The *Argo*'s leaking heat and oxygen. We need to seal it. I'm going in."

"Be careful," said Krueger. "I'm sending a welder."

She picked up the flimsy mesh ladder and tossed one end through the opening so that it caught on the hatch. Wolfson and Smithwick quickly joined her and gave her a boost to help her get up the ladder. Once inside, she noticed three dead crewmen, their exposed skin already discolored by the intense cold. She then checked the hatch leading to the main crew compartment and noticed that it was still locked, but a hissing sound suggested that the seal was less than airtight. They had to act fast—precious oxygen and warmth might be leaking out faster than it could be replaced.

"Do you need a medic?" It was Anya; her voice crackling weakly over the transceiver.

"Negative," said Megan. "Where's that welder?"

"We've got someone coming up," said Wolfson behind her. "Make way." A slightly built man carrying something that looked like a flamethrower struggled up the ladder, his equipment obviously too heavy for him. Megan reached down, took his hand, and, using the strength of her exoskeleton, pulled him into the cockpit in one fluid motion. The man seemed startled by her strength but quickly regained his composure and set to work.

"Stand back," he said. He pointed a long, gray nozzle at the seams around the hatch separating the cockpit from the rest of the ship and pulled the trigger. Yellow foam sprayed out, caking the gap between the door and the walls with a thick, frothy goo. The foam hardened almost instantly, creating an insulated barrier.

"That should hold for a while," said the man. "A welder's on the way. We'll seal the hatch once this one's welded shut."

"The crew, are they going to be okay?" asked Megan.

"There should be enough oxygen in there to last a day or two. But it's really just a matter of time before we have to go in and rescue them."

Megan took a last look at the dead woman, suspecting it was the copilot. She remembered how scared the woman had been and how she had tried to help her. Then it struck her that she had seen *four* figures exit the emergency hatch. When she had been in the cockpit before, there was only the pilot, the copilot, and the two mechanics.

The cockpit must have been breached, she thought. She scanned the cockpit for more bodies, hoping not to find Ridge.

There was a sudden shout over the transceiver. "He's got the ATV!"

"Who?" cried someone else. Megan instantly recognized the voice. It was Hendrix.

"Vic. And something's coming toward us!"

She leaped feet first out of the cockpit's emergency hatch and landed on the ground with her knees bent, the exoskeleton absorbing the shock of impact. As she sprinted to the rear of the ship, she saw the ATV speeding away, a cloud of red dust billowing around it.

Simultaneously, two large hovercraft sped toward them, one slowing near the ATV and the other halting in midair less than a hundred meters from the *Intrepid*. Its engines were loud, and the craft shook as it hovered in place. A pair of yellow lights glowed from its roof.

"Take cover; don't shoot," ordered Krueger.

Megan scrambled behind a half-buried bulldozer. The hovercraft nearest them began rocking from side to side as though struggling with turbulence. A beam of light flashed twice from its cockpit, paused, and then repeated the sequence three more times.

They're trying to send a message, she thought. She wondered if the craft had come from Burke. Several hundred meters beyond it, the ATV stopped near where the other hovercraft was preparing to land, and a man got out. She recognized his build; it was Vic. Nobody else was that tall and strongly built. He began pulling several large duffel bags out of the ATV. Neither Ob nor Cassandra was with him.

"Vic, return to the ship immediately," warned Krueger's voice over the transceiver. "You are not authorized to do this."

Vic ignored him and kept on working. Krueger fired a shot over his head. Immediately, the hovercraft closest to them aimed a massive spotlight their way, temporarily blinding them. Then there was a loud roar as it shot jets of hot air at the ground below it, kicking up a huge cloud of red dust that concealed Vic and the hovercraft from view. They had to act fast.

"Fire in short bursts!" shouted Krueger.

Instantly, everybody began shooting at and around the dust cloud. It was at that moment that a swarm of glowing blue lights poured over the rear of the ship and enveloped them from behind. Megan saw Wolfson shoot into it, but without effect. In the distance, she thought she saw the two hovercraft retreating through the cloud of dust and sand.

The Light Beings continued to flock around them, frustrating the team's attempt to stop Vic. That's when it hit Megan: *They wanted him to get away. They were actively assisting his escape by creating a diversion.* A single glowing speck settled on her arm and pulsated with bluish light. She lowered her weapon, wondering if it was one of the same ones she had seen on the *Argo. They remember me*, she thought, recalling Vic's words. *But whose side will they be on if I try to stop him?*

Unlike Megan, the others were terrified, firing randomly into the swarm while scrambling for cover. There was a scream, and she saw a man grab his leg as he fell to the ground. Then the swarm regrouped and left, disappearing over the horizon.

"Hold your fire," Krueger commanded. "Intrepid One, we need a medevac."

The dust had mostly settled. There was no sign of Vic or the hovercraft. The ATV sat idle in the distance, abandoned, its huge rubber tires covered in red dust. Gregor and Cain carried the injured man to the cargo hatch. As they passed, Megan noticed that the man had a tear in his survival suit just above his right knee. It was Ob. His exposed skin was already black with frostbite. Anya looked worried.

"Will he be all right?" she asked, switching her transceiver to speak to Anya privately.

"Yes," responded Anya. "Only the helmets are pressurized; the suits can tear without leaking oxygen. But we needed him. I don't know if I can do what I'm supposed to do without him." The hatch slid open, and Gregor and Cain disappeared inside the cargo bay with Ob and then returned a couple minutes later without him.

Megan approached Krueger and switched her transceiver's settings to private so that she could speak to him without being overheard. "I don't think we should worry about the lights, sir," she said. "I saw them on the *Argo,* and they tried to help me. I think they're just here to distract us."

"What about Ob?" answered Krueger. "They sure did a number on him."

"Maybe it was an accident. Maybe he tore his suit trying to get away from them."

"I hope you're right." Krueger surveyed his team from where he was standing. "At any rate, we can't seem to do anything about them." He clicked a switch on his transceiver and spoke to the group. "Proceed with the mission. Red Team, secure a vehicle and head to the mines. Blue Team, follow me."

While several members from Red Team searched the abandoned vehicles for any that worked, Krueger gathered his crew and they hiked to where Vic had left the ATV. In front of them towered the volcano. Its height was beyond anything Megan could have imagined—sheer cliffs, two kilometers high, topped with an immense dome-shaped protrusion of rock. Puffs of smoke billowed out of it. Standing in its shadow, she suddenly felt small and insignificant. Anya was beside her. She pushed the switch on her transceiver so that only Anya could hear her.

"Where did Vic go?"

"Can't say," answered Anya.

Or won't? thought Megan. She shifted her attention to the ATV that Vic had left behind. The turbulence caused by the hovercraft had nearly buried it in sand. They would have to dig it out.

"Watch every rock and hill," warned Krueger. "The ones who came out of the *Argo* will be getting desperate for oxygen soon, and they'll be weak. Tell them we'll give them air if they surrender their weapons. Then hit them with tranquilizers; otherwise, we'll have to kill them."

Megan's team pressed on until they reached the ATV. Hendrix pulled a shovel out of the back and began clearing out the sand. He was quickly joined by Wolfson and Krueger, and after about ten minutes, the ATV was ready to roll again.

"Where could that idiot have gone?" grumbled Krueger, dusting off the driver's seat. He sat and switched on the ignition. "Everybody in. We'll pick up extra oxygen and then head for the colony."

Glancing back at the landing site, Megan noticed a truck moving slowly away toward the mines that lay beneath the volcano, followed by another and then another. It seemed as though both teams were now on the move.

Chapter 35

Execution Orders

The order came in the middle of the night, when the doctor least expected it. Two short words: terminate project. It came directly from the top. The doctor knew what to do.

She left her post and hurried to the lab. An orderly handed her two vials of clear liquid, each labeled with a skull and crossbones. She took the vials to a freezer and pulled out two slices of pizza. Next, she poured the odorless liquid over each slice and warmed them in an oven. No one, least of all a child, would suspect that they were poisoned. She set them on a tray and pulled out her phone.

"It's a go," she snapped. "Park the van around back. Call me if you suspect anybody's watching you."

She placed two bottles of water on the tray and carefully

walked down a long hallway until she reached a metal door with a guard sitting beside it.

"Mealtime now?" inquired the guard, curious. "It's the middle of the night."

"Not exactly," replied the doctor. "We've been ordered to liquidate the assets."

"You mean get rid of the kids?"

"You know what I mean. Open the door."

The guard fumbled with his keys until he found the right one. Then he unlocked the door and pushed it open. Two frightened young boys stared back at them. The doctor stepped inside and placed the tray in front of them.

"Guard, close the door," she demanded. "And bring me a cart. That's an order."

Fifteen minutes later, the door opened, and the doctor stuck her head out.

"Did you bring the cart?" she asked. The guard nodded.

"All right. Help me load the bodies." Together, they dragged the two boys out of the cell and dumped them on the cart. Once loaded, they rolled it down the hall to a side exit where a sign read EMERGENCY EXIT ONLY. The guard pressed a button, and the doors opened, revealing a back alley. It was dark, and a van was parked just outside the doors. As they tossed the boys in the back of the van, one groaned and moved his arm.

"Doc!" exclaimed the guard. "This one's not dead!"

"That's impossible. Check his pulse."

"But, Doc," continued the guard as he looked closer at the boys. "I heard him. And I saw him move." He turned to look at the doctor and was startled to see her pointing a gun at him.

"What's going on?" he asked. "I thought—"

"You thought wrong," came the reply, and the doctor fired once at his chest, dropping him to the ground. She ran around to the front of the van and got in the driver's seat.

"You can open your eyes, boys," she said, starting the engine. "I'm getting you out of here."

As she pulled away, Jack and Spencer observed her closely. Her hair was pulled up, and they noticed a tattoo on the back of her neck. It was a pyramid with an eye above it.

"Who are you?" asked Spencer.

"I'm the one they sent to rescue you," replied the doctor. "Now hang on. We're going to be going pretty fast."

Chapter 36

Opportunity Awaits

There was only room for eight inside the ATV, so Megan had to stand on the runners, her duffel bag with the plasma rifle secured to the roof. Anya was sitting in a seat beside her, her medical pack resting on her lap. Krueger was driving. Hendrix, Wolfson, and a guy named Morales were also in front seats. Seated behind them were, Wick, Fletch, and a stocky female sergeant named Davis.

They drove cautiously over the bumpy rust-colored terrain, avoiding craters and ravines. As she studied the ravines, she imagined them full of water, as they must have been thousands or millions of years ago. She wondered what the planet looked like then. As the shadows grew longer and darker, the possibilities seemed endless.

The remaining sunlight soon faded, replaced by darkness. They drove even slower now, practically at a snail's pace, the ATV's spotlight lighting a narrow path in front of them.

Finally, they caught their first glimpse of the colony. Its translucent dome glowed faintly from small fires burning within, proof that there was still at least some oxygen inside. Yellow lights, powered by solar cells, shined dimly from the roofs of several of the buildings.

As they neared the colony, it began to take shape. The dome was much lower than Megan had imagined, perhaps no more than thirty meters at its highest point. The structures were mostly one story, although she was aware that there were multiple basement levels dug deep into the Martian soil for insulation against solar radiation and the extreme cold. Apart from the fires, the colony looked tranquil, as though its occupants were soundly asleep in their bunks.

They reached a gravel road that led the rest of the way to the colony and arrived at the main entrance a few minutes later. When they stopped, Megan jumped off the vehicle and approached the dome, touching her gloved hand to its smooth surface. The others gathered around, peering inside, while Krueger drew the ATV to a stop just a few meters short of a massive steel door.

"Look!" cried Anya, pointing to a strange object above them and to their left, clinging to the dome. She shined a light on it, and it stirred—a simple metal torso connected to eight mechanical legs. One of the legs twitched menacingly, and it crept forward slowly.

"The way it reacted to the light—it must have a built-in solar cell," remarked Wolfson. "Clever. That way it won't shut down if it can't find biomass."

Hendrix took aim with his pistol and prepared to squeeze off a round, but Wolfson raised a hand to stop him. "It's on the other side," he whispered. Hendrix lowered his weapon, and they all stared at it. This robot was different from the ones they had trained with—it was larger, and its movements seemed more natural, as though it were alive.

Krueger found an access panel and was attempting to open the massive door at the base of the dome. It was wide enough and tall enough to accommodate large trucks and hovercraft. "Give me a hand," he ordered. "Wick, Fletch—pry open the door. Get the crowbar."

While they worked, Megan noticed Wolfson pick up a small rust-colored rock. He studied it closely, turning it in his gloved hands and illuminating it with a fluorescent chem-light.

"Basalt," he said, turning toward Megan. "It's volcanic. Same stuff that makes up much of the ocean floor on Earth." He threw it side-armed at the mechanical spider on the other side of the dome. It struck the dome hard and fragmented into tiny pieces. The spider leaped from the dome onto the ground and quickly disappeared into the shadows. Krueger and the others looked up in alarm.

"Why did you do that?" demanded Krueger.

"I'm sorry, sir, I thought . . ."

"Did I tell you to think?" continued Krueger. "Don't do a thing unless I tell you!"

"Yes, sir," stammered Wolfson. "I'm sorry."

"The door won't budge, sir," interrupted Fletcher. "Any ideas?"

Krueger walked around to the other side of the ATV. "We're going to need a forklift. Okay, let's take a break and refill our O2 tanks. Wick and Fletch, you're on lookout. Hendrix, call mission control and have them get someone out here ASAP."

Megan scanned the inside of the dome using her thermal imager. She thought she detected movement on the roof of one of the concrete structures. The object was small and stealthy and seemed to be aware of their presence. "I see something," she called. "It's a spider. No, wait, there are two of them." She stared transfixed as the roof came alive with movement. "There's a whole bunch of them, sir. They're clustered together."

Krueger and Smithwick approached cautiously, guns ready, their eyes tracing an invisible line from Megan's outstretched finger to a concrete structure less than thirty meters away. As they watched it, a door flung open, and a man raced through the darkness toward them. He was wearing no protective gear, no oxygen tank, and had no weapons. He sprinted to the inside edge of the dome and began shouting, but they couldn't hear him. He took out a stick of chalk, fell to the ground, and began writing a message on his side of the dome.

"*Pleh*?" said Hendrix, looking perplexed. "What's that supposed to mean?"

"It says help," said Megan. "It's backward because it's on the other side."

Krueger pointed at the door and motioned that it wouldn't open. The man quickly sketched a circle on the ground and placed an X at one point along its circumference, pointing at Megan and the others with his free hand. He then traced a path around the circle to its western side and made another X. Something startled him, and he spun around. Megan noticed a small black metallic object creeping in the shadows. It stopped.

The man did not see it. He turned back to his work, drawing a map and scribbling words on the asphalt-covered ground. The robotic spider crept nearer and stopped again. Megan and the others began pounding on the dome to get his attention, but he couldn't hear them.

They're coming up through the tunnels, he wrote. The spider took a few more quick steps toward him and leaped.

"We've got to help him!" screamed Anya. Her eyes were wide with terror.

"Can we blast the door open?" asked Wolfson, frantic.

"No," snapped Krueger. "It'll only make it worse. Their air supply would go down to zero in no time."

While the spider clung onto the man's back, another jumped on his belly, while a third attacked his legs. Megan watched as his mouth formed a scream but could not hear him.

The man rolled on the ground, clutching at the spider on his stomach, while the one on his back scurried upward to the back of his neck. It retracted a thick jagged needle from its mandibles and shot it into the base of his skull. The man stiffened in pain and dragged himself to the edge of the dome. He placed a blood-stained hand against the inside of the dome and stared horror-stricken into Anya's eyes. They were only centimeters apart, but there was nothing she could do. Suddenly his face grew calm and he slumped to the ground, his cheek pressed against the black asphalt. His chest heaved one last breath, and he stopped moving, tiny streams of blood trickling from his wounds. More spiders emerged from the shadows and crept toward the bloody puddle forming around him.

"Now they'll feed on him," remarked Wolfson. "Harvesting biomass. That's how they recharge their batteries—well, that and by using the solar cells when the sun's out."

"I can't look," groaned Megan. She turned away and shut her eyes. When she finally opened them, she tried not to look at the carnage. Anya had collapsed to the ground and was shaking uncontrollably. Hendrix helped her up, placing a hand under each armpit and hoisting her to her feet. Although she was now standing, they could all clearly see the terror in her eyes.

"Are you going to be all right?" he asked.

Anya was shaking. "I don't know," she said. "It's worse than I thought it would be."

Megan was surprised by her reaction; back on the ship Anya had always been calm and in control. The thought of her losing it made her even more uneasy about what was in store for them.

Krueger was busy deciphering the man's hastily scribbled message. "*Survivors on sub-level 4,*" he read, "*find tunnel. Code 4-56-46-57-8. Need food, g—*" The rest, including the map, was obscured by the growing puddle of blood. Dozens of spiders were now crawling over the man's body, greedily devouring his blood through straw-like protrusions in their mandibles.

"Let's go," said Krueger. "We'll head around the dome counterclockwise until we see a tunnel. It might be camouflaged so stay alert."

Megan took a deep breath, remembering her dream and the prophecy. If she did manage to get inside the dome, what then? Would the spiders do to her what she had just seen them do to the man?

Hendrix lifted Anya into the ATV, and Megan climbed in behind her. That's when Smithwick noticed them.

"Look," she whispered, shining the spotlight around them. In every direction, the powdery red soil rose and fell in zigzagging lines coming straight for them. They were only several meters away and fast-approaching.

"Guys, we've got company."

Megan switched on her thermal imager and watched as the lines snaked toward them. Whatever it was, the heat signature wasn't human. *Spiders,* she thought. The soil briefly parted as three spindly metal limbs punctured the surface. Behind it, the ground remained pushed up in a line several meters long as a column of unseen robotic arachnids pushed their way forward. They were now within striking range.

"Spiders!" someone screamed. "Let's get out of here!"

"They've got us blocked," yelled Krueger. "Open fire!"

Megan snapped the duffel bag from the vehicle's roof, unzipped it, and pulled out the high-powered plasma rifle that Vic had left her. Spiders were emerging everywhere and had them surrounded. There were hundreds of them. She hurriedly strapped on the battery pack and switched off the safety.

Shots rang out from inside the ATV as the team began firing with reckless abandon, but most of their shots seemed to have little effect. Anya sat petrified, too frightened to move. The noise was deafening. Megan took aim and fired directly through the windshield at a large cluster of spiders in front of them. The explosion shook the ground, sending torrents of soil, rock, and robotic parts flying everywhere.

"Drive!" she screamed as a path opened in front of them.

Krueger hit the ignition and slammed his foot down on the accelerator before new spiders could fill the gap. Megan felt her body jerk backward as the ATV rocketed past the remaining spiders and disappeared into the darkness.

Chapter 37

Another Landing

Unknown to Megan, another ship had landed on Mars only moments earlier.

After a relatively uneventful voyage, the *Ares III* touched down in a region known as the Northern Lowlands, about a hundred kilometers north of Olympus Mons.

Harper had no recollection of the journey. After being sedated prior to lift-off, she had been put into a medically induced coma and monitored by the ship's medic, whose name was Aleksander.

During the three-month voyage, Aleksander and his cyborg assistant opened her skull twice to perform brain surgery. The first time, they added a microchip to the one that was already there and embedded a neural net into her skull. The second time, they removed a rapidly growing tumor that would have eventually killed her had they not done so.

Harper's eyes flickered briefly as she began to awaken. She tried to look around, but everything was blurry. She struggled to remember where she was. Memories of her escape with Wiley and her arrival at Space Innovations began coming back to her in small bits. Gradually, she became aware of two voices. One was friendly, yet authoritative; the other, precise and analytical.

"She's waking up, sir."

"How do her pupils look?"

"Healthy. Do you want me to administer adrenaline?"

"No. Let her wake up naturally. Make sure she doesn't fall off the table."

"Yes, sir."

Harper turned her head to the side and blinked several times until the image of a man gradually came into focus. He was seated on a stool and had dark, wavy hair. His white lab coat looked several sizes too big for him. As she stared, unable to speak, he picked up a tablet and scribbled something on it. A younger man with reddish-orange hair walked over and stood beside him, staring at her with the most inquisitive expression. He was tall and had blue eyes.

"Should we tell her about her condition?" asked the second man, still staring at her.

"Negative. We'll wait until she's lucid."

She could now make out glasses on the seated man's face and a stethoscope around his neck. *Am I in a hospital?* She blinked a few more times and took in her surroundings.

"Where am I?" she whispered weakly.

"You're on a ship called the *Ares III*," answered the man who was sitting. He didn't look up. "Do you remember getting on board?"

"No. I mean, yes. I think so." Memories began trickling

back, slowly at first and then faster. Australia. Space Innovations. Dave Bridges. Dr. Beaudet. Being stabbed with a hypodermic needle. "Who are you? What's happening?"

"I'm Aleksander, the ship's doctor. I've been taking care of you. This is my assistant, Lukas." The man who had been standing knelt and smiled. His face looked youthful, almost boyish, and he had the bluest eyes she had ever seen, like a pair of sky-blue marbles.

"Hi, I'm Shannon," Harper said, remembering the fake name she had used in Australia. She lifted her arm to shake hands with him but was amazed at how weak she felt. She didn't even notice when a third person, a blonde woman with glasses, entered the room and changed the bag attached to the IV in her other arm.

Aleksander put down his tablet and wheeled his chair over to her. "We know who you are, Harper, and that you work for the State Intelligence Service. How are you feeling?"

She sighed, too tired to care that they had figured out who she was. "Okay, I guess. Weak. My mouth is dry."

"Get her a glass of water, Lukas," continued the doctor. "You're on Mars, Harper. Can you believe it? And you know what? There's somebody here who's been waiting to see you for a very long time."

With Lukas's help, she sat up and swung her legs over the side of the table. The floor felt cold on the soles of her bare feet as she tried to stand, but she wobbled and nearly fell over. The doctor's assistant sat her back down immediately. She stared at the doctor, still trying to process what he had just said.

"We're there already? How is that possible?"

"We put you into a medically induced coma, Harper. Standard procedure. It was the easiest and safest way. We do the same thing with the livestock that we transport here."

Lukas handed her a glass of water. "We understand that you were born here. Do you have any memories?"

"No." She took a sip and let the fact that she was at this very moment on Mars sink in. "I was only eight or nine when I left. I forgot all that stuff long ago." She wondered if they could tell that she was lying.

"Well, here's your second chance."

"Harper." It was the blonde-haired woman with glasses. Harper recognized her as Dr. Beaudet, the one who had revealed herself earlier as the mysterious X who had written her the note. "You're suffering from muscle atrophy. You've been in a state of suspended animation for the past three months, and it's going to take time to get you back into shape. Until then, you'll be wearing an exo-skeleton for extra support. After you've eaten and had a chance to adjust, I'll help you put it on."

Harper stretched and took a few tentative steps with the doctor and his assistant holding her arms. Although her legs felt weary, her steps had a certain lightness to them due to the reduction in the gravitational pull. She tried to move faster, but her legs buckled beneath her, and the doctor carried her back to the table.

"Just wait till you strap on the exo suit," remarked Dr. Beaudet. "For now, though, let's get you something to eat and some warm clothes. We'll be leaving the ship tomor-row morning."

The doctor, Aleksander, and his assistant ran additional tests on her for the next couple of hours, assessing her reflexes and general health. Although she didn't know it, they also scanned her brain for memories—anything that might give them insight into her motives. Their orders had been to take her to Mars, but they still weren't sure if they could trust her.

Later that evening, she ate dinner. All around her, crew members were busily at work. She caught a glimpse of Windsor, the young woman she'd met just before lift-off, and realized that she, too, must have been in on the plot to lure her onto the ship and sedate her. Strangely, none of it seemed to matter now; Space Innovations had, after all, brought her to Mars, which had been her goal all along. Maybe they could still be friends. She felt herself relax as she shoveled a spoonful of broccoli into her mouth.

When the meal was finished, she walked to the women's quarters to change into some warmer clothes. Looking at herself in a mirror, she was surprised at how short her hair was—it was practically a crewcut. She ran her hands over her scalp, feeling the short bristly hair, and then turned around at the sound of approaching footsteps. It was Windsor.

"Hi," she said a little awkwardly.

"Hi," replied Windsor cheerfully. "It's good to see you again. Do you remember me?"

"Yeah, of course," said Harper. "I was hoping maybe we could start over. My real name is Harper."

"Pleased to meet you, Harper. Oh, and Windsor is my real name. I'd love to chat, but I have to make sure the vehicles are ready. The engines lock up if they don't have enough anti-freeze. Let's talk later."

"Sounds good," replied Harper, smiling as Windsor left. She was excited at the prospect of leaving the ship soon and had a lot of questions. It occurred to her that Megan might also be on Mars at this very moment, and she began to worry about her. Just then, Dr. Beaudet entered the room pushing a crate on wheels. She popped off the lid and pulled out something resembling a mechanical arm.

"This is an exoskeleton," she said abruptly. "The SIS uses them, so I'm assuming you know the drill." She untangled a few wires and extended the right arm to Harper.

"Do I have to lose the rest of my hair?"

"No. Aleksander operated on you while you were asleep and connected a neural net to your brain. You can control your exo remotely by thinking, as long as you're wearing it."

"You did what to my brain?" She glared at Beaudet and felt like killing her with a swift blow to the neck right then and there. "Who gave you that right?"

"What's done is done," replied the older woman, barely pausing. She pulled out another mechanical arm and placed it on the table. "You can either put it on and come with us or stay here. We'll be gone at least three days. If you choose to join us, you'll be glad you did."

Harper was speechless. *No time to be getting* angry, she told herself. *Must stay focused.* She needed to find Dr. Burke and Megan—the rest was secondary. Putting her anger aside, she attached the right arm of the exoskeleton to her own arm by tightening a series of clasps and locking them into place, and then started on the left. Beaudet reached to help, but Harper pushed her hand away.

"Don't touch me," she growled. "I can do it myself."

It took her nearly an hour to put on the entire exoskeleton. Her muscles were weak, and she had a hard time maneuvering the heavier pieces into place. Once she had it on though, she found that it followed her own movements fluidly, as though it were a natural extension of her body. It was strong, but flexible. As she moved around the room, she marveled at how powerful it made her feel.

The ship hummed with activity all day as the crew prepared to venture outside. Some moved supplies to the cargo bay, while others monitored computers and discussed mission details.

At one point, Harper thought she heard the unmistakable bleating of a goat and remembered what Aleksander had said about livestock aboard the ship. But why were they being awakened now? After all, it didn't make sense to wake them up just to kill them. She realized that there was a lot more going on than she could guess, and she was determined to find answers. Her life, and Megan's, might depend on it.

The next morning, Windsor joined her at breakfast. Harper was suspicious of the young woman's motives but put on a friendly face and tried her best to be pleasant.

"You're riding with me today," said Windsor.

"When do we leave?"

"Soon. I can't say exactly when, but you'll know when it's time."

"So, how about telling me where we're going?" Harper asked as she leaned forward and smiled hopefully. It was a technique that she often used in SIS interrogations to put a suspect at ease, but Windsor saw through it immediately.

"Sorry. No can do."

"Okay." Harper sighed as she held a cup of garrack to her nose and savored the rich aroma. "I'll go put on my exo suit again. I'd hate to be late."

Chapter 38

The Search

After a stretch of frenzied driving to elude the spiders, Krueger slowed the ATV when, at last, there was no sign of them.

They began searching for the entrance to the tunnel. Everybody was covered in red dust and had to brush it from their visors to see. The night sky was dark save for a scattering of brightly lit stars in the distance; Megan couldn't have even seen her own hands in front of her if it weren't for Wolfson's chem-light and the faint glow of fires inside the dome. Hendrix shined their vehicle's spotlight from side to side, searching for both the tunnel and spiders.

Anya was still shaking. The coolness she had displayed on the ship was long gone, replaced by sheer terror. Megan put an arm around her and tried to comfort her.

"I think it's going to be all right. Where's your pack?"

"I'm—I'm holding it in front of muh-me," Anya stammered. She then lowered her voice and switched her transceiver to Megan's private channel. "There—there's something I need to tell you in case I don't make it. It's about what's in this bag."

"Don't talk like that, Anya," whispered Megan. "You're going to make it. We both are." The ATV hit a bump, and the beam of Krueger's spotlight leaped upward suddenly.

"Can they hear us?" somebody asked in a hushed voice.

"Don't know," replied Krueger. "Probably. What do you think, Wolfson? You're the scientist."

"Geologist," interrupted Wolfson uneasily. Megan noticed his eyes darting about nervously behind his helmet's glass visor. "But if they're like most robots, they use thermal imaging, much like our night-vision gear. They see heat signatures, not three-dimensional objects. I don't think they can hear us."

Megan got an idea. "If they sense our body heat, maybe we can fool them. You know, cause them to get a false reading. Maybe a flare gun—"

"Our best bet is to kill 'em," interrupted Krueger impatiently. "Let's not play around with these things." He followed the spotlight with his eyes, searching for the tunnel, then turned and looked at Megan. He seemed annoyed. "Where did you get that?" he asked, nodding toward the plasma rifle.

She froze, unsure what to say. "It's a long story, sir, but Vic gave it to me a few days ago." She paused and looked away. "I was going to tell you eventually."

"Give it to one of the men," he ordered. "Just because

you hit something a little while ago doesn't mean you know how to use it."

She bristled with anger. Just when she had proven herself, when she had saved all their necks, someone was disparaging her once again. Memories came back of being forced to sit on the sidelines at school while the other kids played. Everyone had always underestimated her—even Harper. And now Krueger too. She shrugged and handed the weapon to Wolfson, but Hendrix intercepted it.

"I'll take that, Wolfie," he said, smirking. "I'm the shooter." He slung the weapon over his shoulder and adjusted his helmet. Wolfson grumbled but didn't object. Just at that moment, Krueger slowed the vehicle.

"There it is, right in front of us."

At first, Megan couldn't see it, but then it began to take shape. Lying flat on the ground and half covered by dust and stones were a pair of large metal doors on hinges. The vehicle stopped, and Krueger leaped off to take a closer look.

"There's an access panel," he announced. The rest of the team waited while he punched in the code. There was a loud click, and Krueger and Hendrix pulled one of the doors open. A dark cave appeared in front of them. *Just like in my dream*, thought Megan.

"Okay," said Krueger. "Switch to infrared viewing. Hendrix, you go first."

Chapter 39

On the Move

When it was time to exit the ship, Harper was standing next to Windsor, just inside the ship's enormous cargo doors. In front of them were Dr. Beaudet and Dave Bridges, who would be the expedition leaders, as well as Aleksander, Lukas, and several others she didn't recognize. Behind her, a team of animal handlers was corralling a small flock of sheep and goats into an airtight truck with tank treads over its wheels. Everyone except Lukas was wearing a thickly padded survival suit and oxygen tank, so she guessed he wouldn't be going with them. A few were also wearing exoskeletons, but not many.

Nobody would tell her where they were going, but she had a hunch that it was to see Dr. Burke. The voice inside her was speaking to her again, telling her that she was almost home.

A red light flashed, and a voice blared over the transponder. *"At this time, we request that everybody test their oxygen-delivery system."* She took a breath and gave a thumbs-up.

"Remember, the tanks only hold about a two-hour air supply. When the needle on your gauge hits yellow, attach the secondary hose to the vehicle's ventilation system for a refill."

"What vehicle?" asked Harper.

"They're outside waiting for us," answered Windsor. "You'll see."

There was a low rumble as the cargo bay's doors opened slowly. The light outside was dim, and they could feel a sudden drop in temperature. Outside, the ground was mostly flat and rocky, with a scattering of craters. Dr. Beaudet surveyed their surroundings.

"Looks okay," she announced. "Move to your assigned vehicles."

Harper followed Windsor out of the cargo bay and felt the crunch of the frozen Martian permafrost under her feet with each step.

The ground to one side of the ship appeared to have several large mounds of piled-up dirt. A man approached one of the piles and threw back a tarp that had been concealed by a thin layer of red dust. Underneath was a lightweight aluminum dune rider with wide tires and a glass-enclosed passenger compartment. He then repeated the process at each of the other mounds until a total of four vehicles was uncovered.

As the group began moving to the vehicles, Harper was surprised to see that Lukas was still with them. He wasn't wearing any protective gear at all. She followed Windsor to the third dune rider and strapped herself into the passenger seat.

"How's he doing that?" she asked, pointing to Lukas. "He should be dead, shouldn't he?"

"He's a cyborg," replied Windsor. "Doesn't need air. Radiation and extreme temperatures don't bother him either. Pretty awesome, huh?"

"I've never seen anything like that. How long has this technology been around?"

Windsor smiled as she switched on the ignition and pulled the vehicle to a stop behind Bridges and Beaudet. "Here's where you attach your secondary oxygen hose when you need a refill," she said, tapping a small opening in the console. "Don't forget—it's important."

"Unless you're a cyborg," muttered Harper.

One by one, the vehicles pulled away into the flat, desolate Martian landscape, slowly at first and then faster. In the distance they could see the volcano, Olympus Mons. Harper knew that just on the other side lay the colony where she and Megan had been born. She was surprised to notice smoke rising from its domed peak. *How had a volcano that had been dormant for over a million years suddenly become active?*

The livestock transport, which was slower and less nimble than the dune riders, trailed behind them so that they had to stop every so often to let it catch up. As Harper gazed into the distance, memories from her childhood began trickling back. Happy memories of Dr. Burke and of the younger children whom she considered her brothers and sisters. Memories of hiking to the volcano to search for caves. There were bad memories too—of the rebellion, her separation from Burke, and of being sent away to live on what was to her an alien planet, Earth.

"What are you thinking?" asked Windsor.

"Nothing," said Harper. "I know you can't tell me where we're going, but how long until we get there?"

"About twelve hours. We should get there before dark."

"Why didn't we just land closer to where we're going? It doesn't make sense to waste fuel and time driving so far."

"You'll see," answered Windsor. "Just be patient."

When they hit the dunes, Harper was amazed. They were every shade of red, pink, orange, and violet that she could imagine, and even the smallest ones were as tall as three-story buildings. Some soared to heights of a hundred meters or more.

Aleksander and Lukas sped up the face of one and became airborne as they blasted over the other side. Bridges made a sharp turn that caused his wheels to spray sand and then raced to the top of the tallest dune before slamming on the breaks.

"What do you think?" said Windsor. "Should we let her rip?" Harper gave a thumbs-up, and they carved a few donuts in the sand with their tires before jetting over the tops of some of the smaller dunes. Harper asked for a try, and they swapped seats for a while so she could drive. Finally, they were interrupted by the sound of Dr. Beaudet's voice over the transceiver.

> "That's enough, everybody. The livestock transport has caught up. Get back on course. We still have a long way to go."

As morning turned to afternoon and the sun rose high

in the Martian sky, monotony set in. Harper found herself staring out the window and wondering if Dr. Burke would be there when they arrived. Her inner voice had stopped talking to her, and she no longer felt like she had any answers. Her mind drifted off until eventually she fell asleep.

When she awoke, the vehicles had stopped. Bridges and Beaudet were outside their dune rider, squinting at a distant speck in the sky. Others scrambled to camouflage the vehicles with rust-colored tarps. As they scurried about, she noticed that their survival suits had morphed from white to a dull orange, as had her own.

"What is it?" she asked.

"Drone," remarked Windsor grimly.

"Whose?"

"We don't know. Not ours."

Harper got out and approached Bridges, who was tracking the object's movement with binoculars. A few flecks of sand swirled past them in the breeze.

"Whose drone?" she asked.

"That one belongs to your government," said Bridges. "The Commonwealth of American States. I can tell by the markings on its wings. They must have guessed we'd be coming."

"Has it spotted us?"

"Yes, I think so. That might pose a problem. Excuse me while I talk with Dr. Beaudet."

Chapter 40

Into the Tunnels

Hendrix was first into the tunnel, followed closely by Krueger, Megan, Anya, Wick, Fletch, Morales, Davis, and Wolfson. When the last one was inside, Wolfson closed the steel door behind them with a thud, and they heard a loud click as it locked. He tried to push it back open, but it wouldn't budge. There was a shriek, and Anya backed into Megan.

"Oh my God!" Anya exclaimed, still backing up. "Look!" On the ground in front of them lay a mangled, partially decomposed human corpse. Another lay nearby, its gloved hands still clutching a primitive shotgun.

"Get it together," hissed Krueger as he grabbed Anya by the shoulders and pinned her against a wall. "This is no way to behave when our lives are on the line." Then he called Megan over. "I need you to take care of this one," he said, nodding toward Anya. "She's going to get us all killed if she doesn't settle down. Talk some sense into her. Otherwise, we'll have to tie her up and leave her here."

"What do think happened?" asked Hendrix, nudging one of the corpses with his boot. "I mean, besides the obvious."

"Maybe they were trying to get out," suggested Fletch, "but they couldn't unlock the door."

"Like us," added Wolfson. Megan sensed by his voice that he, too, was on the verge of panic. Hendrix and some of the others had their weapons drawn and were scanning the area for spiders. Meanwhile, Krueger had knelt and was in the process of radioing the ship for backup.

"Come in, *Intrepid*. We need assistance," he said. On the other end there was only static. The layer of rock, dirt, and sand surrounding the tunnel was too thick, and Wolfson wondered aloud if perhaps the door was magnetized to prevent electronic communications getting through.

"How are we going to get out?" he asked. "There's no access panel on this side."

Krueger's gaze was fixed on the tunnel in front of them. "We don't," he said. "We're going in, not out. Follow me."

As the others moved ahead, Megan hugged Anya and took her hand. "It's going to be okay," she said. "We'll be fine if we stick together."

"M-M-Megan," said Anya, the name catching in her throat. She had switched her transceiver over to private again to avoid being overheard. "Re-remember when I said there was something I needed to t-t-tell you?" Her voice was shaking again. She hunched her shoulders forward to allow her pack to slide off her back and onto the ground. She unzipped it, revealing a transparent cylinder about thirty centimeters long and twenty centimeters in diameter. It was connected by hoses to an oxygen tank. Inside was something brown and furry.

"Is that . . ."

Anya nodded, her hands trembling as she turned the cylinder until it revealed the sleeping face of a small primate. Shem. Megan stared at her in disbelief.

"Are you crazy?"

"Shem's a v-v-vervet monkey," explained Anya nervously. "They're climbers. I'm su-supposed to get him inside the colony. There's a device with a switch at the top of the dome, on the inside. It's an EMP—electro-magnetic pulse weapon. Sh-shuts down anything electronic within a two-kilometer radius. We trained Shem in a dome the same size. He kno-knows how to do it." She was growing calmer now and her voice was less shaky. "If it works, it should knock out the spiders."

"Let me guess," said Megan. "Krueger doesn't know anything about this." Anya nodded. "This is crazy, Anya. I mean, look at him, your monkey's not even awake."

Anya pulled a syringe out from the bottom of the cylinder. "This is adrenaline. I put him in a sleep state to keep him quiet. Once you're inside the dome, give him the shot and he'll wake up. He'll take care of the rest—he's too fast for the spiders unless they swarm him in large numbers."

"Me?" gasped Megan. "You want me to give him the shot?"

"I need you to get him in there, Megan. I can't—I can't do it. I don't think I'm going to make it. Take him, please. There's also a crossbow. It has to be assembled. The arrow has a super-magnetic tip and is attached to a cable. If Shem doesn't make it, just aim for the top and shoot. Then climb up there and flip the switch yourself. It should hold."

Megan took a deep breath. It was obvious Anya wasn't

up to the task. Someone else would have to do it. Without answering, she took off her own pack and emptied its contents to make room for Shem and the small oxygen tank as well as the disassembled crossbow. Anya kept the medical kit and placed Megan's discarded gear in her own pack. They could hear Krueger and the others farther up the tunnel. Megan took her friend's hand again and began leading her toward the rest of the team. They walked slowly at first, but then faster as Anya seemed to partially regain her composure.

As they neared Krueger and the others, Megan heard a crunch and grimaced as something cold and sharp pierced her boot and penetrated the bottom of her foot. She bit her lip to keep from screaming—the pain was awful—and then dropped to the ground and grabbed her injured foot with both hands. Anya knelt beside her.

"What is it?"

"I stepped on something. It's gone through my boot. Get Krueger!"

"We need help," cried Anya. "Colonial Krueger, Megan's down."

Within seconds, both Hendrix and Krueger were by their side. "Let's have a look," said Krueger, holding her foot closer so he could see it. "It's gone all the way through. Are you doing all right, kid?"

"Yeah," gasped Megan. "My foot's numb. Do I have frostbite?"

"I don't—I don't think so," said Anya, her voice still shaky. "The foam insulation in your boot would have resealed itself. I'm more worried about infection. Does anybody have pliers?"

"If the boot resealed itself, how will we be able to pull it out?" grumbled Hendrix.

"It'll come out if someone pulls hard enough."

Hendrix pulled out a tool kit. After rummaging around for several seconds, he found a pair of pliers. Krueger took them from him and clamped them onto the end of a sliver of metal protruding from the bottom of her boot.

"Hold on," he said. "This is probably going to hurt."

Megan closed her eyes. She felt a tug, a flash of intense pain, and then relief.

"Got it!" said Krueger. "Looks like a spider part."

Megan sank back to the ground and relaxed, exhaling softly, but Krueger was already preparing to move out. "Hendrix, you stay with the ladies until they're ready to go, then join me in front." Within seconds, he was gone, disappearing into the cave's shadowy depths.

"Look at this," whispered Hendrix as he picked up the fragmented remains of a mechanical spider a couple meters away. "It's been blown to bits." Anya approached him nervously, as though she suspected it would suddenly spring to life. "Someone's been here—there's been a fight." He drew his pistol, the one that fired exploding rounds, and glanced around for more signs of trouble. "I'll bet that dude up there with the shotgun got it. I wonder how many more are down here."

"Take this," he said, handing her the plasma rifle. "You've earned it. Just don't fire on anything too close or you'll blow yourself up." He paused, looking farther up the tunnel and then back at her. "I'm really sorry you got dragged into this, and I want to make it right." Megan nodded and gripped the weapon tightly as he strapped the battery pack on her back.

Just then, Anya reached into a pocket and pulled out a handful of small gray spheres. "Neodymium magnets," she said, stuffing them into Megan's hand. "Really high powered. Stick one on anything electrical, like a spider, and it'll fry its circuits. I've got six. Take them."

Suddenly, they were interrupted by the sound of shouts and gunshots farther up the tunnel. Moments later, Krueger and Wolfson came hurtling toward them, running for their lives. Morales and Davis were right behind them.

"Spiders!" shouted Krueger. "Take up defensive positions. Fire at will!"

"Where's Wick?" yelled Wolfson. "And Fletch?"

"Don't know!" cried Krueger. He took aim with his plasma rifle and fired into a cluster of rapidly approaching spiders. The round exploded, sending debris everywhere.

More spiders raced toward them, some on the ground, others scurrying along the walls and ceiling. There was another barrage of gunfire followed by a second explosion. Through the deafening noise, Megan thought she heard a female voice call from farther up the tunnel.

A spider sprang from the ceiling, and she spun out of its way, falling down and kicking it with all her strength. Before it could attack again, she hurled one of the magnetic spheres at it, hitting it squarely on its metallic back. The spider spun around and stopped, motionless.

Gunfire continued at a relentless pace until the spiders finally stopped coming. When the smoke cleared, she noticed a figure kneeling beside her. It was Wolfson, his face pale and his body shaking. Anya was flat on the floor, immobilized by fear.

"Did we get 'em all?"

The voice was Krueger's. It sounded faint and muffled. He scanned the darkness with his thermal imager, searching for a green blip that would indicate more spiders. Megan caught another glimpse of the terror on

Wolfson's face and knew that she had no choice but to be brave.

"I don't know," said Hendrix. He was kicking something on the ground with his foot. "I hope so."

"Did you guys hear someone farther up the tunnel?" whispered Megan. "I think Wick might still be alive."

"No way," replied Krueger, shaking his head. "If they got her, she's dead by now. But we'll check it out to make sure."

"Sir," interrupted Hendrix. They could see by the glow of his chem-light that his foot was touching the remains of one of the spiders they had destroyed. Wires with frayed ends stuck out of a jagged hole in its side. It was motionless, its circuits fried.

"Don't touch it!" gasped Anya, backing away from it. Krueger came in for a closer look.

"They have a weakness," remarked Megan, her voice rising. "They must have a weakness. Otherwise, we couldn't have killed even one."

"Wolfson," said Krueger. "Get over here. You know something about robotics, don't you?" The geologist hesitated.

"I know a little . . . I studied robotics in college. Nothing much." He unfastened a small tool kit from his belt, but his hands were shaking so badly that he inadvertently spilled its contents onto the ground. The sound of metal tools hitting bare rock echoed through the tunnel.

"Shhh!" whispered Hendrix. "Get it together. Do you want to get us all killed?"

"Sorry. Hand me a screwdriver . . . no, wait a second." Wolfson ran his hands along the spider's broken shell. "I don't feel any screws. Give me the welding torch."

Hendrix handed him the torch, a metal cylinder with a tube protruding from the top. Wolfson took a deep breath to steady his hands and turned a valve counterclockwise. As the gas escaped, there was a flash and a brilliant blue flame leapt from the tube. He then laid the spider on the ground belly-up and used the flame to cut through its outer shell and remove its head. Once it was opened, he pulled gently on a wire coming out of its neck until a miniature circuit board and a few small components popped out and fell into his open hand.

"Interesting. It's just as I suspected," he said. "A thermal imager."

"So that means they read heat signatures," mused Krueger. Wolfson disconnected the wire from the motor and began probing its solar cell. "You know, Megan could be right. We might be able to fool these things."

"How?" asked Hendrix.

"We find something that masks our heat signature. A foil survival blanket might do the trick. There should be one in the first-aid kit. Anya . . ."

The frightened young woman hurriedly took off her pack and handed the medical kit to Krueger. Megan noticed that her hands were still trembling.

"I thought our suits already did that," muttered Hendrix. "You know, trap in heat."

Wolfson shrugged. "Yes, but a survival blanket does a better job. Not only does it trap in body heat, but it's also made of a highly reflective material that will scatter the spiders' infrared signals and confuse them. They shouldn't be able to detect a heat signature through it."

"Okay," said Krueger. "Wrap it around me, and I'll try to get inside the colony and radio for help. We don't have enough ammunition to kill every spider, and we're going to run out of oxygen pretty soon. We've got to keep moving."

"Sir," protested Hendrix. "Let me do it. We can't afford to lose you." Krueger ignored him and rummaged through the first-aid kit until he found a blanket made of thin reflective foil. It was too small to cover him. Hendrix reached for it, but Krueger shook his head. "It's no use. If it won't fit me, it won't fit you."

"Let me try," said Megan, stepping forward and grasping the foil blanket. "I'm the smallest."

"No," said Hendrix. "I won't let you do this, Megan."

Krueger intervened. "She's right, Hendrix. She's the only one it could possibly fit, and right now we're out of options." He turned to Megan. "Are you sure you can do this?" Again, her past flashed before her. Images of sitting on the sidelines, of not being taken seriously, of feeling inadequate. She thought of Shem, now tucked away in the pack on her shoulders, and how she needed to get him inside the dome. And the prophecy—she remembered the prophecy.

"Yes, sir. I can do this."

Hendrix wrapped the foil blanket around her, but it was still too small.

"Try taking off your exoskeleton," suggested Anya.

She did, and it fit, even with the pack on her shoulders. The foil was so thin that she could see through it, but there wasn't enough room inside to carry the plasma rifle. All she could manage were a few of the magnets Anya had given her and her slow-to-charge L-Stat gun. She knew that if the spiders swarmed her in large numbers, she wouldn't be able to stop them.

"It's too risky," muttered Hendrix, looking down and shaking his head. "One tear and you're toast. You'll never make it."

Megan smiled grimly. Without the exoskeleton, her

arms and legs felt noticeably heavier and weaker, but her courage gave her renewed strength. She turned to Krueger and spoke with as much confidence as she could muster. "Sir, with your permission, I'd like to see what's at the other end of this tunnel. I'm ready to go."

Chapter 41

Contact

Harper watched as the drone soared past them and disappeared into a patch of clouds. Once it was gone, Bridges and the others removed the camouflage tarps from the vehicles and resumed their journey.

As the minutes and hours ticked by, the sun dropped low in the sky, casting long shadows. The landscape became bleak and rocky again, and they had to watch out for craters. Suddenly, Bridges stopped his vehicle and signaled for everyone else to do the same. He got out and stood for a moment, squinting into the distance through binoculars. And that's when Harper saw it—a long trail of glowing blue and white lights speeding toward them, flying low over the horizon like a swarm of insects. They came in fast and silent. As she stood watching them, she could sense Windsor's growing anxiety.

The lights slowed when they reached them and changed from blue and white to green. They coiled themselves around Bridges and moved up and down his body before backing away. He motioned for everyone to exit their vehicles. Harper turned to Windsor.

"What are those things?"

"We call them Light Beings," replied Windsor. "They help us. Mostly."

"What are we supposed to do?"

"Stand outside. They need to inspect us."

"Inspect us?" Harper felt her blood pressure rising. "Why? What for?"

"No more questions. Just do it. You don't want to make them mad."

One by one, the lights circled each person, shimmering as they moved over them. They stayed on Lukas, the cyborg, the longest. When they reached Harper, they paused. Then they surrounded her and pulsed with a warmth unlike anything she had ever felt. She was no longer afraid. A voice spoke to her, and she realized that it was the same one she'd heard inside her head for years. But now it was louder, clearer, and coming from right in front of her.

Welcome home. I've been waiting for you a long time.

"Who are you?" stammered Harper. "What are you?"

The swarm pulled away slightly and coalesced into a glowing, slightly transparent figure with graying hair and dark eyes. It was a woman, or rather a holographic image of one. Tears were in her eyes.

"Dr. Burke?" gasped Harper, her eyes widening. "Mom?"

The woman nodded, a smile creeping across her luminescent face. Then she changed, becoming youthful, the same person as before but without wrinkles or graying hair. Her eyes sparkled.

Forgive me, Harper. You were dying and no one knew. There was a tumor. The only way to save you was to bring you here.

Dr. Burke reached as if to touch the glass of Harper's visor, but it passed clear through, and she could feel the warmth of her fingers as she gently brushed the stitches on the back of her head.

Aleksander and Lukas have taken good care of you.

"Taken care of me how?"

The tumor. It was lodged in your cerebral cortex. That is what was causing your migraines. If we had waited, it would have been too late. They removed it.

"Why did they put a chip in me?"

You've always had a chip. It's how I've remained close to you all these years, and it's how you've been able to communicate telepathically with the other children. The new one is just an update, to help you live here if you choose to stay.

"Stay?"
Suddenly everything began to make sense to her. The voices, Beaudet's note, getting hired to work on board the Ares.

You're the voice, she thought, as the truth sank in. The holograph—Burke—nodded.

"Are you real?" she asked. Again, the figure nodded.

As real as you, but I no longer have a physical body. I've become one with the cosmos and am now as you see me. There are billions of us throughout the universe, and we will never die. And now I'm asking you to join me.

Harper was speechless. She had been on Mars only a day and had already found Dr. Burke, or at least her essence. She'd been cured of a malignant tumor. And now she was being asked to stay. But she still had questions, like why was she trying to destroy the colony and how had she become a collection of swirling lights. Her head was spinning. The figure morphed again and became a teen-aged version of itself. It—she—sensed Harper's distress and spoke to her again.

Do not be afraid. Follow me. Your questions will be answered soon.

The figure then broke apart into thousands of tiny blue and white lights that merged with the rest of the swarm, and together they flew off in the direction from which they had come. Harper walked over to where Windsor was standing and shook her head in disbelief.

"You didn't tell me it was Dr. Burke."

"Burke?" Windsor raised an eyebrow apprehensively. "What makes you think that?"

"Because I just saw her with my own eyes, just like you and everybody else."

"All I saw was a cluster of lights," said Windsor, puzzled. "They swarmed around you just like they did everybody else, and now they're gone."

Harper sighed, unsure of what to believe. Could she have been hallucinating? She didn't think so, but she had to consider the possibility. The only way to find out for sure would be to continue following Bridges to where he was taking her.

Chapter 42

News Reporters, Conspirators, and Traitors

When Bellamy got off the phone, he was elated. "That was the former secretary of defense, William Blythe," he said, the cigar still in his mouth. "This is huge. He suspects this goes all the way to the White House, and he says he'll help us. When this story's out, I'll win the Pulitzer Prize for sure. I'll—I mean, *we'll*—be rich!"

Raven cast a sideways glance at Wiley, unsure if she should trust Bellamy, but he didn't look back. She found Bellamy disgusting—he was obviously more interested in fame and wealth than he was in finding justice for them. "If the president's involved, what's to stop him from getting rid of us?" she asked mockingly.

"Ha!" cackled the reporter, setting his cigar on an ash-tray. "I already thought of that, and we've got you covered. Blythe's sending over a car for you. He's going to put you up in a safe house a short distance from here. His own private staff. Nobody will know a thing."

"Thanks, but I'd rather look after myself."

"Come on, Raven," said Wiley. "You're not safe out there by yourself. They have too many agents looking for us." They argued for several minutes until Raven agreed to go to the safe house, but she made Bellamy give her his gun just in case.

"I want you back here tomorrow morning," grumbled Bellamy, sore at losing his gun but still optimistic. "Blythe's coming with you. I'll write up your story and get it to the editor in time for it to be published the following day. Just think, in two days we'll have the president and the director of the SIS squirming like they have ants in their pants!"

Meanwhile, back at SIS headquarters in Langley, Herrington had received disturbing news.

A search of the burned-down warehouse had revealed no bodies. Raven and whoever she was with had escaped. To make matters worse, Irons had called an hour later angry and demanding more money. He picked up his phone and dialed the president, who answered immediately.

"This is the president."

"Mr. President, the Mars mission has arrived. They've already sent a team to retrieve the resource stockpiles, and a small rescue party has arrived at the colony. No word of Burke's whereabouts yet."

"Burke will be there soon enough," replied the president. "I can feel it. And the girl, the one you sent, she's to be eliminated as soon as you find her. Let the spiders do it, or use the avatar if you have to. She's the last of those freaks people call the Wonder Kids, right?"

"Yes," lied Herrington. "I'm on it." He hung up, then dialed Irons.

"Get over here right away. I have your money. There's something else we need to discuss."

Chapter 43

Cloak of Invisibility

Megan adjusted the foil blanket so that it covered her completely. If it worked, it would reflect her body heat back to her, making her undetectable to the spiders. Even her head was covered, and the foil was so incredibly thin that she could see through it. Inside, she clutched a handful of the super-magnets Anya had given her.

Hendrix walked around her with a thermal imager and checked for escaping heat. "Looks good," he said. "As far as the spiders are concerned, you're invisible." There was a tinge of regret in his voice. Despite the way he had treated her for most of the trip, he now seemed genuinely worried for her.

"Wish me luck."

She started down the tunnel without looking back. It was dark, but her visor's night-vision technology enabled her to see everything clearly, albeit with a greenish glow. The foil blanket made a crinkling sound each time she took a step, and she hoped the spiders couldn't hear her. She wondered what would happen if Shem woke up early. *Could he escape from the cylinder?* If so, he'd suffocate or freeze to death in seconds.

Rounding a corner, she stumbled upon a cluster of spiders—perhaps as many as twenty—but they failed to notice her, even when she accidently stepped on one. As she crept past them, staying close to the wall, she stepped in a puddle of slick, viscous fluid, causing her foot to slide a little. She looked down. There lay Smithwick, dead, her protective suit torn open and blood oozing from open wounds on her throat. Several spiders were greedily consuming her blood.

"Wick's dead," she reported over her transceiver. "They got her."

She picked up her pace, encountering more spiders as she continued down the tunnel. There were hundreds of them—too many to count—but they, too, did not detect her presence.

As she neared the tunnel's end, she noticed a closed metal door, beneath which lay the fragmented remains of destroyed spiders and a badly decomposed human corpse. Reaching it, she stopped and listened for sounds coming from the other side but heard nothing. She banged on the door with her fist and shouted. "Is anybody in there?"

"Who's there?" replied a muffled voice.

"Rescue team," shouted Megan. "We're here to help you." She winced as yet another spider climbed over her. "I'm going back for the others. I'll be right back."

She started back toward Krueger, wishing she could

move faster. *If only I still had the exoskeleton,* she thought. She knew their oxygen would be gone soon, and speed was of the essence.

"Sir, I found a door at the end of the tunnel," Megan said over her transceiver. "There's someone in there—I heard them."

"Okay. Hold tight, Megan," replied Krueger. "We'll be right there."

She did not hold tight. As she made her way back up the tunnel, her foot came down on a spider, and as it moved her leg slipped out from under her. She fell and tried to remain perfectly still. The spider turned and moved haltingly toward her. That's when she noticed the tear in the foil blanket. The spider could sense her escaping body heat. They all could. Her mind racing, she flung a magnet at it and ran as fast as she could.

She wasn't fast enough. Without the exoskeleton, the best she could manage was a quick limp. At least a dozen spiders were now after her. She hurled the remaining magnets at them and screamed.

Hendrix heard the scream and ran to help. He felt a sudden stabbing sensation in one of his legs, but he ignored it and kept running. When he saw her, she was limping toward him with an army of spiders closing in for the kill.

Taking aim, he fired the plasma rifle, and the resulting explosion decimated half the spiders but also threw Megan to the ground. He then pulled out his pistol and fired one exploding round after another at the remaining spiders, taking aim at the ones closest to her. He felt another sharp pain in his leg and knew that the spiders were on him. He didn't care—all that mattered now was saving Megan.

"Get up!" he yelled as he fired his last round. "Run!"

He felt another flash of pain, this one in his neck. Two spiders were climbing up his body, and one had stabbed him with its thin metal feeding tube.

Krueger arrived and placed his pistol's muzzle directly on the spider and blew it to bits. Hendrix grew faint and fell to the ground. As Morales beat off the other spider with a flashlight, Hendrix remembered the pride he had felt when his uncle told him he could go on the mission. Herrington had been like a father to him, and he desperately sought his approval. He was now only vaguely aware of the gunshots and screaming around him and no longer felt any pain. Megan knelt by his side and held his hand.

"You saved my life," she said. Her eyes were filled with tears. "Thank you."

He tried to talk but couldn't. He was losing blood fast. He mouthed the words *I'm sorry* and then shut his eyes for the last time.

Megan squeezed Hendrix's hand and stared at Krueger, who was also bleeding.

"We need to get him out of here."

"It's too late. He's gone." Krueger picked up Hendrix's pistol, the one he had been so proud of, and handed it to Megan. "Take it. How far to the door?"

"Not far."

"Okay. Let's go!"

The rest was a blur. As they fought their way down the tunnel, they blasted away at the spiders, destroying dozens. Then Wolfson went down.

A moment later, Morales screamed and fell to the ground, followed by Davis. They were swiftly consumed by the spiders. The noise was deafening, and the smoke and flying debris made it difficult to see.

Finally, they reached the door and pounded on it. It opened, and a pair of hands pulled Megan inside, with Krueger and Anya tumbling in after her. Then the door slammed shut. There was another blast, and a spider that had gotten in behind them exploded into tiny pieces. Megan caught her breath and looked around her. A dozen strangers stared back.

Chapter 44

The Compound

After the swarm of lights departed, the Space Innovations team returned to their vehicles and continued their trek toward Olympus Mons.

An hour later, they abruptly turned east and drove for another two hours until the rim of a large crater came into view. The horizon appeared strangely close, and the vivid reds and oranges that had so characterized the landscape during the day disappeared in the lengthening shadows. The setting sun appeared small and faint, and Harper noticed a tiny moon rising in the west.

"That's Phobos," said Windsor, pointing at the moon. "It orbits Mars every seven and half hours, so you get to see it rise and set three times a day. There's another one called Deimos that rises in the east, but it's a lot farther away. We won't see it until tomorrow."

"Such unusual names."

"Mars was the Roman god of war," explained Windsor. "Phobos and Deimos were the horses that pulled his chariot. Kind of fitting, huh?"

The terrain turned from sand to rock, making the last leg of their journey uncomfortable. Harper was glad to be in one of the dune riders with their oversized inflated tires and shock absorbers—the trucks must have been intolerable. When at last they reached the crater's edge, they drove down a steep hill to the bottom. She gauged the crater to be approximately twenty meters deep and another hundred meters in diameter.

Bridges led the convoy of vehicles to a tunnel carved into the opposite slope, beside which stood a strongly built man with blond hair motioning them to come forward. She guessed that he was a cyborg because he wasn't wearing an oxygen tank or protective clothing. A pair of large steel doors slowly opened to allow them inside.

One by one, the vehicles entered, and the doors closed. Inside was a vast subterranean bunker with rock walls and rows of vehicles, including a pair of dust-covered hovercraft. On the other side were more doors.

"Atmospheric equalization," explained Windsor. "They'll pump in heat and oxygen until it matches the atmosphere inside the compound."

"The compound?" asked Harper.

"Our headquarters on Mars."

"Who's he?" Harper pointed at the blond man she had noticed just minutes before. He was talking with Bridges.

"His name's Vic. He kind of runs this place now."

"Cyborg?" inquired Harper.

"Only slightly. I can't tell you much more. Bridges will fill you in on the rest later."

It took an hour for the air inside the room to be adequately warmed and oxygenated. During that time, Harper remained in the vehicle with Windsor and studied her surroundings carefully.

The room had a concrete slab for a floor and resembled an enormous garage. The walls were natural rock, as the room had apparently been carved right into the side of the crater, and there were long rows of yellow lights overhead that cast an otherworldly glow. Half the room was taken up by parked vehicles and hovercraft, while the other half was dominated by an enormous generator and signs saying DANGER: HIGH VOLTAGE. A handful of workers darted around, refueling vehicles, and replenishing their air supply. She searched for signs of Dr. Burke but did not see her.

When he was finished talking with Vic, Bridges approached Harper's vehicle. He looked tired. After brushing dust off his thermal suit, he opened the door on Windsor's side.

"Windsor, will you please sit with Dr. Beaudet for a few minutes? I need to explain some things to Harper."

"Yes, sir," replied the young woman. She undid her safety harness and got out. Bridges sat down next to Harper.

"This is the compound," he announced, beaming. "This is where we do our work on Mars." He pressed a button on a small tablet, and a holographic image of the entire complex took shape above it.

"We're here," he said, pointing to a red dot on one of the larger rooms. "This is where we keep the vehicles and generate electricity. Robots transport the uranium—it's too dangerous for humans." He then motioned to a vast atrium on the other side of the doors. It was carved into the bedrock and was many stories deep.

"What you're going to see on the other side of those doors," he said, nodding at the pair of tall steel doors in front of them, "is nothing short of amazing. Dr. Burke began building it before the last rebellion. It's a virtual Noah's Ark, with plants and animals from all over Earth. The swarm of lights you saw this afternoon helped her—we call them Light Beings."

"A Noah's Ark . . . but why? Is the world going to end?"

"You've seen it, Harper. Pollution, wars, corruption—it's not going to last more than a couple more centuries. Mars is humanity's future, but we can't let the same governments that have ruined Earth destroy this place too. That's why our founder, Burke, kept it a secret, and it's why we're now defending it."

"You mean attacking the colony and killing everyone in it? Isn't that a bit extreme?"

"If you're talking about the spiders, I have nothing to do with that," said Bridges. "Some say Burke sent them and others say they were manufactured by your country, with your president's full knowledge. It sounds crazy, but maybe he wants to destroy the colony and start over without having to share it with other countries. He could certainly make himself very rich by selling the natural resources. Either way, it doesn't matter though."

"Why?"

"Because the volcano's about to erupt. The spiders, the colony—everything will be destroyed by the lava."

"But won't we die too?"

"That's where faith comes in," he continued. "Faith that He who created us will protect us. Just the fact that this place was built is nothing short of a miracle. And I have faith that we will be protected."

"Can you take me to see Dr. Burke?"

"I'm very sorry, Harper, but she's dead. We don't know

exactly what happened, but she died last year. Vic was with her when it happened—you'll meet him in a few minutes.

"Oh," sighed Harper. She wanted to ask just who it was then that she had seen when the Light Beings visited them, but she thought better of it and kept it to herself. "I'm sorry to hear that."

She exhaled a long breath, causing her helmet's visor to fog up. She noticed other people removing their helmets and took off hers.

Bridges smiled. "I know," he said. "It's a lot to take in. Take your time."

After a few more minutes, the steel doors opened, and they exited the vehicle and entered an elevator that took them down a shaft hundreds of meters deep. When it opened, she stepped out and stared in amazement at what she saw.

The atrium was immense—more than a thousand meters in diameter and three hundred meters high—it resembled an enormous birdcage with a domed ceiling. Inside was the largest garden she'd ever seen, a virtual forest of towering trees whose leaves and needles sparkled in the artificial sunlight. Below, the ground was scattered with bushes, grass, and wildflowers. There was a chorus of chirps, and she looked up to see a pair of bright yellow birds fluttering among the branches. A dragonfly landed on her arm and then flew off, its body flashing brightly as it caught the light. As she followed it with her eyes, she noticed scores of butterflies and hummingbirds flittering among the flowers like tiny jewels.

Windsor joined them, along with the blond man they had seen outside the compound. Harper noticed something strange about his face. It was his eyes. They didn't go with the rest of him. She was sure she had seen him before, but she couldn't remember where.

"Harper," said Windsor. "This is Vic. He's been running the compound for the past year." Harper put out her hand, but the man looked away. As he turned, she noticed a small tattoo of a pyramid and an eye on the back of his neck, just below his hairline.

"Look," said Windsor, pointing. Through a gap in the trees, they saw a flock of goats grazing on a patch of grass. Scurrying around them, a dozen or so chickens combed the ground for food. The air was thick with humidity, and she soon found herself wiping droplets of sweat from her forehead.

"How many different species do you have here?"

"Hundreds," said Windsor, beaming. "We're still nowhere near having all the species on Earth, but it's a start."

"But how is this even possible?" gasped Harper. "We're underground, aren't we?" She craned her neck to look up at the distant ceiling but had to squint. The light shining down from it was intense, nearly as bright as the sun, and she could feel the warmth of its rays on her skin.

"The Light Beings have created a substitute sun for us," said Vic, spreading his arms above him. "Behold!"

She closed one eye and covered the other with her hand, spreading her fingers just enough to see through a tiny opening between them. Still squinting, she saw it—a bright glowing orb hovering beneath the atrium's ceiling like a miniature sun. The entire luminous structure was made up of a cloud of swirling yellow and white lights that endlessly circled a bright core. Every few seconds, one would break free from the orb and shoot out over the trees, disappearing through the atrium's rock walls, while another shot in to replace it.

"Allow me to show you to your room," said Vic, interrupting her observations. "Follow me." Harper, Windsor, and Bridges walked behind him, down a narrow path cutting across the forest floor.

"You'll need to rest," he called back to them. "We have much to do tomorrow."

Chapter 45

The Safe House

When Wiley and Raven reached the safe house, they were relieved to find it air-conditioned and well-stocked with food. Located on the top floor of a sixty-story office building on the far side of town, it had taken them nearly an hour to reach it. A guard was posted outside the front door.

"Looks a little suspicious," observed Raven once they were inside. "The guard draws attention to us. I'd feel better if we didn't have one."

"Just go with it," said Wiley. "It's only for a couple days."

There was a knock, and the door opened. A man with a thick neck and gray eyes stepped in. He was wearing a blue navy uniform.

"I'm William Blythe. You must be Wiley and Raven. Do you not have last names?"

"No, sir," replied Wiley. "We—"

The man held up a hand, signaling for Wiley to be quiet, and walked across the room to a window where he pulled out his phone and quickly typed in a number. While he waited for someone to answer, he pulled the blinds closed.

"How long until they get here?" he asked curtly. There was a pause, and then he added, "Okay." He switched off the phone and turned back toward Wiley and Raven.

"Is someone else coming?" asked Raven, growing uncomfortable.

"They'll be here in a little while," snapped Blythe. "For now, why don't you tell me exactly what happened." He said the last part as a statement, not a question.

"Again?" asked Raven, rolling her eyes. "We just told that reporter everything."

"Young lady, I've fought in wars for this country. I was the secretary of defense until just a few weeks ago. I'm in a position to help you. If you don't want my help, there's the exit." Blythe pointed at the door for emphasis. He wasn't used to being defied and was clearly annoyed.

Wiley got in front of Raven and tried to calm her down. Meanwhile, Blythe took out his phone and prepared to make another call.

"Come on, Raven," said Wiley. "I don't want to stay in hiding the rest of my life. This is our chance."

Raven rolled her eyes again and sat down on the edge of a couch. "Okay," she said with a huff. "Where should we start?"

"At the beginning," said Blythe, putting away his phone. "I want to hear everything."

It was an hour later when they finished telling their

story. Blythe had listened intently, occasionally asking a question or stopping to take notes. Finally, he put down his tablet and stood up.

"This is good. This is very good. If my instincts are right—and they usually are—the president and his SIS director are behind this. I've had a bad feeling about them from the start." He paced the floor, then added, "All right. I'll help you. Here's what we're going to do."

Just then there was a knock on the door. Blythe unlocked it, and the guard stuck his head in partway and spoke.

"The package has arrived, sir."

"Well, okay—send them in."

Two identical young boys entered the room. Their heads were bandaged, and they looked tired and scared. Wiley smiled at them; Raven glared.

Chapter 46

The Survivors

As Megan lay on the floor, she noticed that only Krueger and Anya had made it in behind her. Krueger was bleeding badly. There were faces all around them staring down at them. Their eyes were bloodshot from stress and exhaustion, and they were all very thin. They weren't wearing helmets or protective gear. A woman pointed the barrel of a gun at her face.

"Who are you?" she asked. Her accent was clearly American. There was a low murmuring and the shuffling of feet, and then a bearded man held up his hand.

"Put the gun down, Jess," he demanded. "They wouldn't have risked their lives to come here just to kill us."

Megan sat up and removed her helmet. "We're the rescue team," she said faintly. "Or at least what remains of it." She moved to Anya and helped her take off her helmet. The young woman was shaking and couldn't speak.

Krueger tried to stand but fell.

"Anya," Megan said, looking her friend in the eye and gently shaking her. "Snap out of it. Krueger's bleeding. You're our medic, and you need to help him." She took the medical kit from Anya's pack and rummaged through it searching for bandages. There were murmurs around them, and one of the surviving colonists stooped and helped her.

"Are you guys it? The entire rescue team?"

"I'm afraid so," said Megan. "There were eight of us at the start, but—"

"Well, it looks like we're finished then," said the woman holding the gun. Megan noticed that it was an old shotgun, just like the one they found at the entrance of the tunnel. A few of the others had them as well.

"Those guns look ancient. Where did you get them?" he asked. Anya had partially regained her senses and was dressing the wound in his leg. Krueger grimaced slightly as she packed gauze into it.

"The warden favored low-tech weaponry," answered the bearded man. "Stuff that's simple and easy to fix if it breaks. Plus, the rounds are buckshot—more likely to wound than kill. Perfect for putting down a rebellion. Why kill a prisoner when you can just maim him? After the rebellion's over, you can still get work out of him."

"Are you guards or prisoners, then?" asked Krueger. A few of the people looked at each other nervously.

"Prisoners mostly," replied the man, and someone told him to shut up. "Well, at least I am. I won't speak for the others. Some of us are afraid that we won't be saved if—"

Suddenly, the ground began to rumble, and everyone covered their head with their arms. The shaking continued for several seconds, causing shards of concrete to fall from the ceiling, and then it stopped.

"What was that?" asked Megan.

"Tremor. The volcano's getting ready to blow."

"How is that possible? I thought it was extinct—unlikely to ever erupt again—that it hasn't been active in over a million years."

"Was extinct," snapped a voice from the corner. It was tinged with despair.

"The tremors started a couple months ago," said the man with the beard. His voice sounded husky and tired. "At first it was one every week or two; now it's more like once or twice a day."

"How much time do we have?"

"Don't know. Could be days or weeks. That is, if the spiders don't get us first."

"How much ammo do you have?" asked Krueger.

"A couple dozen rounds—not much. Maybe enough for one last fight."

"Our ship is a few kilometers away," said Krueger. "I can radio for reinforcements, but I'm not getting a signal down here. Where's the best place to get a signal?"

Several of the surviving colonists conferred among themselves, and then the woman with the gun answered. "The communications tower. It's above ground. You'll need to take the elevator or stairs, but there are a lot of spiders out there."

Megan looked around the room. It appeared to be a storage area, with lots of crates and barrels. There was a forklift in one corner. Several of the barrels were labeled DANGER: FIRE HAZARD, and there were two fire extinguishers nearby. The surviving colonists numbered only about twelve—seven men and five women. They looked hungry and worn-out. One took over caring for Krueger while he discussed the situation with a group that had gathered around him. Anya pulled Megan aside.

"Meh-Megan," she whispered, her hands and voice still shaking. "There's something else I need to tell you. I-I don't think Vic is who I thought he was. He-he's evil. He was l-lying to us the whole time."

"Oh," said Megan, remembering Vic's threat to kill everyone if she told on him. "What makes you think that?"

"W-when he recruited me, he said Dr. Burke had a plan to restore Mars' atmosphere. He was l-looking for volunteers to c-come to Mars so humanity could survive here once Earth was no longer able to support life. He-he showed us pictures of the prophecy and told us about a secret compound they had on Mars. I got to go there with Ob and Cassandra once. It was magnificent. We joined his secret society, the Order of the Pyramid, and pledged to huh-help him."

"Did you meet Dr. Burke?"

"No, but I sa-saw her once. Then Vic said she died in an accident. He said he was with her when it happened."

"Okay, Anya. But what makes you think he's evil?"

"The ki-kids on the ship. The ones you saw—they were in a st-state of deep sleep. Ob said that while he was doing a s-systems check for Vic, he caught a glimpse of some of Vic's notes. They mentioned a plan to infect them with a Mar-Martian virus and then return them to Earth, so they could spread it. Ob says that something like that could wipe out ninety-nine percent of the world's population. Megan, he doesn't want to j-just save Mars, he wants to destroy life on Earth. I just learned all this two days ago. Ob told me. I think he's just using us. The prophecy said you'd come, but once you've made it inside, what then? What's going to stop him from just killing us?"

The spiders, if they get us first, thought Megan. She didn't answer, but she put her arm around Anya and tried to calm her down.

"Anya," she said quietly. "I need you to be brave and come with me. I need you to help me with Shem. He knows you. If you stay down here, you'll probably die, but if you stick with me, there might be a chance."

"No!" screamed Anya. Several heads turned to look at them. "Are you crazy?" she whispered. "You're going to get me killed!"

Still grimacing from the pain of his wound, Krueger lumbered over to them. He was helped by one of the surviving prisoners. A few others followed, curious.

"Is there a problem here?" he asked, glaring at Anya. They could tell he was furious.

"No, sir," answered the young woman. "I-I-I ju-just was—"

"Shut up!" ordered Kruger. "If you don't get your act together, I'll throw you to the spiders myself." Anya gazed at him, petrified.

"Okay, everybody," he announced. "Here's the plan: Edwards, Lee, and Young are coming with me to the communications tower. We'll take the stairs." He glanced at the three standing around him. "Freeman, Harris, and Jang, you three are also going to the tower, but you're taking the elevator. I'm sending two teams in case one doesn't make it. Whoever gets to the tower will radio the ship and request immediate evacuation. For this to work, we need a diversion. While we go for the stairs and the elevator, the rest of you are going to open fire on the spiders and clear a path for us. Then stay here. We'll come back and get you as soon as help arrives."

The man with the beard spoke next. "Before he died,

one of the guards told me there's a switch somewhere around here that activates an EMP—an electro-magnetic pulse weapon. It sends out a signal that shuts down anything running on electricity, even if it's produced by solar or biomass. If we can find it, we can use it to stop the spiders."

"Sir," said Megan, looking at Krueger. "I think I know—"

"You're staying here, Megan," Krueger barked, interrupting her. "You're too slow without your exo suit. I really don't understand how you got on our team in the first place."

"But . . ." She was stung by his comment. How could he cast her aside after everything that had happened? Hadn't she proven herself?

"My decision is final," continued Krueger. He turned away and began inspecting the weapons with some of the others. Megan stood still, staring at a wall, trying to calm herself. She felt tears running down her cheeks. She noticed Anya crying in a corner and immediately wiped away her own tears. *I'm not going to be like that*, she thought. *I'm going to the dome whether they like it or not.* Her eyes went to the fire extinguishers, and she got an idea.

A few minutes later, Krueger called everyone together and distributed weapons. He ordered Megan to hand over Hendrix's cherished pistol and gave it to one of the men who would be going with him. She couldn't help but notice that Krueger kept her plasma rifle for himself.

She felt a tap on her shoulder. It was the woman named Agnes, the one who had pointed a gun at her earlier. She handed Megan a chocolate bar.

"For energy," she said, managing a grim smile. Then

she looked over to where Anya was sitting. "Maybe you can share it with your friend over there. Looks like she could use it."

Suddenly, Megan remembered what Herrington had told her about her parents. *Could they be here now?* She glanced around the room looking for someone with features like her own. Krueger looked anxious to start the mission, so she had to act fast.

"Did any of you have a child here fourteen years ago?" she called out loudly. At first no one answered, but then a man spoke up.

"I had a son. We called him Michael, but they took him away, and I heard they changed his name to Wiley. Of course, I never saw him. Is he . . . with you?"

"No, but I know him—he's one of my friends. I'm sure he would love to meet you."

She noticed that some of surviving inmates were glancing cautiously at one of the women. Her face looked weary and gaunt.

"I also had a child," answered the woman after an awkward pause. "A girl." She got up and approached Megan cautiously, cocking her head slightly to the side and taking a closer look at her.

"Do you know what happened to my child? Are you her?"

Chapter 47

Dr. Burke and the Atomizer

As Harper lay in her hammock that night, she could scarcely believe she was on Mars.

The chirping of crickets echoed throughout the vast underground cavern. It was nearly dark, and she marveled at the way the Light Beings had created the illusion of dusk. The birds had stopped singing, and the surrounding trees cast long shadows across the atrium's floor.

The lodge, constructed almost entirely of wood, blended in perfectly with its surroundings. Her room was small but cozy. It had a balcony and an open window with a view of the forest. Outside her door was a hallway and a narrow circular stairway. Her room was on the third floor, two doors down from Windsor.

Unable to sleep, she reflected on her childhood on Mars. Though she had always seemed distant and mysterious, Dr. Burke had been the closest thing to a mother she had ever known. There had been others too—a short, energetic man whose name eluded her but who had played games with the children, and a dark-haired woman named Maya who taught her how to read. But there was another—a jealous man—who seemed to resent her and the other children, especially when Burke was around. His name was Victor. He had an angry, violent side, and she had been afraid of him.

She recalled Vic, whom she'd seen earlier that day, and she wondered if he might be the Victor of her childhood. He had the same name and the right hair color. However, the Vic she'd met in the compound was larger and clearly not fully human. There was also something strange about his eyes, something disconcerting.

As she lay there, a single blue light materialized beside her, then another, and then another. Within seconds, there were dozens of them, and they began to change color— blue to green, green to red, red to blue. They hovered above her, an arm's length away. She tried to touch them, but each time they managed to flit just out of reach.

"Dr. Burke?" she whispered. "Mom?"

At first, the figure was indistinct, like a ghost or a shadow, but gradually it came into focus. It was Burke, an older version than the one she had seen earlier that day. Her hair was graying and there were wrinkles around her eyes. The voice inside Harper spoke.

When I first came to Mars, we discovered a network of tunnels running through the volcano. They were lava tubes, carved long ago by volcanic eruptions.

It was when I was in the tunnels that I met the lights—what some of us call Light Beings. They spoke to me as I now speak to you. They led me to a cave far from the colony where they showed me the prophecy. I will now show it to you to help you understand.

"Where is it?"

It's here, but it's secret. Victor and I are the only ones who know how to find it. The Light Beings guard it, but they'll let you in. They've been expecting you. We all have. Follow me.

Dr. Burke's image broke apart and reformed as a cloud of swirling lights. The lights turned a dark gray and grew dim. Harper followed them out of her room and down the steps, walking as quietly as she could. She followed them through the forest until they reached the atrium's inner edge, a wall of solid rock. The lights landed on it and were joined by others.

You may enter.

"Where? All I see is rock."

Harper watched as the lights passed straight through the rock wall. She reached out to touch it. Rather than feeling stone, her hand passed right through. She walked through it and found herself in a cave. The lights were waiting for her. They had grown brighter, illuminating her way. It was cold and quiet. They led her deep inside through a series of narrow, twisting passageways and then stopped. The figure of Dr. Burke reformed in front of her.

Here it is. The prophecy.

As she glanced around her, she noticed that the walls were covered in brightly colored drawings and writing. They were on both sides and went on as far as she could see.
"Who made this?"

The Light Beings. They came here millions of years ago, before the first Martians. The prophecy begins with them. They say the early Martians looked a lot like us, and in the beginning, Mars looked a lot like Earth.

Harper noticed forests and rivers in the row of drawings closest to her. There were also strange animals that looked like nothing she had ever seen, and there were people too. Amid the drawings were several gaps, as though someone had erased parts of it.
"Why are some parts erased?"

The prophecy is more like a timeline of possible events. Where there's a gap, it means that what was described there didn't happen. The Light Beings remove those from the record.

"So, the prophecy isn't always right?"

Not always. Sometimes people exert free will and change its direction slightly, but the timeline inevitably corrects itself and gets back on track. The future never changes much.

Harper followed the pictures on the cave walls and learned of the first Martians, the civilization they built, and how it declined. She saw scenes of war, plague, and Mars's transformation into a barren wasteland. Moving farther into the cave, she saw pictures of the Light Beings and of the Martians' migration to Earth and the construction of mighty pyramids in Egypt. There was a long stretch of inactivity on Mars, and then humans arrived from Earth and established a colony.

Keep going. The part you need to see is farther up.

A speck of blue light drifted toward a section of the wall with a picture of a girl inside a translucent dome. *Megan*, she thought. *That must be Megan.* There was someone with her, and a small animal with a tail. The volcano was erupting behind them.

Then the light settled on a panel earlier in the sequence. It showed a man excavating the frozen remains of people who had died long ago. He was taking something out of them. Another panel showed him injecting something into living people. The rest was erased.

That's Victor.

"The same one I knew when I was a child?"

Yes, and you saw him again today, although he calls himself Vic now. Victor is one of the last survivors of the Martian race. He grew up on Earth, as did hundreds of generations of his ancestors. They left Mars long ago following a plague that killed all but a few of them. Victor came to Mars to work in the colony when I did. We had no idea who he was. While we were working together, he fell in love with me. He revealed his secret and told me about the prophecy, which he had seen in dreams. He spoke of a girl who would be born here, a girl with a damaged leg and her own dark secret. Mars's fate would lay in her hands.

He told me he loved me, but I didn't love him. He became angry and violent. After you were born and I took you in, he grew jealous. That's when I noticed the Light Beings. They followed him when nobody else was around. I asked him what they were, but he wouldn't say. Then one night they appeared to me. They showed me the prophecy. They said that Earth was doomed and that they were building a place where humans and animals might survive. Victor was helping them, but they knew he would betray them.

"Why would he want to betray them?"

Victor blames humans, and especially me, for all his problems. He wants revenge. He found the frozen remains of ancient Martians who perished in the plague, and he extracted remnants of the virus from them. He's experimented with a weakened strand of the virus, but now he's in the process of fully infecting three young humans who he will send back to Earth to destroy humanity. In doing so, he will have destroyed everyone I ever cared about or loved. Then he will return to Earth and rule over the survivors, if there are any, because he's given up on Mars too. Now that you're here, and Megan's here, he will also try to kill you. But we won't let him.

Harper glanced at the picture of Victor and the three young humans again. "How can he breathe outside without an oxygen tank? Is he a cyborg?"

Victor has a genetic adaptation that allows him to breathe the air here. He can also survive the extreme cold for short periods. It's a Martian adaptation. Before they left, they were acclimatizing to life on Mars. He has also had microchips implanted in his muscles to improve functioning. I installed them myself when we were still friends.

The blue light moved to the other side of the wall where it appeared that some of the images had been crossed out or erased. Then it arrived at a series of pictures that showed the Mars of the future—one with trees, forests, rivers, and oceans. There was a city without a dome over it, and the people weren't wearing protective helmets or oxygen tanks.

"Why are the pictures before this one erased? I mean, it's all in the future, so how can the Light Beings know what won't happen?"

I destroyed them so Victor couldn't see them. One foretells his death. If he saw it, he would try to use free will to change the outcome. But as you can see, everything leads to a single outcome: Mars will be reborn as a life-sustaining planet. My job is to help the prophecy come true in the best way possible. That's why I brought you here.

"And fate brought Megan?"

Yes. But we can still help her. Come with me. There's one more thing you need to see.

Dr. Burke's transparent image shimmered and disintegrated once again into tiny specks of light that joined with the Light Beings. The lights led Harper out of the cave and back into the atrium's underground forest. They followed a stream until they reached a waterfall, whereupon the specks of light vanished and reappeared on the other side. Harper darted through the wall of water and found herself in a narrow rock-walled room on the other side. She was half soaked. In front of her was a bronze-colored capsule large enough for several people to fit inside. Beside it lay three unconscious teenagers. Wires connected their bodies to a nearby machine.

"Who are they?" asked Harper, walking over to them. The lights reassembled into human form.

Victor's latest experiment. They're the ones you saw in the prophecy. He will be infecting them with the super virus any day now.

"What's that?" She pointed at the capsule. There was a door on one side that was partially torn off. Inside were seats surrounded by wires and glass tubes. The tubes were shattered, and the wires looked as though they had been ripped out.

The Atomizer. It's how I was able to shed my physical body. Electricity tears you apart, atom by atom. Once you've been broken down into individual atoms, you reform as complex particles.

"Does it hurt?"

The pain is irrelevant. Once you're in that state, you can travel to other planets, galaxies, and parallel universes in the blink of an eye. You can travel into the past and future. After each experience, I'd return to the Atomizer and be made whole again.

Then one day, Victor found it. Knowing I was inside, he took his revenge. He destroyed the machine, preventing me from returning to my physical body. Without a body, I can't rebuild it, but it doesn't matter. I can now go almost everywhere, and I've learned many of the secrets of the universe. I watched you grow up and helped you when I could. And I'll never die.

And now here we are. The volcano's about to erupt and the colony is under attack. If the spiders don't destroy it, the lava flow will. Other volcanoes will also erupt, sending vast quantities of carbon dioxide into the atmosphere. As the atmosphere thickens, it will trap in solar radiation and warm the planet. We'll build factories and introduce oxygen-producing algae. The permafrost and ice caps will evaporate, creating rain that will fill the rivers and oceans. The air will become breathable, and life outside will be possible again.

"How long will it take?"

A thousand years. But if you stay and become like me, you'll live to see it all.

Harper closed her eyes and tried to imagine this future. She wasn't sure about losing her body, but the idea of living for a thousand years and surviving to see a restored Mars enthralled her. While she pondered the option, Dr. Burke's spectral image came closer.

But first I need you to do something for me. Kill Victor.

Harper gasped. "But why me? Why can't you—"

I can't. The rules forbid it. Only you or Megan can, and right now Megan is in a lot of danger. There's a knife under the floorboard below your hammock. Stab him in the heart while he's asleep. Do it tonight.

Before Harper could ask another question, Burke dissolved into a cloud of swirling lights once again and was gone. She felt a chill come over her. Reluctantly, she made her way back to her room, all the while wondering if she could carry out the bloody deed.

Chapter 48

Deus Ex Machina

Megan was speechless. She had always half suspected that Raven was right, that their parents had died
years before. As she stared at the woman, she began to see
parts of herself in her—the chin, the nose, the eyes. She
took a step back.

"I'm Megan. I'm fourteen. Do you really think I'm
your child?"

The woman threw her arms around Megan. Tears were
streaming down her cheeks. "I'm sure of it," she cried,
hugging her tightly. "You were the only child born that
year. I never wanted to give you up. They took you away
from me."

"Is my father alive?"

"No, honey. They broke him. They broke him after the
rebellion." She let go of Megan and stared into her eyes.

"My name is Abigail. I was born in Denver." Then she laughed.

As they embraced again, Megan momentarily forgot about Krueger's stinging remark and the danger that lurked on the other side of the sealed door. However, the reunion was short-lived.

Krueger announced that he and his new team were going in. Everybody else was to shoot at the spiders and clear a path for them. They had five minutes to check their weapons and get into position.

She took off her pack and handed it to Abigail.

"Don't say a word—there's something I have to do." Then she turned to Anya, who had been watching her and who appeared calmer than before. "Anya, come here."

Megan unzipped the pack and pulled out the cylinder containing Shem. She pried off its top, revealing a small furry head with closed eyes. She slid the sleeping primate the rest of the way out of the cylinder. Abigail watched, bewildered. She removed a syringe, stuck it in Shem's thigh, and pushed down on the plunger.

"Adrenaline," she said, as much to herself as to anyone else. "To wake him up." The monkey stirred immediately, blinking his eyes and flexing his tiny muscles spasmodically. His eyes followed Megan's every move as she slid him back into the clear plastic tube and then placed it back inside her pack. Anya was now beside her.

"Anya," she whispered, "I'm going in whether Krueger likes it or not, and I need you to come with me." The young woman's eyes were wide with fear, but she didn't protest. "We'll give them a head start and then follow them up. I'll take care of Shem, but I need you to assemble the crossbow and shoot it. Besides, I have an idea." Her eyes flashed to the fire extinguishers. "The spiders have sensors, right?

Well, let's spray them with foam and cover those sensors so they can't see anything. It might also make it hard for them to get traction."

She grabbed one of the extinguishers and clipped it to her belt and then kissed Abigail on the cheek. "I'll be back."

As she moved into position behind the door, a man handed her one of the shotguns. "It's loaded," he said. "Eight shots."

"How well do these work on the spiders?" she asked.

"Not well. Mostly just slows 'em down a little."

"I don't want it then," she said, handing it back. She unclipped the fire extinguisher and held it close.

There was a low rumble, and the ground shook again causing a pair of crates to tumble off a shelf and crash onto the floor. The tremor opened a crack in the ceiling, showering all inside with dust and stone-sized fragments of brick and mortar.

"Come on, let's get this show on the road!" roared Krueger.

He and the others who would be going upstairs stood just inside the closed door. Each person clutched their weapon nervously. Megan was behind them. She noticed Anya picking up one of the remaining fire extinguishers.

Krueger unbolted the door, pushing it open just enough to get a peek at the hallway. To the right lay two corpses, a man and a woman, but no spiders. The left was clear. He could see the entrance to the freight elevator, its doors spattered with dry blood.

"All clear."

The door burst open, and Krueger and his team hurried toward the stairwell on the right, making sure to avoid stepping on the pair of badly decomposed corpses on the floor. The other team sprinted toward the freight elevator on the left. Another tremor struck and they froze, fearing the worst, but the corridor remained intact. When the shaking stopped, Megan followed them out, Anya trailing close behind.

Krueger reached the stairwell doors and froze. There was blood under it, and he could hear strange ticking sounds coming from the other side. Before he could stop him, another man pushed a button, and the doors hissed open. The stairwell was teaming with spiders—hundreds of them—and the bodies of dead prisoners littered the stairs. Krueger and his team opened fire and retreated down the corridor, but for the man who opened the door, it was too late. The spiders were already on him, tearing his flesh with their mandibles.

Krueger and two other men sprinted past Megan and Anya as they raced for the elevator. As the spiders closed in, others fired at them from behind her with shotguns while Megan pulled out the fire extinguisher and sprayed them with foam. Anya, seeing its effectiveness, began using hers too. It worked, at least momentarily. The spiders slipped and floundered about as they struggled for traction, a few even flipping over, their spindly mechanical legs helplessly clawing at the air. Some froze as their sensors were covered in foam, but hundreds more were right behind them.

She hurried to get away from them. Anya was in front of her, a step or two ahead. When they reached the storage room that they had come out of, somebody inside slammed the door shut and locked it. At the far end of the corridor, the elevator's door was still wide open, and Krueger and his surviving team members were already inside.

Don't close, she thought, screaming the words in her mind and knowing it was just a matter of time before the spiders would be upon her. *Don't close, don't close, don't close.*

Anya had raced ahead and was now also in the elevator, and she shouted for Megan to hurry. She struggled forward as fast as she could, but it was too late—the door closed with an ominous thud. There was no way out. She spun around to face the spiders, most of which had regained their footing as the foam spread out. *This is it,* she thought. *This is where I meet my end.*

Before she could even scream, a panel on the wall opposite her hissed open, and something resembling a man stepped out. Its face was only partially human, with a small nose and deeply set eyes that glowed, and it moved with robotic precision. Suddenly, the spiders stopped moving. She raised the now-empty fire extinguisher and prepared to throw it, but the mysterious manlike creature stopped her.

"Come with me," it said. "I'll help you."

Chapter 49

Double-Cross

When Irons burst through the door of Herrington's office, his clothes were scorched from the warehouse fire and his hair was singed. A pair of guards stumbled in behind him, their weapons drawn, but Herrington ordered them to close the door and stand outside. He pushed a button that locked the door.

He had Irons exactly where he wanted him, and he didn't want witnesses. As he leaned back in his chair and pretended to relax, he placed his right index finger on the trigger of a small handgun concealed behind his desk.

"Have a seat, Mr. Irons," he said heartily. "It's always a pleasure to see you!" He studied the man's charred face indifferently and nodded toward a box of cigars. "Care for a smoke? Or have you had enough of that today?"

Irons scowled at the joke and remained standing. He pointed a finger at Herrington's face and shook it angrily.

"I've come for my money," he snarled. "And I want double what I agreed to."

"And if I don't pay you," asked Herrington coolly, "what then?"

"I'll tell everybody about your little extracurricular activities involving those kids."

Herrington scowled and lowered his voice. "Then I really don't see much reason to keep you alive."

Irons took a step back in surprise as Herrington drew the gun and pointed it at him. A silencer was attached to its muzzle.

"But we can still work out a—"

Herrington fired once, and the bullet pierced Iron's throat. The man fell to the floor clutching his neck and gasping for breath. He stood and fired two more rounds into the dying man, then knelt beside him to check for a pulse.

"You unbelievable moron," he scoffed. "To think you could come into my office and—"

Suddenly, he felt a flash of pain and fell over backward clutching his stomach. In his dying gasp, Irons had stabbed him with a knife that he had hidden inside his shirt. As Herrington lay on his back writhing in pain, he wondered how this man—this complete and total moron—had managed to sneak a weapon past security.

The guards, alerted by the commotion, kicked in the door and stormed the room with guns drawn. One ran over to Herrington and tried to stop the bleeding, while the other put an extra bullet in Irons to finish him off.

"Call an ambulance," the guard yelled to his partner.

"No," gasped Herrington, blood trickling from his

mouth. "There isn't time for that. Help me get to the basement. There's something—" He winced in agony before trying again. "There's something I need to do first."

Everybody at SIS headquarters knew that to cross Herrington could spell the end of your career. Though the guards were uneasy about his odd request, they knew that they had no choice but to comply. They picked him up and carried him to the elevator, which they took down three levels to the basement. When it stopped, Herrington pointed to a concealed panel near the ceiling.

"Push there," he said.

One of the guards did so, and it sprang open, revealing a hidden switch.

"Now flick the switch."

The elevator plunged down one more story and the doors slid open, revealing the secret room with white walls. In the center was the large black chair, above which hung a helmet connected to a supercomputer. The room was strangely cold and quiet.

"Help me into my chair," said Herrington, grimacing. "And get a bandage on this wound. There's a stack over there." He pointed to a table on which lay a tray of surgical instruments. They placed him on the chair and bandaged his wound, barely noticing as he pulled back a flap of synthetic hair, uncovering a port in his skull.

"Now get me a glass of water."

He pointed to a small refrigerator in the corner. While one of the guards carried out his request, he pulled the helmet on and stiffened in agony as it thrust a bundle of wires through the port and into his brain. Once the wires were in place, a robotic arm positioned a pair of virtual reality goggles over his forehead so that all he had to do was pull them down when he was ready.

"What is this place?" asked the guard standing beside him. "What are you doing?"

Herrington drank the glass of water, his head throbbing with pain.

"Serving my country," he growled. "Lock the door."

Without hesitation, the guard crossed the room and bolted the door.

"Now hand me your gun."

The guards looked at each other nervously. The one closest to him handed over his weapon, fumbling to get it out of his holster before placing it in Herrington's hand. The director took a deep breath and then shot both men in quick succession. They fell to the floor, where they lay motionless.

"Sorry, boys," he said, closing his eyes. "You saw too much. It just wasn't your day."

He turned a dial that switched on the avatar. Gradually, the sensations of his injured body were replaced by a new feeling, one of strength and vitality. He opened his eyes and glanced around the room where the avatar awaited his commands. He thought about wiggling his fingers and looked down to see the avatar's hand move accordingly. Then he willed it to walk to a door and open it.

With each step, the mechanical body felt more like his own. He followed a narrow passage upward until it ended at a cleverly disguised panel, then stopped and listened. Someone on the other side screamed. The panel slid open, and he stepped out. He had made it just in time.

"Come with me," he said to a terrified girl who was backing away from an onslaught of approaching spiders. "I'll help you."

Chapter 50

The Deal

When she returned to her room, Harper pried up the floorboards under her hammock and found the knife Burke had said would be there. Its blade, serrated on one side, was just long enough to puncture a man's chest and impale his still-beating heart. She felt its leather grip and rubbed her fingers nervously along the blade, feeling its sharpness. Her mind was made up; she would kill Victor and stay on Mars with Dr. Burke. Still, she shuttered at the idea of thrusting a knife through his heart and wished she could use a gun instead. She fought to steady her nerves.

You can do it, she thought.

Gripping the knife tightly, she snuck out the door and down the hallway to the room that was Victor's. The air was thick with humidity, and the sound of crickets chirping masked the creaking of the floorboards as she walked stealthily across them. When she reached his door, she was surprised to find it ajar; her lock-picking skills would not be needed. In front of her lay Victor, asleep on his hammock. As she crept forward, she noticed several glowing blue specks darting in and out of the darkened room like miniature fireflies.

When at last she reached the edge of the hammock, she raised the knife above her head, ready to strike. Victor's chest rose and fell calmly with each breath as though taunting her to strike. He was snoring softly. Killing him this way seemed cowardly, dishonorable. It reminded her of the Shakespearean play in which Macbeth, at his wife's urging, murdered the king in his sleep. The guilt had driven Lady Macbeth insane. Would she too be haunted by the deed?

I'm not the villain, she thought, focusing on the task at hand. *He is. Just do it.*

Before she could strike, a single glowing speck materialized on Victor's chest, and then another and another. He opened his eyes and gazed peacefully up at her. Losing her nerve, she brought the blade down and held it to his throat.

"Don't make a move," she whispered.

"Go ahead," he said in a low voice. "I deserve it." More glowing specks landed on him. They began pulsating and changing from blue to green to red. As she held the knife to his throat, he closed his eyes again and relaxed.

"You *want* me to kill you?"

"No," he whispered. "But if you let me live, I'll take you to Megan. I know where she is. You—I mean we—can save her."

"Why would you do that for me?" She pressed the blade harder into his throat. A small stream of blood trickled out.

"Megan's gone to the colony," he said hoarsely. "She won't survive. Let me help her. I have a vehicle and special equipment."

"And what about the ones you're infecting with the virus?"

"What virus?" he gasped, the knife still firmly pressed against his throat. "I'm saving their lives. Their families begged me to take them. Each one is dying from something that's easily treatable here, and when they're cured, they'll become pioneers, like us." He swallowed involuntarily while struggling for another breath and then continued. "Someone's been telling you lies."

"And Dr. Burke?" asked Harper.

A troubled expression crossed his face. "I was in love with her once, but she rejected me. I was angry, so I destroyed the Atomizer while she was in it. But we can bring her back. Let me make it up to her and win her back. I'll help you save Megan. She's alive—I can feel it—but there isn't much time."

"How much time?" asked Harper, pulling the knife away slightly from his throat.

"I don't know. Maybe days. Maybe hours."

Something about his tone was believable, but she remembered the prophecy and Dr. Burke's warning. Still, she wouldn't kill him. Not yet. She needed his help to reach Megan in time to save her. As she slipped the knife under her belt, another tremor shook the atrium, this one more powerful than the last, and she stumbled. The crickets became silent, replaced by the sounds of people taking cover.

"Okay. Agreed."

Although she didn't know it, Victor was also planning on killing her, but not before reaching the colony. He needed her in the same way that she needed him. If he showed up at the colony alone, Megan might hide or possibly even try to kill him. But if Harper were with him, she would come willingly. Then he could drive them to a spot Burke least suspected and kill them both. He was confident the Light Beings wouldn't intervene. He was, after all, one of the last Martians, and he knew they loved him as no human could.

Harper watched as the glowing specks twinkled and reappeared on Victor's neck, healing the wound she had made with the knife. The blood disappeared. They hovered around him a moment longer and then raced off through an open window.

Victor rose from his hammock and threw on a robe. "Come with me," he said. "We're going to need a vehicle and weapons. Put on your thermal suit. We're leaving now."

Chapter 51

Captured

Megan glanced at the strange artificial man-creature behind her and then back at the spiders. They were moving again and closing in fast. She pointed her L-Stat at the man-creature's chest. Whatever it was, it wasn't human. Not a trace of emotion showed on his smooth, synthetic face, and his eyes glowed faintly. What she didn't know was that he was, in fact, an avatar and that he was being controlled by her nemesis, Herrington, fifty-eight million kilometers away. All she knew was that she didn't trust it.

"Stand back," she warned. "I'll shoot."

"Come with me," repeated the avatar. "I'll help you."

He—or rather it—stepped in front of her and aimed a small device at the spiders and flipped a switch. The spiders suddenly stopped moving again.

"Who are you?" she asked nervously.

The avatar ignored her, indifferent to the weapon aimed at its chest. It calmly walked to the freight elevator and pressed a button. Megan drew closer.

"How did you do that? How did you make them stop?"

"That is no concern of yours. Come with me."

Megan took another step toward it, suspicious, but she realized that she didn't have much of a choice. If it hadn't intervened, the spiders would have already killed her. The elevator opened, and what she saw inside was horrible. The blood-stained bodies of two men lay motionless on the floor as spiders tore at their flesh and siphoned their blood. The avatar pointed his device at them, and they, too, became still.

"Get in," it demanded, kicking the spiders out of his way. "The spiders will become active again soon. I can only stop them for several seconds at a time."

She stepped inside. As the elevator door slid shut, she could hear the spiders outside returning to life, their metal legs scratching the floor. Then the elevator began rising, and the avatar placed a hand firmly on her shoulder, sending shivers down her spine. Its scent reminded her of the smell of new tires.

"Give me your gun."

Before she could react, it wrenched the L-Stat from her hands with superhuman strength. There was no point in resisting. It was too strong. As the elevator climbed steadily upward, she closed her eyes and mentally rehearsed her plan: escape, hide, and release Shem. Beyond that, all she could hope for was to survive.

When at last they reached ground level, the door hissed open, and they stepped out into a room with glass walls and a control panel. The smell of rotting flesh filled the room, and she covered her nose with her hand. At her feet lay a dead security officer, his taser carbine still clutched tightly in his hands and his body half eaten by spiders. She glanced out the window and noticed that it was still dark outside. In the distance, someone sprinted toward a guard tower and began desperately climbing a ladder. Another person lay dead just outside the window. She suspected it was either Krueger or Anya.

"Wait here," said the avatar, shoving her to the floor. It knelt beside the dead security officer, wrenched the weapon out of his lifeless hands, and seized his steel handcuffs. Before she could get away, it grabbed Megan by the foot and ratcheted one of the cuffs around her ankle, and clasped the other around the dead man's wrist, locking them together. The stench was appalling, and she fought the urge to gag. She kicked the cyborg hard in its face with her other foot, leaving an imprint of her boot on its forehead, but it only grinned. Then it went outside.

She watched through the window as the avatar found the plasma rifle and strapped on its battery pack. It lifted the weapon to its shoulder and took aim at the guard tower. She turned her head, unable to watch, and instead focused on trying to free herself from the handcuffs.

She pulled with all her might, and the officer's body began to slide across the floor, which was slick with blood. Reaching the control panel, she began hurriedly flipping switches, hoping to trigger something that might cause a distraction. Suddenly, there was static, and she realized she had stumbled across a transceiver. Outside, there was a loud crack followed by an explosion as the cyborg fired the plasma rifle. She pressed the transmit button and shouted into it, hoping someone aboard the *Intrepid* would hear her.

"Mayday, Mayday. Come in, *Intrepid*."

There was nothing but static on the other end, followed by a second explosion outside. There wasn't much time. She tried again.

"Come in, *Intrepid*. My name is Megan. I'm with the team inside the colony. We're surrounded, and we need—"

She heard footsteps and looked up. The cyborg was right behind her, its reflection visible in the window. Outside, the guard tower was consumed by flames. Thick black smoke billowed out of it, filling the topmost portion of the dome.

"Why are you doing this?" she pleaded. "Let me go!"

Her ankle, the one that was cuffed to the dead man, hurt, and her foot was going numb.

"Be quiet," said the avatar, "or I'll kill you right now." It adjusted a series of dials on the transceiver. There was more static and then a low whine as it changed frequencies.

"Burke," it said coldly. "I know you're out there. Speak to me. I have one of your children—the one named Megan—and I will kill her unless you meet my demands." Instantly, Megan remembered her conversation with Herrington a few months before. He had said they were sending her to Mars to force Dr. Burke to negotiate.

There was more static, and then a voice answered him.

"Dr. Burke is dead."

There was a pause as static faded in and out. Then it returned, clearer and louder than before.

"I'm her daughter. What do you want?"

Megan recognized the voice immediately—it was Harper.

"I don't believe you," replied the avatar. "Burke's alive and I know it." It grabbed Megan by her hair and pulled her to her feet, twisting her arm until she cried out.

"Tell them your name," it ordered.

"Don't listen to him, Harper; he's a liar!" The avatar shoved her back to the ground before she could say more.

"Okay, *Harper*," it hissed, "you have three hours to meet my demands. If Burke is dead, bring me her body, her ashes, whatever. I want you and everybody in your little compound to begin evacuating this planet. If you do not, the girl dies, and I'll hunt the rest of you down until every last one of you is dead too."

"How do we know you'll keep your end of the bargain?"

"You don't," answered the avatar, "but right now you don't have a choice. Meet me outside Opportunity, just outside the main entrance. Bring Burke dead or alive." It switched off the transceiver.

"If she's alive, what makes you think you can kill her?" asked Megan, not expecting an answer. "She's smarter than you—a lot smarter."

The avatar smiled slyly, just as Herrington did back in his control room millions of kilometers away. Though he knew better, he couldn't resist bragging. "There's a satellite orbiting Mars at this very moment, armed with long-range ballistic missiles. One push of a button, and they launch. No more Burke, no more rival colony."

Megan grew bolder. "I thought Dr. Burke was supposed to be the bad guy, but it's you, isn't it? Why are you doing this?"

The avatar seemed on the verge of answering but then stopped.

"What's in the pack?"

She froze. If the avatar found Shem, it was all over.

"Medical supplies," she stammered, struggling to mask her alarm. "Food."

Just then, it glanced out the window, and something

caught its eye. Megan guessed that someone who had gone with Krueger was still alive and trying to find a place to radio for help. She hoped it was Anya.

"Stay here. I'll be right back."

She watched nervously as it strode out the door and disappeared around a corner. She then dragged the dead security officer to where her pack lay. She unzipped it and pulled out the tube containing Shem. He was still awake, shivering but alert. She unscrewed the top and he climbed out and perched on her shoulder. He seemed confused and disoriented.

"Shem, we're inside the colony," Megan whispered, remembering that he understood as much English as a young child. "The dome is out there. It's time for you to do your thing."

The tiny primate's eyes darted around the room, and it leaped onto the control panel and peered out the window before returning to her side.

"Okay, let's get you out there."

She dragged the dead security officer's body back across the room to the door that the cyborg had exited. She pushed it open. Shem hesitated. *Did he know what to do?*

"Go on, boy," she said in her most encouraging tone. "You can do it. I'll join you as soon as I can."

The tiny monkey uttered a series of timid squeaks and disappeared out the door. She blew a sigh of relief.

You can do it.

Chapter 52

To the Rescue

Racing over dunes and rock-strewn valleys through the dark of night, Victor maneuvered the dune rider with expert skill. Beside him sat Harper, her knuckles white from gripping the utility bar in front of her. Their vehicle shook violently as they raced toward the colony, at times going airborne as they rocketed over dunes and small craters. They had been driving like this for the past two hours, stopping only once to reply to the call they received on their vehicle's two-way radio.

"Meet me outside Opportunity," the voice had said, "right outside the main entrance. Bring Burke dead or alive." They had also heard Megan's voice loud and clear. She was alive, but she was being held hostage, her captor threatening to kill her.

"How long until we're there?" asked Harper.

"Not much longer. Hold on."

She was alarmed at the increasing frequency of tremors caused by the volcanic activity. As the dome came into view, Victor slowed the vehicle. The guard tower inside was glowing softly with the remains of the fire that had consumed it, and the reflection of stars gleamed on the dome's clear surface.

"Where do you think Megan is?"

"Most likely above ground. I'm guessing whoever has her is waiting near the entrance and is watching for us. They probably suspect a trick."

She ran a finger along the polished steel barrel of the neutron pistol that now lay beside her. Although she had never seen one before, it looked powerful.

"Let's go over the plan again," advised Victor. "I'm going to get out and let you drive to the rendezvous point. When they demand to see Burke, hand them the canister of ashes and agree to everything they want. Then say you want to see Megan. As soon as they bring her out, I'll start shooting. You grab her and get her in the vehicle."

"What do you think our chances are?"

"Fifty-fifty, if we're lucky."

Victor stopped the vehicle. They were hidden in a shallow crater, with the colony only half a kilometer away. He jumped out, and Harper scooted over into the driver's seat.

"Wish me luck."

Victor shrugged. "I don't believe in it, never have. But I do believe in redemption. Thanks for giving me a chance."

It was a lie. He knew Dr. Burke would never love him, not even if he brought Megan back alive, so he would have his revenge instead. Soon, both Megan and Harper would be dead, and Burke—or what remained of her—would be torn with grief. To add to her suffering, in a year everyone she had ever cared about on Earth would be dead too. He grinned smugly and watched as Harper drove the rest of the way to the colony, the silver dune rider silhouetted against the colony's faintly glowing dome. Then he started walking.

Chapter 53

Confrontation

As soon as Shem was out the door, Megan concentrated on making her escape. She rummaged through the dead man's pockets in search of a key to the handcuffs. Finding it, she slid it into the locking mechanism, gave it a twist, and the cuffs popped open. She repeated the process, removing the cuffs from the corpse as well, and stuffed them in her pocket. Then she grabbed her pack and hurried to the exit.

She was too late—the avatar had just stepped through the door. It was carrying a helmet and oxygen tank, but it dropped them as soon as it saw her. She tried to run past it, but it seized her arm and slung her down onto the hard, cold floor. She lay stunned for a moment but then noticed the oxygen tank lying beside her. She got up and hurled the tank at her captor, striking it on the head and causing it to stumble. Again, she tried to flee, but the avatar was quickly upon her, this time punching her hard on the side of her face. She fell to the ground with a thud. It reached down and grabbed her by the hair and began dragging her to the other side of the room. She screamed and closed her eyes.

"You want to die, do you?" it asked mockingly. "I was going to kill you later, but I can do it now instead. If I suffocate you, they won't even know you're dead until it's too late."

It pounced on her like a lion and began choking the life out of her. Megan struggled for air, digging her fingernails into the avatar's rubbery skin, but it didn't let go. Rapidly losing consciousness, her mind flashed to a dream of Dr. Burke telling her to breathe. *I can't die now*, she thought. *The prophecy . . .*

She opened her eyes. The avatar was kneeling on top of her with both of its hands around her neck. Behind it flitted a swarm of glowing blue and white lights, just like the ones she had seen on the ship. There was a loud rumble, and the room began swaying violently. Large chunks of concrete fell from the ceiling. The avatar stood up but was immediately struck on the head by falling debris and knocked to the ground. The windows shattered and the ceiling caved in on them.

As Megan gasped for air, the swarm of lights settled onto her, and her pain went away. She heard Dr. Burke's voice again saying *breathe* and she inhaled deeply. She looked around her.

What she saw surprised her. The avatar was pinned under a steel beam, and the room lay in ruins. Remarkably, not a single bit of debris had fallen on her. She sat up. Outside, the dome's inner surface was swarming with spiders, and there was no sign of Shem. Several bodies lay dead on the ground. Inside, the Light Beings were now gone, and she could hear the avatar struggling to extract itself.

Get up, she told herself. *There's still work to be done.*

She stood up and put on her pack. Then, grabbing the oxygen tank and helmet, she limped out into the large open area under the dome. In the distance, fire and smoke poured out of the volcano, and several bright red rivers of lava streamed down its sides. *We don't have much time*, she thought.

She started for the center of the dome, hoping to find Shem and somehow get him to the EMP switch. Just then, two spiders darted out from under a mining truck and began pursuing her. She looked for a place to hide. There were stacks of crates all around as well as a large water storage tank that was now broken and gushing water. Beyond it lay a power station and several parked mining trucks. The spider was gaining on her, and she had to act quickly.

As she scurried toward the crates, she noticed a man lying dead in a pool of blood. Beside him lay Hendrix's beloved pistol and a clip of ammunition. She dove for it, snatching it off the ground and simultaneously sliding in the ammo clip while rolling behind a crate. She fired a shot just as a spider leaped at her, blowing it to bits. She then took aim at the other one and hit it dead center, destroying it too.

"Megan!" screamed a voice from behind one of the crates. It was Anya. She was crouched on top of a pallet and waving frantically. "Help!"

Megan hurried to the crate where she was hiding and took off her pack. Anya was clutching Shem, who was alive and well but clearly terrified. A puddle of water was rapidly spreading around them.

"Sta-stay away from the water," whispered Anya. "It's almost to the capacitors."

"The what?"

"The capacitors. They store electricity. If they get damaged and the water touches them, anything touching the water gets fried. Ge-get on top of the pallet."

Megan stepped onto it and looked at Shem.

"Is he injured?"

"I don-don't think so. The spiders almost got m-me, but then he came, and they started chasing him instead. He was too fast for them and came back."

Megan pulled the disassembled crossbow out of her pack, along with the coil of nylon cord attached to a bolt. She put a hand on Anya's shoulder to reassure her and then gently stroked Shem's furry head.

"Let's do this, Anya. I don't know how to assemble the crossbow, so you'll need to do that for me."

Anya took the parts and began putting them together. Although she was still shaking, she had practiced assembling the weapon so many times that she could practically do it in her sleep. When she was finished, she handed it back to Megan.

"You do it."

"But I've never shot a crossbow in my life. I—"

"I'm shaking too much, I'll never hit it. Ju-just aim for the very top of the dome. It's laser-guided. The bolt has a magnet. It's enough to hold the line and Shem."

Megan took the crossbow and handed Anya the pistol. She aimed at the dome's apex, but the crossbow was heavy and she couldn't hold it steady. She tried propping it against the top of the crate, which helped. Lining up the laser with her target, she squeezed the trigger. The bolt and line shot up to the top of the dome where the bolt's magnetic tip latched onto a steel beam.

"Give me Shem," she said.

"How long until—"

Suddenly, a hand reached out and seized Anya by the wrist. She screamed as the avatar hoisted her above its head and threw her. She came crashing down on a nearby crate, putting a large dent in it. Shem had leaped out of her hands just in time and disappeared behind another crate. The avatar then turned and stared at Megan.

"Do you know who I am?" it hissed.

"No." Megan glanced around her for a way out.

"I'm the one who sent you here. You're here to lead me to that renegade, Burke."

"You're Herrington? But . . ."

The avatar grinned and uttered a hollow, sadistic laugh. It was standing in the rapidly widening puddle, glaring at her as though deciding how best to kill her.

Behind him, Anya, bloody and battered, was slowly climbing onto another pallet. She was looking at the capacitors, the bases of which were now submerged in water. Above them was printed the warning DANGER: HIGH VOLTAGE. She aimed Hendrix's gun at one of them and fired.

There was an explosion, and sparks began flying everywhere. The avatar shook violently as electricity surged through the water and into its body. Smoke came out of its mouth and ears, and it fell into the water where it lay motionless.

"Are you okay?" shouted Anya. She was still clutching the pistol and trembling all over.

"Yes," said Megan, still trying to comprehend what had just happened. "Thanks."

She looked around for Shem. *Had he been electrocuted too?* She climbed on top of a crate and began calling for him.

"Come here, Shem," she hollered.

"Come here, little buddy," echoed Anya, waving her arms above her head.

There was a sudden flash of motion, and the monkey leaped onto Anya's shoulder. She then guided him to Megan, who was directly under the cord hanging from the dome's highest point.

"Okay, Shem, you know what to do."

The tiny monkey leaped onto the cord and began climbing quickly. Thick smoke now filled the upper portions of the dome, and they lost sight of him as he neared the top.

"Will the smoke be a problem for him?" asked Megan.

"Let's hope not."

Moments later the lights went dark, and they could hear the thuds of spiders hitting the ground after falling from the dome. The damaged capacitors were no longer giving off sparks.

"He did it!" Anya smiled and laughed. "He really did it!"

"Is it safe?" asked Megan, pointing at the water below them.

"Yes, it should be."

Anya climbed down off the crate. She had calmed down considerably. "There's no more electricity."

They stared at the erupting volcano in the distance. Streams of lava had now reached the base of the mountain and were flowing outward towards the colony.

"Let's gather the survivors and get out of here. Is there a way to get one of those trucks going?"

"The older ones have an insulated backup battery. So,

yes, I believe so," replied Anya. "There should also be an alternate way to open the front entrance. I'll figure it out."

"Okay," said Megan. "You get a truck ready, and I'll get the survivors."

Chapter 54

Ambush

A few minutes earlier, Harper had been at the wheel of her dune rider when its headlights shut off and the vehicle unexpectedly lost power. As she coasted to a stop a short distance away from the dome, she thought it strange that the lights inside had also suddenly gone out. Behind her, the volcano, Olympus Mons, erupted with a savage explosion that shook the ground and sent enormous clouds of smoke skyward. Streams of bright red lava poured down its sides like raging rivers of fire.

She knew there wasn't much time. Victor was out there, concealed by the darkness, probably stalking her at this very instant. She had only spared his life so that he could take her to Megan, and now that she was here, she regretted not having shot him the moment he stepped out of the vehicle. She imagined him watching her over the barrel of his plasma rifle, just waiting for the moment Megan emerged to blow them both into oblivion with a single shot. Her only hope was to move fast.

She grabbed the neutron pistol and walked briskly toward the colony. When she was about fifty meters away from it, she stopped, knelt, and watched for signs of activity. A truck was parked by the entrance, and people were getting into it. Everyone had on thermal suits and helmets—it was impossible to tell if Megan was one of them. She glanced behind her, but there was still no trace of Victor. Instead, all she saw was the erupting volcano, with streaks of lightning flashing intermittently around its peak and rivers of molten lava streaming toward her.

Suddenly, the dome's main entranceway slid open, and the truck slowly rambled out onto the bleak Martian plain. As the door slid closed again, she noticed two figures hurrying on foot toward the truck. One of them appeared to have a limp.

Megan! Harper began running as fast as she could toward her friend. When she reached her, Megan looked up, surprised, and then smiled when she realized who it was. Before they could embrace, they noticed a figure racing toward them out of the darkness, plasma rifle in hand. It was Vic.

"Run! It's an ambush!" screamed Harper. Vic was now only a few meters away. His eyes flashed with cruelty as he pointed his weapon at them. A swarm of blue lights swooped in behind him and hovered overhead.

"Artemis Burke!" he screamed. "Revenge is mine!" He took aim and pulled the trigger.

Chapter 55

Evacuation and Escape

Megan thought it was the end. As she braced herself for the explosion, she wondered if she would feel anything. Time seemed to slow down, and she was surprised that she wasn't dead yet. However, the blast never came.

Vic pulled the trigger again and then threw the plasma rifle to the ground. Harper drew the neutron pistol and tried to shoot him, but it also failed to fire.

The EMP, thought Megan. *It's disabled their circuits.*

Anya pulled out Hendrix's pistol and pointed it at Vic. He froze. It was a simpler weapon, requiring no electricity.

"What do we do now?" she asked, looking at Megan.

"We need to get out of here. The lava's going to be here soon."

"I've got a dune rider up there," added Harper. "But it stopped working."

"I can fix it," said Anya. "What do we do with him?" She nodded at Vic.

"Kill him," said Harper.

"I can't do it." Her arm was trembling again, and she took a step backward. "I've known him too long."

"Don't trust these people, Anya," said Vic, taking a step towards her. "I'm your friend. Give me the gun." He stretched out his hand.

"He just tried to kill us!" screamed Harper. "You saw it."

"I shot at *them*, Anya, not you. Give me the gun."

She took another step back.

"I don't know her," she said, glancing at Harper and then back at Vic. "But I'm not going to let you hurt Megan."

With her eyes on Vic, Harper inched closer. She was closer to Anya than Vic was, and she sensed an opportunity. She charged Anya and grabbed her by the arm, wrenching the pistol from her. During the struggle, Vic ran, disappearing into the darkness. The swarm of Light Beings vanished with him.

Harper sighed. In the distance, they could see the truck's headlights moving away from them. The lava was getting closer, and they were already beginning to feel its heat.

"Let's get in that dune rider," said Megan.

When they reached the dune rider, Anya crawled underneath and switched the power source over to the backup battery. Harper stood guard while Megan checked their oxygen levels. The ground shook intermittently as the volcano continued to spew smoke and lava. With each passing moment, they grew increasingly nervous. Finally, Anya crawled out from under the vehicle and stood up.

"It should work now."

"What's that all over you?" asked Megan, holding up a chem-light.

Anya was covered in red fluid. She looked down at herself and then back at Megan. A look of horror crossed her face.

"It's brake fluid. I must have accidently cut the brake line."

"What does that mean?"

"We have no brakes."

"It doesn't matter," said Harper. "All we need is to get out of here. Megan, you drive. I'll keep a lookout for Victor. Anya, you're in the back seat. We'll worry about stopping later."

They got in and started the engine. Just then, a torrent of bright red lava burst over a hill and came rushing toward them, engulfing everything in its path. They could already feel the heat radiating from it. Megan pressed down on the accelerator.

"What if the road's blocked? I mean, the lava . . ."

"The compound will be safer," said Anya. "I know how to get there. Turn right here."

Megan turned the steering wheel and increased their speed. It was still dark, and she had to be careful not to crash their vehicle as they fled the lava, which was now on both sides of them.

"It's just hit the dome!" exclaimed Anya. "It's melting!"

As Harper turned to look, the passenger-side door beside her flung open and Vic leaped in. Before she could react, he grabbed her and shoved her out of the moving vehicle. In the same instant, Megan reached into her pocket and pulled out the handcuffs. With Anya scream-ing behind her, she turned the dune rider hard to the right, throwing Vic off balance. As he grabbed onto the safety bar in front of him, Megan took both hands off the wheel and snapped one of the cuffs around his wrist and the other around the bar. A look of terror crossed Vic's face. In front of them was a wall of lava. She punched the acceler-ator and screamed at the top of her lungs.

"Jump!"

She pushed the door open and jumped out, as did Anya on the other side. She hit the ground hard and rolled sev-eral times until she came to a stop.

The dune rider, with Vic trapped inside, drove straight into the lava and was consumed by flames. Megan strug-gled to her knees and gasped for breath. Even with her helmet and survival suit on, the heat was stifling, and her ribs hurt where she had hit the ground. Her hair was soaked with sweat inside her helmet. Droplets of perspi-ration ran into her eyes, stinging them, but there was nothing she could do about it.

As she struggled to catch her breath, she heard Dr. Burke's voice telling her to breathe, just like in the dreams. She turned up the dial on her oxygen intake hose and in-haled slowly. Harper was running over to her.

"Are you okay?" asked Harper.

"Yes, I think so."

"We've got to get out of here. I'll help you."

They noticed Anya staggering around with her hands on her neck. Her eyes were opened wide and her skin was turning blue. The Light Beings returned and swarmed around her.

"What's the matter?"

"She's out of oxygen," said Harper. "The jump must have broken her tank."

Anya sank to her knees, gasping. Megan knelt too, holding her hand and trying her best to ignore the intense heat around them. Again, the image of Dr. Burke telling her to breathe flashed in her mind.

"There's nothing we can do for her, Megan," said Harper. "We need to leave now."

"No. I can help her."

Megan inhaled deeply, taking in as much air as she could, and then held her breath. She detached her tank's hose and attached it to Anya's helmet. Anya began breathing, fast at first and then more slowly. Megan removed her tank and placed it in Anya's arms. With the Light Beings now surrounding her, she took off her helmet and inhaled the deadly Martian air.

At first, it felt strange. The air entering her lungs was cold, despite the heat radiating from the lava.

Harper and Anya both stared at her in disbelief. She, too, was shocked, not so much at the fact that she was breathing, but that she had made the leap of faith and taken off her tank and helmet. It defied everything she had known and believed.

The ground shook again, and it began tearing apart in zigzagging lines, opening a deep chasm. She stumbled but quickly regained her balance.

"Let's go!" she yelled.

The three young women began hurrying away from the lava and the growing chasm. In the distance, two spaceships—the *Intrepid* and the *Argo*—rose high into the night sky as they made their escape without them. The further they went, the colder the air felt on Megan's unprotected face and in her lungs. When they were a kilometer away, Megan took out a flare gun and fired it into the sky. A bright white light burst above them.

They could no longer see the truck ahead of them, but they did notice the swarm of lights emerging from the lava. It sped toward them, then broke apart and reformed as a single large orb, from which emerged a young woman.

She had glowing, slightly transparent skin, dark hair, and sparkling eyes. Megan recognized her immediately. It was Dr. Burke, not as she had appeared in her dreams, but a much younger version. Tears were in her eyes.

"You did it," she said. "You fulfilled the prophecy. You and Harper both. I'm so proud of you."

"Are you who I think you are?" asked Megan, bewildered. Harper walked over and stood beside her.

"Yes, it's me. I've missed you, Megan. I knew you'd both do the right thing."

Harper looked surprised. "But you told me to kill Victor, and I didn't do it."

"You couldn't have," sighed Burke. "I thought you could, but I was wrong. It had to be Megan. I'm sorry, Megan. I'm sorry you had to experience so many terrible things. But the prophecy ordained that only one born of Martian blood could do what you did."

"Martian blood?" exclaimed Megan. "Me?"

"Yes. That's why you're able to breathe the air. I've been trying to tell you—"

"But I'm just an ordinary girl. In fact, I'm not even that. I can't even walk properly. My leg—"

"No, Megan. You're special. You were chosen before you were born to save humanity and to protect Mars too. It always had to be you. That's part of why Victor was so jealous."

"But my mother. I-I just met her."

"She was a Martian spy who had infiltrated the colony. She didn't realize she was pregnant when she went there."

"Why did Vic say he was the last Martian then?" asked Anya.

"Jealousy consumed him long before the flames ever did. It burned out the last spark of goodness in him and left only evil. By the time you met him, he wanted only revenge, and he told you whatever he thought you needed to hear to help him."

Harper checked her oxygen gauge and stared at the erupting volcano. More lava flows had made their way down its sides and were carving new paths of destruction. She glanced at the colony; its dome was melting and would be gone soon.

"Can you help us get to the compound?" asked Harper.

"Yes. Help is already on its way."

"My mother is on a truck with the other survivors," said Megan. "Her name is Abigail."

"Don't worry," said Burke. "They'll be safe."

Later, just as the sun was beginning to rise, a hovercraft appeared on the horizon. It landed near them, and Megan, Anya, and Harper got on board.

When they looked behind them for Dr. Burke, she was already gone. As they flew in search of the truck carrying the other survivors, Megan noticed what looked like a tiny comet darting away from them. She tried to remember something—anything—about her childhood on Mars, but it was all a blur, and she drifted off to sleep.

Chapter 56

Trapped

His avatar on Mars destroyed, Herrington sat slumped in his subterranean control room beneath SIS headquarters. He was strapped to his chair and bleeding badly.

He opened his eyes and surveyed the room. To his right, a guard lay dead on the floor with a bullet lodged in his heart. To his left, there was blood on the floor, but no man. He wondered what had happened to the second guard. Drops of blood dotted the floor. *Had he had escaped?*

He removed the helmet connecting him to the supercomputer, barely noticing as the bundle of wires detached from his brain. He tried to stand but couldn't. Exhausted and weak from blood loss, he sank back into his chair.

As he lay there, helpless, he remembered his final moments on Mars with the avatar. He had been so close. He thought of Megan and her friend and was furious. *If only I had killed them when I had the chance,* he thought. *It would have been so easy.*

When the police arrived, Willian Blythe was with them. They found Herrington motionless in his chair, his eyes closed. It was only by a stroke of luck that they found him at all—the guard who survived after being shot had lived just long enough to radio for help. Blythe placed his hand on Herrington's neck and felt for a pulse.

"He's alive, but barely."

"I'll call for paramedics," replied a police officer.

"Wait," said Blythe, opening a briefcase. He pulled out two hypodermic needles and held them up to a light.

"What do you have in mind?" asked a sergeant.

"We're going to find out the truth about what's been going on here."

Blythe injected the first needle into Herrington's neck, and his eyes opened. He stared around wildly, like a captured animal.

"That was adrenaline," said Blythe sternly. "To wake you up." He held up the second needle for Herrington to see. "And this is SP-117, otherwise known as truth serum." He stuck it into the wounded man's arm and pushed down on the plunger. "It impairs the brain's ability to lie. Now, you're going to tell me everything about what's been happening on Mars, and what you did with the kids who were born there."

"I'll die before I tell you anything," snarled Herrington, but his eyes were already becoming glossy, and he was losing control of his thoughts. Blythe pulled a chair up next to him and sat down.

"First question: What were you doing in this room before we got here?"

Chapter 57

A Choice

After arriving safely at the compound, Megan slept for hours. She was unaware that nearly sixty million kilometers away, Ross Herrington had given a full confession that implicated the president.

Under the truth serum's influence, he told Blythe all about the deceptive nature of the rescue mission and how he had operated a cyborg avatar to oversee the colony's destruction. He explained that they had sent Megan there to lure out Dr. Burke, but that their plan failed. He also described the plot to kill the Wonder Kids and how he had defied the president by abducting them and having them brought to a lab for surgery instead.

The volcano continued to erupt, shaking the ground and releasing vast quantities of smoke and ash into the sky, but the rivers of lava never reached the compound.

Whether through luck, divine intervention, or the efforts of the Light Beings, life inside went on much the same as it had before the eruption. Its occupants could barely have guessed at the destruction going on around them.

The Light Beings healed Megan's wounds while she slept. When she awoke, she met Anya in the dining hall, where they were later joined by the survivors from the colony. She and Abigail, her mother, ate apart from the others and talked for hours getting to know each other.

Later that day, Megan visited the compound's animal hospital, where a small vervet monkey lay unconscious in a respirator. It was Shem. His tiny chest rose and fell gently as oxygen was pumped into his lungs. Anya was sitting nearby.

"I thought he was dead," exclaimed Megan. "I mean, when he didn't come back . . ."

"I found him before we loaded the truck. He was in bad shape—smoke inhalation. I put him back in his cylinder and replenished his oxygen."

"Is he going to make it?"

"They say he's got a chance, but it's not good." Tears welled up in her eyes. "I really hope he lives."

"I didn't think he meant that much to you. The first time I saw him, you said he was just a monkey and not to get attached to him."

"I did say that, didn't I?" Anya wiped a tear from her face. "I guess what we went through changed me. It doesn't seem fair for him to die after what he did for us."

"What are you going to do if he lives?"

"Stay here and take good care of him. I don't want to go back to Earth."

That night, long after everyone else had gone to

sleep, the Light Beings led Megan and Harper through the forest until they reached a wall of solid rock. A single speck of light landed on the wall and glowed softly.

"Follow me," said Harper. Taking Megan's hand, she walked straight through it, pulling her friend along with her, until they found themselves in a dark cave. The swarm of lights entered after them, illuminating their surroundings enough for them to see.

"I know this place," said Megan. "I saw it in a dream."

"Keep walking," replied Harper. "The prophecy's farther up."

They followed the Light Beings down narrow, twisting passageways until they came to a spot where the walls on both sides were covered in pictures and hieroglyphs. The lights merged together, and Dr. Burke stepped out of them.

"Megan, Harper—there's something I need you to see."

She pointed to a section of the wall that was illuminated with a bluish glow. There, the prophecy showed the volcano erupting and figures fleeing a domed colony. There was a girl and a small monkey. In the next panel, a man met a fiery death, and in the next, everyone was safely inside Burke's underground compound. After that, there was a long stretch of wall with nothing on it, and then it resumed with pictures of a future Mars, one teeming with life.

"What's the gap for?" asked Harper. "When you showed it to me before, there were drawings there."

"I've removed them," said Burke. "The distant future remains unchanged—Mars will be reborn, but the immediate future is in your hands. You have a choice: you can stay here with me or return to Earth."

"If I stay, will I become like you, or can I stay the way I am?" asked Harper.

"That's up to you. I'll show you how to rebuild the Atomizer, and then you can make the choice."

"I'll stay then. I belong here with you."

"Very well. You will stay. Megan, what do you choose?"

"I don't know. I don't want to go back, but I don't want to stay, either. I just want a normal life, if that's even possible."

"What would you consider a normal life?"

"On Earth, but when things were better—before all the pollution and shortages. And I'd like to have a family."

"That just might be possible if we rebuild the Atomizer," continued Burke. "I can send you back thousands of years to ancient Egypt where your ancestors built a magnificent civilization. You'll meet the first Martian settlers and have a place of honor among them."

"No," said Megan. "I don't care about any of that. I want my own life. If Abigail agrees, I'd like for her to come with me. She's been a prisoner on Mars for longer than I've been alive. She deserves better, and what could be better than a simple, normal life?"

"But, Megan," protested Harper, "if you stay here, think of all the adventures we could have. We could be a family right here."

Megan felt tears running down her cheeks.

"I'm sorry," she said, choking on the words. "I can't stay."

"Is this what you really want, Megan?" asked Dr. Burke.

"Yes."

"Okay. Go talk with Abigail. As soon as the Atomizer is ready, you can go."

Chapter 58

Going Home

The day before she left, Megan went to find Harper. A year had passed since they had arrived on Mars. She had recovered from her injuries, and the Atomizer was finally ready. Now it was time to say goodbye. She found Harper upstairs in the control room.

"Hey," she said. "I'm leaving tomorrow morning. Will you take a walk with me?"

"Of course," answered Harper. "Where do you want to go?"

"The path through the forest. When we're finished, we can get something to eat."

As they walked among the trees, it almost felt like they were back on Earth. The birds were especially active that afternoon, fluttering from branch to branch and chirping their songs. The rock ceiling and the occasional appearance of tiny lights darting above them were all that reminded them that they were still on Mars.

"I'm going to miss you," began Megan. "You've always been like my big sister, you know."

Harper smiled. "And you've always been like a little sister to me. I honestly don't know what I'll do without you." She paused and wiped away a tear. "You know, you don't have to go. If you stay here, we can still be a family."

Megan imagined growing old in the compound and having her friend with her every day. It could be a nice life, but something about it seemed fake. The forest was beautiful, but you could walk across the whole thing in fifteen minutes. Even night and day were an illusion here, created by the Light Beings.

"I'm sorry, Harper. I just need something more real than this. I may be a Martian—whatever that is—but Earth is my home. I can't wait to see what it was like a couple hundred years ago. From what I've read, people were nicer then, and there were still lots of beautiful places to explore. It's not the same on Mars. Outside of this compound, it's just dust and sand and rock, and that's not enough for me."

"But all that's changing. More volcanos are erupting, and the atmosphere is thickening. It's going to get warmer. We'll introduce microbes and—"

"And in a thousand years," interrupted Megan, "Mars will be this beautiful, awesome place. I'm sorry, but I can't wait that long." She fidgeted uncomfortably and then added, "You know, you could come back with me."

"I wish I could," sighed Harper. "But I'd only go if Dr. Burke could, and without a physical body that's impossible. People would freak out if they saw her." She stopped and faced Megan. "I'm happy you found your mom,

Megan. I guess I found mine too. It's just weird that I'm a human and I'm staying on Mars, and you're a Martian, but you're going to Earth. Shouldn't it be the other way around?"

"Probably, but then again, we're the same, you and me. The only difference is that I can breathe here, and the cold doesn't hurt me as fast. Other than that, I think humans and Martians are pretty much the same. We feel and want the same things."

"You're right, Megan." Harper squeezed her hand. "You'll always be my sister."

The next morning, they had breakfast and enjoyed talking about old times. Abigail and Anya were there too, as were Shem and the survivors from Opportunity. Finally, when it was time to go, a swarm of Light Beings descended on them and formed a large glowing orb out of which stepped Dr. Burke. She looked sad.

"Are you ready to go?" she asked Megan.

"As ready as I'm ever going to be."

Megan hugged Harper and Anya, and they shared a tearful goodbye. Then she took Abigail by the hand, and they followed Dr. Burke to the Atomizer. Its door was open, revealing two seats.

"This is your last chance," said Burke. "Are you sure you want to do this?"

"Yes," said Megan, and Abigail squeezed her hand gently. "I'm positive."

"There's a chance this could create a time paradox," continued Burke. "That means that by going back in time, you could change something that affects the future. Or it could create an entirely new timeline in an entirely new universe. But the Light Beings say it will be okay, and I trust them."

Abigail climbed in first, and then Megan. As she sat down, she remembered boarding the *Intrepid* and how scared she had been. She wasn't afraid this time though. She exhaled a long steady breath and nodded at Dr. Burke.

"Ready."

"Okay, sit back and relax. What's meant to be, will be." Dr. Burke closed the door and typed a set of coordinates into a keypad. Then she entered the year: 2025. There was a sudden flash, and the Atomizer was empty.

Chapter 59

Reunion

That evening as she lay in her hammock, Harper felt empty inside. Megan had been like a younger sister to her, and now she was gone, a world and more than two centuries away. Even if Megan lived to be a hundred, her life would have been long over by now, her body dead and buried decades before she had even been born.

She felt tears welling up in her eyes and wished there was something she could do. She lay like that for hours, tossing and turning, until, finally, she drifted off to sleep.

When she awoke, a faint light was pouring in through the window and the songs of sparrows filled the air. She sat up, surprised to find herself no longer in a hammock, but in a bed with sheets and covers. Everything about the room was different—it was painted lime green and there were posters on the walls of people she didn't recognize. She got up and ran to the window.

Outside, the night sky was giving way to the first orange and pink-hued rays of dawn, and she could make out a street and houses and a forest behind them. There was an obnoxious buzzing sound and she spun around, spotting an old-fashioned alarm clock on a dresser. She switched the alarm off and noted the time. It was 6:00 a.m.

"Honey?" came a voice from outside the closed bedroom door. "Are you up?"

Harper paused, startled. Where was she? Was she dreaming?

"Come on, honey," repeated the voice. "Megan and Bryce are already up. Breakfast is on the table, and your dad says he'll drive everybody to school if you can get ready in time."

Still startled, she managed a frightened "okay" and sat back down on the edge of the bed. She felt something brush her shoulder and turned to see what it was. There beside her was a single glowing speck of blueish light, pulsating with warmth. *She did it*, thought Harper. *Megan changed the timeline.*

Someone knocked on the bedroom door and pushed it open. A petite dark-haired woman stuck her head in and smiled. It was Dr. Burke! She was not a hologram, but flesh and blood.

"Harper," she whispered. "Everything okay?"

"Yes." She looked back at the tiny speck of light, but it was gone.

"Come on. We need to get going. I have that interview this morning. Everyone else is up."

"Everyone who?"

The door closed again, and she looked for some clothes

to put on. As she opened a closet, a streak of luminescent specks shot out of it and disappeared out the window.

She really did it, thought Harper, mouthing the words without actually speaking them. *But how?*

There was another knock on the door, and a girl entered. It was Megan, and she didn't have a limp.

"Hurry up, sleepyhead," she joked. "Breakfast is waiting!"

Harper was speechless; all she could do was stare. Megan sensed her confusion and sat on the edge of the bed.

"What's wrong?" she asked.

"I don't . . ."

A single speck of bluish light reentered the room through the window. It wandered slowly around the room and came to a rest on Harper's knee. She glanced back at Megan.

"Can you see that?"

"You mean the Light Being? Yes, I see it."

"What's going on? I feel like I've woken up in a different life."

"Don't worry," said Megan. "You're okay. You've finally remembered, that's all. The same thing happened to me once."

"Remembered what?"

"The other life that we shared—in the future."

"But who am I, in this life?"

Megan smiled. "You're the same amazing person you've always been, except that you haven't been to Mars, and you certainly don't work for the State Intelligence Service. There's nothing to worry about. You have a great life. The rest will come back to you soon."

"Are we sisters?"

"No," said Megan. "My mom's Abigail. You remember

her, don't you?" Harper nodded slowly. "We live on the same street, just a few houses apart. I've been staying at your house this week because my parents are out of town."

Harper made a strange face and was about to speak when the speck of bluish light vanished into thin air.

"So, everything that happened before, it was real?"

"Yes, it all really happened."

"But—"

"Stop worrying," said Megan, smiling. "We're not on Mars anymore. Now hurry up. I don't want to be late for school!"

Chapter 60

Epilogue

His story finished, the old man leaned back and checked the time. It was getting late, and only a few stragglers remained on the observation deck. His granddaughter smiled and yawned.

"It's way past your bedtime," he said. "Let's get you back to your room. Your mother will be upset with me."

"Wait," said the little girl, furrowing her brow. "Did you know Megan when you were on Mars?"

"Yes, I did. I was there when she came back to the colony, and I saw her fight the spiders. I was one of the ones who escaped in the truck."

"Did you ever get to talk with her?"

"Many times, and I spoke with Harper and Anya too. That's how I came to learn their story. You know, it took them nearly a year to fix the Atomizer, so we were together for quite a long time."

"But how about the last part, where they went back in time? How could you know that?"

"Ah, yes. The last part. That was from the prophecy. After Megan left, the Light Beings took Anya to see it. The gaps had been filled in to reveal what happened, but of course, they'd always been there. Dr. Burke had just temporarily hidden them."

"So, they had always gone back in time?"

"There was always the possibility of them going back in time. That's what the prophecy revealed."

"But what happened to everybody else? Did they live?" The little girl was now wide awake and brimming with curiosity.

The old man closed his eyes and remembered. Although the events had taken place many years before, to him it was like yesterday. He cleared his throat and began.

"Ross Herrington died after he gave his confession, and the authorities found the warehouse where his accomplices had operated on Raven and the others. Bellamy, the reporter, wrote his article, which revealed the president's and Herrington's crimes to the public. Soon there were calls for the president to be impeached, and he resigned in disgrace, never to reenter politics.

"Wiley and Raven briefly became a media sensation as they told their story on various talk shows, but after a few months the public lost interest, and they went their separate ways. Raven reverted to her cyberpunk lifestyle, hanging out at clubs, and getting into trouble; and Wiley went back to school. He missed his friends. As for the twins, nobody ever heard from them again.

"When Victor died, his plan to bring the virus to Earth and wipe out humanity died with him. The three teenagers he planned to use as carriers survived and lived at the compound. Anya recovered from her breakdown and stayed at the compound for several years. But Mars held too many bad memories for her, and she eventually left and returned to Earth, where she became a medical doctor. When the Orion Space Station was built, she signed on as a doctor, and she's been here with us ever since."

"Can I meet her?"

"You already have! She's your doctor. She gave you your last checkup."

"That was her? But she's old."

The old man laughed. "Well, the story I told you took place fifty years ago. We're all older now."

"Wow! I never would have guessed."

"There's one more thing. Come here. There's something I want you to have."

He pulled a small red collar out of his pocket and handed it to her.

"What is it?"

"Shem's collar. Anya didn't want it after he died, so she gave it to me. And now I'm giving it to you."

The girl rubbed the collar between her fingers and smiled. She liked the way its fabric felt against her skin. She closed her eyes and tried to imagine Shem. Then she gave her grandfather a big hug and a kiss on the cheek.

"Thank you, Grandpa."

As the old man carried the little girl back to her room, the telescope remained focused on Opportunity, the lost colony on Mars. Not much of it remained, just a few dilapidated concrete structures and the tarnished shells of some of the robotic spiders that had once terrorized it. The rest was buried in sand and lava, never to be seen again.

It was a desolate, forbidding landscape, yet something stirred within it, something slow and unnoticed growing quietly along the base of the collapsed walls—tiny blue-green algae feeding on the carbon dioxide released by the eruptions. Over the years, it had developed a resistance to radiation and the hardiness to survive the extreme cold. Like a weed, it had taken root all over Mars. With each molecule of carbon dioxide it consumed, it released a precious atom of oxygen, a process that was repeated billions of times every hour across the red planet.

More life-forms would follow—lichens, radiation-resistant fungi, and a whole host of microscopic organisms. Larger plants—plants completely alien to anything that had come before—would also appear, their roots reaching deep down into the now thawing Martian soil.

As the atmosphere thickened and warmed, rain would begin to fall, slow at first and then in torrents, filling the previously dry creek and riverbeds and flowing downward to the seas, gradually filling them. An entire ecosystem was beginning to emerge, and along with it the promise of new stories to come.

The End

Acknowledgments

This novel originated as a story I wrote for my school's Young Authors Club nine years ago. What began as a short story gradually evolved into a much larger story complete with cyborgs, robotic spiders, and, of course, our clever and courageous hero, Megan. As the plot thickened, I often felt like I was wrestling an octopus. Each change that I made resulted in a ripple effect that forced me to make other changes as well, and I soon wound up constructing a twelve-foot-long story map just to help me keep track of what all the characters in the novel were doing. The process has given me a much greater appreciation for the sufferings of professional authors.

I would like to thank the entire team at BookLogix for their guidance and help in getting this book published.

I also want to thank Will Duda, Kay Wilson, Bendette Moore, and my parents for reading early versions of my manuscript and giving valuable feedback. Thanks, also, to the many students and members (past and present) of the Dodgen Young Authors Club for their ideas and inspiration.

I would also like to thank the high school students who participated in a contest to illustrate the novel's cover and their wonderful teacher, Kathleen Petka, who organized it. The winner was Tori Lehman, whose drawing is suggestive of Megan's triumph over the robotic spiders. Many thanks to Patrick Prendergast for the digital effects he added to the cover illustration.

For general information on Mars, I used *The Smithsonian Book of Mars* by Joseph M. Boyce, *The Traveler's Guide to Mars: The Mysterious Landscapes of the Red Planet* by William K. Hartman, and NASA's website at *mars.nasa.gov*.

To better understand what life would be like on a space journey, I used Mary Roach's *Packing for Mars: The Curious Science of Life in the Void*.

Finally, *The Case for Mars: The Plan to Settle the Red Planet and Why We Must* by Robert Zubrin with Richard Wagner provided helpful information about what a settlement on Mars might look like.

About the Author

Brian Wilson teaches sixth grade social studies in Cobb County, Georgia, where he also runs his school's Young Authors Club. He enjoys reading, tennis, and studying history.